Queen of Ista

I0678207

Thaddeus Nowak

Copyright © 2024 Thaddeus Nowak
All rights reserved.

www.ThaddeusNowak.com

Published by Mountain Pass Publishing, LLC.

ISBN: 978-0-9863946-7-6

First Printing: Feb 2024

Set in Adobe Garamond Pro
Cover art Copyright © 2024 by Thaddeus Nowak
Maps Copyright © 2024 by Thaddeus Nowak

This is a work of fiction. All characters, names, places, and events are the work of the author's imagination. Any resemblance to events, locales, or persons living or dead is strictly coincidental.

This work is copyrighted. Scanning, uploading, and distribution of this book via the internet or any other means without the permission of the publisher and author is illegal and punishable by law. Please purchase only authorized electronic editions and do not participate in or encourage the electronic piracy of copyrighted materials.

Your support of the author's rights is appreciated.

Books by Thaddeus Nowak

Queen of Ista Series
Queen of Ista

Heirs of Cothel Series
Mother's Curse
Daughter's Justice
Daughter's Revenge
Daughter's Search
Father's Legacy

Bound Series
Bound

Snow Cat Series
Snow Cat's Shadow

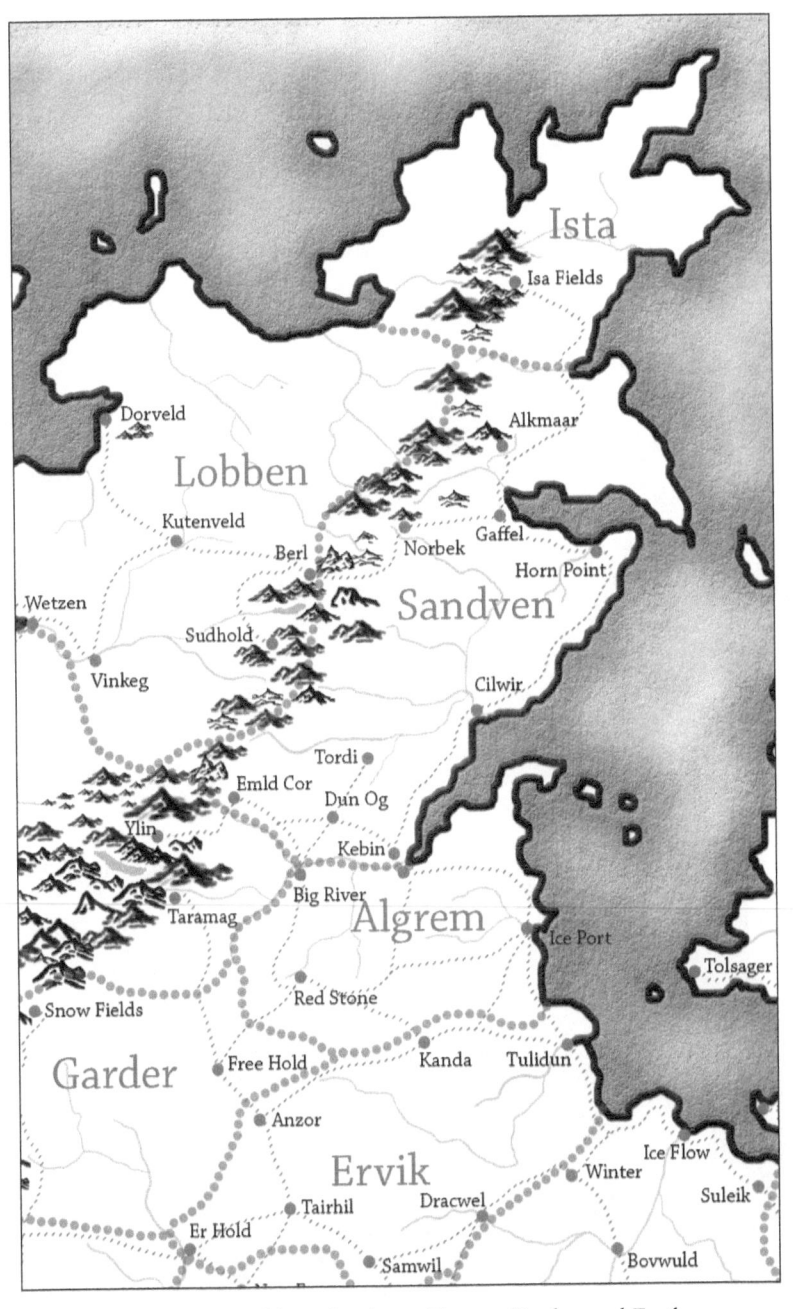

Map of Ista, Lobben, Sandven, Algrem, Garder, and Ervik.

Acknowledgements

I would like to thank the many people who have helped make this work possible. My wife Sherri, my best friend Chad, and my parents. I would also like to thank my editor Judy Reveal as well as the others who have inspired and offered advice. Any errors left in the work are entirely mine.

Also, any mention of trebuchets and flinging flaming projectiles remains a side effect of the fact that I'm not allowed to have one.

Chapter 1

Stephenie moved forward into the throne room. The stone walls under the faded and soot-stained tapestries held a chill even though the summer season had started. The dark floor, darker ceiling, and dingy walls drained the light from the lamps and candles scattered around the room. Not even the long rectangular fire pit in the center of the room provided warmth. It only filled the air with the heavy odor of burnt coal and a layer of smoke hovering above everyone's heads as the hazy cloud slowly permeated the thatch of the roof.

She came to a stop a dozen feet in front of Trovin's second son, King Ivan, a middle-aged man with thick blond hair and a neatly trimmed beard. The slightly overweight man sat on a wooden throne covered in carved runes and symbology worn down by time. The king's expression remained wary and uncertain, unchanged since she had entered the room. However, his eyes held a sharpness that told her he observed everything.

A wrinkled and aged man dressed in a bearskin tunic and heavy wool pants stood to his right. This man's brown eyes calculated everything he saw, equally observant, but with a trace of cruelty not found in the king's expression. Neither man looked soft from age, despite the king's added weight.

The emotional energy both men emitted remained muted and Stephenie did not bother trying to probe into their thoughts. Those schooled in dealing with people who used magic could reduce the intensity of surface thoughts and emotions that most people radiated freely. *Would they call me touched by their Goddess? Witch?* She mentally snorted at herself. *Definitely not mage.*

Until her world fell apart three years ago, she believed in the mythology of the southern gods and felt herself cursed by the imaginary demon god Elrin. At the time, she knew her fate was most likely a painful death on a pyre. *These northerners believe in a different set of gods and don't burn people alive. But they still don't know the truth of magic.*

As she waited for Ivan to acknowledge her, she once again assessed the mental energy from the forty-two minds of the men and women gathered along the walls of the throne room. The people watched and examined her and her husband, Kas, uncertain of the threat they represented. *At least fifteen of the people feel as reserved as Ivan and his mage. Likely soldiers,* she silently assessed, knowing the trials of intense training hardened most.

Ten women mixed in. She doubted they held any personal autonomy beyond their households. The men she encountered in Sandven seldom abused their female family members, but neither did they grant them full freedoms. *Then again, my life was not my own in Cothel either.* She never liked the idea that her father and mother married off each of her older sisters without their involvement. *Only my mother's cruelty and fear spared me that fate.*

In addition to the mental activity leaking from people into the world, Stephenie examined the energy potentials of all the physical matter. Unlike almost every other living person, she could actually visualize the forces that held the world together. Matter and energy; everything consisted of a ratio of the two. Dense materials—like the metal of the swords, daggers, and knives worn by everyone in the room—stood out in her mind's eye from the cloth, wood, and flesh. The cold stone of the walls behind the tapestries felt different from that of the stone around the central fire pit, which held a greater reservoir of energy absorbed from the hot coals.

When she focused her attention, she could see all the hidden currents as a spectrum of color that flowed through the solids, liquids, and air as the energy moved from concentrated sources of higher potential to less concentrated areas. Like water, the energy that existed in and around everything wanted to flow and spread out. *Cold and hot mixing to become warm.*

She did not investigate anything too closely, focusing instead on confirming potential threats. Most specifically, anyone else in the room born with the ability to manipulate the energy of the universe. These people appeared to her senses as a spot of low potential energy, or a hole in the fabric of the world, because the surrounding energy flowed into them.

Centuries of purges killed off most people who had an ancestor that could pass on a natural talent for magic. Now those who could use magic had so little ability that they might not even realize they possessed any powers at all. *And then I come along. A bastard daughter.*

She marked the king and his old advisor as threats because they appeared as slightly dimmer spots to her mind. The limited flow of power meant they had either learned to consciously control their draw of energy, or that they had limited capabilities.

Only four other people in the room drew energy into themselves, but she did not turn her head to look in their direction. Her mental senses did not need her eyes to see them. One of the four she knew intimately, as Kas stood one step behind her and to her right. The other three stood together in a cluster near one of the large posts holding up the roof. *Likely a family that managed to pass on the genetic ability, but reducing their capacity for magic with each new generation.*

Stephenie shifted her focus, spreading her awareness further, going through the rough stone walls of the throne room and even through the stone of the adjacent buildings. Her mind peered through the solid material as though she looked through fog. Hundreds of minds filled her senses, and she could not separate those at the periphery into distinct people. They appeared only as a mass of mental activity.

I hope the others are okay, Kas whispered telepathically to her in Dalish, a language long dead to the world. With their close proximity, and the limited strength behind his projection of thoughts, it remained unlikely anyone else would hear the communication, but using his native language ensured their privacy.

Stephenie did not respond to the inquiry and continued to search for Ryia. Dense obstacles, like stone, significantly reduced her range and sensitivity. Coupled with the large grouping of minds in the adjacent buildings, she had trouble picking out her friend. Her familiarity with Ryia made her more attuned to the younger woman, but that did not overcome the environmental noise. After a moment, she noticed energy flowing into someone and isolated Ryia's mind from the others. She forgave Ryia for not exercising more caution. Her friend, along with Henton and Perain, had stood surrounded by Ivan's soldiers when Stephenie and Kas had left them. *She's bound to feel threatened.*

Has anything happened to them? Kas continued his inquiry.

Stephenie finally responded, knowing his own limited ability meant he could not sense Ryia or the others. *They seem safe.* To herself, she added, *there is at least no magical fight taking place. A step in the right direction for Ryia.*

Stephenie noticed a slight shift of the King's posture and then his roaming gaze rested on her eyes. She gripped both of her forearms with her hands and held them level with her chest. After a momentary pause, she offered a slight bow of her head to the only person in the room who sat. "Your Majesty," she said in Sandvian as she released her arms and let them drop to her sides. Her words held a slight sharpness carried over from Cothish that almost three years of practice had not removed.

Ivan shifted slightly in his chair, and he crossed his arms. "You're younger than I expected. A child, really. Have you even reached your majority?"

Stephenie moistened her lips. The smoke clung to everything and left the slight taste of sulfur in her mouth. She pulled her shoulders back and shifted her head, sending a ripple through her long red hair that now went past the middle of her back. Henton no longer called her vain to her face, but she knew he thought her obsession with maintaining her hair foolish.

"I'm older than I appear." She found it hard to believe that she would turn twenty-two in less than four months. That she looked only sixteen or seventeen meant most people had that question, though no one ever voiced it aloud within her hearing. *And if what I've been told is correct, I won't look any different for centuries.* The thought did not offer comfort.

Ivan leaned slightly forward, his hands moving to the arms of his worn throne. "And you now claim the lands of Ista as your own?" He snorted. "You've even crowned yourself queen?" He held open his hands to indicate the people about the throne room. "Sandven traded with Ista for time beyond memory. The people we met at the border every year were men and women of the north." He narrowed his eyes. "That is, until twenty-three years ago, when the people of Ista suddenly ceased coming to trade." His chin tensed and the man standing next to him shifted to the left. "We sent people into those forbidden lands, fearing they had come to harm and needed help. Sandven's people never returned. For years, anyone foolish enough to enter never returned." His tongue traced the inside of his lips. "Merchants stopped coming. Trade dried up." He held her eyes in his gaze. "Three years past, a handful of southerners sneaked through my lands uninvited, crossed the border to Ista, claimed this once mysterious land as theirs, stole hundreds of my people, and now suddenly show up at my door demanding an audience." He shifted in his seat, and she sensed an increase of energy flowing into the man. "Who are you to claim rulership, let alone demand anything of me?"

Stephenie ignored Kas' mental request for Ivan's words to be translated. Her husband never took the time to learn the local language and she had little sympathy for him in that regard. "King Ivan, when I came to Ista, I came to learn about the events of two decades earlier. Those events impacted me as well, thousands of miles to the south, though I did not yet live at the time. I came north to find answers. Some of which I did." She forced her shoulders down and her hands to relax. "The people that once lived in Sandven and followed me into Ista did so on their own. I've not held them against their will." His brow tightened and she decided not to elaborate more on that subject.

"You have not answered my question. What gives you any right to claim those lands? You who come from lands so far south that we do not know the names, or even the count, of the countries between us."

Stephenie pushed away the memories of all the skeletal remains scattered over what had become her country. Tossed about in their homes, on the streets, and hiding under beds and behind crates. She knew exactly who had slaughtered Ista's entire population and left the bodies to rot before her sire raped her mother. She despised the connection to the being capable of such a heinous act. *I'm not the monster he is.*

After a moment more, she responded. "If pedigree is important, I'm the last born in Cothel's royal household. I'm the daughter of the former king and sister to the current king of Cothel." She would claim the king as her father because he knew she did not belong to him, yet he still loved and claimed her. "If action means more, I have led my soldiers back and forth across the world to stop those who threatened my family, my friends, and my birth country." She did not look at the people standing around the edges of the room, but she felt their eyes upon her. "A great tragedy befell the people of Ista when you lost contact with them. The land needed someone to care for it and I happened to be allowed to pass through the protections the former ruler instituted. I have claimed what was once lost because I was uniquely capable of doing so." *Just as Ista has claimed me.* She felt the subtle agreement of the castle at the heart of her country in her mind. Despite the hundreds of miles of distance, the intelligence living in the stone, named the same as her country, remained a constant presence in her head. *And will be until I die.* The initial fear of having to share her mind with another intelligence had long ago faded. Ista did not want to control her, just to have a partner.

What is being said? Kas asked again.

Stephenie nearly broke the connection with his mind, finding it a challenge to focus on so many things at the same time. However, she had asked him to watch for threats and wanted to allow him to warn her if needed. She also knew how isolated he remained, even around her circle of friends. *Later.*

"And why should I not claim those lands for myself?" Ivan sat back and looked around the room at his subjects. "I surely have more rights than a child from lands that hardly know what it is to live at the top of the world. Besides, unless my information is wrong, only my people remain in Ista right now."

Stephenie smiled. She had a need for secrecy, but some of the people who had come to Ista in the early days had shared stories with their families and friends that remained in Sandven. "Your Majesty,

Ista would not have allowed you to do so then, and she would definitely not allow you to do that now."

Stephenie, Kas demanded. *What is being said?*

Not now, she growled silently at Kas.

She considered Ivan for a moment. *Is he testing me to see if I'll divulge information or lie to him? Surely, he is aware of Islet, if not Douglas and Walter as well.* She had decided before she had fully considered the question. "The people who once called Sandven home now consider themselves subjects of Ista. But regardless, your information is wrong. My beloved sister is regent while I have come here. Her husband, and protector, also comes from Cothel." She decided not to mention Douglas. *Three people of Cothel origin among three hundred and forty two—or one—from the north,* she corrected herself, remembering Perain had traveled with them. *An entire country of less than four hundred.*

She glanced at the edges of the room and the faces of the people closest to the throne. The cacophony of emotions remained a mix of eager anticipation and dread. "We have been neighbors for the last three years and even enjoyed some minor trade last summer. I've come to you today with the proposition of expanding that relationship. I want to establish a fair-trade agreement that benefits everyone."

Ivan considered his words before speaking. "Southerners don't tend to like things that benefit others. They always have hidden agendas." He gripped the arms of his throne again, and this time, the wooden joints shifted slightly. "What is your true aim? Is it to bring your gods here and convert and burn my people as witches, Prophet of Catheri?"

Stephenie raised an eyebrow. *He's done research. Few people here should have heard that title.*

I heard him say Catheri, Kas demanded. *What is going on? He does not feel, or sound, happy.*

She ignored Kas and addressed Ivan without pause. "I would suggest you do not allow any of the southern gods to take root in your country. The truth is, I'm no prophet of anyone. The title was thrust on me most unwillingly. It served a purpose at the time, and no one believed me when I refuted the claims." She exhaled, trying not to allow the old frustrations to surface in her tone. "If anything, I would align more with your beliefs in your Goddess, but I must confess, I don't believe in her or your Dalkin. I do not believe in any of the gods." *Just flying demons. Flying demons that take any form they want and rape mothers to create half-breed cuckoo children.* She pushed aside the rage that boiled up within her, not wanting to allow it to control her.

The man at Ivan's side took a step forward, his voice rough and gritty, as if he had spent his life shouting. "We know you have power. Where you get it from is not clear."

Stephenie allowed herself a moment to refocus her attention on the energy currents around the king and his advisor. Both of them now drew more power into themselves than when she had first entered, but it remained a trickle compared to what she could manage. *That meant that neither would have been considered real mages in Kas' time. Or they are very good at controlling themselves.*

She shifted her feet slightly as she addressed the old man. "I make use of the energy that flows through and exists in all things. I pray to no one for my power. As you would say of the Goddess, those touched by her must take what they want, for the Goddess does not respond to weakness." She turned her attention back to Ivan. "What say you? I would like to establish a relationship with Sandven. I come as a friend and want to renew the long history between our countries. While those you dealt with previously are gone, I would like to honor their memories by working with you and your people."

Ivan snorted. "Twenty-three years ago, Ista dealt with my father, not me. However, I remember all the wealthy merchants from lands far away that flocked to the northern edge of my country to exchange goods and coin for trinkets of gold and gems that other men coveted. They spent some of that coin here, paying taxes and fees and giving purpose to many of my people. When that trade disappeared, my people suffered." He considered her for a long time. "If I refuse you? What then? You will take your trade to the other side of the World's Backbone? Trade with Lobben?" A long frustration hung on the name.

Stephenie shook her head even though she had once considered that as an option. "That formidable range of mountains runs all the way north to the Endless Sea. Sure, I know of passes through the mountains inside of Ista, and in Sandven, but I'm not here to threaten you or issue demands." *I just need free passage of goods into Ista and someone to act as a messenger.* "I want to establish trade and official relations. It will benefit both of our countries."

Ivan let the silence hang in the air. Only the sound of people breathing remained audible. Stephenie did not give in to the silence and eventually Ivan spoke. "You've turned away my people at your border and few who enter leave. How do I know what you do in your conquered country? I have heard about fields of strange plants and stone beasts that move on their own. What powers these? Human sacrifices?"

Stephenie sighed, but kept her focus on Ivan. *Sacrifices do nothing. What will it take for people to learn the truth? The schools we want to build,* she reminded herself. *That's the long-term goal.*

For Ivan's question, she did not want to allow just anyone into Ista, but she needed to rebuild the population and skilled industry. Some of her advisors had contentiously objected to the idea, but Ista's single city could support over twelve thousand inhabitants based on population records going back dozens of centuries. "Our borders, just as they were two decades ago, are closed for internal security reasons. However, I do not hold anyone against their will." She tried to soften her stance, lowering her shoulders that had again tensed. "What worked before can work again."

"You would not even allow me entry?"

Stephenie bit her lower lip to pause before responding. Although she already had an answer prepared for the request, she wanted to make him think she only now contemplated the demand. With a visible sigh, she responded. "I would be willing to allow you to visit. With a small contingent of people," she added quickly. "But first, I would like you to rescind the order that no one can approach Ista. There are people living in Ista that still have family and friends in your country. Your soldiers in Alkmaar, and at the border encampment, prevent them from even talking."

Ivan looked at her. "It begs the question of how you reached Horn Point with no one providing advanced notice of your journey out of Ista."

Stephenie smiled but said nothing. The three-hundred-and-thirty-mile journey had been a pleasant escape from the day-to-day tasks of running the country.

Ivan's advisor spoke again. "You came here with three men and one woman. No army, just the five of you on your tall horses. What makes you think we will let you leave without great concessions on your part? You stand weaponless with your consort in this hall. What would your sister give us to return you?"

Stephenie allowed the possessive rage that always simmered within her to surface in her eyes. "Never threaten my friends." Her voice contained the undercurrent of the inhuman growl her sire had imparted into her. The low rumble left some in the room wondering if the ground had vibrated as well. She held the advisor's gaze until the man looked away and then she turned back to Ivan and spoke normally. "The snow hides many a crevasse."

Ivan grinned. "You are learning our ways. Indeed, the confidence you show is not that of foolish youth. I know a warrior when I see one and there are tales of you slaying many enemies. You are more than you seem." He rose to his feet and his smile widened. "Come, let us dine. I delayed our meeting for the last day and a half to order a feast. We can discuss this trade you want to establish more over food and entertainment." He let the smile drop for a moment. "Though I will have something in return for anything I grant."

Stephenie nodded her head. "I would expect nothing less. Your Goddess offers nothing to the weak."

"Indeed!" Ivan raised his arms as a young boy hurried forth with a scabbarded sword and belt. The boy wrapped the belt around Ivan's waist and Ivan took the two ends into his hands and then looped the tooled leather end through the brass circle before pulling it tight. "Food is set out in the great hall."

"My friends?" She asked.

"Of course. We'll sit them according to rank."

"Henton and Ryia are at least equivalent to your jarls. Perain is a trusted advisor."

"Then they can sit next to you." Ivan and his advisor stepped off the dais and walked past her as they headed toward the doors Stephenie and Kas had entered through.

"What is happening?" Kas asked aloud in Dalish.

"A feast," Stephenie responded aloud. She smiled as she followed Ivan, keeping Kas at her side. While he could sense any potential dangers around them and defend himself, he remained a bookworm and not a fighter. "I'm hopeful we can strike an agreement."

Chapter 2

The journey from the throne room to the great hall took them down a dimly lit passage that bore the hallmarks of age. Stephenie could tell the tiles underfoot had at one time been decorated with brightly colored glazes. Now a woven rug covered most, but not all, of the chips and cracks. The once white walls, while free of cobwebs, remained darkened with soot and stains of countless candles since the last whitewash.

Stephenie kept pace behind Ivan and his advisor as they entered the great hall. The stink of cooked fish assaulted her nose, but she maintained her composure. *That's one thing I haven't grown used to,* she mused to herself. Beef and venison held a special place in her heart because they reminded her of the man who raised her as his own and dining at his table. The northern staple of fish, augmented by other animals, including bears and seals, did not sit as well with her tastes. *Though,* she begrudgingly admitted, *many in Cothel enjoyed their fish.*

"Come, sit down here with me," Ivan said, turning left. He led her past eight long tables that stretched three quarters of the length of the hall. Servants had already spread the food out on platters or directly onto the aged wooden surface. Candles scattered between the piles of smoked fish, kettles of fish stew, plates of roasted meats, and piles of bread illuminated the room.

She glanced around the room and took in the open ceiling with exposed timber beams reaching up to support the sharply angled thatch roof. Six fireplaces, three on each side of the room, emitted heat and additional light.

The door at the far end of the hall, now behind her, opened, and she sensed Henton, Ryia, and Perain enter. She tracked them better with her mind than her eyes, so she continued with Ivan toward the head of the tables without turning to look at them.

"This is a large feast," she remarked, as servants huddled in the corners and out of the way. "What would have happened if you'd chosen to dismiss me?" Stephenie allowed her voice to rise at the end of her statement, offering a subtle tease.

Ivan turned to face her when he stopped at the end of the table, and she had to look up slightly to meet his eyes. "I would've had more food for myself." He stood at the head of the tables, a chair with padding was turned to face everyone else. He sat down and indicated she should sit on the bench on the long side of the table directly to his left.

Stephenie felt the forty-two other people from the throne room, plus an additional sixteen more filling the hall. The fifteen soldiers moved to take positions along the walls, giving the diners space to maneuver to spots around the tables. Everyone remained standing and watching her. Dressed in clean wool riding pants, a heavy blue linen shirt, and leather boots, she did not dress as a typical woman of the north or the south.

Ignoring the stares, she led Kas around Ivan's chair to the other side of the table and then swung her leg over the end of the bench to take her assigned seat. The unladylike action made a definite statement. Kas followed her lead and stepped over the bench in a far more dignified manner to sit next to her.

The king's aged advisor sat opposite from Stephenie on Ivan's right. His mouth showed no disapproval, but his eyes betrayed him. Once he sat, others already at their places also climbed over the benches to sit down.

"Our kind of place, eh Sarge?" Ryia commented in Cothish as she followed directly behind Henton, her reddish blond hair tied back in a masculine queue. "Hope the drink is better than the piss we had last night." Stephenie hoped that the language limited Ryia's sarcastic comments to only their group. The six-month journey to her birthland should minimize the chance anyone here spoke Cothish. *But I need to remind her to watch what she says.*

Henton, dressed in a padded gambeson that dropped to his mid thighs, stopped at the spot next to Kas. He grasped his forearms with both hands, held them at chest level, and bowed his head to the King Ivan. "Your Majesty," he said in Sandvian, with just a trace more accent than Stephenie.

Ivan nodded. "Sit, everyone. We will have entertainment while we dine!" The king leaned toward Stephenie and looked at the end of the hall. "My jarls have chosen champions to battle for us." He grinned. "Just to first blood, of course. And we have healers standing ready should anyone get overly injured."

Stephenie leaned forward so she could look around Kas, Henton, and the rest of the people who had sat down at the table. Ten men dressed in chain armor with swords and spears just entered the great hall. *Well, entertainment for Ivan and the cheap seats perhaps,* she thought to herself, as many of the people's views would remain obscured by their neighbors.

Ryia walked over to Stephenie, her steel-capped staff with dragon motifs in one hand and Stephenie's sword and sword belt in the other. Dressed in wool pants and a gambeson to match Henton and Perain, she appeared more a soldier than a noble in Stephenie's court. No one would mistake her for a man, but neither would they call her a lady. Stephenie took her weapons and leaned them against the bench behind her, allowing Ryia to return to her seat.

"So, tell me about your friends," Ivan said as he grabbed a whole smoked fish from the platter in front of him. He dropped the warm food on his pewter plate.

Stephenie returned her attention to the king. "Kas, as you must already know, is my husband."

Ivan looked at Kas and examined his short brown hair and clean-shaven face. "He's older than you, but not by much."

Stephenie smiled. *You have no idea.* Though Kas appeared no older than twenty-five, he had only had this second body for less than three years. "We have a lot in common." She turned to him and smiled honestly. "And he's mostly just as I would like him to be."

Kas looked at her and mentally asked her to explain the conversation.

I'm just telling him how perfect I made you.

Only my body, my mind is original, he retorted.

"And your respectful giant?" Ivan asked with a nod to Henton as he started pulling apart the fish on his plate with a fork and knife.

"Henton is one of my closest friends. Duke of the Waves is his title. Where we came from, he spent many years on the sea."

Ivan examined the tall Henton. "The sea here is unforgiving. Ice, bears, and seals will ravage our long ships if one does not pay attention." He stuffed a chunk of fish into his mouth as Stephenie skewered a stack of what looked like venison with the two-pronged fork that they provided her. "I know the woman with you is not your sister, but she looks no older than you."

Stephenie wondered if Ryia's eyes had rolled. So far, all the king's statements had been loud enough to carry, and few others spoke in anything more than a hushed whisper. "Ryia is the Duchess of Fire. She might as well be one of my sisters. I've claimed her as such. But you are correct. My older sister Islet remains in Ista." Stephenie cut off a chunk of the roasted meat and put it in her mouth, hoping that no one had decided to poison any of them. The typical way to deal with people who had power involved toxins that would overwhelm the body, forcing it to constantly heal and use energy, giving the poisoner a better change to kill them.

Stephenie looked at the king. "Perain is originally from Sandven and is an advisor on my royal council. He lent us some of his dog teams and sleds when we first came north, and I've done my best to repay his kindness. However, I fear I do that poorly by asking even more from him."

Ivan chuckled. He nodded his head to his older advisor. "This is Jarl Vanic. He's the youngest son of my father's father. He advised my father Trovin for many years."

The older man nodded his head but said nothing.

"Ivan," Stephenie said, "if I may call you Ivan." The king nodded. "Then call me Steph. I know that my sudden appearance at your castle, and the change in status of Ista, has come as a surprise."

Ivan looked up at the men at the end of the hall. The sounds of grunts and clashing steel signaled the entertainment had begun. Ivan glanced at Henton and then back to Stephenie. "There is room for one of your men to show their skill. The winner will take home a hefty purse."

Stephenie leaned forward to see the two combatants come together, swords bound. As they turned, each trying to get an advantage, one of them punched the other with a gauntleted fist. She turned back to Ivan, who had been watching her. "I've come to talk and reopen trade. I did not come to perform, and I would not ask any of my friends to do so either."

Ivan grabbed a chunk of broken bread from the table and bit into it. "In the north, that is part of the negotiation. It's tradition." He nodded his pleasure at seeing one combatant stumble backward. "Expected."

Stephenie groaned silently. *The foolish need for men to measure their dicks and women to watch.*

"Even your advisor, while skinny, is built with enough mettle to at least try." Ivan's gaze moved from Perain, momentarily considered Ryia, lingered on Henton, and skipped Kas. "No one gets seriously hurt."

Stephenie felt the grin Vanic had on his face, but she refrained from looking in his direction. *They just want to see what powers we have.* "Ivan, I'm not entertainment. I didn't come here to perform for you or anyone else. I know my worth and the skills of my people. We have nothing to prove." She shifted her gaze to Vanic and then back to Ivan. "If you've heard that people in Cothel call me the Prophet of Catheri, I'm sure you've heard other things about me as well." She stabbed another chunk of meat with her fork and put the bland food in her mouth. "My proposals would help both of our countries, and if you would listen to them, I'm sure you'd see that." She watched Ivan mull over her statement as she finished chewing and swallowed.

He glanced down the table at the combatants as a second set of men engaged in some exaggerated sword work. "Just what are your propositions?" His voice lowered and his tone hardened.

Finally. She felt Vanic's annoyance, and disappointment leaked from others near enough to have heard the conversation. *I won that round.* She smiled. "They are really simple. First, the soldiers you sent to the border. They prevent the people living in Ista from visiting and seeing their relatives. My people need free and unmolested travel. They want to see those that are dear to them, not invade your country."

"You permit no one into Ista. Why should I be the one to allow your people into my country? I want my share."

Stephenie had expected that push back. "It is for internal security, and it has been a long-held tradition." She tilted her head. "That's why the encampment has existed at the border for generations." She sighed. "You may not believe me, but limiting those who enter is for everyone's protection. Yours as well."

Ivan looked at her. "What demonic things do you do that need to be hidden from all?"

"None." She put her elbows on the table and leaned toward him. "The city of Isa Fields, and the waypoint along the road to the border, would seem very foreign and strange to others. I'm willing to let people who want to live there move into the city. I'm willing to let them change their minds, but I ask if they leave, that they do not talk about what they have seen and know. The last thing I want is a bunch of people trying to come north to see things and try to take advantage of my hospitality. As you definitely know, people that historically crossed the border without an invitation did not return. The land is very unforgiving."

"The land is hard," Vanic growled. "But you murder, imprison, or sacrifice those that enter Ista uninvited. There can be no other cause that none of them return."

Stephenie turned her attention to the older man. She wanted to say that the trespassers had not been killed, but in truth, the guardians had indeed killed those that crossed the border without mercy or quarter. The wrinkled and leathery skin around Vanic's eyes made it hard for her to gage his age, but the heat in them made her believe he lost someone crossing the border.

The earlier trickle of energy Vanic drew into himself had grown faster, and she knew his body could not contain the power indefinitely. How he would expel it, she did not know, but she remained confident she could protect herself and the others if needed.

"Ista has defended herself long before I arrived. You know this. Ivan stated as much in the throne room." She turned her attention back to Ivan. "Fortunately, few have pressed their luck in the last three years."

"So, you admit their deaths?" The knife in Vanic's hand shook.

"Any who entered before my arrival died before my arrival. Their bodies buried in rock and ice." Stephenie had surveyed the scattered bones and ordered the guardians to gather the remains into a mass grave once she had bonded with Ista. "Any who have tried to enter since I made Ista my home have been turned away. If they did not then return, the wilds claimed them in Sandven."

Ivan cleared his throat, drawing Stephenie's and Vanic's attention. "I insist upon an advisor visiting to see your city for himself and report back to me."

Stephenie nodded her head. Henton and others felt the risk too great, but she knew it had to be granted at some point. *Besides, it's obvious some people have talked to others even though we ask them not to.* She lowered her head slightly, making a visible point of giving a concession. "I will permit a small group to visit." She looked up. "However, I have the right to refuse your choice if I deem the person unfit. They also need to abide by keeping what they learn secret, with the exception of reporting to you."

Ivan considered her for a moment. "I will share what they learn with my advisors."

"I expected no less. But I warn you to do so with caution."

"Your next demand?" Ivan asked, apparently considering the first item settled.

"I want to establish trade again. Including allowing skilled artisans and experts to immigrate." She reached for the cup in front of her and took a small drink. "You know that I have a small population living in Ista."

"People stolen from my country." Ivan grabbed a handful of roasted meat with his right hand and dropped it on his plate.

She did not want to argue the point. The people came because they thought her touched by their Goddess with powers they had never seen before. Some had come around to the truth, but most had not, maintaining a near worship of her. She ignored the statement and continued. "While in time we can learn the trades we are missing, I would rather not take the years needed to develop those skills internally. But even with select craftsmen immigrating, perhaps from south of Sandven, I will still need to purchase more than I sell for many years. I want access to buy cloth, grains, and other durable goods. I'm not looking for special pricing or concessions, just a fair rate and access to people willing to sell me supplies."

Ivan grabbed another loaf of bread and ripped off a chunk. "What of the trinkets and jewels and pieces of art that Ista used to sell? Are you saying you no longer have what attracted wealthy merchants to come to your door?"

Stephenie pursed her lips. When she had gone through the city, removing the skeletal remains of over nine thousand people to bury them, she had found many items that could be sold. It felt wrong to take from the dead, but these dead would not come back for what they had lost. *And Ista even suggested we take anything of value.* She felt the intelligence agree with the statement and hoped it would not grow tired of her self-doubt. "There are plenty of the treasures the nobles and merchants want."

Ivan drank from his own mug. "I will tax the merchants as I see fit. They are traveling through my country." He placed the empty mug on the table and a young woman with a pitcher moved away from the wall and refilled it. "But I will not be unreasonable. Is that all you want?"

Stephenie shook her head. "Just one more thing. I need to find a couple of teams of messengers that are reliable and are willing to embark on a year's long journey. I have packages I want to send to Cothel, and I want to make sure they arrive safely."

"What kind of packages?"

"Mostly letters and a couple of trinkets." Stephenie sat back, feeling confident that he would meet her demands. "I will pay handsomely, but I want two separate groups to travel separate routes to prevent any single event from impacting both groups. Upon successful return," she met Vanic's hard gaze with her own, and then turned back to Ivan, "I will pay a bonus of ten times the original amount." She crossed her arms. "What say you?"

Ivan studied her for a long time and then nodded his head. "You will trade only with my people, and I will trade with others. That will ensure I get my cut."

"You could set up a larger encampment at the border and act as the broker. It would speed up the process and prevent your people from buying things that other merchants might not value as highly."

Ivan picked at some meat stuck in his teeth with his tongue. "That would be fine." He leaned back as well and held up a hand covered in grease. A young boy with a clean cloth rushed forward and rubbed the king's hand clean. "We will agree who will visit your hidden city tomorrow. Once that is done, they will go back to Ista with you. If they do not return, we will be at war."

"I will not harm anyone, and I will certainly have them expelled after they see Isa Fields."

Ivan nodded his head in agreement.

"Can we also select the messenger's tomorrow? I brought the packages with me and would like to get them headed south. The journey is about six months each way. If they leave now, they could return next summer and not have to travel in the northern winter."

"I do not know how any messengers will find their way to Cothel, but we can look."

Stephenie leaned closer to him. "I have very detailed maps that I will give you. I've marked the route we took to get here. However, there may be options to take ships for a longer part of the journey and perhaps speed things." She saw Ivan's eyes grow bright with possibilities and smiled herself, stating the obvious to drive the point home. "They would definitely give you advantages in dealing with others in the region and with others to the south."

Ivan raised both of his hands into the air and boomed, "Done!" He smiled and stood up. "We have an agreement with Ista. You men," he pointed at the combatants that had stopped to look at him. "I'm tired of the banging of metal. Bring out the dancers. I would rather watch women."

Chapter 3

Dacian ran his hand over his shaved head. "Are you sure?" he asked Vikram. The image of his younger cousin standing outside a building and next to a dogcart overlaid his small bedroom. He ignored the cart emerging from his bed as an inconsequential artifact of the communication stone. The device projected images and sounds of the general area around the corresponding stone into his mind across hundreds or thousands of miles. *At least it didn't have the capacity to transmit smells.* "Did Stephenie really arrive in Horn Point?"

Vikram scratched the black hair on his chin. His skin, several shades darker than Dacian's own deeply tanned complexion, blended into the shadows. "Everyone in the city is talking about it. She showed up two days ago and demanded an audience with Ivan."

Dacian swore. "The troops have massed in Berl. We march in three days. How could this have happened before we were ready?" Dacian bit the side of his left index finger as he paced. He knew massing the army at the Sandven border posed risk, but the one hundred and ten miles through Sandven's desolate countryside to the nearest city had mitigated the concern. *As long as the soldiers don't wait in Berl for days and cause the merchant traffic we've locked up to become noticeably late, we should still be fine.*

He continued aloud for Vikram. "If we delay too long, the risk that Sandven realizes there is an invasion force waiting at their border grows. The current plan is based on them not being aware." He pursed his lips. "We've already locked up half a dozen merchants to prevent them from returning." Dacian sighed. The Sandvians did not represent his primary concern. "We know little of her except rumors." Dacian stopped pacing. His changing position would appear to his cousin as the world shifting around him and Vikram now looked a little uncomfortable.

His cousin took a moment to steady himself and then lowered his voice. "If she blew up a mountain top, then she's not the child of some fifth or sixth gen. She routed the entire Senzar invasion."

Dacian frowned. "Grandfather believes, as do others, that the mountain exploded because she somehow caused a chain reaction with the Gimtar's artifacts buried under the rock slide. The entire purpose of the Senzar invasion was finding something to crush the other houses."

Vikram raised his thick eyebrows. "That is a convenient tale to keep those of us, namely me, who are in the same city as her, from leaving."

Dacian nodded his head. "Yes, but not even a fourth gen can bring down a mountain like that. And we both know that Pusnintarik has grown old. He's the only third gen left and Ordamanis House is all but gone. He's not likely to have sired any offspring. So, the theory makes sense."

"You're sure she's unclaimed?" Vikram asked. "No ties to any family? Yreka left her in the north from what I heard. Chased her across the world, confronted her, and still did not execute her for all the family members she killed."

Dacian frowned. No one would confirm the truth of it, but that story remained. *That must mean she's identified Stephenie's line somehow and Stephenie had to be significant enough to not kill for all the turmoil she caused.* He took a deep breath, tired of repeating the same arguments with Vikram. "Grandfather said we are not to engage with her at all. We are not to let her even know we are here. Who she is should not impact us."

Vikram shrugged. "What do you want me to do? From what I have heard, she came south with four others. I've not gone looking for them."

Dacian nodded. "We need to wait and hope she returns to the north. We are supposed to make sure she stays in Ista. We've not spent the last two years recruiting priests of Fotia for this plan to fall apart before we can put it into action."

Vikram shook his head. "I'm eighth gen. There is nothing I can do if she decides to continue south. But the rumor is she's here to make a treaty and trade agreement. Perhaps if you delay the invasion for a few days, then she'll go back north soon."

Dacian struggled to calm his mind. *You're two hundred and two. Don't act the fool,* he told himself. *Likely, some of Vikram's emotions had bled through the stone.* He knew some devices had better protections and prevented unwanted feedback. However, house Hezin had been declining since before he had been born and they did not always have the best artifacts at their disposal. While they all aged slowly, Vikram had not yet turned fifty. By any of the families' standards, he remained a youth, regardless of appearing slightly over twenty.

With Dacian being two generations closer to a source, his own two-hundred years, and significantly greater power, left him appearing only thirty. His mind cleared, and he continued. "Vikram, I'll find a way to delay as long as possible. I imagine I'll need to wait at least seven days after she heads north again before it can start, otherwise, our forces risk running into her on the way back home."

"Likely."

"What are they saying about her? I would be curious to learn more about Sandvian opinions."

"There are politics at play." Vikram's breathing slowed and his voice evened out. "It is said Ivan wants the trade agreement, but some of his more powerful jarls secretly oppose it. They don't want him to gain strength by filling his coffers with tax money." Vikram shrugged. "The population is definitely not in open unrest, even if they aren't happy with things. If an agreement is signed, some jarls stand to lose a lot."

"Understood. For now, stay away from her and those with her. I blend in a little better than you do, but all three of us are obviously not natives to the north." Dacian pulled the holy symbol of Fotia out from under his robe and let the metal disk rest on his chest. He could feel the non-intrusive intelligence of the device waiting for his command. "I'll go make the case now to the High Council Member to delay. Let me know as soon as she leaves so I can allow the invasion to begin." Dacian continued, more to himself than Vikram. "Andre is going to be problematic."

Vikram nodded his head and then broke the connection.

"This whole endeavor is a fool's game." Dacian could not disobey his grandfather's orders, but he also could not help but think that had he been less eager to answer the call to action, he might still be studying the cultural history of those that lived in Mestad before that country had formed.

Dacian secured the communication stone in a fracture of the stone wall next to the head of his bed. People many hundreds of years ago carved an entire city into the side of the mountain overlooking the pass to the eastern side of the range. Hundreds of rooms, both large and small, spanned eight levels up from the ground. The soft stone allowed for chambers with detailed carvings and imagery. Natural veins of harder stone inspired murals and pieces of art within the very walls of the city. Based on the chisel marks throughout, he did not believe the builders had deployed magic to form the stone. *A research project for another day.*

He grabbed a dagger made with a dark obsidian blade and sliced a cut across his palm, drawing a significant flow of blood. The ceremonial dagger's serrated edge glistened in the lamp light. He set the blade aside, grabbed the linen rag he had used earlier to dry his face, and wrapped the material around his hand, tying off the ends. Once the blood had seeped through to be obvious, he drew power into himself from the environment and directed his body to heal the damage.

The sharp blade meant the wound did not hurt as much as if he used a dull weapon, but the euphoria that often came from healing did not offset the annoyance of having to cut himself.

He checked his robe and then left his bedroom, passed through a larger room used for study, eating, and conversing with others, before exiting into the public space through a wooden door. The long corridor he stepped into had over thirty doors leading to similar accommodations. The holy warriors and priest of Fotia had claimed the eighth level of Berl's Stone City. At this time of day, most of the inhabitants of the Stone City would either be at one of the temples or preparing the three thousand soldiers to march into Sandven.

Dacian made his way out of the long corridor into a wider street with one end exposed to the exterior of the mountain. Not only did it allow in fresh air, but the opening provided access to a wide walkway cut into the exterior of the mountain. The walkway provided stunning views of the surface city west of the pass as well as curved around the mountain's side to overlook the pass itself. A parapeted wall preventing people from falling two-hundred feet to their death had a clear military purpose.

A hundred feet before the exit to the walkway, he turned down an equally wide street that led back into the mountain. At the end of this long street, with multiple doors and side passages, a dozen soldiers in their brown uniforms stood guard in front of a pair of large doors. Their clothing, trimmed in yellow with a yellow circle in the center of the chests, marked them as those without power. They bowed to him as he approached. Once again, he wondered if enemies of Fotia had convinced Fotia's followers to adopt a yellow sun emblem on their chests to create a target. *Their teachings are foul enough that they deserve a little culling.*

"Prophet," the soldiers chanted as he walked past them.

"Faithful," Dacian replied as he entered the grand chapel room reserved for wealthy merchants, nobles, and senior members of Fotia's following. The original builders of the city had likely used it as a throne room or perhaps a market space. Two dozen stone pillars supported the thirty-foot-high ceiling. A twenty-foot-wide gap separated the pillars down the center of the room, with smaller ten-foot spans between the pillars and the long walls. At the far end of the room, the Council of Fotia had placed a fifteen-foot-tall statue of a bald man on a stone platform. The silvery metal shone brightly in the lamp light.

Dacian knew these people's holy shrine represented the peak of magical innovation. The device acted as a relay, transmitting power through it to all the holy symbols the priests and holy warriors used to augment their natural abilities. Instead of drawing power through themselves and wearing down their body, they would command the devices to do what they wanted, and only if needed, would they have to tap into their natural abilities. *Which is really important now that hardly anyone has any actual power, and fewer still know how to use it.*

His research in Mestad had included trying to determine how the people around the Sea of Tet went from understanding magic to believing in gods that never existed. Few documents survived, but he expected the relays and augmentation devices shifted to a holy nature about six or seven hundred years earlier during an extended period of societal collapse. Even now, none of the families had the knowledge of how to craft such devices. *So much lost. But at least the families are not as ignorant as these fools.*

A pair of young priests bowed to him as he walked toward a side chamber at the end of the hall where the council had offices for those who lived in or visited Berl. Dacian walked past another pair of guards, traversed a narrow passage, and entered a twenty-foot by twenty-foot room where a large square table filled the center of the room. The table had numerous maps scattered across it, along with small miniature men to represent troops. "High Council Member," Dacian said, bowing his head to Master Andre.

Andre looked up from his position leaning over the table and then straightened. "Prophet Dacian. I am glad you could join us." Andre's tone did not match his words. The High Council Member crossed his arms. "Your disciple Warner has been causing concern among the nobles. His overly cautious talk of needing to deploy troops all along the supply line needs to stop." Andre did not give Dacian a chance to reply. "He's too young to know anything about tactics, and you were just a scholar, before Fotia called to you." Andre moved around the table and shifted some of the miniatures. "The supply wagons will have plenty of troops to defend them. We don't need to waste soldiers and priests standing on desolate roads."

Dacian held his tongue. *If the goal was purely to take Sandven, you would be correct, but I need a wall across the country.*

"Well?"

Dacian considered his response. The forty-year-old Andre had shaved his dark blond hair since the last time Dacian saw him. The shine on Andre's head distracted him. Anger in Andre's eyes prompted Dacian to speak. "Yes, High Council Member, Warner is indeed advocating caution. The portents indicate our success requires it." Dacian hated the role of prophet. The title had not existed until two years earlier when he showed up at the council and demonstrated powers that only someone whose linage had not been diluted over many generations of breeding with those outside a family line possessed. He claimed Fotia had spoken to him and showed him how to find those that could be called upon to join the ranks of the empowered. *Andre should appreciate that I'm the one that turned his fortunes by providing soldiers. Instead, I get contempt.*

"I question your interpretation of the readings. I have years of experience leading armies and what you are advocating isn't necessary. Perhaps you should go back to finding more priests and leave the war to me."

You think you don't need me, Andre? Dacian pursed his lips. As a sixth-generation descendant, he merited respect as one would give a senior noble of any country. "Without Fotia's guidance through me, there would be no invasion. I brought you over four hundred holy symbols and the people to use them." Without the ability to craft new augmentation devices, the followers of all the gods around Tet protected their holy symbols jealously, for any one lost became one less priest or holy warrior they could deploy. *I found the trap room in the mountains because I know where to look. Or was that my misfortune? Without the augmentation devices, I might be back in Mestad right now.*

Andre's eyes narrowed. The man kept himself fit and practiced with a sword and war dog team daily. Dacian knew Andre thought of him as a younger man without proper discipline, because while they stood about the same height, Dacian's preference for reading left him about twenty-five pounds heavier.

"Is that so?" Andre crossed his arms.

Dacian nodded his head. "I have performed another seeing before I came here." He held up his left hand so they could see the bloodied cloth. "Fotia told me if we invade now, disaster will befall us. Death will come to half the nobles and the Faithful will sicken and die. We must wait until the portents are favorable."

"Unlike you, I've led companies of warriors into battle before. The portents I see say moving now is favorable. While your ability to locate men who Fotia would admit into the ranks of the empowered is nothing less than divine, most of the people have only a year of training, many even less. They are green and restless. Waiting will undermine their confidence further." Andre looked over at Talon, another council member who tended to agree with anything Andre said. "As the High Council Member, I'm inclined to ask the other council members to override the Prophet's warnings and act now. Do you agree?"

"Their lack of experience," Dacian offered before Talon could respond, "is likely one of the reason Fotia wants them to wait." *I just need Stephenie to go back north.* "You declared me Fotia's Prophet when I came to you with his words. I'm simply bringing Fotia's latest message." Dacian moved to the opposite edge of the table. "The invasion will happen. If we take Fotia's advice, it will be successful."

Andre frowned. Talon said nothing. The younger man nearly worshiped Dacian after he first arrived, but Andre bristled at Dacian's influence with the other seven council members, and Talon quickly toned down the admiration. Andre stared as he weighed a decision. After several moments, he spoke. "Very well. I expect you to check the portents twice daily and advise me immediately when Fotia determines the time is right.

Dacian bowed his head. *That look is just more evidence that Andre knows the truth that there is no Fotia.* Over his two hundred years of life, he had met with multiple high priests and leaders of churches. His passion remained the study of how so many people had universally come to believe in a false narrative. Originally, he thought those at the top of their organizations would have the most faith and devotion. However, that youthful ignorance had crumbled after meeting the high priest of Ari in lands south of the Sea of Tet. *That priest knew the truth and perpetuated the lie to control the entire country. He wanted me dead for even the possibility of knowing. So many others I met after him were the same way.*

Chapter 4

Stephenie sat on the short stone wall attached to the boarding house. The aged wall enclosed a storage yard designed for wagons, but now contained weeds. Despite the many buildings in this section of the city, she felt only a handful of people close to them. With the decrease in trade, many of the larger buildings that housed travelers and their pack animals now sat empty and unused. When they had arrived three days earlier, Perain had taken them to another part of Horn Point, where the merchant guild had arranged for them to rent the entire building for themselves.

She glanced over her shoulder at the stone building whose walls extended further under the ground than above. The limited exposure helped keep the wind from penetrating the thick walls and causing drafts. The sod roof, which she could simply step onto from the top of the wall, proved watertight and the rains in the early morning had not found their way inside.

Bigger than most of the buildings in Horn Point, the interior space held pens in the back for more than their five horses. It also had four semiprivate rooms along the left wall and open storage on the right hand wall. A long firepit in the middle of the floor provided warmth and a place to cook. She had counted at least thirty similar boarding houses on the outskirts of the city and found only two others that had current residents.

Unlike the cities in the south, which had two- and three-story buildings packed next to each other, Horn Point's buildings remained detached and scattered about. Nearly all of them, aside from those contained inside the castle walls, were just smaller versions of these boarding houses: a large interior space where multiple people lived, slept, and worked. Perhaps one or two small walled off spaces for storage.

She set down the journal she had tried to write in and turned her attention to the others who now came out of the building and headed in her direction.

"Did you sit out in the rain?" Henton asked in Cothish since they all spoke the language, Perain having learned it as they learned Sandvian.

She shook her head. "The rain had stopped. Though I had to dry this spot on the wall."

Kas pulled out a folded piece of parchment. "Based on my studies, there are three probable locations for a trap in Horn Point. However, this city has changed significantly since the books in the library were written."

Ryia shook her head and looked at the puddles of water on the wall next to Stephenie. "Didn't dry enough for the rest of us?"

Stephenie frowned, pulled energy from the ground inside the pen and concentrated the power into the water. While she could narrow her concentration and focus on the tiny structures that made up the water, doing so normally gave her a headache. Instead, she just pushed heat into the stone. The potential energy of the water climbed quickly until steam rose from the surface of the wall. She forced the power to move faster, and then the water suddenly vaporized into a cloud that blew away. The remaining damp spot on the rock receded, leaving the stones dry and far too hot to touch. She reversed the flow of energy, slowing the small particles of the stones that had become excited. She pushed the excess energy back into the ground, melting the frost that had formed from where she had extracted the energy.

"Thanks!" Ryia jumped up, her own power augmenting the upward force so that she spun in the air and landed with her rear on the wall next to Stephenie.

Henton shook his head. "You should have made her do that herself."

"Go hump someone else," Ryia responded, adding a hand gesture to punctuate the comment.

"I believe the most likely place to find the trap would be buried under the castle, but it would be hard to look for it without someone noticing." Kas tilted his head and looked at Stephenie. "That is, unless you can sense it."

"We're not here to hunt for traps," Henton challenged, causing Kas to turn to face him. "Plus, with the castle overlooking the gulf, you'd likely hit water if you dug too deep."

"Stephenie agreed to help eliminate all the traps," Kas said. "I have spent most of the last two years looking through as many books in the libraries as I could find that had any mention of them. Sandven had one in this area."

Perain shook his head. "Sandven never worshiped any of the southern gods."

Kas turned to the northerner. "That you remember. Before you converted your beliefs into your Goddess, and this Dalkin character, there were people here that used augmentation devices."

Stephenie despised the lies the priests told. The fact that most priests and holy warriors also did not know the truth did not make her feel better. She did not know how or when the reality of the old technology designed to grant mages an additional source of power became divine, but those that controlled the message benefitted from the deception for centuries. *Of course, the original makers had to craft them into medallions that people now think are holy symbols didn't help.* She sighed. *But even if they were shaped differently, whatever they looked like would be undoubtedly have become the symbol of the gods.*

"And what if some people here still use the augmentation devices to get power?" Henton raised an arm toward the heart of the city. "We are trying to form an alliance with Sandven. We can't just do things to cause trouble."

Ryia bounced her feet against the wall. "Yeah, there could be people running around with holy symbols thinking they were getting their power from the Goddess, but they're getting it from other sources."

Kas mumbled his favorite Dalish curse. "You know I hate it when ignorant people call the augmentation devices holy symbols. My ... Wars were fought by people who knew the truth to stop the murders of innocent beings in another world. Your so-called holy symbols are slowly bleeding away the life of a being stuck in the traps people created centuries ago. The evil devices suck away their life to provide pathetic people energy through augmentation devices. There are no gods involved."

Stephenie cleared her throat. Ryia's provoking almost caused Kas to let Perain in on the secret of his age. Perain, and the rest of the northerners, did not know Kas' origin, or that his first birth had been more than a thousand years earlier. They only knew he simply appeared at the way-station after Stephenie had traveled ahead of them when she had led them to Isa Fields. The people that knew the truth simply ignored questions about how he had arrived there. She knew the northerners talked, but none of the stories Ista overhead came close to the truth. *So many damn secrets,* she complained to herself.

She spoke, stopping the continued arguing. "Kas, Henton is correct. We can't go about doing things that will jeopardize our treaty. We need the trade to happen." She raised a hand before he could interrupt. She wanted to chastise him mentally to avoid doing it in front of their friends, but she feared conveying far too much of her frustration over his obsession if she shared a mental connection with him at the moment. "I know we agreed to destroy the traps. But whatever trap was created and placed in this area is likely dormant."

"That won't stop another being from falling into the trap. We are condoning the slow death of a creature in another world so that people can get a little extra power. These devices exist in multiple worlds and will not stop searching for a victim until it is destroyed. Would you leave a dog in a bear trap?"

Ryia mumbled her own favorite curse and shook her head.

Stephenie breathed deeply and kept her thoughts in her own head. *If it's not Henton complaining about allowing people into Ista, it's your obsession with the traps. I can't do everything everyone else wants.* She felt Ista's sympathy at her frustration. "You've asked the people of Ista. You've asked Perain. You've looked through books. Whatever was here might be gone. We've not seen anyone with anything that looks like an augmentation device. We've not seen anything that looks like a relay. I can't simply sense a trap by walking around unless I actually stumble across it. We'd need to work backwards, find an augmentation device, use that to find a working relay, then triangulate from the relay, or ideally multiple relays, back to the trap."

"I've told you, Kas," Perain said. "The markers people carry for the Goddess are made from smooth stones or bone. The Goddess' statues are carved stone. Her shrines aren't made of that special metal the southern gods use in their temples. Whatever crimes you think happened in Sandven are long gone."

Kas shook his head and turned to Stephenie. "You swore to me you would help put an end to this."

She slipped off the wall and landed nimbly on her feet. "And I will, once we have something to act upon. You are free to look about the city and find the trap while you buy the supplies we need. I have to spend the morning at Ivan's castle reviewing possible ambassadors to allow into Ista, and hopefully find messengers to go to Cothel." She walked through the group and headed toward the ramp cut into the ground that led to the front door of the boarding house. "I'm going to the castle alone."

Islet dipped her quill into the ink well and transcribed the notes collected during the last two days into the ledger. She tugged at the end of her brown braid that hung over her shoulder. "That will not be enough," she mumbled as she recorded only two bags of wheat grains collected. The handful of people who worked in the fields had done a good job cutting the summer harvest, but it had grown mold when they tried to dry it. No one really knew how to properly harvest and thresh the southern grain, as this version of the crop did not naturally grow this far north. "And any of us from far enough south never worked a field even once in our lives."

She scanned down the notes and looked for the amount of oats that remained and stopped when she felt the hand sized stone in the pocket sewn into her dress pulse with warmth. With the sun barely setting each day, she had lost all track of time and thought the day had not gone beyond the very early morning.

She removed the thin oval stone and opened herself to the tingle that let her know one of the corresponding communication stones had been activated. The stone's intelligence burrowed into her mind, forcing her mind to see and hear the area around the other stone hundreds of miles away. Islet steadied herself as the office and desk she sat at merged with a dimly lit building that had the appearance of a converted barn. Rushes now covered the stone floor beneath her feet, and a haze of smoke filled the air. Henton stood in the middle of the chair in front of her desk, his legs merged with the cushioned seat in a disconcerting way.

Islet stood up and moved to the other side of the desk, shifting Henton and the building into the middle of her office. "That's better," she said.

"I take it I was in the middle of your desk," Henton said.

"The chair, actually." Islet returned Henton's frustrated grin. "I hope you have some good news. I'm about to ask Ista to send some guardians out to hunt more deer and bears. If only I could ask them to find grains—or dried fish, since most of the people here prefer fish."

Henton grunted. "I've told Steph she needs to establish a small encampment near the shore and allow people to do some fishing." He looked to the left and then Ryia came into Islet's view.

"Hey, hope things are well." Ryia held up a mug of something that steamed. "We got to watch morons fight for sport last night and then women twirl around. The most useful waste of an evening if I knew one." She shrugged. "Steph made some progress, but I was bored and would have rather been in a pub."

Islet raised an eyebrow and decided pointedly not to ask. "Tell Ryia that her students miss her." Islet knew only Henton could see and hear her. The stones transmitted the sights and sounds around them only to the person holding a corresponding stone.

Henton chuckled. "I think I'll leave that one alone. She's been enjoying the time away. You can tell because she isn't cursing."

"I told you to hump the wall," Ryia's voice came to her from outside the stone's view. "Just don't spread the mites to your hands."

Henton ignored the comment, but his jaw stiffened. "The meeting went well yesterday. Steph's gone back to the castle this morning to continue the finer points of the negotiation." His head shook slightly, and Islet knew he tried to hide an underlying anger. After a moment, he gave up. "She agreed to allow some of Ivan's people to come visit so that they can report back on Ista. She's screening the people this morning."

"Henton, you keep walking the same ground. We knew that was likely going to be a condition for opening up trade. The soldiers at the border have demanded entrance since they first arrived late last year and returned this spring." Islet noticed the wet ink that stained her fingers and turned around to grab a rag before she ruined her dress. The change of position swung Henton and his location through much of the office's furniture. She spun back to put him in the middle of the room.

Henton wobbled a little. "Give me a warning. I just saw the world spin."

"Sorry," she said. "But my point still holds. If we expect to have people immigrate, we have to accept that not all of them will want to stay, and when they leave, they will probably talk."

"I know." He sighed and shook his head. "Some already have." He paused a moment, then continued forcefully. "But we have powerful enemies. Probably not anyone in Sandven," he conceded, "but those further to the south? What if one of the Senzar decide to pretend to be a farmer and then gets a free invite into the country?" He tensed his body. "Steph's not learned enough to compensate for the centuries of experience they have."

Islet bit her lip and pushed away the images of those that died at Senzar hands. *I will not remain in that cell,* she demanded of herself. They had broken her in their dungeon, and only because of Stephenie, Henton, and the others, had she gotten free. *I am free. I am free.* She pushed away the panic that could overwhelm her, not caring that Henton would see her reaction. "Let's not tread this path anymore." She grabbed her left arm with her right hand while holding the stone before her. "Do you see trade opening up right away?"

He shrugged, defeat evident in his slumped shoulders. "It would be hard to get word spread to enough people, and then for them to purchase materials before the end of summer. We're ten days from you as Stephenie travels and at least fifteen or more as most others move. Ivan would have to send word south. Those people would have to believe what they heard, decide there is money to be made, buy the things we want, then transport them north." He shrugged. "Late summer at the best, late fall or next year, more likely."

Islet nodded her head. "What about the rest of you? Kas holding up under Stephenie's blistering pace?"

Henton frowned. "He had a fit about hunting for traps earlier. He insisted Perain take him to a couple of places in the city. No regard for the things we need to accomplish." He sighed. "Sorry, I should be more respectful. I don't know what's come over me anymore. I feel like I'm just a bitter man."

Islet softened her expression. "Moving here has not been easy for any of us. You want what you think is best for everyone, but you aren't able to convince everyone—"

"Stephenie, you mean."

"Yes, her most specifically—that you are right." Islet sighed. "I value you as a friend. To be fully honest, I think you need a break. Some time for yourself so that you can figure out what you want. You're struggling."

Henton shook his head. "You're not wrong, but even though I'm fairly useless, everyone seems to still need me."

"Useless? That you are not," Islet replied.

He turned his head to look at something outside of her view, but he did not move the stone in his hand. He shifted his focus forward again. "We're going to gather more supplies while Steph continues to negotiate. We'll try to get some oats and other grains that Sandven imports before we leave. I'm hoping we can head north in a day or two."

"Don't forget to get some fish."

Henton shook his head. "You know what Steph thinks of that."

Islet chuckled. "Tell Steph I love her and to be safe. And you do the same. I want all of you home sooner than later."

Henton smiled. "Same. I'll contact you again before we leave, or if there is some change in the situation." He waved a hand at her and then the connection separated.

Islet felt the intelligence withdraw from her mind as the entangled particles in the stones no longer transmitted energy and information between the pair. She slid the stone into her pocket and moved to the window in the south wall. The room had originally been a bedroom on the fourth floor of the castle, but Islet had preferred this to an office on the first floor because of the large window and expansive view of the mountains. The interior offices left her with a sense of confinement.

Outside the clear glass, she could see thin clouds moving with the southerly wind. A flock of birds remained low and close to the castle, avoiding the strong winds outside the protection of the city. The snow-covered peaks of the World's Backbone filled her view of the horizon. "I am safe," she mumbled aloud as images of the dead passed through her thoughts and tears leaked from her eyes.

She crossed her other arm and hugged herself. Not finding relief, she bit her lip hard enough to hurt and forced herself to look out the window and believe that she indeed saw the outside and not the dark walls of a cell. "I am not a prisoner."

Her breathing grew shallow as the memories looped through her mind. The time she spent as a Senzar captive felt like an eternity, and it formed an insurmountable wall between the phases of her life. Too often, it dragged her in and refused to let her go.

She slammed the heal of her fist against the edge of stone around the window. She repeated the strike three more times before hitting the wall with all her force. The sharp pain broke her free, and she turned away from the window with tears in her eyes.

How can I feel so old? She conceptualized the fact that she had just turned twenty-three fifteen days ago. Stephenie had celebrated with her only a couple of days before Stephenie had left to negotiate with King Ivan. She wanted to have a sense of safety and happiness. She just could not find a way to smile without forcing her face to move.

What is wrong with me? Why can't I stop hurting? Her position as a princess of Cothel had required her to age quickly. Married to an old king at fourteen, widowed and imprisoned at eighteen, freed almost two years later, only to find her father dead and her mother a monster. *And now I'm regent of a new country.* She wanted to find a small cupboard and crawl inside to hide. However, she knew if she did, she would only be returning to the cold, dark cell that Stephenie had removed her from.

"Are you okay?" Sir Walter asked from the door.

Islet turn around and wiped the tears from her eyes. When she looked up, she saw him walking toward her with Sachi in his arms. She rushed toward her redheaded husband and wrapped her arms around him and her six-month-old daughter. "I'm walking memories," she admitted.

"I'm here for you." He squeezed her back and put his lips on her forehead. "Anytime you need me."

"I know," she admitted, tears still flowing from her eyes.

"You should rest. You don't need to put so much pressure on yourself."

Islet breathed in his musky scent and knew he had been outside helping to train the six men who made up Isa Fields' security force. The population generally got along with each other, but a few fights and thefts had occurred.

She pulled away from him and wiped her eyes again. "I need to be of value and my time as queen means I'm better suited to this work than Steph."

"Who again is running around having fun."

Islet frowned at Walter and shook her head. "You might not see eye to eye with my little sister, but she does not rest either." Islet allowed her emotions to fade and pushed down the pain that always threatened to overwhelm her. "We each are acting to our strengths."

"I'm sorry. I don't mean to imply Stephenie is not doing what needs to be done. I just want you to be able to find peace and relax some yourself." He handed Sachi to her and she quickly took her daughter. "You wake too early and bury yourself in work."

Islet played with her daughter's small fingers. "I get up when I can no longer sleep." She looked up at her husband. "I love you."

"I love you too." He forced a smile and stood next to her. "I've got the kitchen preparing some food for you. Come down to the dining hall."

She smiled. "You are the best."

Chapter 5

Stephenie sat in an interior room with Ivan, Vanic, and four soldiers standing guard. She expected her friends experienced a better morning than her, even if they had to go about the city to purchase supplies. Unfortunately, she doubted they would purchase anything of significance until after Ivan officially proclaimed goods could be carried to Ista.

Stephenie rubbed her forehead and looked up. "No, I won't accept that man either." She did not have a way to articulate why the last man had bothered her. His thoughts had been as quiet as the last four they paraded in for her to consider, but something about his nature irritated her and she would not have him enter Ista.

"You agreed to allow someone I chose to inspect Ista and report back to me." Ivan's face had grown more tense as a dozen people so far failed to meet her approval. "You didn't even let me suggest Vanic."

Stephenie looked at the older man and felt his animosity toward her. "And he knows why."

The man sneered at her but said nothing.

"Bring in the next one," Ivan said, loud enough for the men outside the door to hear. He shook his head and continued softer. "I would love to sign the papers that are being drawn up. But I won't give on this."

She had pushed back on him hard enough that his frustration leaked from his mind, and she worried about potentially causing the treaty to fall apart. The door opened, and she turned to see another man walk into the room. The man's dark blond hair hung to his shoulders and a short beard covered his lower jaw. He looked slightly overweight, but definitely not obese.

"Your Majesty," the man said to Ivan, grabbed both forearms and bowed his head. He turned toward Stephenie and repeated the gesture. "Your Majesty."

Stephenie tugged at the energy around her and directed it into her muscles, easing the stiffness that had accumulated in her back from sitting in the uncomfortable chair. The man before her appeared to be about Henton's age, give or take a couple of years, and perhaps an inch taller than her.

"You want to go to Ista? Why?" She asked her question again, hoping some emotional energy would leak from his mind.

"Because I have not been there." The man moistened his lips. "I want to put my eyes and ears on what legend has imagined since before my people can remember. I want to believe that Ista is a land of the Goddess and the spear point that drives Dalkin back to the north every year. I want to know if Isa Fields is the winter home of the Goddess." He glanced at Ivan. "I also want the trade agreement to happen."

"I'm glad that is a priority," Ivan said and then drank from the goblet he lifted from the small table next to his chair.

Stephenie found their belief system of the Goddess controlling the weather and bringing warmth to the land antiquated, though much of that came from her upbringing with southern gods. *Her sleeping and resting allows Dalkin to blow in the cold of winter and then she wakes and brings back life. It is very idealistic.* The southern gods' tenets had far greater complexity, though she now knew those originated mainly from the personalities of the intelligence in the traps. *Or that of the high priests influencing people's thoughts through the augmentation devices.*

She felt a tendril of energy flow into the man. *A mage, either weakly powered or confident enough to control his draw.* She did not sense a dismissive nature from him, as the prior man projected. *The last man did not like dealing with women.* She sighed, knowing her ability to reject people had likely reached an end. "Okay, this man is acceptable."

"Dalkin's balls, that is a breakthrough." Ivan lifted his goblet in salute. "I'll drink to that."

Stephenie sighed. "How many more?"

"Jarl Dufnall the Younger, meet Queen Stephenie of Ista." Ivan's words contained an echo of his drink.

"Brother, I was at the feast last night." The man turned his gaze to Stephenie and bowed his head again. "Though somehow no one formally introduced us." His grin widened as Ivan's lips compressed. "I'm the second spare and last son of our father, Trovin."

Stephenie smiled. "I'm pleased to meet you as well."

"To answer your questions, I'm always escorted by at least five others. I can introduce you to them. Kor is the most interesting of the others."

"There will also be some men to lead our snow ponies," Ivan added. "There is what, three hundred miles between Horn Point and Isa Fields, with Alkmaar the only real city between the two."

"About that far," Stephenie admitted, hearing a bit of dismissal regarding Alkmaar. The community had dwindled far more than other cities in Sandven when Ista had closed her borders. To Dufnall she said, "Well, introduce me to your men and we can get that over with."

"Every single person?" Ivan shook his head. "You said you wanted skilled crafts people to come to your city in the northern wastes. I doubt you will want to look each person in the eye first. A queen has more important things to do all day."

"Indeed," she admitted. They had honestly not agreed on a means to screen new immigrants.

Ivan stood up. "I'll send for your people. We should eat before the dinner feast." Stephenie's stomach grumbled, almost on cue, and Ivan smiled. "It's settled."

"We have one last item." Stephenie leaned over and lifted a small leather satchel from the floor. She reached inside and pulled out two small bundles wrapped in cloth and tied in a netting of silk cords. Multiple wax seals covered the knots in the cord as it wrapped around the cloth. Both bundles fit into her pair of outstretched hands. "I will pay whatever rate they demand to take these south. I want two groups going different routes. Upon successful return with a package from Cothel, I will pay ten times the initial fee. To both of the groups," she added, to prevent one of them from trying to sabotage the other.

Ivan raised his eyebrows. "I should go into the business of delivering messages."

Stephenie knew she sounded desperate, but she had sent people from Ista to Cothel two years ago. Most of them returned last year with brief messages from her brother and the friends she had left behind. However, she had expected more and hoped her brother would have sent messengers back with her people, which he had not. Her heart raced, and she found her breath weak when she thought about how long they had gone without word from him. The feeling grew worse when she realized they had to wait six more months before these packages would arrive.

Foolish worry, she admonished of herself. *Josh and Will would be fine. Perhaps they did send someone, and they got lost.* She handed over the bundles to Ivan, who then handed them to Vanic. She then pulled out three more bundles of folded parchment. "These are the maps I promised, as well as instructions for routes that will lead to Cothel. The journey will take six months to get there and another six to return." She handed over the parchment. "I'd recommend leaving soon so that it's summer in the north when they leave and return. I arrived later in the year and that made things harder." She tilted her head. "Though the sea route might cut time off the journey."

Ivan grinned and handed the parchment over to Vanic. "Definitely. Dalkin's breath does not cease while the Goddess slumbers." He looked at the door and back to Stephenie. "I have people looking for volunteers. We'll let you know what they will ask for payment."

"Thank you."

"Food?"

Stephenie bit her lip and signaled her agreement. *Please something besides fish.*

Stephenie stepped out of Horn Point Castle's outer wall and looked back at the thick fortification. The top of the wall rose over thirty feet from the ground, and while the vertical outer face consisted of large stones, the interior side sloped away from the face with a covering of sod. At the base, twenty-five feet of stone and dirt protected the inhabitants. The top of the wall had a five-foot wide walkway with large boulders that created cover the defenders could duck behind.

The castle complex had impressed Stephenie from the amount of work Sandven's rulers put into the construction of the defenses. It reflected a country that toiled with war far too often. *Though I imagine, it provides some protection from the wind as well.*

Henton took up the lead, directing them across the cobbled plaza surrounding the castle and toward a larger street that ran through the main part of the city. The sun had finally set, but it hovered just below the horizon. Complete darkness at night would not truly return for at least two more months. The twilight nature of the sky meant no lamps lit the city's streets.

She yawned as they walked down the street. Outside of the buildings in the castle, everyone else in the city appeared to live three quarters of the way below the ground. Stephenie looked around and paused for a moment. With the limited design styles and sod roofs, she had to rely upon the ten-foot-tall towers of painted stone to provide a means to navigate.

"Keep going straight," Perain said from the back of their group. Having traveled regularly to Horn Point before he had moved to Ista, he filled the role of guide and royal advisor.

"Thanks," Stephenie said and resumed walking. The ever-present light meant that many people still moved about the city, even in what amounted to the dead of night. Most people they encountered avoided them, the awareness of their origin having spread rapidly through the city. Three years earlier on their journey north, few had bothered to acknowledge the strangers that could not speak the local language. Now fear of them caused people to turn down different streets.

"Too bad Ivan didn't ask for anyone to fight tonight. I'd have volunteered," Ryia said in Cothish. She twirled her staff before her, making Perain step away for fear of getting hit. "I'd have loved kicking a few of them in the balls."

"Ryia." Henton's use of her name carried his annoyance and frustration. "You know, we've been trying to keep people from knowing the extent of what we can do. With your sword work not where it needs to be, I'm sure you'd have relied upon magic—yours or the staff's—and given away far more than you should."

"Whatever, Sarge." She moved faster, nearly having to jog a step to come even with Stephenie and Kas. "Steph, I could have bested a couple of the ones from yesterday without magic."

Stephenie looked over at Ryia. Her friend's early life on the streets had limited her growth, and even at nineteen, the younger woman barely exceeded five feet in height. Henton had more than a foot of height on her. The last three years put muscle on the thin girl, but that reduced the already limited curves she had. "I'm thankful the entertainment was just singers tonight."

"You're no fun," Ryia said. "I wonder if there are any pubs open at this hour. Perhaps I'll find someone to dance with."

Henton ignored Ryia and slowed a step to allow Perain to catch up to him. He raised his voice so Stephenie could hear. "The horses won't enjoy carrying it, but we'll likely be able to reach home with a sack or two of spare oats, as well as two extra sacks of grain." He failed to stifle a yawn. "Any news on when Ivan will tell everyone that trade has resumed? I fear if it takes too long, we won't have anyone bring us goods until next year."

Stephenie sighed. Growing up as the youngest member of the Cothel royal family had limited her exposure to political negotiations, but her father and brother had discussed treachery with trading partners multiple times. "The best I got was that once Dufnall does his inspection of Isa Fields, he'll have the soldiers called off. As for spreading news that business is open ..." She shrugged. "I wish I knew. However, I expect he'll put some effort into it. I think he needs the income."

"What about the messengers?" Kas asked. "Of the items you wanted done, that was at the top of your list."

She shrugged again, ignoring the unspoken complaint about the trap not being on her list. "I handed over the parcels and understand they are still looking for someone to take them south. If everything leaves Horn Point without trouble, I will trust Ivan a bit more." She leaned into Kas, dropping some of her weight onto his arm. "Through Ista, I can sense the communication stones in each bundle. I can track the progress and make sure they are going the correct direction."

"Good thing I found the stones," Ryia remarked, ever proud of her own prowling through Ista's castle.

Stephenie frowned at her friend. "You could have found them two years ago before we sent the first messengers south. I wouldn't now be wondering what is going on in Cothel." She directed Kas around a corner that she recognized. "Instead, I'd have just reached out and talked to Josh to make sure no one has attacked him."

"Well, you better tell me now what you'll need in two more years. I'm not a fortune teller." Ryia's tone remained neutral, neither of them wanting to mention the other items Ryia's explorations had found.

"Any other mages?" Henton asked.

"No surprise, but Dufnall and his man Kor are," Stephenie responded quickly. "Since Ivan and uncle Vanic have it, it seems to be strong enough in that family."

Perain cleared his throat. "Ivan's father's father, Ulgar, could bend the wind. At least that is what the stories say. Perhaps Ivan takes after him. His father, Trovin, was a powerful warrior, but no one says that the Goddess favored him."

Stephenie nodded her head. After enough generations, magic grew weaker in each person and not everyone in a family would present the ability.

Kas looked over his shoulder at Henton. "I am not anywhere as sensitive as Stephenie, but I believe a couple of the jarls might be as well. Or at least some of the people that serve them. It was not uncommon for people in my ... with power to gravitate to position over others."

Stephenie knew Kas had grown tired because he almost inferred his age and history again. She considered admonishing him, but he rarely spent much time with any of them, preferring to spend most of his day in the libraries. *Too many deadly secrets.* She put the thought from her mind and turned at the next intersection.

"I did not get a clear understanding of when you expect we will leave in the morning," Kas said, still supporting Stephenie as they walked together. "Did they agree to have everything written in Pandar, since none of us can read or write Sandvian?"

Stephenie nodded her head. "We'll sign the final documents in the morning and should be able to leave shortly thereafter."

Henton shook his head. "When I stood guard for the ambassadors your father sent to other lands, nothing ever went quickly. I'd expect they will insist on eating a midday meal before allowing you to leave. I would put coin on that."

Stephenie sighed and removed herself from Kas. She had barely considered the problem of documenting the treaty before that morning. The benefits to both sides had made her certain Ivan would agree, but getting it in writing had actually been Ivan's suggestion to her. *I really would prefer not to be queen,* she admitted to herself. Having grown up believing herself a cursed witch who would burn if people learned her secret, she never expected to live long enough to be married, let alone rule anyone. Only after Kas had explained the truth of magic—that the gods and Elrin did not exist—could she grow to understand herself. And with understanding, the constant fear diminished. Never in those early years of life did she envision being central to protecting a country. *A massive threat to a country, sure. Definitely not a positive influence.*

Her exhaustion deep enough that she hoped sleep might come easily, she headed down the ramp and through a wide door just tall enough to allow horses to enter. The building's interior smelled of horse, sweat, and burning. The central firepit smoked in a few places from where someone had added coal earlier in the day, but now the fire appeared mostly spent. Rushes covered the packed earth floor, providing some insulation, but its age trapped odors created long before their arrival.

Wooden posts down the middle of the room supported the roof and provided a hook for a series of oil lamps, only one of which still burned. A table against the right-hand wall had some cold biscuits, a pitcher of water, and a dozen mugs that the owners of the building provided them every day.

"I'll check on the horses," Henton offered.

"Thank you," Stephenie said. It had taken a bit of work to get the former marine to truly enjoy riding. The first time she had suggested the need for horses, he had protested vigorously.

She walked over to the pitcher of water and poured a mug for herself. "Whatever that dessert was, it tastes like I ate someone's dirty socks."

"It's considered a delicacy," Perain said. "You get used to the lingering flavor. Its main ingredient's a root that grows near the hot springs and smells of rot. But when cooked with fish guts, it renders the foulness to something desirable. It's not cheap. I only ate it once before tonight."

Stephenie shook her head. "I'll try most things, but I won't eat something terrible twice." She took a deep drink of the cold water, hoping to wash away the lingering sulfur taste. She paused and stopped drinking after swallowing half the mug. A tingling in her mouth and throat seemed to hide a bitter alkaline coating that lingered on her tongue.

The disconnected sensation spread out from her gut and her body instinctively flooded itself with energy. The sudden pull of power dropped the temperature in the building. Her mind panicked as the poison spread through her. She felt, but did not see, Kas bringing a mug of the water to his lips. Her body protested, but she lashed out with a gravity wave, knocking the mug from his hands and sending the pitcher to shatter on the floor as she crumpled to her knees.

"Steph!" Ryia called.

"Steph?" Henton demanded, rushing toward them.

Stephenie waved everyone away, unable to make her voice work. She could not feel her lips, mouth, or tongue and she found her chest did not want to expand to draw in air. Rage exploded from the beast within her as she pitched forward onto her hands. She made herself a void and power flew from the ground through her arms and legs. She wanted to control where the energy came from to avoid harming her friends, but her own survival instinct overrode her caution. The spilled water froze solid. The moisture in the air crystallized and fell to the floor as a dusting of snow.

"Stephenie!" Kas shouted.

Stephenie wanted to scream from the pain of her lungs and her stomach burning from the inside out. *Bastards! I will eat your hearts!* The stones of the building vibrated. She spared one moment more and flung everyone away from her just as flames flew up her throat and out of her mouth. The raw energy, having burned away the contaminated flesh and poison, needed to escape. Her body's instinctual response changed the nature of her cells and the organs inside of her. Because of the man who raped her mother, her body adapted to the gluttony of power coursing through her.

No! She swore, desperately trying to contain the energy to the core of her body, avoiding sending it through her outer flesh and the clothing she wore. Pain wracked her from head to toe as her lips, nose, eyes, and face transformed. The flames flowing from her mouth burned the floor. The rushes between her hands disintegrated instantly, and the packed ground that had been under the bed of vegetation steamed as the moisture evaporated.

She swore mentally as she fought to limit the transformation. Raw energy burst from her fingers and blistered hands. Iridescent scales spread from her mouth to her hairline and down her neck. Her shattered teeth reformed as rows of pointed fangs and her jaw extended slightly. Her eyes became grey slits and the nails of her fingers hardened and grew into one-inch talons.

The agony of burning stopped.

A moment later, she gasped for air, drawing in smoke and soot from the vaporized rushes. She coughed and shook her head, keeping her tongue from the tips of her razor-sharp teeth.

Kas moved forward, and she waved him back as she dropped her butt to the floor. A burp of fire, much less intense, burst from her lips.

She sighed. Her earlier exhaustion from dealing with dinner was now a fond memory. Every fiber of her being hurt where human flesh met the new flesh of what she had become. With the bulk of the energy expelled, she pushed the remaining energy back into the ground at an orderly rate to allow her body to return to normal.

The talons at the end of her emaciated fingers shifted back into human nails and the iridescent scales that had covered her exposed skin turned to a powdered dust that fell onto her clothing.

"Where are you injured?" Kas demanded, kneeling beside her. "Have you been able to heal?"

Ryia rubbed her temples with her left hand. Her right gripped her staff with white knuckles. Her face lacked any color. She shook off the pain of hitting the support post and breathed slowly.

Perain stood next to the wall she had inadvertently thrown him against. He watched Stephenie as she slumped back against the leg of the table that had held the poisoned water. His discomfort at her transformation was not well hidden.

"Stephenie?" Kas demanded, his hands on her face. "Are you unharmed? I do not want you to come to harm."

She brushed away some of the shimmering dust on her hands. Her tongue glided over her flat teeth. Her desire to contain the power inside herself and not radiate it outwards in all directions had cost her more than if she had allowed her body to fully change. *But at least I'm not naked on the floor.*

"Stephenie!"

She patted Kas' hand. "I'm fine." She turned her attention to Ryia. Henton had reached out to hold the young woman steady. "Ryia?" she questioned.

Her younger friend pushed Henton away from her and clenched and unclenched her left hand. Stephenie's mind hurt too much for her to open her senses, but she expected Ryia's hand and arm showed signs of bruising.

"I'm fine. Leave me be." The younger woman closed her eyes and then used the staff for balance. "What happened?"

Stephenie breathed slowly and then finally managed to speak. "Someone poisoned the water." *If I find out who ...* She worked to contain the rage that would see her shred people with her bare hands. Her power made her deadly, and she did not want the guilt of killing innocents. Instead, she focused on a positive. "At least I no longer taste that crappy dessert."

"I'll kill Ivan," Ryia snarled. "The coward couldn't face you like a man."

Perain took a step toward Stephenie as he overcame his reluctancy to acknowledge the evidence she had one nonhuman parent. "I'm not sure it would have been Ivan. There are a lot of possible threats." His voice was uneven.

Stephenie drew a deep breath and let it out slowly. "Whatever had been in that water would have done any of you in quickly." She closed her eyes for a moment as Kas continued to caress her face. After enjoying his gentle touch, she returned to the question. "Whatever was in the water numbed me, but I think it would have killed me after a short time. I couldn't breathe."

"They might have wanted you incapacitated," Henton offered. He had moved to the first of the rooms, carefully opening the door while checking for anything that might do damage to a person.

Stephenie felt her strength coming back to her and leaned forward. "It acted too quickly to get all of us." She replayed the events in her mind. "The effects would have been evident after one or two people took a drink." She shrugged and pushed herself to her feet. "Had I not gulped it down, I think I would have tasted the poison before drinking too much."

Perain walked over to the table but touched nothing. "They'd have no way of knowing who would have been poisoned. I wonder if the point was to disrupt the negotiation." He turned to Stephenie. "Sandven has many factions. This trade agreement will benefit Ivan greatly. Others might want to prevent that, perhaps even trigger a war. Killing only one of us would spark a conflict faster than killing all of us."

Ryia crossed her arms. "If they'd killed Steph, I'd have killed as many as I saw."

Stephenie felt her own possessive rage and had to force herself to stop drawing in energy, as it would only tax her for no purpose. *None of them were hurt,* she told herself, but her mind would not ignore the idea one of them might have died. *Only Ryia and Kas have any magic, and neither of them could withstand the energy I used.*

"Steph," Perain said, a tremor still in his voice at seeing the predator that existed under her normal facade. "Anyone could have done it. The outer door doesn't even have a lock."

Stephenie closed her eyes and slowed her heart and breathing. After a long period of silence, she nodded her head and opened her eyes. "I also don't think it was Ivan. Vanic?" She pursed her lips.

"Perhaps, but not Ivan." She brushed the short rushes from her pants. "The castle and city need repairs. The lack of regular maintenance is a classic indication they don't have enough funds. They need this agreement as much as we do."

Henton rubbed the back of his neck with his left hand. "I know we've been over these waters a thousand times, but we have too many enemies. The more people learn about Ista, the bigger the risk is." He dropped his arm and looked at the smoldering rushes. "What if someone tries something again and you transform where others can see you? The last thing we want to do is attract the notice of the man who sired you."

Stephenie looked at the dried vegetation on the floor and extracted the energy from where small fires still smoldered, extinguishing any latent threat that posed a risk to them or the horses. All of them knew the truth, and in what Henton considered a moment of weakness almost three years ago, she admitted just what kind of monster lived within her to many more people. *Half dragon. Why do I feel less human every day?*

Her breathing remained calm as she tamped down the instincts that could make her a danger to those she cared for. The fact her body ached from head to toe helped, but anger always simmered within her. For the majority of the world, dragons had died off over sixteen hundred years earlier. That they lived and walked among people, playing games with kingdoms as if they merely represented pieces on a board, had been a surprise to everyone who had learned the truth.

"So, who do we kill?" Ryia punctuated her demand by hitting the end of her staff on the hard ground. "What bastard dies for what they just did to you?"

Stephenie looked around the room, trying to see with her mind's eye anything that stood out. Ryia continued to draw energy into herself, building up a reserve that would eventually burn her from the inside out. Like drink to a drunk, the feeling conveyed a sense of power, but would quickly turn devastating to the young woman's body. The fact that she had the ability to draw upon energy meant that somewhere in her family tree a dragon had mated with a human. Unfortunately for Ryia, her body's tolerances for the power became significantly diluted over the generations.

Stephenie turned her focus to looking at the energy patterns of all the surfaces. Anything that had different potentials from the rest and might show something had been applied to the top. A wire that might trigger a weapon or anything else that might present a danger to them. She peered through the walls and examined the floor and ceiling.

She frowned. *I'd rather have found at least one thing than nothing.* She looked at the water that had spilled on the floor. Most of it had soaked into the hard ground or been absorbed by the dry rushes. Her head hurt too much to determine what someone had added.

Henton paced, something he rarely did. He then stopped and continued an argument that started months ago. "Ista is filled with statues and images that will challenge most people. And that is nothing to explain how an entire city remains a green island in a sea of white in the middle of winter."

Stephenie tamped down her frustration. "You've sailed in circles over that topic." She wished the threat of destruction did not hang over her head, but adapting to whatever came remained her only option. *If only I could go home now.* However, they had to endure at least the morning before they could leave.

She exhaled slowly. "We don't have enough people in Ista to sustain the population. Sure, with generations, the population can grow, but we're starting with only three hundred and forty-two. There are only three people with magic that Ryia is training. And what, six people in Isa Fields, and another eight on the border, who will take up swords as soldiers."

"We are looking to establish a school for mages," Kas added. "We tested everyone in Ista, and those three are the only ones with any potential."

"Kill?" Ryia prodded. "Someone needs to die."

Stephenie knew Ryia's rage did not come from her distant dragon parentage. Instead, her hate matured into a personal desire for vengeance at the hands of people who had harmed and betrayed her from an early age. "No one. For now." Stephenie walked over to Ryia and hugged the shorter woman. "Unfortunately, we need the trade agreement. We can't risk it failing." She looked toward everyone else. "I'll push for leaving in the morning."

"What of the supplies we bought?" Henton asked.

The money spent did not concern her. Ista had more than enough wealth. The wasted time and risk did. "We can't trust any of it. I want the four of you to go out first thing and purchase all new supplies. Do it from merchants that would not expect you and make sure you pick out the goods yourself."

She released Ryia, who moved to an arm's length away. The younger woman had learned a lot about containing her emotions, but right now Stephenie could feel the fear radiating from her. Fear of one of them coming to harm. Fear of being alone in the world. "If I sense someone that's surprised we're still alive, I'll rip the thoughts from them, and then we can deal with the bastards."

"I get to help kill them." Ryia walked to the back of the building with the horses. She stared at the horses for several moments. "Sorry Dancer, no treats tonight."

Chapter 6

"Won't you stay for a midday meal?" Ivan asked as he reviewed the pair of documents on his desk. Scribes wrote both documents in Pandar, the language of the city state of Pandaras, which had become the unofficial trade tongue adopted by many countries around the Sea of Tet. Sandven, and those on the other side of the World's Backbone, tended to exceed the reach of Pandaras' influence, but enough trade had come through Sandven that at least some people spoke the language, and Ivan had learned to read it. "I'll send for your people to be brought to the castle."

Stephenie shook her head. "My friends are replacing our supplies."

Ivan sat back. "Has someone treated you badly in my city? If someone stole from you, I'll have it replaced and remove the head of the thief."

Stephenie watched Ivan with her eyes, but she kept her senses on Vanic and Ivan's soldiers. She doubted any of them had any awareness of what had happened, but they still had not fully earned her trust. "Much worse. Someone poisoned the water in our rooms. I have no intention of risking anything that might have been tainted. I would suggest you have everything we left there burned."

Ivan's shock appeared genuine. Vanic twitched. Concern slipped from his mind before he could school himself. She did not believe it came from a sense of guilt, but fear of what might occur in the room. *Uncertain if I'd try to kill Ivan in front of them? They would have to know a lot more about me than they've let on to think I'd consider myself powerful enough to get away with that.*

"I will have soldiers stationed to guard your friends." Ivan had been about to shout an order, then turned back to Stephenie. "I hope no one was harmed."

Stephenie shook her head. "Fortunately, I drank the tainted water first." A grin formed on her face, but no warmth reached her eyes. "I'm not easy to kill."

Ivan looked around the room. "Guards, please leave and send a dozen men to guard the barn Stephenie's friends are staying in." He waved them out when they hesitated. "Make sure you tell them it is for protection only and let them go where they want. The soldiers are to protect the horses and supplies."

Stephenie shook her head. "They are no longer at the boarding house. You'll have to look for them in the city." She did not look over her shoulder. "And make sure the soldiers know to make sure Ryia knows they are not being detained or restricted. It would not go well. She's far quicker to violence than I am."

When the soldiers left, Ivan cleared his throat. "To step out from the snow cover, I will admit that we do not want hostilities with Ista. I'm angry that someone would try something against you." He swallowed and his voice rose slightly. "In truth, we've heard little from Alkmaar and even less from those who've seen Ista and returned. What we know is that people fear you and worship you at the same time." He struggled to keep his eyes from shifting away from her. "We know you drove off what people called an agent of Dalkin, and they claim the Goddess shown through you. The rest is rumors from people, who talked to people, who talked to other people where you came from." He hesitated. "From the south, stories abound that you are a demon of the southern god Elrin, a witch they could not burn. Others say your title makes you a warrior of another god, Catheri." He swallowed. "The most disturbing tale is that you brought down a mountain on an army of witches and warlocks, single-handedly killing thousands."

Stephenie considered Ivan. Vanic had remained silent the whole time, almost frozen in place. *No mention of dragons?* She wondered if the secret had held or if they intended to keep that knowledge to themselves. *That won't last after Dufnall visits Isa Fields.* "You value strength in battle and defeating enemies. I know from Perain that most of your legends are about great warriors." She softened her expression. "To be honest, many of the tales told in Cothel and other lands to the south are about the same things. In that sense, our people are not very different." She leaned forward. "However, while I'm entirely capable of bringing war to those that deserve it, I have little desire to do so without cause." The memories of those that she grew up with and would never see again ran through her thoughts. "I'm looking to be an ally to Sandven and a peaceful neighbor to everyone else." She smiled. "But I also want to get back home, so I will kindly turn down the offer of a feast. That way I can put my feet on the road."

The tension left Ivan's face and hands. "I will honor that request. The summer days grow long, but they pass all too quickly." He reached for the quill on his desk, dipped it in ink, and then signed the parchment that spelled out their trade agreement.

"On the issue of the messengers, there are a pair of brothers who have traded with the countries south of us." He set aside the first document, sanded the ink to dry it, and pulled the second one close. Vanic lifted a candle and melted wax to drip onto the document so he could apply Sandven's seal.

"They each have teams that agreed to travel to Cothel." He looked up before going back to the inkwell. "They looked over the maps and one brother will sail from Horn Point to Ice Flow, a city in Renot that he has some trade with. They will then head south to Pandaras and take a ship all the way to Antar."

Stephenie nodded her head in understanding. "That will reduce the time it will take them to arrive."

Ivan returned to signing the second document. "The other brother will follow your recommended route along the World's Backbone until they reach some city you had called Jura. They'll head south from there and take a ship to Antar once they hit the Sea of Tet." He looked up, set the document aside for Vanic, and pushed the first one toward her. "With them each starting on separate paths, I thought to allow them to leave around the same time."

Stephenie accepted the quill and inkwell from Ivan and signed her own name on the first document. "I'm fine with that."

Ivan cleared his throat. "For the difficult part—and I tried to talk them down—I managed some, but they refused to go lower." He paused a moment more. "They have asked for a total of ten measures of gold coins between them to cover all the costs and pay their men. I …"

Stephenie set aside the first document to let the ink dry and grabbed the second document once Vanic finished. She had a rough idea of the weight of a Sandven measure and knew that a single measure would exceed the yearly income of a dozen families. *Ten measures of gold?* She considered it for a moment. *It does have to get them to Antar and back before they get the rest. But a bonus of a hundred measures of gold …* She pursed her lips. *Henton and Ryia had called me a fool when I made the offer so publicly. They probably weren't wrong.* She signed her name and set aside the second parchment to dry, Vanic adding sand to speed the process. "I believe the gold in Ista is a bit more pure than that of Sandven, but I'm fine with the amount." She bent down, opened her satchel, and removed a heavy leather pouch. The dragon that had once ruled Ista had amassed much wealth. "Do you have some scales?"

The morning had grown late by the time all the pleasantries and official business completed. Stephenie again refused the offer of a midday feast, to the dismay of Dufnall. However, Henton and the others had long since gathered replacement supplies, and the horses had no patience left to stand around waiting.

Dufnall joined them, carrying an eight-foot-long spear and dressed in a leather jacket over a linen shirt. No longer dressed in the colorful clothes he had worn to the feasts, he looked like a smaller and less fit version of Ivan. The four soldiers she had met the day before stood behind him, each wearing chain armor over light gambesons. They also carried matching spears with swords and daggers on their belts and a helmet on their heads.

Kor stood off to the side, seemingly amused at the light linen shirt and wool pants she wore. Kor wore leather from head to toe and appeared ready to wrestle a bear. The tall man had an assortment of weapons and an unstrung bow attached to his body. Deeply tanned, his blond hair and blue eyes provided a distinctive contrast to his appearance. She had almost refused to allow him to come, but Dufnall insisted he could not go far without his hunter, cook, and healer.

Five additional men came up from the rear. Stephenie had not approved of them entering Ista, but she agreed to allow them to manage the seven ponies that carried all of Dufnall's and his guards' gear to as far as the border camp. She spared a moment of sympathy for the stocky animals and the multiple bundles of supplies that almost doubled their height.

She doubted any of drovers were older than Ryia. None of them exuded the confidence of the guards, and their minds remained far less disciplined. She sensed their discomfort with having to journey to Ista. *This should make my life fun.* Stephenie pushed aside the self-pity, knowing Ryia had grown sensitive enough over the years that she would also feel the fear of these men and that would make her friend grumpy.

Stephenie rubbed Argat's neck and slipped the tall chestnut a ball of oats stuck together with honey. Her southern horse stood sixteen and a half hands high and towered over the northern ponies. Built for running and southern temperatures, Argat's thinner form had shed most of his winter coat, while the ponies still carried a thick layer of hair. *We'll get you back home to the warm fields,* she silently told the horse, knowing Argat missed the opportunity to spend his days grazing.

"Ready," she said more than asked, having already started walking forward with Argat's lead. Her chestnut gelding and the rest of her party could make the three-hundred-and-thirty-mile trip to Isa Fields in ten days. These others, she suspected, would cause the trek to take at least fifteen, *if not more.*

"Indeed, your Majesty." Dufnall attempted to bow in a more southern style, but he looked awkward, imitating motions that he probably never saw before. Then he rushed forward to walk at her side after he realized she had not stopped. His soldiers hurried after him. Henton and Kas fell in directly behind her, with Ryia and Perain at the end of their column. The drovers hastened to get their ponies moving and ended up trailing thirty feet behind everyone else.

"Call me Steph," she said as she turned onto the cobbled street that headed west from the city. She kept herself from turning her head to examine the buildings and people as they walked. Instead, she used her mind to make a mental image of the world she sensed around her.

"As you desire." Dufnall's grin widened. "Though I find Stephenie an unusual name and enjoy the sound of it. Please call me Dufnall, as I have no shortened form."

Stephenie felt the stares of Kor and the soldiers on her back. They seemed eager to protect their charge, but not willing to offer verbal comments. Stephenie watched as Dufnall moved the spear back and forth between his hands, presumably to give his upper body something to do while walked. She expected he actually had some training with the weapon, but she felt he likely remained more at home with books than on a battlefield. "Why did your brother call you Dufnall the Younger?"

"Ivan is the second son of Trovin. Dufnall the Elder, first born, died the year after I was born and so my father renamed me."

Stephenie nodded her head. The idea her parents might rename her because one of her sisters had died disturbed her. *I had nothing in common with any of them and would not want to be a replacement.* Her mother had borne many ahead of her. *Josh, then the twins, Kara and Julia.* She had never known Julia, who died after only a month. Stephenie remembered Kara as a reasonable older sister, but Kara had married a prince of Esland when Stephenie had been very young. *Regina was a bitch, but mother should never have killed her.* Islet, who came into the world just sixteen months before her, had let Regina and her mother influence her before she left home to become a queen.

Stephenie stared into the distance. *Sis.* Only Islet and her older brother Joshua still lived. Everyone else had died. Recent events had changed her feelings for both of them, drawing her closer to Islet and further from her brother.

"I will say that I regret not seeing any of you fight." Dufnall's statement brought Stephenie out of her introspection. "Though my brother lied about it being a normal custom, I had fully expected at least one of you to give in and show your skills."

"We did not come south to perform," she responded evenly.

"A shame," Dufnall said, and then he looked over his shoulder at Henton. "He's taller than most of us and moves like he knows what he's doing."

Ryia snorted from where she followed behind Henton's horse. "I'd have kicked someone's ass. And I'm not tall at all."

Dufnall walked sideways as he looked back to consider Ryia before turning to Stephenie. "Ivan told me he admitted to you we've not heard much from the north, but there are rumors you won't back down from a fight."

Stephenie sighed. "Only when there is no better way." She glanced over the top of the sod roofs at the choppy water to the north. Several sails dotted the horizon, but the far shore remained too distant to see. She enjoyed looking out on the long gulf, even though it forced them to travel nearly due west for almost ninety miles before they could truly turn north. To the east, she knew from the maps, a narrow channel allowed these icy waters to mix with the Endless Sea. Perain had told her that in the dead of winter people could sometimes walk across that channel hopping from iceberg to iceberg.

She shifted her focus back to Dufnall, wishing she could retreat within herself to enjoy a quiet journey. "I know life here is difficult. The cold and ice only relenting in the summer, but the city seems quiet. You don't seem to have large conflicts, at least not over the last couple of years."

Dufnall considered his words for a moment. "Sandven is not a country filled with resources. Our ships sail and catch fish as soon as the ice melts from the harbor. When it freezes over, we cut holes and pull up what we can. Bears and elk and deer and seals add variety. There are trees to harvest closer to the World's Backbone and a pass through the mountains to Lobben. We trade with them for salt and coal. They were lucky enough to find deposits and cut mines into their side of the mountain range." He shook his head. "None of my people have survived the mountains long enough to find value beyond a few animal skins." He nodded his head, silently agreeing with an inner thought. "What that means is we have few people and little to fight over. But when we do fight, we mean it."

Stephenie felt the wistfulness of his statement and changed the topic. "Perain once told me that Horn Point had been renamed from something else a long time ago. What was the original name?"

Dufnall's brown eyes twinkled. "Ivanveld. Or so I would like to believe. It means home of my magnificent brother who teased me as a child."

Stephenie made a point of looking back over her shoulder at Perain and then frowned. His name for it had been equally absurd. The thin man tilted his head in confusion, having not heard what they had said. To Dufnall she said, "I take it the name is quite personal to each person."

Dufnall shrugged. "I know not what you mean." He nodded his head to a group of women walking past with baskets full of something heavy and unseen. "What was the name of the city where you grew up? Antar, I thought I heard?"

"I lived in Antar, the capitol of Cothel. At least until war came from the south." Stephenie hesitated a moment, remembering the night she fled and the pain of learning her mother had betrayed Cothel. "When everything fell apart, I left Antar to save my father and brother. I rescued Joshua and got him back on the throne. Eventually, my travels led me over two thousand miles north to Ista."

"You will have to regale me with the tale. We've days of walking ahead of us."

I should have told Ivan we'd meet Dufnall at Ista's border. "Perhaps." She looked behind her at Argat's inquisitive eyes and wished they had not sold the riding saddles on their initial journey north. While the harnesses to carry supplies had saved their lives, she would rather have covered the ground in the saddle instead of on foot. "I'm just hoping you and your men can keep up with us. We managed over thirty miles a day on the way south."

Dufnall's eyebrows rose. "That is a lot of miles for our short ponies' legs on the rocky roads. The campsites and small villages come about twice as often."

Stephenie smiled and increased her pace. "Indeed."

Chapter 7

Away from Horn Point, rocks, ravines, and ridges filled the broken land. Nothing they could see reached the size of a mountain or canyon, but the land remained challenging enough that only the most determined people looked for routes through the wilds. Rapid travel required remaining on the road, whose construction and marking occurred outside of memory.

Dufnall stopped them at the first campsite west of Horn Point. The standing stones that marked the road for winter travelers also encircled a fifty-yard oval with multiple firepits. Grass and weeds grew in much of the flattened ground, highlighting the reduction of traffic along the roads in Sandven.

With the sun remaining above the horizon well into the night, Stephenie had hoped to get another ten miles in before stopping. However, the drovers and the ponies seemed unwilling to push on further and the small pens inside the campsite would contain the animals easier than tie downs along the road. As she led Argat over to a corral, she opened her mind and connected her thoughts to her equine friend. She examined his mind for pain and indications of injury or exhaustion. As expected, Argat had held up well, so she only pushed a little energy into his body to relieve the effort of the day.

She then silently did the same with all the other horses, except for Ryia's Dark Dancer. Even though Ryia's capacity remained limited, her skill at using her powers had improved greatly over the last two years and caring for her own bay had become commonplace.

Once she addressed the horses' needs, Stephenie reached out to the minds of each pony in turn while one drover brought them food. The animals, not familiar with her, resisted initially, and even snorted in irritation, but their mental defenses could not keep her out. After relief seeped into their tired backs and legs, the ponies settled down and continued to eat the grain the drovers provided them.

The activity took little time and the rest of the camp still had people running about. Kor, she noted, made a fire, and now worked on Dufnall's food in a small pot. The drovers divided their tasks and two of them erected three tents. Another one tried to coax a fire from the coal they carried. The last drover assembled a pair of wooden chairs while the four soldiers stood watch.

Stephenie kept from rolling her eyes and she joined Henton and Kas in setting up her group's pair of tents. The two of them worked quickly and efficiently as Kas explained to Henton how he spent the morning trying to think of a way to calculate accurate distances from written references that lacked numerical details.

"Give me that," Ryia demanded of Perain. "You couldn't light a stick from a blazing fire." She snatched a small burlap bag of coal from Perain and dumped a pile out onto the ground.

Stephenie started to walk over to Ryia to understand the sudden outburst when Dufnall called out to her.

"Come, sit." Dufnall pointed to the first of two chairs. "I made sure to bring a second chair."

"Go, we've got this," Henton said in Cothish.

"This is going to be a long trip home," she whispered in response.

"I cannot say I disagree with his approach of sitting in a chair," Kas said with a smile. "It would definitely be more comfortable than finding a rock to rest against, as the rest of us will need to do once again."

"It looks like rain," she mumbled to him and turned away. When she reached the chair, she looked at it and switched to Sandvian. "Setting up camp goes faster if everyone helps."

Dufnall grinned. "It might, but when we stop at each campsite, then we don't need to rush." He pointed to the sun that still hovered well above the southern horizon. "Kor is making enough fish stew that I can share with you."

Stephenie sat down in the chair, the joints creaking as it took her weight. "Ryia makes a pretty wonderful stew with dried venison and vegetables. It even has some seasoning. I can make sure there is enough for you as well."

Dufnall licked his lips and sat down as the drover working on his chair finished. "Indeed. However, I expect that means neither of us like the food the other is fixing."

She let a small laugh escape. "That is likely true."

"I had observed you that first feast." He took a mug of something from Kor, who went back to the small pot sitting above the coal fire. "Even though my brother had me quite a way down the table, you avoided the fish my brother kept pushing in your direction." He grew more serious. "I had planned to joke with you about it. However, Ivan told me what happened before we left." He paused, but Stephenie said nothing. "He will find out who tried to harm you and have them executed. My brother feared you took great offence at the attack. I can confirm he had nothing to do with it."

Stephenie watched Dufnall and tried to sense his emotions. Mostly, a little fear leaked out of the seemingly playful persona. *But fear based just on what people think of me or fear that I'll learn something about him?* She considered her response. "I hope Ivan only takes action if there is a certainty of guilt. Killing an innocent person would not sit well with me."

"You are quite calm about it. I'm not sure I would be."

She leaned forward and allowed some of the calmness to drop from her face. "If I had found the person responsible, Ivan wouldn't need to act." Her hands tightened. "Had one of my friends come to harm instead of me, you can be certain people would have died before I left Horn Point."

Dufnall swallowed. "Understood." He glanced over at Kor and then back to Stephenie. "Changing subjects. I find it interesting that none of you believe in the southern gods. I thought I understood any heresy resulted in burning. Belief required from everyone."

Stephenie bit her lip. Most southerners hearing the things she now said regularly would indeed declare her an Elrin worshiper and try to kill her. While she did not fear a threat from the priests of Felis, if word got back to Cothel, it would undermine her brother and friends she had left behind. *However, I have always hated the lie.* "Some people of my homeland would indeed call me a witch and a follower of Elrin. Several did advocate for my burning. It is one of the reasons I decided to remain in Ista instead of returning home."

"Interesting." Dufnall looked to the west before turning back to her. "That would explain why you weren't interested in trade with Lobben. You know," he indicated the distance west, "with their renewed fervor in their god Fotia."

Stephenie raised an eyebrow to prompt Dufnall for more information. He had seldom stopped speaking as they had walked through the day, and only a little enticement kept his mouth moving.

"We've traded with them for generations. They don't like those of us that honor the Goddess and despise those who can take her power. However, they would only do things to those who crossed into their lands and made a show of disrespecting their god. Otherwise, they've tended to not interfere with us or others in the area." He shrugged. "War being less profitable than trade, the stance makes sense. However, the last couple of years, they seem more ardent. They even named someone the Prophet of Fotia."

Great! Some other prophet to inspire fools to believe. "I know little of Fotia." Stephenie tried to keep the disdain from her voice. "It's not been a point of any conversation with those who came to Ista, and we've been somewhat isolated these last couple of years," she added, allowing a trace of annoyance to leak out. "I don't demand any particular belief of those who immigrate, but as most of them came from Alkmaar, they have tended to believe in the Goddess."

Dufnall nodded in understanding. "They say Fotia holds the cauldron of rebirth and through pain comes knowledge. Through trials, one can be reborn in his image." Dufnall took another drink from his mug and then rubbed his thick hair. "Fotia is supposed to be some bald guy with eight hounds to run down his foes. Not sure I'd want to lose my hair."

Stephenie nodded her agreement.

"While King Boraue holds the crown of Lobben, in truth, the country is ruled by a council of eight priests."

"You're right. They probably would not like trading with me. However, the more important aspect of Sandven is, you have a road."

She pointed to a thirty-foot-tall rise in the land a hundred feet away that trailed off to the south. "The rough ground makes transporting goods a problem."

Dufnall snorted. "A practical woman." He shifted slightly, straining the chair's joints. "Lobben isn't all bad. We do trade with them. The goods come down this very road. In a few days' time, we'll come to a small community where the road splits, going either north to Alkmaar," he inclined his head, "and on to your Ista. Or heading west to Norbek and finally on to a pass through the Backbone into Lobben. I've been to Berl once a few years back. It's their city just on the other side of the mountains. Half of the buildings are cut out of the mountain itself. There are rumors that caves and tunnels go deep into the belly of the Backbone."

Stephenie immediately thought of Ista. Her castle sat at the base of a mountain peak and had rooms and passages that not even Henton and Ryia knew about. "Is that where they get the coal and salt from?"

Dufnall shook his head. "No, Sudhold, to the south, is where they have their mines. No heathens are allowed there." He gave her a knowing smile.

"Perain, eat shit." Ryia's statement turned everyone's attention. "I know how to cook dinner. Get out of my face."

Dufnall remained silent for a moment and turned back to Stephenie. "Why don't you tell me more about Antar and where you grew up? I love hearing of other places."

"There's far too much to tell." She considered getting up to check on Ryia, but Henton already moved in her direction.

Dufnall drank from his mug. "I heard a story that I don't know I should believe."

She raised her eyebrows.

"It is that you executed your mother after you single-handedly defeated an invasion force."

The real question finally comes out. She considered what she wanted to confirm. The rumors that had spread through Cothel did not sit well with her, but they did make her appear more powerful. She sighed. "It was not a single-handed defeat of the invaders. I accidentally triggered a chain reaction that caused a landslide.

Another war destroyed the mountain top centuries before, so it was already unstable. Plus, the invaders, who call themselves Senzar, had forced their prisoners to dig through the rubble, making it easy to collapse." She decided not to mention the flames that had consumed her body, triggering her first partial transformation. "The morons had their encampment at the base of the mountain and died when the rubble top fell on them."

Dufnall nodded his head and Stephenie wondered if they had heard more detailed facts or far wilder tales that suffered from exaggeration. He waited a few moments to see if she would continue, and then he spoke. "These Senzar I heard are like gods themselves, stealing away the power of your priests."

Stephenie frowned. "No. They are not gods." She glanced over at Ryia, who stirred the food in her pot while holding her staff in her left hand. She turned back to Dufnall. "Some of them are very powerful. Actually, many of them are. Unlike my people, they did not spend centuries killing anyone with a hint of what those in the south call witchcraft and I call magic."

"And you defeated them." He hesitated. "And you executed your own mother."

Stephenie sat back in the chair as she suppressed the anger she still held. "I executed the bitch for betraying my country, causing the deaths of thousands, including my father. Then she started going directly after the rest of my family and friends." She calmed herself. "And I didn't defeat the Senzar. I only stopped their invasion force. They are still a threat."

Dufnall's eyes remained wide. "I am sorry for bringing up a painful subject. I ..."

She shook her head. "You need to know who you are dealing with and have heard things. I understand the questions and that they are not all your own."

Dufnall let out a knowing grin as he leaned forward. "Still, forgive me. I can see now how others can underestimate you. When I look at you from afar, I see a young woman, barely old enough to live outside your father's house, if even that. But when I look in your eyes, I see you are much older."

She chuckled. "I have seen a lot, but I'm not yet twenty-two."

"I very much want to learn more of what you've seen in your twenty-one years."

Stephenie turned her face into the chilly breeze and allowed it to blow against her face. "In time."

The sun kissed the horizon when they finally turned in for the night, and Stephenie wanted nothing more than to crawl into her tent with Kas and tune out the world. However, Ryia's unease and temper had continued to get worse. Her normal joking and sharp humor had been silent, dulled by the presence of strangers, leaving only sarcasm and anger.

Stephenie walked over to Ryia, who sat on a stone near the far side of the clearing. The moisture on Ryia's cheeks remained despite the cool wind. "Want to talk?"

Ryia looked up from where she sat with her staff tucked against her shoulder and under one leg. Fresh tears leaked from her eyes. She sniffed and used her upper arm to wipe her eyes. "I'm sorry."

Stephenie sat down on the stone, using her rear to push Ryia over just far enough to make room for her. She put one arm around Ryia and pulled her younger friend in close.

"I'm scared and I can't get it out of my head." Ryia swallowed the mucus draining from her sinuses. Stephenie just held her. After a while, Ryia continued. "I haven't felt like this ..." She looked down at her hands, her right one just slightly larger than her left one.

"I will always protect you," Stephenie said, knowing Ryia thought about the pain and turmoil she faced over the six months it took for Stephenie to coax Ryia's right forearm and hand to regrow. The physical pain her younger friend had experienced paled compared to how vulnerable Ryia had become by allowing Stephenie into her mind almost daily. By the end of the effort, few of Ryia's dreams, fears, and humiliations had not been exposed.

Ryia looked up, meeting Stephenie's gaze, something she had only been able to do in the last year. "What would have happened if they had killed you?" Ryia gripped her staff with dragons emblazoned on the steel ends. "I need to kill whoever did it to make sure they don't get to try again. You should have done something."

Stephenie bit her lip and then nodded her head. "I feel it. My own fear about something happening to any of you has me constantly scanning everything around us." She raised her head and looked north to the choppy waters that filled the horizon. "We've had a good couple of years to grow complacent; well protected in Ista. Unfortunately, even that is an illusion."

"Exactly. Someone could harm us at any time." Ryia squeezed her eyes shut. "I let myself become too comfortable."

Stephenie leaned against her. "I don't want you to be scared all the time. You've grown a lot, and the staff will forever be yours."

Ryia pulled the weapon closer and leaned her head against Stephenie's shoulder. "What would happen in Ista if you died? Would she drive everyone out? Would she kill everyone?"

Stephenie felt Ista's response immediately. "Ista was created to protect her people. She'd look for someone to replace me. It would probably take a while, and unfortunately, everyone's fate would depend on who that was, but she would not accept just anyone. She has a particular set of criteria."

Ryia shook her head slowly as she leaned against Stephenie's shoulder. "You should have found who attacked us."

Stephenie pulled Ryia tight against her. Her eyes focused on nothing in particular in front of her. "I would rather let a guilty person go free than harm someone innocent. If I don't keep myself in check, far too many who don't deserve it could die."

Ryia slowly nodded her head. "I know. It just sucks."

Stephenie stifled her own emotions. She took a deep breath and gave Ryia a gentle shake. "How about you try not to take things out on Perain? He's not your enemy."

Ryia sniffed and wiped away more tears. "I should apologize." She released the tension in her shoulders. "I just can't face him or Henton tonight."

"You need to get some sleep."

Ryia nodded her head. "I will once they go to sleep."

Stephenie gave her friend a firm squeeze and then stood up. "I'll see you in the morning." She patted Ryia's shoulder and then walked to her tent, where Kas had already retreated.

"My Love," Kas said in Dalish as she slipped through the flap. "Are you finally coming to bed? You do not look well."

She rubbed her temples and pulled in a trickle of energy with the hopes it would relieve her headache. "I'll live," she replied. In truth, she had little left to give. With Ryia slipping back into a despair they both thought she had resolved, and entertaining Ivan's younger brother, she simply wanted silence. She hunched over, as the tent did not provide room to stand, and pulled off her boots. "How about you?" Of the group, he had the most trouble on the journey south. While he physically appeared to be in his mid-twenties, this body had only existed for two and a half years. Much of that time he spent in the library and not on the training field; his endurance reflected that. His magic had sustained him, repairing damage to exhausted muscles, but magic taxed a body and mind in other ways.

He exhaled and turned on his side to face her. "I am feeling a bit left out of things, if I am honest. I am not sure your bringing me on the trip was the best use of our time. I have been completely useless to you and way too tired to continue my research." He seemed to consider not saying more, but then spoke. "Besides, we did not even look for the trap in Horn Point. If there is something caught in it, it will suffer. If nothing is caught, something could stumble into it later."

Stephenie considered her words. His commitment to the ideals his people had over a thousand years ago had grown irritating to her. From everything he had said, the trapped beings lived for centuries and the life-force drained away slowly, similar to how a mosquito extracts blood. *We have time to deal with the traps. It's the pressing issues of the people of Ista that cannot wait.* Aloud, she answered the first statements. "It wasn't a mistake for you to come. You needed to get away." She climbed under the blanket and moved next to him. "And I enjoy having you here. However, I'm still going to give you a hard time for not bothering to learn the language."

"I'm just not the big brute of a man I remembered being before I died." He forced a smile. "Before I lost my body."

"Thank you," she replied to his correction, as she disagreed with the idea he had died. She adjusted the sack of her clothing she used as a pillow and then scooted even closer to him. When she had first met

Kas, he had existed only as an energy cloud held together by his force of will. Extraordinary events more than a thousand years earlier led to him becoming a ghost at twenty-seven instead of simply dying. *If only he'd been aware for those thousand years and had learned everything in his library.* Those that exist purely as an energy cloud tend to fall into a trance and relive powerful memories until they eventually disassociate into nothing. She sighed, knowing her exhaustion contributed to her sense of frustration with him, and she softened her response. "I'm enough of a brute for the both of us. Your obsession with books has always been your most attractive quality."

Kas smiled and rubbed her hair.

"Thank you." She closed her eyes and allowed herself to drift off to sleep.

Islet heard the scratching at her bedroom door and slipped from the bed. Walter stirred beside her, but he did not wake. The former King's Guardsman had lost some of his edge. Nightmares haunted both of their dreams too often, but he medicated his pain with a drink before bed that helped him sleep. Islet did not like how the medication made her feel and hated the thought of being unable to wake if something happened.

She approached the door and opened it. A large stone cat blocking her path did not startle her. The stone surface of the guardian cat's face and neck rippled as though living flesh and scales existed within it. Its solid eyes blinked up at her, though its head sat level with her chest. The leathery looking wings extruding from its shoulders flexed and the stone cat, weighing more than a full-sized horse, turned and walked down the marble hallway with only the softest of clicking.

Islet exited the bedroom and closed the door behind her. The illumination in the windowless hallway brightened slightly, allowing her to easily see in both directions, but it remained dim enough that it did not overwhelm her sight. She did not know where the light actually came from, and Stephenie's explanation never made sense, other than to say, magic.

Ista's guardian led her to the wide stairs at the end of the hall and then down past the second floor to the first floor. Islet knew the guardian would take her to what she called the speaking room. While Stephenie could communicate directly with the intelligence living in the castle, no one else had that privilege. *Or curse,* Islet decided. Stephenie had told her that formalizing the bond had required that Stephenie embed small fragments of metal and stone within her body. The entangled particles, Stephenie had explained, allowed her to communicate with the castle across vast distances without having to travel the distance between them, just like the communication stones did. What that truly meant for Stephenie's sanity, Islet did not know. But the idea of inserting something into her body and leaving it there made her uncomfortable. The idea that the castle had constant access to Stephenie's thoughts terrified her. Islet experienced enough people in her head, leaving her with no sense of privacy, even for her deepest secrets. *I'd rather die than live through that again.*

Ista used the guardian's giant stone paw to push open the doors and navigate several rooms and corridors until they finally reached what had been a large storage room. Islet had to blink away the brightness as the intensity of the illumination rose when she entered. Words and phrases written in Cothish covered the stone walls and floor. The marks in the center of the room represented individual letters and numbers, allowing for the guardians to spell out less common words if needed.

The castle moved the guardian along a path that went around the edge of the room, allowing access to the words. Like a house cat, the stone creature stopped and looked at Islet, waiting to ensure it had her attention.

"Ista, what do you need to tell me?" Islet asked aloud, knowing the intelligence in the castle would hear her through the walls as well as the stone cat itself.

The guardian's left wing unfolded, and it used its thumb, or the leading part of his wing, to point to the word danger. It then shifted to a series of marks that showed a scale of urgency and the guardian indicated a moderate concern.

"Where is the danger?" Islet asked.

The guardian moved a quarter way around the room, pointing at various words and moving on as Islet spoke them aloud. "Someone was murdered in the city." She gasped. While a couple of fights had broken out in the nearly three years they had lived in Isa Fields, no one had ever died, even of natural causes. "You don't know who killed ..." She waited for the guardian to use its paw to spell out a name. "Nokki, son of Heggr, was murdered. Do you ... no, you don't know who did it."

With the limited population, Islet had learned everyone's name, even if she did not interact with them regularly. She stopped watching the guardian and mused aloud. "I remember his brother is called Hugo. Which one had the family?"

The guardian tilted its head and then quickly used its paw to spell out Nokki.

"Did anyone see who did it? Where did it happen? When?"

She watched the guardian frown and wondered if Ista had suddenly wished the construct had an actual voice that the castle could speak through. The guardian quickly moved back to the walls to answer the questions.

"No one knows for now," Islet read from the wall. "In Nokki's shop. Early morning, but that is a guess." Islet accepted the head nod of the guardian as an affirmative to her assumption.

"Please wake Douglas and ask him to come to the castle." She bit her lip. I should tell Steph, but there's nothing she could do from where she's at. "If you talk to Steph first, let her know I'll take care of it." She turned to leave the room. "I'll grab something to eat while you convince Douglas to come."

Islet sat at a table in the main kitchen. Erika, one of the castle's primary helpers, had been up early and offered to prepare breakfast. She provided a small plate of eggs and a roasted root vegetable that Islet found to be not quite sweet enough to truly enjoy. She had already finished her meal and rose to her feet when Douglas followed a guardian through the door.

"Why have I been dragged from my bed and brought to the castle?" The twenty-four-year-old crossed his arms. His disdain for nobility, aside from Stephenie, had caused the former soldier to retire and take up the role of tailor. At six feet tall, the brown-haired man assumed his imposing stance, but Islet did not let him intimidate her.

Islet glanced around the room, noticed Erika and another maid, and then ushered Douglas back the way he came. Once in the hall outside of hearing from those inside the kitchen, she motioned for Douglas to follow her to Stephenie's offices as she spoke. "A guardian woke me to tell me someone murdered Nokki. Ista didn't see it happen and doesn't know who might have done it. I'm not sure if anyone else is aware yet or not, but word will spread quickly. I need someone I can trust to figure out who did it."

Douglas stopped walking. "What's wrong with your husband? Or any of the six constables? Shouldn't this fall to them?" He shook his head. "I gave up chasing people around with swords."

She turned to face him. "Look Douglas, I know you'd rather be sewing someone's shirt, but I need someone impartial. I need someone who understands our customs. I need you. Henton isn't available. Neither is Ryia, Steph—"

"I know they are all in Sandven. I'm not a fool." He shook his head. "You all think you can order anyone about whenever it suits your needs."

Islet straightened her back and closed the distance to him. Even though she had to look up, she jabbed a finger into his chest. "You're damn right we make requests of those who claim an allegiance. What is wrong with you? What if it was Steph that asked?"

Douglas looked away. "Steph wouldn't ask. She'd take care of it herself."

"I'm not my sister. I can't fly. I can't blow a hole through someone's head with a thought. I can't do any magic. I can't swing a sword. I can't just wander through the city asking questions. So, I rely upon those I trust to help me do what I can't." She turned and started walking again. "I'd do it myself if I could, believe me." She heard Douglas following behind her and held in a sigh of relief.

"I'm sorry, Islet. I shouldn't be so—"

"So much of an ass," she finished for him as she entered the office that had a model of the city on a large table.

"I gave up this life before I ended up like so many others." He sighed and then brushed a hand through his long hair. "I could've turned into one of those rebels that opposed your brother for the things he had done. I've killed people in cold blood for what they did to Ryia. You told me to walk away from that life before it consumed me. I did what you said."

Islet softened her expression, though the anger at Douglas' stubborn side still heated her blood. "Steph made you a duke, and you accepted that responsibility. If you wanted to have no obligations at all to Ista, you should have turned down the title."

He frowned and then nodded his head. "What do you need me to do?"

"Get ahead of this. The guardians said it happened in his shop, but they don't seem to know when or who. We need to find out who did this." She raised an open hand. "We need to be certain. We're now down to three-hundred and forty-one citizens. If people take sides, or think justice isn't carried out, we'll have a lot of trouble."

Douglas looked over at a guardian that lounged against the wall of the office. "Won't they protect us?"

"Most of them are patrolling the borders." Islet looked over at the cat that had not moved from that spot since well before Stephenie had left for Sandven. "There are enough in the castle and city to make sure we don't die, but that is not my concern. We need to have a viable country, which means attracting more people. Murders and open conflict will turn people away." She looked at the model. "I wish I could tell you where Nikko's shop is, but I'm sure you can get a guardian to escort you."

"I'm sorry I'm an ass," Douglas said. "I'm just afraid something will happen to take away everything I've worked to build here."

Islet put a hand on his arm. "Preventing revenge killings will go a long way to make sure that life doesn't go away. You have positional authority. Use it."

Douglas nodded his head and quickly left the room.

Islet looked down at the model and shook her head. *So much rested on so few.*

Chapter 8

Stephenie yawned and wanted more sleep, but she decided to throw off the blanket and get up. *I definitely know why Ista's walls block my ability to sense through them.* Every time someone rose in the night to relive themselves, the guards rotated shifts, or someone had a nightmare, the change in the environment woke her. The random mental signals coming from the people around her intruded on her mind and interrupted her own dreams.

She pulled on her boots and slipped out of the tent. The sun had long ago risen above the horizon, and at the pace the others traveled, they needed to get an early start if she hoped to make better time. One of Dufnall's guards, a man named Thale, turned his attention to her as she emerged, but he did not move from where he sat on a rock near his jarl's tent.

Argat, she thought, reaching out to her horse's mind to make sure he had no complaints beyond the normal lack of food and boredom of being confined in a pen. Before she could fully check in on him, she felt Ista reaching out to her, and through that connection, noticed her sister using a communication stone to speak with her. She acquiesced to the request and immediately Islet and her office superimposed itself into her mind. She knew Islet would only see her and not the world around her, as the fragments in her did not act like a normal communication stone.

"Steph," Islet said, her voice strained.

What's wrong? Stephenie asked mentally, seeing the dark circles under her sister's eyes. Stephenie continued to walk over to Argat, dividing her attention between what existed in front of her and what manifested purely in her mind. She knew changing scenery bothered most people, but Stephenie could easily separate the two disjointed inputs to her senses.

"Someone murdered Nokki last night." Islet shivered in her seat and closed her eyes.

Stephenie confirmed the details with Ista before Islet had finished speaking. *Thank you for asking Douglas to handle this. I know he can be trouble, but he worries over Ben.*

"Everyone is good with him and Ben. Even the more stodgy people. He just makes everything so damn hard." Islet let out her breath and opened her eyes. "Steph, I just don't want to see people lose faith in us. It had to happen when you were out of the country. No one here is skilled enough to read the minds of any suspects to make sure we know for certain who did it."

Stephenie rubbed Argat's soft nose and then pushed aside his searching lips. "I don't have a treat for you right now. Give me a minute and I'll feed you." To Islet, she continued their conversation. *These Sandvian visitors want to travel like slugs. I'm half tempted to leave them behind and meet them at the border, but ...*

"We need the trade agreement more than they do."

Stephenie shrugged. *At least as much as them,* she responded as she moved around to check Argat's feet. *Keep me appraised, but I know you've got it under control.* She did not want to admit that she might have invaded a lot of people's privacy had she been there, which she knew would damage the people's sentiment with her as much as the murder, if not more. *Love you.*

"Love you, too."

With that, Stephenie cut the connection and sighed. *Murder. Why now?* She patted Argat's side and heard the rumble of his belly. "Yeah, I get it, you're hungry." She would quietly let the others know about the troubles after she cared for the horses.

Islet went to the fourth floor of the castle and stepped out onto an open patio that provided a view of Isa Fields. The cool breeze blew across her face, and she allowed herself a moment to take in the long bowl-shaped valley before her.

Two and three story pinkish-grey buildings with tile roofs filled the core of the valley. Orderly streets of cobbled stone provided the residents with plenty of room to move about. Green spaces and tall trees scattered throughout the grid of buildings provided places for people to relax and enjoy the outdoors. An outdoor environment made pleasant by the ninety-six black obelisks that covered the valley in a geometric pattern. The magic of the forty-foot-tall towers created a bubble of consistent warmth and blocked the worst of the wind, snow, and ice.

Fields with stone dividing walls occupied the land beyond the area reserved for the buildings. A forest, more at home in the south, filled the northern most edge of the city. The outer edge of the valley carved out of the mountain had a sharply defined edge created by a line of three-foot tall obsidian obelisks spaced twenty feet apart. That boundary connected to the tall obelisks to form an unbroken and invisible dome. The castle's awareness extended from them, letting it know if anyone entered or left the city.

Islet moved to the edge of the parapeted wall and looked down at the courtyard that surrounded the castle. She saw Douglas standing on the white granite flagstones next to one of the many planters filled with flowers. He appeared to take in the numerous trees and statues that decorated the grounds. Islet reminded herself that a dragon had formed all of it with his magic and that human hands had not labored to craft what she saw. *Though two gardeners did now tend to the flowers.*

After some time, Douglas moved, heading to the first set of steps that ran the length of the east side of the castle courtyard and allowed people access from the main entrance to a plaza filled with a massive granite water fountain. The opulent structure had seven levels of pools for the water to land in before it drained into a large oval basin that surrounded a complex scene of a forest glade. Different vignettes depicted animals, including large cats, horses, and fish. Others showed elves, humans, and strange humanoids lounging together happily.

She watched as Douglas paused again, looking at the sixty-foot-wide fountain. She suspected his attention fell on the pair of two elven men entwined in a passionate embrace. However, many groups of beings engaged in acts of pleasure existed in the stone. At one time, the sensibilities imparted by her mother and tutors would have made her blush and turn away from such a hedonistic display. However, a year in a cell where many people had seen her in compromising situations had left her ambivalent to the imagery.

Douglas left the fountain at a hurried pace, using the second set of stairs on the other side of the fountain to descend into the city proper. She noted the half dozen guardians that sat watch around the castle. She wished more of the stone beasts existed to protect the city. On her own personal tours of the city, she observed many empty alcoves where one of the winged cats that no longer existed had once waited patiently. Stephenie's sire, Duvargintik, destroyed many of them when he rampaged through the city, killing every living person. "The murder of Kervigar had not been enough. Everything around us seems to want to destroy. Why can't happiness exist?"

Islet sighed as she lost sight of Douglas on his way to Nokki's woodworking shop. She trusted the man and wished she did not need to demand his help. "But we all have our burdens to bear."

Chapter 9

Dacian stood before Andre in Andre's public office deep in the mountain. The prior councils of Fotia had artisans replace the original carvings on the stone walls with imagery of Fotia and his eight hounds. He found the decision distasteful as it wiped away a storied history of the original builders of the mountain city. What had likely represented a completely different mythology became propaganda designed for those now in power to retain it.

Andre sat behind his gilded desk with several smaller maps spread on the surface. "What has Fotia told you?" Andre demanded without looking up.

Dacian did not roll his eyes, though he wanted to slap the arrogance from the man. Two years earlier, when he approached Fotia's council, he had held his true capabilities in check, but even that limited display had far exceeded what the High Council Member could do. The arrogant man had little concept of just how powerful Dacian and his young cousins actually were. *I am not a hostile man, but the day will come when you will regret the disrespect.*

With Stephenie having left the city the prior day, his primary concern remained how fast she traveled. He knew the camping sites along the road between Horn Point and the various cities tended to be around fifteen miles apart. *Assuming the worst case, she'd arrive in Gaffel in five or six days. Our own troops, assuming two days to take Norbek before moving on, would reach Gaffel in eight. Add two days of buffer to make sure she moves on from the small town.* "Fotia said the armies can leave tomorrow. However, all the portents continue to show we need to leave patrols to protect the supply lines. We should station the nobles along the road from Norbek to Horn Point and have them constantly patrol." *I don't like relying on things to work as planned, but I don't think I can delay him anymore.*

Andre looked up, a sneer across his lips. "I'm glad we waited for favorable conditions. The council members here will discuss your report and I expect we can have the troops leave at first light. Perhaps they can make up for lost time."

Dacian sweetened his voice and leaned forward slightly. "Fotia would not likely want you to accelerate the soldiers' travel. It would defeat the purpose of the delay that our wise lord demanded of us."

Andre's eyes narrowed, but the man did not respond to the bait. "Fine, I will report that. We should still be in Horn Point before the end of the month."

Dacian nodded his head. *If the projections are correct, with five days to spare.* "Remember, Fotia wants to convince Ivan to join the flock. The goal is not to kill him, but to siege his castle until he complies. It will be a lot easier to convert the heathens to Fotia with him backing us." *And it will elongate the conflict, giving justification to keep the road patrolled.*

"I'm older and wiser than you," Andre said, presumably assuming Dacian's appearance matched his actual age. "Please leave the strategy to the council." Andre waved his hand in dismissal. "Report to the troops in Berl and reassure them by providing your blessings."

Dacian bowed his head and left Andre's chambers. *Insufferable. When Grandfather considers this task done, I will end that man in a manner that ensures he realized just how insignificant he is.* He sighed as he left the worship hall and turned onto the large street. Many priests and laymen of Fotia rushed about the eighth level, each bowing and giving him their thanks. He responded appropriately, but he did not want to perform for them. Spending time with the troops would amplify that annoyance tenfold.

Instead of heading down to the ground level and into the surface city, he returned to his rooms. *I'm not a dog to order about. But I guess I am,* he admitted as he turned onto the small side passage. *I'm at Grandfather's bidding. I just hope we do not have to maintain this containment of that girl for too long. Two years wasn't a lot of time to develop a robust method of control.*

As Dacian neared his rooms, he felt the mind of someone moving about inside them. With a little more focus, he realized they moved in a manner that implied an active search of his bedchamber. He pulled energy into his body to prepare for the potential conflict. The man in his bedroom reacted to his entering the outer chamber. *A weak mage?*

Dacian felt the man panic and allowed a grin to reach his lips. "What do we have here?" he asked as he flung open the bedroom door.

A young man not yet twenty looked about. His brown robes marked him as an acolyte, but it would not take much effort to steal robes. "Prophet, I …"

Dacian extended his senses and connected his thoughts to the man before him. The young man, who Dacian immediately learned called himself Kev, resisted the mental intrusion, but Dacian had manipulated minds for more than a century and quickly broke down the youth's defenses. "Kev, what were you doing in here?"

The man tried to think of other things, a girl he liked, but Dacian pressed harder. "You were next to my bed … and found a stone in a natural crack." Dacian pursed his lips and shook his head. "Why would you be interested in a simple … ah, you felt the magic. You're a little bit more sensitive than others."

"I …"

"Don't bother speaking," Dacian said, pushing his way further into the man's mind as he crossed the small room. Dacian removed the leather glove from his right hand and grabbed the man's bare wrist, making physical contact, and providing a stronger connection to his mind. "Who sent you? Resisting makes things more painful." The man sagged, but Dacian forced the man's muscles to tighten so that Kev did not fall to the floor.

"You found a bag of coins." The man's hands moved on Dacian's orders and pulled the leather pouch from the satchel at his waist. He also made the man pull out a small journal and the communication stone. The man moved stiffly, putting everything on the bed. "Too bad you only found a couple of coins. Hardly enough to even buy a meal with."

"I found only a couple of small coins," Kev agreed, despite the bulging bag he had dropped.

"The only item of magic you found was the silver dish that the prophet uses to read the words of Fotia and see the future." Dacian projected an image of the dish that sat on the small table covered in water with drops of blood spreading out, the complex pattern that had formed already lost.

"The portents are real," Kev mumbled. The man's eyes stared straight forward without seeing.

"You were smart and timed the search well," Dacian said. "The prophet returned to his rooms. You saw him coming down the passage, but you had already completed your search."

"I am good at what I do," Kev agreed.

Dacian allowed his eyes to show remorse. "You thought you knew Andre had been correct to suspect something, but now you are certain the prophet is not planning anything. There was nothing to find in his rooms. You will be civil to Andre and report back as instructed, but you now realize Andre's only after personal power. You must protect the secret of your knowledge and not let anyone know you are aware. You must protect the prophet." Dacian repeated the statement five more times silently, building a loop in the man's mind that would continue to reinforce itself.

"Andre was wrong, but you cannot act yet."

Dacian carefully created a mental scene in Kev's mind of them passing in the passage close to the main street and far away from his rooms. He developed a new memory of Kev looking through all of his things, checking under the bed, in the chests, and finding nothing of note.

Kev continued to nod his head. "The prophet is here to guide the council. Andre was wrong, but I can't tell anyone."

With a mental shove, Dacian commanded him to leave and to report back to Andre as previously instructed. The young man walked forward with purpose, and Dacian released Kev's arm. The man's gait faltered for a step and then took on a more natural appearance. Kev left without looking back.

Dacian grabbed the items from his bed. "I'll need a better place to hide these." He experienced a trace of remorse for Kev. The implanted thought patterns would eventually cause Kev to rebel against Andre, and possibly even attempt to kill the High Council Member. *However, some things cannot be avoided.*

Chapter 10

Stephenie allowed her thoughts to quiet and simply put one foot in front of the other. On her left, the rocky landscape spread for as far as she could see. Green vegetation grew in any fertile gaps between the rocks. On her right, the waters of the gulf broke upon the shore at the bottom of a high cliff. A few birds floated on the white-capped waves and an occasional sea beast would break the surface and send a spray of water into the air. The background noise of the wind and sea pushed the prospect of ledgers and counting supplies into a distant memory.

Dufnall had spent most of the day walking beside Perain. The distance and distracting landscape kept her from hearing the topics of their discussion, and that brought a smile to her face. Kas smiled at her in turn as he walked beside her. However, he pivoted his attention back to the road and, she suspected, he continued to contemplate the passages he had read at their midday break. His obsessions with ending the sources of power for anyone claiming that deities provided their abilities sometimes worried her. She knew his motivations had purity, but the consequences could devastate countless innocents. *If only he would understand that we can't be rash.* She sighed. His people had died for their ideals. *Which happens too often when you challenge those in power.*

A tingle of consciousness at the edge of her mental range roused her from her contemplation, but she did not slow her pace. Instead, she pulled in energy and expanded her mental awareness. Ahead of them, the rolling land grew rougher, with more jagged rocks poking out of the ground to point into the sky. Although she could not see it from where they currently stood, she knew that in the middle of the chaotic mess a river had cut a wide gorge out of the land. The cold water drained into the turbulent gulf. Someone long ago had dug a roadcut into the banks of the wide gorge, gradually lowering the height of the road to be closer to the level of the river and the gulf. They then constructed a bridge with a manageable span to allow carts, animals, and people to reach a matching roadcut on the west side of the gorge.

She contemplated the three-quarter mile narrow choke point and the confining walls that eventually exceeding forty feet in height. Then she factored in the four or five people she felt to the south. *A perfect place for an ambush.* Straining her mind, she guessed at least two more people waited with the initial five. *Someone in that group is familiar with mages. Positioned well beyond what any normal person could sense.* The likely scenario meant the men watched them with spyglasses and would pursue them into the roadcut that started less than an eighth of a mile ahead of them.

Keep moving, Kas, she sent him telepathically. *There might be an ambush.* A moment later, she felt his surprise and concern, but he acknowledged her mental request and asked no questions.

Stephenie glanced behind her, focusing more on Argat's feet, but caught enough of Henton's attention that his gaze remained on her. Her left hand flashed a subtle signal for danger and then she slowed to a stop.

"What's up?" Henton asked as he overtook her on the narrow road and stopped on her right where Kas had been. Ryia, who had walked beside Henton, stopped behind Stephenie.

Stephenie dropped Argat's lead to the ground and moved to one of his saddlebags. "Six or seven men south on this side of the gorge," she whispered to him as she pulled a hoof pick from the bag. "Hiding from sight and at the edge of my range."

He raised an eyebrow, indicating he had several questions at once.

She shrugged as she went to Argat's right front hoof.

"Anything wrong?" Dufnall called out as he grew closer to the blockage on the road. He stepped off the packed road surface and moved around Ryia with Kor and his soldiers following him.

"Nothing," Stephenie called back to Dufnall before she finished whispering to Henton. "It could be Ivan's people trying to see what we're capable of. Could be something else." Stephenie pried a couple of small stones from Argat's hoof. "Keep going," she told Dufnall, who had squeezed up on Argat's left. "I'm just clearing some stones." She set Argat's hoof down and glanced back at Ryia. Henton had already passed along the signal to her and then on to Perain, who now waited next to Ryia. Stephenie caught her eye. "I think Dancer's picked up a rock as well. You probably need to clear them real good. He's a bit of a baby when it comes to his feet."

Kas, changed my mind, fall in behind me with Perain. If there are people on this side of the gorge, I expect others are ahead of us as well.

Dufnall stopped to wait on her and watched as she checked Argat's other feet.

"So, who dug out the road?" Stephenie asked as she stuffed the hoof pick back into Argat's saddle bag.

"We don't know," he admitted as she grabbed Argat's lead and started walking forward again. "Ivan had to have people remove some boulders that the ice had forced loose over the winter, but the road's existed for generations. It normally takes care of itself." Dufnall pointed into the distance where a large grey-brown stone stood at an angle. "Many believe the trolls that once ruled these lands had moved the unmovable rocks and built the bridge."

Stephenie smiled at Dufnall as they passed Kas. Henton waited with Ryia as Perain and the drovers passed the two of them, silently changing their order of travel.

"Have you seen the troll bones?" Dufnall asked.

Stephenie nodded her head. Perain had pointed out some stone bones embedded in the rocks on their journey south.

Dufnall's grin widened. "Before man came to these lands, trolls ruled for as far as anyone could see. They shared their blood with their pets, giving them rock-like flesh to endure the freezing gales. When the Goddess called forth man, asking for his aid against the threat of Dalkin, she pushed back on the darkness of night and the trolls fled from the sun and warmth she brought to the land. They hid in caves, under boulders, and under bridges. But the Goddess pursued them with the help of her most loyal warriors. The trolls then climbed into the stones themselves. However, this was a trick, and she trapped them where none would see them again."

Kor grunted an agreement and Stephenie saw the slight nodding of at least three of Dufnall's guards' heads. "However, they did not die. They are forever trying to escape from their prison." Dufnall pointed the butt of his spear at a fractured stone laying on the side of the road. "From time to time, we find the bones of those that try to escape and fail, their flesh burning away in the sun's light, leaving only their bones."

Stephenie had heard the story from Perain already and wondered if the guardians of Ista might have sparked some of those legends; Kervigar had created them centuries ago. During the negotiations, Ivan had mentioned the stone creatures that moved, and most of those who were in Alkmaar three years ago had seen multiple guardians. Sadly, Kas had not convinced Perain of the truth, as Perain felt that Ista's guardians did not explain the bones in the rocks. Kas had argued with him that these fossils were simply creatures from long ago that had died and time had covered their bones with stone. Stephenie trusted Kas' knowledge more than local legend, but given what she had seen done with magic, she could not rule out all other explanations.

As they started to descend below the ground surface, Stephenie lost awareness of the men to the south because of the density of the ground. She turned her focus ahead of them, while also monitoring her friends coming from the rear.

"Does the ice break loose rocks from these walls every year?" She asked, changing the subject.

Dufnall shrugged. "Many a change in weather brings forth demons."

What do you want me to do if they attack? Kas asked her, his position now between the drovers and Ivan's soldiers. He did not hide his concern in his mental communication.

Stay close to Perain and protect him and the drovers. She knew Ryia and the staff would protect Henton.

Dufnall continued talking, unaware of Stephenie's split attention. "It's critical Ivan keeps this road open. There once was another road and bridge over the Vamm river to the south. The road headed directly to Norbek from Horn Point, but the damage to that bridge was too great to repair. This passage is now the only path for trade between Lobben and Horn Point." Dufnall kicked a smooth rock off the road and into a gully filled with loose rocks that had slid down the increasingly taller walls of the roadcut.

Dufnall walked over to the edge of the ten-foot-wide path and removed a small round rock from the loose wall. "Legend says the hills of round stones scattered over the lands were created by dragons looking for their lost eggs. They picked up and examined all the rocks, breathed fire on them, making them round, but finding no eggs, they tossed all the smoothed stones into piles that turned into the long hills." He chucked the rock down the path, allowing it to bounce over the gravel road. "They never found the eggs and so they slowly died off countless generations ago."

Has he been admiring Ryia's staff too closely, or has word actually spread? She knew he continued to hunt for a reaction from her. *Trolls. The mention of dragons.* Stephenie smiled despite the concern at his choice of topics. The idea that a dragon would bother with stones amused her. The truth of their narcissistic nature existed in many stories and tales, but even the most damning stories underestimated just how deranged some of them were. *What can I expect of a species that might live forever and can only be killed by one of their own? Definitely not compassion for humans.* For the vast majority of the world, the dragons disappeared almost sixteen hundred years earlier. For her, the father and king who raised her had nothing to do with her coming into the world. Her actual sire had poisoned her mother's mind, manipulated countless others to try to kill her, forcing Stephenie to leave a trail of bodies on her journey to learn the truth. *That creature had no regard for the lives he destroyed.*

"When I was a little boy, I roamed the wilds and would take a dog sled out into the frozen waste to see just how far I could go." He turned his head and widened his eyes with a smirk. "Once, a friend and I went all the way to the World's Backbone in the early winter." Dufnall looked up into the clear sky and pointed with his spear. "I swear we saw a dragon flying over the peaks before dropping out of our sight." He looked at Stephenie. "I admit we had both been into our drink, but I know what I saw." He frowned. "Dalkin be damned.

My friend fell through the ice ten years ago, so I can no longer have him vouch for me."

Perhaps Caridelis, Stephenie considered. *Maybe Kervigar if Dufnall was very young at the time, but I'm guessing that dragon was dead by then. The disappearance of the dragons had nothing to do with missing eggs or dying off. Their elders demanded they conceal their presence under pain of death. Or so Caridelis told me.* Ista confirmed long ago that the female dragon had been a friend of Kervigar. *She was supposed to teach me, but then she just stopped coming.* Stephenie wondered if Caridelis still wandered the world in the form of a human or if another dragon had killed her. But the idea that either of those two would allow others to see them in their natural form surprised her.

"Drink and snow blindness," Kor said from behind Dufnall. "No one has ever believed either of you."

Dufnall turned and walked sideways so he could roll his eyes at the man in leather. "I was young, not simple in the mind."

Stephenie tuned out Dufnall and the others as she felt additional minds enter her range ahead of them. It took a moment, but as they grew closer, she sorted out a distinct form of intelligence from the people. *Nineteen dogs,* she sent to Kas. Her husband groaned mentally, but she felt his acknowledgement and she knew he would pass the warning on to the others. After another thirty paces she added, *And twelve people.*

The roadcut turned slightly before opening into the lower third of the gorge. The road surface that had dropped forty feet below the ground level now emerged into the open. Much of the stone removed from the ground to make the cut now formed a narrow trackway mounded up to connect the roadcut to the stone bridge ahead of them. Short stone walls prevented people from falling off the road's surface to the rocky riverbed. After sixty feet, the mound of rock turned into a stone bridge with multiple supporting pillars and arches that spanned one hundred and fifty feet over the fast-flowing icy water.

On the other side of the river, the pack of dogs filled the roadway. Most of the men she felt remained within the confines of the roadcut on the other side of the gorge. The dogs and three handlers stood at the edge of the bridge.

Stephenie pulled more energy into herself, holding it in reserve so that she could react quickly. At the same time, she mentally watched Dufnall and the members of his party for their reactions.

"What's going on?" Dufnall demanded. The sudden and abrupt falter in his step made Stephenie believe in his surprise. *If Ivan had arranged for this attack, Dufnall hadn't been informed.*

The dogs rushed forward. Their leashes released by the handlers. The two hundred feet that separated the two groups shrunk quickly.

Stephenie pushed herself, projecting her thoughts as far as she could and then some more. Her left eye twitched despite the fact her mind ignored anything her eyes physically saw.

"Back," Kor demanded, pulling Dufnall behind him as the larger man scrambled to free the unstrung bow from his pack.

Stephenie felt the fear and concern leak out of a couple of soldiers. "Dogs ahead," she called out as she pushed against the minds of the whole pack. She did not want to reveal too much of her ability, even if neither Ivan nor Dufnall had put this into motion. Her bubble of awareness then registered dogs coming from behind them as well, and she shouted in Cothish, "Ryia, dogs from behind!"

She did not hear a response from the rear guard, but she expected Ryia and Henton had it covered. *At least the roadcut limits the enemies' numbers as well.* She offered herself the reassurance while continuing to assess the threat.

Kor worked to string his bow and the four other soldiers made a wedge position across the road, primarily protecting Dufnall with their spears leveled to engage the dogs. However, one man stepped in front of her to offer protection. She recognized the gesture, but she kept her focus on the animals.

Argat stood motionless, despite the snarling dogs sprinting toward them. The pack's eager aggression evident in the barking and snipping at each other. The other horses and northern ponies radiated fear and Dufnall's drovers fought to keep control of their animals.

"Arrows," Kas yelled in Cothish. Stephenie sensed him form a gravitational barrier above them that would deflect anything that rained down off to the sides.

Stephenie closed her eyes. She counted twenty dogs charging in from the rear. The nineteen ahead of them had closed to sixty feet.

Mine! She mentally shouted at the dogs in front of her. A rumbling growl vibrated through the ground and into the air. The soldiers ahead of her spun their heads, looking for the source of the inhuman sound. She ignored them and continued to project dominance and power at the animals, knowing they would not understand words. The dog's minds resisted her intrusion, especially since it lacked a specific target. However, as predators, they recognized her power. She pushed harder, ignoring everything else around her. The energy swirling around her body created a haze, but no one noticed because their attention remained on the arrows raining down from above.

Her hands tightened slightly as the energy burned. She unleashed the possessive anger that she inherited from her sire, and as one, the dogs stopped their forward movement. Their ears shifted back, and their tails dropped between their legs. Wines of fear and submission issued from most of the pack.

One of the former pack leaders snarled and Stephenie channeled a trickle of power to create a gravitational snap, inflicting pain into the brown-haired dog as if she had bitten him from afar. The former alpha dropped his belly to the ground and whimpered. Several of the others had rolled onto their sides, looking away from Stephenie and making themselves small.

Behind her, she heard the echo of thunder and felt the energetic release of electrical energy filling the air. A second blast followed immediately after the first. The horses, ponies, and Dufnall's men jumped with panic.

Stephenie turned her attention to the dogs coming up from the rear. The range to them made her whimper with the effort, but before she could tell Ryia to stop killing the animals, movement in front of her drew her focus. A small object raced horizontally across the gorge directly at her.

She opened her senses, and while it seemed to be a crossbow bolt, unlike the other projectiles that followed an arched trajectory, this metal object accelerated in a direct line, as though gravity had no influence on it. A heartbeat later, it reached Kas' gravitational barrier and cut right through it.

Shit! She instinctively forced a field to deflect the bolt, but the object ripped through her protection. Power coursed through her as she flung the soldier before her out of the bolt's path while doing the same to herself.

The bolt shifted course and instead of flying over her right shoulder, it smashed into it. Bone shattered, muscles tore. She felt a surge of power, and memories of exploding magical devices filled her mind. She instinctively tried to form a field to pull it from her body, but it deflected her attempt.

A fraction of a heartbeat later, pain raced through her body. Instead of exploding, lightning and pure energy shocked her system. Her heart and other muscles spasmed. She reacted without conscious thought, drawing in the raw power and absorbing it like she would from any other source. Flames cracked around her hands as her left hand reached up and ripped the bolt from her shoulder.

Argat had shuffled backwards as she staggered into the short wall at the side of the road. She lost her footing and slipped to her rear. Breath refused to enter her chest, and she shifted her focus to the immediate issue of her muscles not wanting to work correctly. More power surged through her, healing the damaged nerves, but it also burned muscle in its wake. Her body wanted to transform. The energy exceeded what a human could normally tolerate, but she forced herself to remain as she was.

A few moments later, relief filled her as she breathed deeply. Pain radiated from every part of her, but as her lungs continued to bring fresh air into her body, she focused her thoughts on things other than the pain. *It will pass.*

"Stephenie!" Kas screamed.

She paused long enough to reassess the situation. A normal crossbow bolt hit the road ahead of her, no longer bouncing off Kas' protection as he rushed forward.

Hold your position! She shouted at him mentally. She felt him slow and the field he had been maintaining returned in time to deflect the next bolts that arched in their direction.

They hurt you. I must help you!

Help by holding your position, she told him and then tuned out his response. Kor just released his first arrow at the group of men rushing across the bridge in their direction. She tried to stand, but her right side resisted her attempt. The bones in her shoulder remained shattered and blood poured from the open wound.

She noticed the metal bolt still in her left hand, the skin of her fingers blackened by the energy that had heated the shaft. She tossed the bolt away as more thunder and lightning erupted from the rear of the group. Stephenie hoped Ryia did not have to face something like that bolt, knowing the staff would not likely be able to protect her.

"Goddess, watch our fight," Dufnall shouted, his own spear joining those of the soldiers.

Kor fired another arrow at the same time she felt another metal bolt fly from one man at the rear of the group on the other side of the bridge. The bolt continued to speed up after it left the weapon and appeared to head toward Dufnall.

Bastard, she swore. She created a gravity field around a large rock at the top of the short wall next to Dufnall and used her mind to rip it from the mortar. The stone flew up just as the bolt closed in on Dufnall. A deafening crunch filled the air and a flash of light erupted on the other side of the stone that had fractured into five unequal pieces.

Stephenie held the fragments aloft and kept them together until the metal bolt fell to the ground. A snarl driven by pain escaped her lips and she launched the five fragments of stone at the attacking men. She then channeled an energy field to pull more stones from the wall. The stones flew toward their attackers. More stones followed, quickly ripping the wall apart and down to the road's surface.

Most of the barrage missed their marks, but at least five men tumbled to the ground, three did not rise again. The two that scrambled to their feet retreated in the other direction, one taking an arrow in the back from Kor.

Stephenie continued to launch stones even after she could no longer see anyone to hit. The excess energy in her body cooked her from the inside and she needed to release it before it did more damage or forced her to transform.

"Kill the dogs and get some prisoners," Dufnall shouted to his soldiers as he moved toward her. "Kor, she needs healing."

Stephenie used the energy in her to lift herself to her feet. Her shirt soaked to her waist in blood and her right arm was limp at her side. "Leave. The. Dogs. Alone." The growl echoed through the gorge.

She directed some of the remaining power in her body to heal the damage to her shoulder. Her body worked quickly, taking minerals and resources stored within her to reassemble the destroyed parts of her body.

"I will not remain in the back!" Kas demanded in Dalish as he beat Kor and Dufnall to her side. "That magic is not something these simpletons should have access to."

She swallowed and looked at the hesitant soldiers. "Leave the dogs, they won't harm you," she yelled in a more human voice. She moved the fingers of her right hand and tried to lift her arm. The soldiers eased around the animals. "I'm in no danger at the moment," she told Kas as he tried to turn her toward him. "And yes, someone has something powerful."

Kas looked at the eight-inch metal crossbow bolt on the ground. "Was that what hit you?"

She stared at the pointed projectile. She focused her senses on the energy currents and saw the void within the device, pulling in a small, but constant, stream of power. "It appears to be recharging itself," she told him in Dalish, keeping the conversation private between them. "It controlled the gravity around itself and pushed a ton of energy into me." She flexed her fingers again. "I thought it would explode like those overloaded batteries. Fortunately, it didn't."

Kas pulled her shirt away from her shoulder. "You have healed." He released the bloody cloth but did not wipe his hands. Instead, he turned his attention back to the projectile. "It would be harder to reuse them if they exploded."

Stephenie grinned at the practical observation.

"Your Majesty?" Dufnall asked from five feet away. "Are you well? Kor is a healer." He looked at her haggard appearance. The cloth at the ends of her sleeves showed signs of burning.

"Thank you, but Kor might look at the man I threw out of the way instead of me." She looked at his soldiers. All four were now on the other side of the dogs. One limped behind the others.

"I believe you saved my life, Your Majesty." Dufnall bowed from the waist.

Stephenie's head throbbed, but she reached out with her senses while she pushed excess energy into the short stone wall behind her. The stones heated until they steamed. The sounds of Ryia's attacks had stopped, and she needed to know her friends' condition. She sensed Perain at the edge of her range. He did not seem agitated. "Kas, please check on the others."

"I should be watching over you." He frowned at her expression and then nodded his head before he took off at a run toward the rear of their group. They still had a mental connection, and she knew he would warn her if they needed her.

She rolled her shoulder. The rapid healing had fixed most of the damage, but the newly healed flesh and bone ached. "Who attacked us?" She asked Dufnall as she gingerly bent down to pick up the bolt. Her hand paused before touching it. She looked for a dominant intelligence in the projectile, but she sensed nothing. As a permanent item of magic, it had to have an internal structure that allowed it to control the energy around it like she did. Without the internal intelligence, at best, an object could only hold potential energy for someone or something else to use. Not all items possessed a personality, but she prepared herself for one just in case. Just like when making a full mental connection with a person, a dominant mind could take over the body of the mage initiating the connection.

She wrapped her fingers around the still hot metal and righted herself. Nothing reached out to her mind.

Dufnall drew a deep breath. "The weapon, I believe, was fired by an assassin named Kanin." He met her eyes. "Who hired him?" He shrugged, though the tension had not left his face. "Hopefully, we can capture someone who still lives. There are several people who might not want to see your agreement with Ivan succeed."

Ryia and Henton went after the others, Kas told her from the rear of the group.

Stephenie felt Kas' unease at the destruction Ryia had delivered upon man and dog. Where Kas felt revulsion for the shattered bodies, she only felt sadness at the mental images he shared with her.

She crept over to the other bolt just a dozen feet away. This one absorbed no energy. The front half of the metal rod resembled a deformed mushroom. She picked it up, knowing before she had that the internal structures had been damaged beyond function.

"I see the concern in your face," Dufnall said as he had moved to follow her. "That assassin is why Ivan seldom leaves his castle. Those bolts travel too far and can bend around things." He shook his head. "Kanin had not been seen for nearly eight seasons. Stories that he died have floated around. Perhaps a son or someone else now has his weapon." He raised his hands in uncertainty. "Perhaps he still lives."

"Kanin?" Stephenie turned and then bit her lip to avoid grimacing. The excess energy had harmed most of her internal organs. Had she not resisted the transformation, her shoulder and the rest of her body would have fully healed. *But the last thing I want is Dufnall to see me as a naked woman with scales, sharp teeth, and claws.* She breathed slowly, knowing Kas had moved further away as he went to check on Ryia and Henton. "Where would an assassin get a weapon like this?"

Dufnall shook his head, but Kor moved closer, avoiding the hole Stephenie had created in part of the road. "Sometimes when the Goddess' battles are at their worst, weapons fall from the land of the gods into our world." The man said nothing more.

Dufnall glanced at the gulf now visible through the river gorge and then continued for Kor. "The Goddess collects the fallen warriors and brings them to the land of the gods. The strongest ones she gives weapons of power to fight against the might of Dalkin while she sleeps through the winter. Not in these waters, but further north, out in the sea, there are islands where legendary weapons have been found. Sometimes ships will come upon these islands and find the things that fell between the worlds." Dufnall looked at the metal bolt in her hand. "My grandfather spoke of Kanin and his mark of death. When Kanin used the weapon upon someone, they never lived."

"You are the first," Kor said.

Ryia is dragging someone back, Kas told her.

Stephenie let go of the tension she felt, directing most of the excess energy into the environment.

Dufnall nodded his head. "My father, Trovin, died at Kanin's hand. One of those bolts shot from impossibly far away. I did not see it happen, as I'm normally sent to live in Cilwir, but I learned of his death a month later."

Kor placed a hand on Dufnall's arm. "The bolt that killed Trovin was stollen away. Some say that Kanin called it back using powers he stole from Dalkin."

Stephenie looked at the rod that had struck her. She wiped away her blood that remained on it to examine it closer. The silvery metal had several scratches, but otherwise appeared undamaged. She knew none of these people had the skill to manufacture magical weapons. The skill of embedding the proper lattice structures into an object had been lost to most people. *Something from before the fall of civilization. Or perhaps something a dragon made recently.* "It would make sense that if this assassin only has a limited supply of bolts, he'd want to recover the ammunition."

The four soldiers dragged an injured man past the dogs and toward them. Blood ran from the prisoner's face, making his light brown beard red. Blood also seeped from a wound on his right leg, but the heavy wool concealed the extent of the injury.

"Jarl," the lead soldier named Anso said, as the group dropped the man at Dufnall's feet.

Stephenie felt the slight draw of power from the man and watched for any fields he might create.

Dufnall nodded for the men to stand up the prisoner and the soldiers immediately complied, two holding the middle-aged man upright between them. The other two stood ready with their spears. The injured man could not contain a grimace and his right leg hung at an odd angle without supporting his weight. "What is your name and who sent you?" Dufnall demanded.

Stephenie noticed the cut and bruise on the man's forehead where a rock had hit him. He continued to draw in power. She refrained from drawing more into herself, trusting the reserve still in her to be enough.

The man swallowed and then spit at Dufnall's feet. Anso, on the man's right, kneed him in the leg and the man sagged in agony.

"Answer!" Dufnall stepped closer.

The man whimpered. "The Goddess will claim me for her battle against Dalkin. I fear nothing."

"Not if we scatter your bones," Dufnall growled. "She'd never waste the time to collect you."

Stephenie noted the man's eyes widen at a threat that few would inflect even on an enemy. She knew no warrior wanted to become barred from the Goddess calling them to battle Dalkin. If someone started scattering bones, eventually they would receive the same punishment.

"Tell me," Dufnall insisted.

She felt the man's fear, but she had no intention of entering a mind she did not trust. Her mind was already crowded with Ista and Kas. "Why attack us? Who sent you?" Stephenie asked with a calm and measured voice, belying her physical state.

The man turned his head away, as if waiting for the death blow to come.

Stephenie turned her head to the rear of their group. She could now see Ryia approaching with a large man she easily dragged by his left arm. The young woman seemed unaffected by the effort, but Stephenie sensed the sweat forming within Ryia's hairline. This demonstration of dragging a hundred and eighty-pound man over the rocky ground came at the expense of drawing power through her body. The earlier lightning had come from the intelligence within the staff and not sourced from Ryia herself. Her friend lacked the physical stamina to form lightning and always would.

"I left Kas on watch as Henton and Perain searched the bodies behind us," Ryia said in Cothish. "I killed all of them." The statement somewhere between a brag and a confession. Ryia took in Stephenie's haggard appearance and then looked down the road at the dogs and the scattering of only a couple of bodies. "You?"

Stephenie glared at Ryia, but her young friend held her gaze without flinching, daring Stephenie to challenge her. Stephenie smiled and shook her head before responding in Cothish. "Just a couple." She glanced down at her shoulder. "I got hit by a magical bolt."

"Kas is complaining about your recklessness." Ryia switched to Sandvian. "They came to kill Dufnall so that Ivan would blame us.

And you so that Ista would go to war." Ryia drew in a lot of energy and then flung the man forward to land in front of Dufnall.

The man held by Anso and Thale drew in energy and tried to crush the head of the man Ryia had tossed at their feet. Stephenie blocked the attack and retaliated by crushing the mage's hand with her own power. The man screamed as his fingers collapsed in on themselves to form a small, mangled ball that now dripped blood. "Don't call upon your powers in front of me."

Stephenie knelt and rolled over the man Ryia had dragged to them. Burn marks covered his chest and she wondered how the lightning had not already killed him. "What's your name?"

"Con—Conor." Blood slipped from the man's lips.

"Who sent you?"

"Rokr."

"Traitor," the man with the crushed hand uttered. "May Dalkin feast on your soul." He snarled at Dufnall and drew in more energy, chanted, and this time trying to attack Dufnall.

Stephenie again disrupted the weak field by drawing away the energy. The two soldiers with their spears ready drove the metal ends into the man's chest, withdrew their bloody blades, and drove the spears home again and again until Anso and Thale dropped the dying man to the ground.

Stephenie closed her mind to block out the panicked thoughts coming from him. The terror and fear people emit as they died lingered in her consciousness too long. She looked up at Dufnall with a raised eyebrow and then glanced at Conor.

Dufnall bit his own lip. "Jarl Rokr normally lives in the south. He's been in Horn Point since the feast for the summer court. Most of the jarls attend. He has spies everywhere." Dufnall looked at Kor. "This is brazen for him. He normally avoids any direct actions." Kor shrugged, but said nothing. Dufnall continued his questions. "Could someone else have used his name to have these men do this?"

Kor frowned. "Unless they knew the attempt would fail, I doubt it."

Ryia wiped her brow. "The men who came from the rear seemed confident until I rushed them." She kicked Conor in the leg. "Tell us your orders again?"

The man struggled to speak. "Kill the bitch queen and Dufnall at all costs. The goal is war with Ista."

Dufnall shook his head. "Never tell the wind your plans. Only Dalkin knows where the gale will carry them."

Stephenie agreed with the sentiment and wondered if perhaps Dufnall's concern about this Rokr's name being falsely presented might be true. "Who sent you to kill us?

The young man on the ground looked up, his eye pleading for mercy. "Ingle One Eye, the captain of Jarl Rokr's main longship." The man struggled to breathe. "He came to our camp."

"What camp?" Dufnall demanded.

The injured man turned his attention to the Jarl. "We've hid out in the wilds. Waiting for Rokr's call."

"Where?"

The man shook his head and coughed up some blood. His voice fading, he whispered, "Hold the bridge." The man's eyes closed as he worked just to keep breathing.

"We cannot take that one with us," Kor said to Dufnall, who nodded his head. A moment later, Kor drew a dagger.

Stephenie rose and turned away before Kor slit the man's throat. She focused on the dogs. *I am not a monster,* she swore to herself. The rage that yet another enemy surfaced to cause harm to her friends burned within her and wanted to make that statement false.

"You think he's the one that poisoned you?" Ryia asked.

Stephenie shrugged. Without evidence, she hesitated to act.

"What do we do about the dogs?" Anso asked. "They are likely to attack anyone that gets close."

"They are mine," Stephenie said evenly, barely suppressing her sense of ownership of them, but not able to reduce her need to protect the pack. She calmed herself and took a deep breath. "They'll come with us."

"You can't be serious?" Dufnall shook his head. "These are not sled dogs. They're bred and trained to kill. They will run wild and kill anyone they see."

Stephenie looked over at the dogs. All the ones before her had collars with leashes. They still lay on the ground, but some of them watched her and those with her. *Stay where you are,* she instructed them, conveying her desire they do not move.

"I'm deadly serious. The dogs are now mine."

Henton and Perain soon approached, their arms laden with weapons and several packs. Worry filled Henton's eyes at the sight of her, but the rest of his face did not betray his thoughts. Stephenie signaled no danger and he set down what he carried. "We pulled these from ten of the men Ryia dealt with. We took what seemed important, but we didn't look for a camp site."

Kor looked at the pile of swords and crossbows on the ground. "We should get moving in case those that escaped from ahead of us find reinforcements. Kanin, or someone with his crossbow, is still among them."

Dufnall nodded his head. "Leave the dogs to Her Majesty." He turned to his soldiers. "Throw any weapons we can't carry into the river. We'll search the bodies ahead of us as we move. Then toss them in the river as well." He took a deep breath and tried to hide the slight shaking of his hands. "Let's get out of this confining space."

So that we can be a better target for long-ranged attacks? Stephenie wanted to laugh. Despite the obvious contradiction, they could not remain idle no matter how much she wanted to take a few hours to rest, and she also did not like feeling confined.

Chapter 11

Islet entered the street outside of Nokki's shop with Walter at her side. She told Ista to keep the guardians away from the crowd that had gathered. As she feared, word spread quickly and nearly everyone in Isa Fields had come to see what happened. "Pardon me," she said in a level voice as she moved through a group of people speaking in a dialect she did not understand. Their tone conveyed displeasure. *Or fear,* she decided.

"Douglas," she called out when she reached the large wooden door of the shop, which stood mostly closed. A woman cried inside and out of sight.

Douglas emerged and then bowed to her. "Your Majesty." He kept his own voice level and spoke in Cothish.

Aware of the crowd pressed in close enough to hear them, she responded in Sandvian. "What did you find?" She tried to flash a signal Stephenie used to indicate discretion, but at his puzzled look, she expected she got it wrong. "We don't want to accuse anyone of a crime until we are certain."

Douglas nodded his head. "He was stabbed in the chest with a chisel. The workshop is a bit of a mess, but his wife said it normally looks like that. She and his kids are with him now."

"Any indication of why?"

Douglas motioned for her to follow him back into the shop, and he opened the door just enough for them to enter. Islet followed behind him and came to a stop once she could see the body of Nokki. The deceased's hands and shirt were now red and soaked with his own blood. A chisel protruded from his chest. Wood shavings covered his black beard and hair.

"When I found him," Douglas said quietly in Cothish, "his eyes were open and one hand still held the chisel. I think it took him a while to die. The blade missed his heart."

"Could he have done this himself?"

Douglas shook his head. "There is a knee print in the blood on the floor. As well as a handprint over there." He pointed to the stone tiles under sawdust and shavings several feet from the body. "And a bloody footprint there and there," he pointed to a trail leading toward the door. "As you know, a guardian happened by earlier and stood watch until I arrived." He sighed. "Beka arrived looking for her husband shortly after I did, then word spread quickly."

Islet looked at the thin woman. Her light complexion was a sharp contrast to Nokki's dark skin and hair. The woman looked up, saw Islet, and quickly tried to scramble to her feet. Islet waved her back down. "Please, do not worry about that. I am only here to offer my sympathies and try to find out how this happened."

"Nokki was a good man," the woman's voice broke and more tears fell from her face. A boy of perhaps seven and a girl at least two years younger stood behind their mother, holding the back of her shirt. "He never fought with anyone."

Douglas switched to Sandvian. "I've asked the constables to check everyone's shoes for signs of blood. Another dozen volunteers are also helping. I've worked with all of them and trust them."

Islet nodded her head. "It should be pretty quick to check everyone." *And we now have one less person than before. Two once we catch the person who did this.*

"One person we want to speak with is Hugo, Nokki's older brother."

Islet tilted her head, unable to look away from the body still laying on the floor. "Where is he?"

"He runs food and supplies to the border and the waystation. Ista conveyed through a guardian that he and Rolf left very early this morning with a dog team and cart."

"Really? Had he been near the shop?"

"Hugo came by often," Beka said, forcing herself to stop crying. She pushed herself from the floor and Islet suspected she must be at least ten years younger than her husband.

"Did they get along?" Islet asked as kindly as she could.

"No history of problems," Douglas responded for the grieving woman. "But so far, everyone else appears to have been accounted for and has a reasonable explanation of where they have been."

"How is this possible?" A loud voice rose from outside the shop. "Don't those stone creatures keep watch? You accuse us of murder when those things are supposed to protect us and know what is going on!"

Islet turned around and headed out of the shop with Walter and Douglas on her heals. A small space had cleared around a pair of men who stood in front of a bearlike man that stood over six-feet tall. The people closest to her tried to move back, but the crowd had become densely packed.

She struggled to recall the man's name as all eyes turned toward her. The two men who faced off against the large man stepped to the side. Neither of them were part of the city constables. *Perhaps Douglas' volunteers?* She cleared her throat. "A tragedy has occurred here. We want to hold those responsible for it accountable for their actions." She scanned the faces of the people around her and raised her voice to carry to those further back. "Beka and her children need your support while we investigate what happened."

"What of your damn cats? Why didn't they see this?" the man demanded. "Then you wouldn't have to accuse those of us who've done nothing wrong."

"Holgar," she said, thankfully remembering his name, "our guardians are numerous, but they watch the borders of Ista and cannot be in all places. Besides, I believe most of you prefer some privacy. The tradeoff is that they did not see who did this, only observed it after the fact."

"He refused to show us his boots, Your Majesty," said one of the two men.

"Holgar?" Islet asked.

The large man lifted one boot and then the other, showing soles that were covered in dirt. She knew he worked as a laborer who carried and moved heavy things for others as well as went into the wilds to hunt deer and other animals. *His feet are far too large for the marks on the floor,* she admitted to herself. "Thank you."

She turned to Douglas. "Nokki's brother needs to be made aware of these events. Can you arrange for a dog team and wheeled cart to bring him back?"

Douglas frowned at her and then nodded his head. "I'll take one or two people with me."

"Thank you. He needs to know his brother is dead." *And we need to know if he might have done this.*

Chapter 12

They only managed to travel another six miles to the next campsite before they stopped. Stephenie hated to admit it, but the power she absorbed to keep the bolt from killing her did a lot of physical damage to her whole body, well beyond the obvious hole in her shoulder. Although the time needed to walk the six miles from the gorge allowed nearly all the physical damage to heal, it left her starving and worn out. She could not simply convert raw energy into flesh. Her body craved food to replace the nutrients she had used.

"Please sit," Dufnall said, urging her to take the first chair assembled. The overall mood of the group remained subdued, and even Dufnall's need for constant talk had remained mostly silent since the attack.

Stephenie used her teeth to tear off a large hunk from the jerky she pulled from a new pouch as she moved closer to the chair. She had finished two whole pouches over the six-mile walk. The blood on her shirt had long ago stiffened and dried in the wind. She waited for Kas and Henton to finish putting together the tent so that she could remove her clothing, get cleaned up, and change into one of her few sets of clean clothing. *I really liked these clothes,* she complained to herself. *Next time, I won't hold back on transforming. It's not like it saved my shirt.*

"Are you well?"

Stephenie sighed. She turned the seat so that she could monitor the pack of dogs, but did not sit yet. The animals rested just on the other side of the standing stones that marked the boundaries of the campsite. She had removed their leashes to prevent them from getting tangled and covered in debris. Without a way to anchor them to the ground, there was no point in trying to leash them together. *Just my charming personality keeping them contained.*

She turned her attention to Dufnall. "Yes. Just a bit tired."

The thirty-year-old turned his head to examine the nineteen dogs and then turned his focus back to Stephenie. "I'm without words to express myself. I would not have expected such control over them."

She ripped another chunk of jerky off with her teeth and sat down. "I'll be fine once I get some rest." *And figure out what we can do about that assassin.*

"You saved my life today," Dufnall said without the flare his voice normally contained. The drover assembling his chair stood up and stepped back with a bow. Dufnall smiled at the young man and pulled the chair closer to Stephenie. "Despite the stories we heard, I never expected anyone to use large rocks in that fashion."

"It is a matter of changing the fields around them to overcome the attraction between the ground and the stones. The technical term for the field is gravity. My field caused a repulsive force, which lifted the stones into the air. Then I curved the field so that the stones would fly at those on the bridge." She stuffed more jerky in her mouth. "I gave it enough speed that it would cross the distance without me having to project a field all the way to the target." Her shoulders relaxed as she allowed some tension to leave her body. "As a child, I'd go out with my father and brother when the armies practiced with trebuchets. I got really good at aiming. I just visualized how the rocks would fly and they did."

He chuckled. "I'm not sure I know the language you are speaking. Fields and gravity, and what was that, a trebuchet? Is that some sort of catapult?" He grew serious again. "You may not be aware, but I'm able to use some of the Goddess' powers, like Kor. He's better at it than I, but I've been able to heal minor injuries and light candles to read by." He shrugged. "Small things. Nothing useful in a fight."

Stephenie pushed aside the pleasant memories of flaming stones flying through the air and came back to the conversation. "I'm aware of your abilities. Both you, your older brother, and your uncle can use the energy around you." She leaned forward as she ate more of the jerky. "One of our longer-term goals is to create schools in the north where people can go to learn how to develop their skills with what we call magic. We have a few people in Ista that have apprenticed under Ryia, but eventually, we would like to build the ranks of those that have power and know how to use it to the point where they could leave Ista and teach people in Sandven. A school that could draw more people to your lands."

Dufnall considered her words. "I wish I had witnessed what young Ryia did. It sounded like she called down the wrath of the sky." He glanced at Ryia putting ingredients into a pot. "I had no idea how powerful she was." He smiled as he listened to Ryia talk to herself. "I imagine she has a biting tongue, unless the language she uses much of the time just sounds like that."

Stephenie laughed. *It is definitely better for them to think she's as powerful as I am.* "She likes to curse. She's tried to learn how to insult people in as many languages as possible. If she decides she likes you, she'll be overly open. Otherwise, you would be best to just stay out of her way."

"I imagine she is not alone in that respect."

Stephenie held Dufnall's gaze but decided not to address the statement. "We could teach you and Kor more about using your powers. However, you might not enjoy hearing what we have to say about how your abilities really work."

Stephenie turned her head back to the dogs as a male growled and snapped at a brown female with half her left ear missing. The female dog jumped up and bared her teeth. The larger male stepped back and moved around another dog.

"They'll need to eat soon," Dufnall said. The initial fear he exhibited now returning with that show of aggression.

Stephenie growled, sending a rumble through the ground. The angry female closed her mouth and sat back on her haunches. The male dropped to the ground. She turned her attention back to Dufnall. "I'll find some of the deer that roam out in the wilds. We brought food for the horses and us, but nothing to feed them."

Perain carried a loaf a bread and a bag of sweets in his right hand and a mug in his left. "They can go a day or two without food. Probably better that they do." He handed her the food, and she immediately ripped off a chunk of bread and started eating it. He watched as she dropped the bag of candies and the rest of the hard loaf into her lap as she took the mug. "They're not anything I'd put into a sled team—been made mean by their prior masters—but they appear to have recently eaten. Though they'll get more aggressive the longer they go without a meal."

"Thank you," Stephenie said as she swallowed the first mouthful of bread. "I should be able to keep them in-line. Perhaps I can get some of the anger and hate out of them." She did not want to manipulate their minds. Adjusting memories and thought patterns often destroyed the personality of the being, replacing it with only a shadow of the former mind. *And leaving many problems behind.* The idea disturbed her because someone had tried to do that very thing to her. *I won't do that to the dogs. Perhaps love and kindness might show them not all humans are cruel.*

Henton, Kas, and Ryia came over together to join Perain. "How much are you going to eat tonight?" Ryia demanded. "A whole pot?"

Stephenie bit her lower lip and then nodded her head.

You know better than to draw too much energy, Kas admonished her telepathically. *You could burn yourself out by being stubborn.* He sighed visibly. *The tent is ready. I can help clean you up.*

"We need to talk about camp security," Henton said, unaware of Kas' communication.

Stephenie bit off a piece of bread with her mouth and nodded her head to both of them. *I know you worry, but I managed the power.* She turned her attention to Henton. If she kept talking to Kas, she would snap at him for a lack of combat discipline when he dropped the field that had shielded them from the crossbow bolts.

Henton continued. "If this Kanin can shoot his weapon from a long way off, we need to make sure he doesn't have a clear view of any of us."

"More you and Dufnall," Ryia said. "I imagine he won't waste bolts on the guards or drovers. At least if what everyone said about him stealing back the bolt that killed Trovin is true."

The bolt is still recharging, Kas told her mentally as she relayed the conversation to him. *I do not know how long it will take to be at the power it needs to function. We also do not know if there is some type of homing signal. It might fly away on its own or even try to hit you again. I am not familiar with this type of weapon and don't know how smart it is. Let's hope it considered its job done after it hit me.*

"It is possible Rokr hired Kanin." Dufnall took a mug from Kor, who had come over to join the conversation. "I know little about the assassin aside from the legend that he never fails in his task and his fee is large enough to sink a ship."

Kor shook his head. "He will not easily give up."

"Which means we should probably keep moving," Henton said. "I don't like being exposed like this. We're not that far from the ambush site. I doubt that even if the assassin stayed off the road, that the broken ground will have slowed him that much. I wish we had gone after them to check out the camp." He raised a hand to stop Stephenie from speaking. "I know. You were in no condition to pursue, and splitting up just increases the risks."

Ryia tightened her grip on her staff. "Are we sure that weapon isn't something a Senzar bitch we know didn't provide someone? Or someone else who sent people after us?" Ryia's focus on Stephenie left no room for doubt that she referred to Stephenie's sire.

Dufnall's eyebrows rose.

Stephenie exhaled. They had too many enemies, and she did not want to face Yreka, or anyone Duvargintik might manipulate into attacking her again. The Senzar woman had less physical capacity than her, being four generations removed from having a dragon parent. However, as Kas constantly reminded her, skill overcomes raw potential every time, and Yreka had several hundred years more experience. *Plus, actual instruction by people who knew what they were doing.*

"This Rokr," Stephenie started, "what do we know about him? How does war help him? And Kanin has used this weapon for years, yes?"

Dufnall did not pursue Ryia's statement. "Rokr is wealthy. His family has been in Sandven for generations. Before my father's, father's father united the lands, Rokr's forbearers had control of what is now southern Sandven. If he can disrupt Ivan's control, he could claim the throne." He leaned forward again. "We almost bled together today," Dufnall said. "That is worth some honesty." He glanced at the drovers on the other side of the camp site and lowered his voice. "The truth is, Ivan needs your trade agreement more than you do. He would have agreed to it even if you had not allowed me to come to Ista. He pushed because he cannot seem weak right now and many of the jarls demanded he get concessions from you. When Ista closed her borders, and our father lost all that income, it felt like the ice would never leave and the Goddess could no longer blow Dalkin's cold from the land. That's likely why someone paid to have him killed."

Ryia crossed her arms. "So, Ivan only sent a handful of people to protect you because he didn't want to appear weak?"

Kor cleared his throat. "We honor prowess in battle."

Ryia frowned. "Dead is dead."

Kor looked at Stephenie, his expression forced.

Dufnall continued. "I'm a spare of a spare. Ivan has two boys in different cities to the south. My death does not affect the throne." He looked around at all of them. "The crossbow. Kanin used it for generations. It is likely that Rokr hired the assassin. We heard the dying confession of an attacker."

Stephenie swallowed the bread she had been eating. "Five guards, or a hundred, with that weapon. It wouldn't have mattered." She looked around the campsite. "I propose this. You've set up the tents. The horses and ponies can use some rest. If the assassin is targeting me and Dufnall, and his ammunition is scarce, he won't waste it on just anyone. However, I don't want anyone to take too many risks."

"I'm not going to let you go off on your own," Henton said, crossing his own arms. "I can see you planning things in your head."

She smiled up at him. *He knows me too well.* "I will have the dogs spread out around the campsite." She glanced at the gulf to the north. Only a hundred yards of open ground separated them and the vertical cliff that marked the edge of the shore. "If Kanin, or whoever has his weapon, plans to take us out, it would be easiest when we are sitting here. I want all of you to remain in the tents. If he can't see who he is targeting, he will probably avoid shooting the weapon. The dogs will give warning if anyone tries to get too close."

"What are you going to do?" Dufnall asked.

"I'll head south off the road and find a place to hide. My guess is he'd want to approach from cover so that he has a path to get away after he's killed one, or both, of us. He won't want to fight the rest of our group. Not when the initial attack failed." She shrugged as she drained the rest of the mug of water. "Heck, he might even think he did enough damage to me that I died or will die. The lack of knowledge about my condition might cause him to be more aggressive with completing the assignment."

"We found a spyglass among the belongings of the rear group," Perain said. "He might have one as well and could be watching us from afar. He might know you survived."

"You're not at your full strength," Henton protested. "You don't know what else you might face."

You've been silent, she told Kas. *I assume you and Henton are talking quietly.*

Are you claiming you have not noticed? Kas asked. *I would assume you would have seen the fields that indicated we were speaking.*

I need you and Ryia here to protect the others if someone comes sneaking past me from a different direction.

Kas pursed his lips. *What if I refuse?*

Please don't fight me.

I am not happy with this course of action.

I know, but there is not a better option. I love you, she offered him.

Aloud, she continued. "My body has healed. I'm tired and I need more to eat, but I've faced worse when I've felt worse."

"This feels wrong," Dufnall said. "It should be I protecting you. You're the ruler of Ista. I'm just an jarl in title only."

She looked at Ryia. "Can you get me a bowl or two of what you're cooking? I'll grab my pack and a blanket or two and head out after I eat."

Henton shook his head. "You make it impossible to protect you."

She stood up and tugged at her ruined shirt. "I won't be far. If I need help, I'll signal as I always do, and then you can come running to my rescue."

Henton snorted and changed to Cothish. "If you make something explode or transform and still need help, I doubt there is anything I, or any of us, can do to help."

She smiled at him. "And that is always my point. So, if that happens, try to escape."

"Is this settled?" Dufnall asked.

"It is," Henton said, though his tone and body language shouted his disagreement. "Everyone, finish up your tasks that need you in the open, then get into the tents and stay low to the ground so your shadow is not visible. Try to get some rest while we wait for Steph to let us know things are clear."

She nodded her head and followed Ryia toward the cooking pot. "Definitely get some rest. I want us traveling thirty miles a day after this. We can't be certain this is the only assassin sent to kill us, and I don't want to give them a chance to catch up after this."

Ryia stopped and put her arms around Stephenie, squeezed, and then continued to the cooking pot without saying anything.

Chapter 13

After Stephenie ate half the pot of food Ryia cooked, she grabbed a couple of blankets, her pack, and headed west along the road. She needed to position herself south of the camp so that she could watch for anyone approaching. However, she wanted to do that without anyone being seen. While she did not sense anyone within her range, that did not mean someone with a spyglass did not observe the campsite from afar.

She moved quickly in a partial crouch until the land started to slope downward. Trusting that the hills and larger boulders would conceal her from any likely watchers, she straightened up and began running.

She wanted to fly. Long before she learned of her heritage, she had found a love of the wind blowing across her face. However, even though an hourglass would call it evening, the sun still brightened the clear sky. Anyone would be able to see her for miles if she lifted into the air.

She ran for a mile more before leaving the road and heading south into the broken ground. Grasses, weeds, small trees, and scattered boulders covered the rolling hills. She slowed her pace from the fast jog, but still moved with haste, relying upon her senses to alert her to anyone's presence before they would hear her. She felt the minds of many small animals, the closest of which would either scatter or freeze, depending on their survival instincts. After another half mile of travel, she sensed a herd of eight deer. She noted the direction, and if they remained in the location, she would take one to feed her dogs, once she dealt with Kanin.

She remained hunched over below the height of the vegetation as she moved, which unfortunately meant she did not know her exact position. Her senses stretched as far as she could make them, but she did not yet sense any humans. She slowed after she felt she had doubled back far enough to place the campsite roughly north of her. *I would never want Kas to return to his ghost form, but I definitely miss his ability to quickly scout without being observed.*

Stephenie angled her path to the north and continued methodically through the rough ground cover. She aimed to put the camp at the very edge of her perception so that she could monitor for any powerful emotions that indicated a threat snuck past her. After a fair amount of traipsing back and forth, she finally felt the horses. With their position fixed, she moved north until she could just make out each mind in the camp. Then she looked for a place of cover where she could get some rest herself. She would not sleep, but she wanted to find comfortable concealment to wait within.

If the bastard has the reputation Dufnall claims, plus a weapon like that, he'll be coming, she told herself, trying not to temper her optimism with all the logical reasons that the assassin would find as risks of pursuing them.

She set the folded blankets down on a patch of rocky ground next to a small tree with leaves that had seven points. A couple of larger stones extended two feet above the ground, and she leaned her backpack against the flatter of the pair. With the grasses, no one would be able to see her unless they came into the small clearing.

"Ryia," she mumbled as her mind wandered, worried about her younger friend and the dark mood that had returned to her. "Don't let the hate consume you." None of them had faced lethal combat since moving to Ista. The earlier fight had been the first combat outside of training in almost three years, and Ryia had not held back. Stephenie sighed. Even her anger at Kas' lack of discipline needed some moderation because of his lack of experience. *I'll apologize for getting angry.*

She pushed her thoughts away and closed her eyes. Her mind reached out to monitor the mental sphere around her as she quietly waited.

Stephenie lost track of time. No one in the camp expressed any powerful emotions, and she hoped they took the opportunity to get some rest. *After I deal with Kanin, or give up waiting, they're going to march through the night.* She did not want to make the Sandvians suffer, but her desire to return to Ista dominated her thoughts. *If they put a little more effort into each day, it would be good for them. It's not like the road is really that difficult to travel on. I could be marching them through the mountains to show them real suffering.*

She opened her eyes and looked up through the tree branches at the clouds that now filled the sky. The clouds remained white and thin in spots, so she did not expect rain. Then she felt something tickle the edges of her senses and she realized that someone approached from the southeast. That presence had roused her from her meditation.

Stephenie breathed slowly and focused on the person. *Persons,* she corrected. *Two people. I really want to be done with you.* She moved into a crouch and picked up the blankets under her. The two people remained at the edge of her ability to feel them. If either of them could use magic, she did not expect they would have the range to sense her.

Once she had stowed the damp blankets in her pack, she moved toward the two people. She kept her focus in their direction, waiting to see if others followed behind them. After she had gone thirty feet, she still sensed no one else. *Do I rush them with the assumption that at least one has magic?* She pursed her lips. Most people possessed no powers and would not be able to sense her if she snuck up on them. However, in her observations of the world, those with powers gravitated toward activities and professions with more inherent risk. Even if they had no conscious awareness of their abilities, it always gave the person with magic an advantage over others.

Don't overthink it, she chastised herself. The last two years of not constantly running from enemies and not living in fear of dying had dulled her confidence. She continued slowly forward, keeping her form below the height of the surrounding cover. If either of the people changed their movement suddenly, or reacted as if they sensed her, she would charge them.

The distance between her and the two people—*one man and one woman*—closed gradually, until only forty feet separated them. Without cause, the woman froze, and a burst of fear escaped her mind.

Stephenie used her mind to lift a rock bigger than her torso into the air just ahead of her and then jumped to her feet. She expected the twang of a crossbow discharging, but the man did not fire the one he carried. She did not know if that weapon had shot her earlier, but she would not take the risk.

The female voice rose in fear and called out to the Goddess. Stephenie sensed a broad gravitational wave fly in her direction. The unfocused energy was strong enough to drive a normal person backwards, but Stephenie tore apart the threads of power emanating from the woman and her gravity wave crumbled.

"Down!" the man yelled; his voice hoarse with age.

Stephenie closed the gap to ten feet, her boulder directly ahead of her, blocking their view of her and any potential projectiles. Her mind took in the greater surroundings, and she reached out mentally to lift two other random stones from behind the two. The rocks flew into their backs.

The woman tried to dodge, but she could not react fast enough. Both stones crashed into her attackers. The twang of the crossbow releasing came almost at the same time as the stone ahead of her cracked with a restrained explosion.

"Grandpa!" the woman choked out as she tumbled to the ground.

Stephenie felt both of the people on the ground and the location of the crossbow. She rammed the largest piece of rock ahead of her directly down onto the crossbow, smashing it into the ground.

The woman struggled to get to her knees. A dagger in her left hand. The man's right arm buried under the stone with the crossbow. He did not move, but Stephenie knew he lived because of the pain radiating from his mind. She shed her backpack and drew her sword and long dagger. She approached the woman, who held the dagger in her direction. The woman forced herself up and kept looking between the old man and Stephenie.

"He's dying!" she cried.

Stephenie noticed the deformed metal bolt that now lay in a pile of smoldering vegetation. Anger flowed through her and she swung her sword to loosen up her right shoulder. Pain lingered from the earlier healing. She advanced on the woman who appeared to be in her late twenties.

"Please, let me save him," the woman said, glancing backward as she retreated. "He's all I have left."

Stephenie used her power to swipe the woman's left leg from behind and the woman fell backwards, landing hard against a sharp rock. The woman's scream of surprise and pain followed the impact.

The old man moaned from the ground, unable to pull his arm free of the stone. "Don't kill my granddaughter," he pleaded, his words barely audible.

"You tried to kill me earlier today. You tried to kill Jarl Dufnall. I've been told you kill his father. How many others have you murdered?" The ground vibrated with the snarl that turned up a corner of her lip. "Now you expect me to allow you to live?"

"Please," the woman begged. "Let my granddad live. Kill me if you must, but don't let him die."

"No," the man forced out the word.

Stephenie could see his left shoulder and arm turned at an unnatural angle and she suspected the stone she had used to strike him from the back had broken several of his aged bones.

The woman threw aside her dagger. "I surrender to you. Just save him."

Stephenie knew both of them could die in a heartbeat. She could generate a pulse of energy inside their heads and scramble their brains, ending their lives with nothing more than a thought from her. She slowed her breathing and forced herself to pause. *I am not like the Senzar. I am not my sire.* She sheathed both of her weapons and used her mind to lift the rock from the man's right arm and held it above the man's head. The woman gasped and Stephenie again knew death only required her to stop holding up the stone.

She exhaled and tossed the rock to the side. The man's arm already had hints of blue. Blood oozed where bone fragments extended through his skin. She did not think the man could move, let alone use the still intact crossbow, but she took no chances and used her powers to move the crossbow to her feet and out of reach of either of them.

The woman scrambled over to her grandfather and put her hands on the man's upper arm. "I'm here. I'll heal you. Don't die on me."

Stephenie could see the power the woman drew into herself as she channeled and then pushed the energy into the old man. The woman's voice breaking as she chanted and pleaded for his body to heal. Her physical capacity appeared to rival Ryia, but the woman obviously had little training in using her abilities, so she remained far less effective.

After several moments, the man's breathing eased, though the broken bone fragments still extended through his skin. The woman sobbed, seeing the damage that remained. She sat back on her heals, sweat covered her face. "Can you heal him? Someone with your power."

Stephenie looked down at the woman and shook her head. "No." The act of healing would require establishing a mental link with the man and that could expose her to a mental attack. "This weapon I understand was in the possession of a man named Kanin. Is that him?"

The man, still laying on his stomach, nodded his head. "I retired."

"And you decided to do one last job by killing me and Dufnall." Stephenie fought against the urge to rip their arms from their bodies. "You came with men to kill my friends. No one harms my friends." She forced her heart rate to slow.

"They took my mother," the woman said. "They gave us no choice."

"Who?"

The woman shook her head. "I don't know. Men came the day after you first met with King Ivan. They told us to go with them and to make sure you die, or my mother would suffer. Later, someone arrived to say Dufnall traveled with you and must die as well."

The man struggled to get into a sitting position and the woman moved to help him up. She tried to shield his crushed arm and offer more healing. After she shifted him so that he sat against her with his feet before him, he spoke. "Rokr's men learned who I was three years ago. I refused to help them then and swore I had given Balkr's bow to someone who watched over my family and would take revenge if any came to harm."

"Quiet, Granddad. Rest yourself."

He shook his head. "She must know you're innocent," he wheezed. "This time, Rokr's men called my bluff. I had no choice. I'd given up the life."

Stephenie looked down at the crossbow. "Where are the bolts?"

The man tried to move his arms but could not do so. A whimper of pain escaped his mouth. "Let me," the woman said. She reached around to a satchel hanging at his waist. She opened it and pulled one eight-inch bolt out and tossed it toward Stephenie's feet.

The man's breathing remained shallow. "That is the last one. The rest were spent over the years."

Stephenie crouched down and held her hand above the crossbow to sense for an intelligence. She felt a slight stirring from within the bow, but the personality seemed mild and not very demanding. She picked up the crossbow and the bolt. The word Balkr echoed into her mind, but she pushed away the intelligence and it retreated. "How does this work?"

"Heal him and we'll tell you," the woman demanded, her arms holding her grandfather upright. Tears moistened her cheeks.

Stephenie looked at the crushed sight at the end of the weapon, wondering if she had damaged the weapon beyond use. Only certain magic items had functionality to reinforce their structure. "I'm sure you realize that healing requires making a mental connection with the person being healed. I won't do that for anyone I don't trust." She looked at the brass release on the underside of the crossbow and noted the bend that had formed from being crushed against a sharp rock. "Back at the camp, the only two people that might consider healing him are Dufnall and his man Kor. Though I imagine the healing would only be to prolong his life so they could kill him more slowly."

The old man grimaced but remained motionless. "You're right. I've killed many. I knew this day would come." He breathed slowly. "The bolts take a couple of days of rest before they are effective after being shot, but as long as you visualize the target when fired, the bolt will hit it." He exhaled sharply and pain continued to radiate from his mind. "Until you."

"Grandpa, no, I need you." The woman glared at Stephenie. "My mother will die and you condemn him to death as well."

Stephenie growled. "Your piece of shit grandfather put a bolt into my shoulder. It hurt." She used her free hand to raise her blood covered shirt for emphasis. "This is my blood covering my clothing. I have no intention of dying because your assassin family drew attention it didn't like."

The man shook his head. "Una, she is right. Your mother and father benefitted from my trade. They knew what I was." He looked up to meet Stephenie's gaze fully. "But Una is innocent. She knew nothing of my deeds until Rokr's men came. Spare her."

Stephenie narrowed her focus to the energy fields around the two of them and looked for anything else that might be drawing power. She found nothing. "Are there others out there waiting to attack us?"

Una shook her head no. "The other men, the six that were left, ran. They swore Dalkin had come for them in your form."

Stephenie decided that the woman spoke the truth. "Did either of you try to poison us in High Point?"

The woman shook her head vigorously.

The man breathed heavily and spoke slowly. "We know nothing about poisoning you. We left with Rokr's men when they took us."

Stephenie released some of the energy she had been holding. She turned her head toward the camp and, after a moment, turned back to them. "Hear this. What is saving your lives is you did not personally target my friends." She hefted the crossbow easily. "I'm going to return to the campsite and will let the others know Kanin is no longer a threat. Don't make me regret that statement." She extended an arm and her pack flew from where it lay on the ground directly onto her shoulder. She then threaded her left arm through the other strap and walked away from the two people. *If she focuses and spends enough effort, she might save his life.*

*   *   *   *   *

Ryia, Kas, Kor, and Dufnall sensed her approach, and by the time she arrived at the site, everyone had emerged from their tents. She took a deep breath, not sure if she felt good about the decision to leave the two assassins alive or not. The choice she made could be reversed, while going the other way would have been permanent. *I just want no one else to come to harm because of it.*

"You were successful?" Henton asked, seeing the crossbow.

Dufnall's voice rose. "Kanin is dead? Or at least the person with the bow is?"

Stephenie moved through the gaps between the standing stones. "That threat is no more. Rokr's name came up again. I doubt the jarl will be satisfied with letting things go at this point. If a baron in Cothel took such actions, it would cross a line far enough that he can't go back. I'm assuming it is the same here." She handed Henton the crossbow and the spare bolt. "I believe this one is charged and ready for use. The one Kas has might take another day or two." His eyes questioned her. "I'm not completely certain, but it would appear all you need to do is see your target and release the bolt." She ignored his deeper question that she had not answered.

Yes, Kas, I left the man beaten and dying. The woman might save him. She might not.

I trust you, he responded, allowing his approval of not murdering them to come through to her.

To the others, she continued aloud. "We break camp now. Even with the clouds, it won't be too dark to see the road. We push through and camp when I feel we've gone far enough."

Dufnall grunted. "You heard her Majesty. Move like the snows are coming."

Chapter 14

Stephenie set the pace on the road, keeping it to a manageable one that would not wear out the drovers or ponies too quickly. She intended to build up their stamina over three or four days and then maintain that speed until they reached Isa Fields. *However, most likely they'll just be getting their wind by the time we arrive.*

The dogs she shifted between drawing into a tight pack where she, Henton, and Perain walked among them, and sending the pack ahead to run free to burn off excess energy. She always kept them within her ability to sense oncoming traffic, that way she could direct them away from any unintentional conflicts.

Their group encountered three sets of travelers heading toward Horn Point from Norbek. The merchants greeted them without realizing the identity of Dufnall and his men, thinking that perhaps the jarl was just a wealthy merchant using southern workers to help move goods.

It required the entire day, but they traveled thirty-two miles before reaching the second campsite along the road. Stephenie healed all the animals and offered relief to Henton and Perain, leaving Kas and Ryia to address their own needs.

What Islet told her about the murder when she checked in left Stephenie concerned. However, she trusted Douglas would catch up to Hugo. Ista reported Nokki's older brother, and a young man name Rolf, had driven their dog team hard, having switched dogs at the waystation even before anyone suggested looking for him. The castle sent guardians to monitor their progress along the road, but on

Stephenie's urging, Ista would wait and use the guardians stationed near the border to detain the men.

"What do you plan to do with Kanin's crossbow?" Dufnall asked as he devoured the meal that Kor provided. "I'm certain it killed my father."

Stephenie glanced at Henton, who wolfed down his food and sat on the other side of Kas. She had examined the bow more during the midday stop and found the intelligence of the weapon quite benign. *As most weapons are. No one wants a chatty sword to distract you when fighting for your life.* "I'm not sure yet," she admitted.

"Weapons that fall from the land of the gods are devastating in the wrong hands," Kor added as he handed Dufnall a mug of ale.

Ryia snorted and shook her head. She then looked up. "What?"

"You take issue with my friend?" Dufnall asked.

"I take issue with stupid statements," Ryia said between spoonfuls of her soup. "That's not how things work." She turned her focus to Stephenie. "When you forced me to teach people, I told you I won't listen to bullshit."

What kind of monster did I create? It's a good thing I love you, Stephenie sent to Ryia and then sighed aloud when Ryia rolled her eyes. She turned her attention back to Dufnall. "She's not wrong." Having already finished her second serving of soup, Stephenie set the bowl and spoon down beside her. "I mentioned before the term for what we do is magic. The truth is, magic is just the manipulation of the energy that is around us. There are no gods, only people who have the physical ability to channel the power, and the skill to do so. Things like that crossbow have tiny structures created inside them." She held out her right hand and small bits of sand and dirt floated up from the ground to land on her palm. "Structures thousands of times smaller than these." She turned her hand to the side and let everything fall back to the ground. "Those structures control how the energy flows. They control how the magical device acts. It is like a tiny brain. They can even have personalities that range from the very basic to incredibly powerful and dominating." She felt a smirk from Ista as the castle had a definite self-awareness.

Stephenie glanced at Kor, who listened intently, but with a deep frown. Anso had an even deeper sense of disapproval that he did not hide. "The crossbow wasn't created recently, but by people who lived a long time ago. The skill to make items that hold magic and can manipulate the world is mostly gone. There are some out there still who can, but it takes people with incredible power and skill."

"Can you make them?"

Stephenie hesitated. *I should be able to. I can see the fields. I just don't know how to craft the structures.* "We can't teach you how to make these kinds of things, but we can teach you how to control the energy around you so that it isn't just an instinctual reaction."

Dufnall nodded his head. "I've never seen anyone move things so small and with such control. Those touched by … Well, those we'd say were touched by the Goddess can crush a man, but nothing so delicate as what you just did."

Kor crossed his arms; his mind leaked his disagreement. "The southern gods give people holy symbols. Without them, they can't call upon their god's powers. They are not the same as those that take power from the Goddess."

Henton stood up. "Both Steph and Ryia can give you the long explanation, and it is worth listening to, but I'll save you some trouble. Those disks of metal are magical devices, like the crossbow. They get their power from special metal statues in the shrines. Which gets their power from something we call a trap." He glanced at Stephenie, and she nodded her head ever so slightly.

"And every shitty priest is simply like you," Ryia said. "People with power, but so weak they can't do anything but make the mental connection to the metal disk. They are the ultimate hypocrites, killing people like me for being different when they are the same as me."

Stephenie took over. "We don't know how long ago, but we think it was about six-hundred years. People with genuine power left the lands around the Sea of Tet and people lost the understanding of the devices. Those that remained behind invented the gods to control the population. They killed off anyone who opposed them, effectively purging the population of people with anything more than a trace of power. As time went on, they became more militant and developed the mythos of witches and witchcraft. They invented the idea of Elrin, their imaginary god of the elves, to explain why some people had power and others didn't."

Dufnall shook his head. "We didn't believe in witches until southerners started pushing their beliefs on us," Dufnall said. "We've always had faith in the Goddess. Not gods with statues and crazy rules."

"You are fairly far from the Sea of Tet, so that doesn't surprise me." Stephenie noticed the distant look on Kas' face and knew he felt left out of the conversation again. He had not reached out to ask her to include him. She knew the long day had exhausted him, but also knew he likely wanted to make a point about being excluded. She stood. "That's enough of a lesson for now. Ryia can continue if you want to hear more, but for now, I'm going to get some rest."

The next morning, Stephenie woke everyone early and had the camp broken down in half the normal time. Ista reported the guardians detained Hugo and Rolf and Douglas would reach the border soon. She asked the castle to report his arrival and then turned her attention to the road.

In a little less than three turns of the glass later, Ista let her know Douglas and his dog team reached the border. She instructed the castle to signal the communication stone Islet had given Douglas.

"What?" Douglas asked as Stephenie's vision became overlaid with Douglas standing before a stone building. Her friend's long hair did not conform to his normal fastidious appearance. "Oh, sorry, Steph. I thought you were Islet."

I'm sorry you got dragged into this. But I can't say I'm not happy to see you in your fine form. She smiled at him to emphasize her teasing tone.

He ran his fingers through his hair, they got caught in the tangles and he pulled his hand free without fixing his appearance. "You look as wonderful as normal. Have you gotten naked in front of everyone yet?"

Fair question, but no, I've managed to go at least two weeks without burning off all my clothes. She grew more serious. *Ista said he traveled with Rolf. They both keep asking why they've been detained and claim they didn't do anything.*

Douglas yawned. "What do you want to do? I've only slept a short time so that I could catch up to this guy."

Just keep the communication stone active while you question them. Ista told me that no one else in Isa Fields appears to be a suspect, so it is likely one, or both, of them are responsible.

"Perhaps a family disagreement?" Douglas started walking toward the door of the building. "Or so we can hope."

Stephenie did not bother to respond. She also wanted a simple explanation for the crime. She watched as Douglas entered the dimly lit building. A traditional firepit sat in the middle of the room with a pile of wood burning to remove the chill from the stone walls. The two men sat at a table with a pair of guardians sitting next to them. Anyone without significant magic would find these stone cats deadly foes, and even those whose lineage remained close to a dragon would struggle to get away.

"Your Grace," Hugo said when he saw Douglas. "What is the meaning of this?

Douglas moved to the table and sat across from the dark-skinned man. Some grey hairs speckled Hugo's black hair and beard. "I am sorry to have to tell you this, but it is about your brother, Nokki."

Stephenie saw Rolf flinch, though Hugo merely expressed a questioning shift of his eyes. *I wish I was there to feel their emotions,* she admitted to herself, without conveying the thought to Douglas. Even as a child, she relied upon her ability to detect the moods of others to navigate most of her relationships. She wanted to say that the additional feedback she felt provided her with little more than what an observant person watching people's expressions had, but she knew that her ability provided far more. And with people closest to her, she found herself far more attuned to them, making them easy to read, even when they kept their emotions contained.

"What happened to my brother?" Hugo eventually asked. "I saw him the day before we left to bring supplies to the border."

Douglas leaned forward. "Someone drove a chisel into his chest and forced him to the floor of his shop. It was a brutal murder."

"What?" Rolf shifted away from Hugo in his seat. "Nokki is dead?"

Douglas kept his attention on Hugo when he answered Rolf. "Yes. I came here to inform the both of you personally."

"May Dalkin take whoever killed my brother!" Hugo rose. "I need to get back to Isa Fields right away. Nokki has a wife and kids. They will need my help."

Douglas leaned back on the bench. "Please sit. There will be time for that. For now, I'd like to see each of your boots."

"What?" Rolf demanded. "I had nothing to do with this. I just help Hugo with the dogs and make sure the food gets delivered."

Douglas turned his attention to the twenty-year-old with barely any stubble on his chin. "You arrived in Isa Fields last year before Ivan closed the border."

"What's your point?" Rolf demanded.

"Why was the dogcart so lightly loaded? The lieutenant said that when he unloaded the food, there was only a fraction of what you normally deliver. Plus, you pushed the dogs to near exhaustion rushing here." Douglas shifted his gaze to the stone cat that had moved closer to Rolf. "You can't outrun Ista."

Rolf shook his head. "I don't know. I don't. I'm just here to help." His voice broke and a sob came out. "Please, I had nothing to do with anything."

Hugo's shoulders slumped. "The boy's telling the truth. He had nothing to do with Nokki's death. If you want the truth, I killed him. I wanted Beka and he did not want to share her. We argued, and he pulled that stupid tool from his workbench." Hugo dropped his head. "I didn't mean to do it. It just happened. The next thing I know, my brother is dying on the floor." Hugo raised his head. "I told him I was sorry. But the light went out of his eyes. I panicked. I took the cart, left as much as I could, then raced here. I hoped to cross the border and plead my case to the Sandvian soldiers. The boy knew nothing about what happened. You should let him go."

I don't trust him, Stephenie said. *Rolf knew Nokki was dead. If the two of them would lie about that, what else are they trying to get away with?*

Do you want to conduct this interrogation? Douglas asked Stephenie mentally. *I mean, it's not like I'm the one here and you're far away on a road or anything.*

Sorry, Stephenie said.

Douglas exhaled. *I'm tired and don't want to be here, but I shouldn't be rude to you. What do you want me to do?*

You are by far my favorite tailor, and I need a new shirt. Plus, I don't think the blood will come out of my pants.

What did you do? Was it the blue shirt?

I'll tell you when we arrive. And yes, the blue one. Needless to say, I got thirty miles out of everyone yesterday.

Damn glad I didn't go with you.

Stephenie let her approval come through the connection. *Let Rolf go. Ista has an additional twenty guardians scattered around the border. I'd prefer the soldiers don't see them move, but if Rolf tries to make a break for it, she will ensure he doesn't escape.*

Do you want me to escort either of them back to Isa Fields right away?

If you can live in the substandard station for a few days, we should be at the border in six or seven days. It depends on how long Dufnall wants to stay in Alkmaar before continuing on. Then I can make sure of their guilt before I level any sentence on them.

She watched the two men staring at Douglas as their silent conversation continued. They both had a trace of hopefulness in their eyes. *They are up to something,* she decided silently.

"Rolf, I believe you," Douglas said, and relief washed through the man's body. "Hugo, for murder, you will remain here until Her Majesty returns from Horn Point."

The older man swallowed and nodded his head. Resignation was evident, but also a trace of satisfaction.

Douglas stood up. "I need to speak with the lieutenant. Please remain here for now." *Satisfied?*

Yes, my friend, Stephenie replied. *Get some rest. I'll leave you to handle things on your end until I arrive.*

Thanks, Steph. Tell Islet I am sorry for being an ass to her.

Done. With that, she broke the connection. "What are the two of you up to?" She mumbled aloud.

"What?" Kas asked in Dalish as he walked beside her.

"Sorry. Just trying to figure out why Hugo killed his brother and what a third person's role is."

"You spend a lot of time communicating through Ista. She is not intruding into your mind too much, is she? I can feel her sometimes when you are sharing thoughts with me."

Stephenie shook her head. "She's like a cat. She wants attention on her terms, but is generally independent and can function perfectly well on her own."

Kas said nothing. The castle's presence in her mind had been a point of contention since she had first allowed it into her mind. She expected jealousy contributed to his objection, but the deeper concern he always expressed remained the risk that Ista would take over her mind. Unlike the crossbow she had handed over to Henton, and even the staff she had given to Ryia, Ista's personality had been created to act as a companion to a strong-willed dragon. While her own sense of self remained solid, it did not compare to the ego and narcissistic dominance of the winged beasts.

"Let me apologize now, but I'm going to pick up the pace."

Kas groaned and drew in energy to help make his legs move faster.

Late in the day, they passed through Gaffel, a small community that sat on the fork in the road that either went to Norbek and then on to Lobben, or north to Alkmaar and then to Ista. Stephenie allowed enough time in the town to buy meat for the dogs and supplies for the people, horses, and ponies. After they had replenished their supplies, she forced them to go another twelve miles to the next campsite.

Stephenie took over leading both Argat and Dark Dancer, allowing Ryia time to explain the basics of magic to Dufnall and Kor as they traveled. Stephenie's own ability to actually see the fields allowed her to mimic effects of others simply by recreating the results. That did not translate well to explaining how to form the correct mental models everyone else needed to perform magic. Ryia had managed to learn from Stephenie, but the process involved a lot of cursing from both of them. Although Ryia claimed to detest teaching others, Stephenie found her more than capable.

The next day they encountered no other travelers and Stephenie pushed them over thirty miles. Ryia's instructions continued through the day, but then trailed off in the evening when everyone had grown tired. They finally arrived in Alkmaar as the sun fell below the horizon. Everyone, including Argat, wanted a break from the endless days walking along the road, and Stephenie agreed to stay most of the next day in the northern city.

Unfortunately for Lami—the healer they befriended when they first arrived in Alkmaar nearly three years earlier—they woke him and invaded his comfortable single room home. The drovers, ponies, and horses found lodging in another building, but with Dufnall and his soldiers, Lami's home became a series of blankets spread on the floor.

In the morning, Dufnall met with the captain of the soldiers Ivan had stationed in the dilapidated city. The Jarl provided updated orders, which included waiting for him to return from Ista before heading south. By midafternoon, Stephenie said her goodbyes to those she knew in the nearly deserted city, and then got everyone back on the road. She gave the group a break by only making them travel fifteen miles before stopping for the night.

Chapter 15

Dacian walked at the head of the column of two thousand nine hundred and sixty-two soldiers led by a group of twenty-one nobles. Fortunately, none of Fotia's council wanted to leave Lobben to lead the invasion. Andre's orders put him in charge of the invasion of Norbek to ensure the soldiers he had helped recruit and train could handle the task. In truth, Dacian knew Andre just wanted him away from the rest of the council for a while.

"Prophet," Warner said as he closed on their group. His younger cousin left Norbek before the city gates had closed to provide his report. Warner bowed to him and then to the nobles. As fit as Andre, the nearly eighty-year-old man looked only twenty-five. Warner's dark brown hair, which two years ago had fallen to his waist, was now little more than a couple days' of growth. "Norbek is not aware of our approach. If our soldiers march to the walls after the sun sets, we can take the city quickly. The men inside the walls will eliminate the guards and open the gates."

That aligned with Dacian's original plan. If they removed the city's primary defenders while they slept, few of Lobben's soldiers should become casualties. Then, over the next two days, they could root out the people who might pose a challenge to Fotia's rule. The secondary wave of soldiers would arrive just as the initial force prepared to leave. That would allow the smaller group of less experienced soldiers to hold Norbek.

"The men are tired," Baron Chilton remarked.

Dacian did not want to hear any more of Chilton's complaints about his body's aches and pains. Although the tenets of Fotia's preaching included a requirement for the Faithful to endure suffering to gain the god's favor, in practice, few actually enjoyed the process. Only the most devout actually inflicted pain on themselves, preferring more to inflict it on others. "Fotia has warned that if we allow the Sandvians to fortify themselves, our endeavor will be at risk." *And I won't have enough troops to station on the roads to deter Stephenie from heading south.* He admitted the actual concern to himself.

"The sun won't set for quite a while yet," Chilton demanded. "We're what, two miles from the city?"

Dacian looked to the north. Norbek sat at the foot of a lone mountain peak that rose out of the ground east of the primary mountain range. He observed a bit of snow still visible in a few of the peak's valleys. The rolling foothills concealed the troops and the approaching road from any defenders. Over a year earlier, he scouted the city and knew his soldiers would only become visible for the last half-mile. With the Mother Moon waning and nearly over the horizon already, there would be little light to give them away. "The soldiers can rest and eat cold food. No fires. We already have over fifty holy warriors positioned within the city walls. They are expecting us to strike tonight."

"The Prophet is right, Chilton. Once the sun drops below the horizon, we march." Baron Daniels had shaved his head the night before. While not someone Dacian considered overly devout, Daniels understood tactics more than most of the other nobles, who generally accepted any order they received from Fotia's council. *The entire country is a puppet for the council and the council answers to Andre, for now.*

"Fine," Chilton said. "I'll go join my soldiers and prepare them."

Dacian nodded his head and considered the discussion over. He turned his attention back to Warner and switched to speaking Malinan, the primary language of house Hezin. "I believe we should make a show of our powers to reinforce our position with the soldiers and these nobles. That damn thorn in my side appears to actively be working to undermine us."

Warner shook his head, knowing Dacian's thoughts on Andre. "The fools really should learn their places in the world. They have no actual power and no protection from any family."

"Let us hope our purpose for being here has headed north diligently. Grandfather confirmed he knows of no family connection that Stephenie claims, or that claims her, but Yreka wants to keep her in the north."

Warner frowned. "Since when has your grandfather bowed to that Senzar woman? They are both fourth gen."

Dacian patted Warner's shoulder and turned the man so they could walk back to the primary group of soldiers a quarter of a mile behind them on the road. "She agreed to return Grandfather Galeno's home city to us, which gives us back our port access. The family has been in decline for centuries and we can use the revenue."

"I still don't like it," Warner complained. "But I'm two generations less than you, so who am I to question things?"

"Warner, it is always proper to question. You just have to exercise great caution in who and when you convey those questions, and more importantly, what action those questions lead you to take."

"Wisdom as always," Warner said with a smile.

Dacian and Warner walked through the soldiers, providing reassurances that Fotia watched over the soldiers and that all the portents predicted a sound victory. Dacian reinforced his words with a mental projection of confidence and power. The emotional energy influenced any of the people in his immediate area, but it lacked the potentially damaging adjustments he had made to Kev. This manipulation would not last long, but when repeated, it reinforced the notion that the soldiers should trust him personally, just like a man rewarding a dog with treats. *When the dust settles, Andre, they will follow me, not you. Not that I plan to stay in Lobben.*

As the sun neared the horizon, he mustered the nobles and the long column of soldiers slowly fell into line along the road. After the sun set, he walked with Warner at his side toward the gates of Norbek. If the timing worked correctly, the fifty holy warriors that had arrived in Norbek over the last two weeks would have started eliminating the soldiers at the gate and along the wall. Using the augmentation devices and having a nearly two-to-one advantage, he did not expect anyone to even raise an alarm.

Faced with tangible action, the soldiers that they had training for months to fight now had a purpose, and their excitement filled the air. Dacian preferred to read and do research, but over his lifetime, his family had required him to participate in many conflicts. The prospect of slaughtering people little more than children offered no pleasure, but he had no intention of ending up expelled from the family for refusing to comply with his grandfather's demands.

They came around a bend in the road, which also marked the top of a rise. The vantage point allowed the walled city of Norbek to come into view. Its stone walls stood forty feet tall with a dry ditch twenty yards in front of that. The stone gatehouse stood higher than any other part of the city, providing a massive structure for defenders to stand on and hide within. However, the large reinforced wooden doors now stood wide open, with a handful of men silhouetted by the city lamps burning behind them.

Dacian approached with the confidence of a man returning to his own home. When he grew close enough for the men standing under the gatehouse to recognize him, they all bowed.

"Fotia will prevail," he said as he led the soldiers into the city. The commandment for his advancing army to remain quiet would end once enough of them had passed through the gates. He just needed enough time to prevent the estimated three hundred defenders from reclaiming the walls or the gates.

On the other side of the gatehouse, the builders of Norbek had left a large, open square. Four roads led away from the open space, one in each direction along the city walls and two more that went deeper into the city at different angles. The streets of Norbek wandered and lacked order, which could hinder invaders. However, the leader of each unit carried detailed maps with their specific targets to overcome that risk.

Dacian and Warner stopped in the center of the square and allowed the first groups of soldiers to break off at a run. With their superior numbers, enough redundancy existed that each of the targets had no hope of resisting long. More troops followed the first groups and the noise level increased.

Deeper in the city, the sound of an alarm bell rang out and Dacian turned in that direction. A group of five soldiers, likely on patrol, fired crossbows toward his army. *Time to show off,* he thought to himself. He flung his arms in the air to draw attention to himself. The movement was a complete waste of effort, as magic, when done correctly, remained a purely mental exercise. However, most people stumbled on magic accidentally, and thought that they needed to cast spells to achieve the proper mental states.

A wall of blue green energy more than a hundred feet wide flew outward from him, knocking the bolts from the air. He felt the chill in the air as Warner drew in energy and released a bolt of lightning at the nearest of the five soldiers. The blinding flash of energy struck the man, dropping him to the ground with burns and a convulsing body.

Dacian clapped his hands together and pushed energy forward from him. He heated and compressed the air so that it grew hot enough that flames suddenly ignited as it flew at the soldiers. The bright flames cavitated and swirled, driven forward by the wind he pushed toward the men. The four remaining men screamed as the blistering-hot fire rolled over them.

Cheers rose from the soldiers, priests, and holy warriors of Fotia that continued to rush into the city. He doubted any of the nobles had entered the gates yet, but expected word of his and Warner's displays of power would soon reach every ear of the invasion force.

Dacian would rather kill the enemy soldiers quickly, with a narrow blast of force that could rip through a man's skull or chest. However, those attacks, while more effective at killing and conserving energy, did not inspire his followers. He chuckled, remembering the augmentation device resting on his chest. He preferred using his own powers because it provided a much finer control of the effect, *but for what I'm doing, broad waves of energy are enough.*

Beside him, Warner directed a gravitational burst into the front of a building at the edge of the square. The two men who had rushed out of the door ahead of the field flew backwards and crashed through the stone wall. A moment later, the sod roof came down on their corpses.

"Good work, Warner," Dacian said. "But do try to keep the casualties to the combatants and not random people. Our goal is to contain the queen in Ista, not kill indiscriminately."

Warner nodded his head, though Dacian sensed his cousin's frustration with the conflicting requests. *Yes, I know,* he admitted to himself. *Impressive displays of power are at odds with not causing reckless destruction.*

Chapter 16

The next morning Stephenie woke to a stiff wind and rain coming out of the north, making their trek bitter, but the ancient road shed the water easily and their footing remained solid. In the early afternoon, the rain subsided, and Stephenie gave in to the misery of the others and allowed them to stop and set up camp after only twenty miles.

After eating, she walked alone among the dogs, petting the ones that would accept her offer of kindness, and growling at the ones that thought to challenge her. She expected that at least thirteen of the nineteen would eventually become easy with people and not pose any real threat. The other six, she feared, might never learn to trust anyone and would only comply while a more assertive leader dominated them.

With the rest of the camp remaining in their tents because of the biting wind, she took a moment to enjoy her privacy. She dried a rock with her powers and sat down. She thought again about Caridelis and wondered what happened to the missing female dragon. Selfishly, she wanted more lessons so that she could get on an even footing with any of their enemies, but her own compassion made her worry that Caridelis might also have been harmed or driven away by Stephenie's sire.

"Damn bastard," she swore softly. She could not fathom the twisted purpose Duvargintik had in first creating her and then systematically manipulating people to try to destroy her. Caridelis warned her not to attribute human motivations to the actions of dragons. *But a motivation is a motivation. Did she just mean that they are all bastards that like to torment others?*

Stephenie looked down at her small hands. The callouses developed from weapons training had faded some. She had not engaged in close combat with anyone since before arriving in Ista, and her time spent training with swords had become a guilty pleasure she seldom found time to enjoy. *I've relied on my powers more and more. Plus, how sporting is it for me to fight someone who has no chance of beating me?*

A tan dog scooted closer and rested his muzzle on her foot. She leaned forward and petted the animal, who desperately sought approval. "Good boy," she mumbled and then leaned back while looking at her fingers.

Control the transformation, she told herself. Caridelis had told her she could not become an actual dragon, but each time her body changed, it felt more and more like it wanted to form wings, a long neck, and a tail. She did not know if the feeling came from envy at seeing how beautiful Caridelis had been in her natural form. A creature of magic and power, sleek and graceful, with scales that held the same iridescent quality of her own transformed flesh. *And the wings.* The idea of flying with wings spread wide to glide effortlessly in the wind continued to haunt her dreams.

She pulled power from the land, drawing it in slowly and concentrated it into the index finger of her right hand. *Change without flames,* she commended her flesh. The pain built until she could not help but clench her left hand. Her right finger glowed, a blue plasma covered it as her nail grew and elongated into a claw. The human portion of her hand shrunk in on itself, becoming thinner, as though she squeezed muscle, blood, and fat from the rest of her hand to become the one-inch-long talon. Pink skin disappeared and greenish-grey scales that luminesced in the light took its place.

The transition line burned and hurt; the human portion of her hand looked almost skeletal, withered away like death had visited her, but she held the partial transformation a little longer. Small flames danced on the surface of her finger, but she had limited the wasted energy far more than she normally did.

The pain grew more intense, and she allowed the energy level in her finger to decrease. Her talon shrunk as the flesh in her hand reformed. The sensation felt uncomfortable, and she wondered if Caridelis' transformations had been so quick and fluid to avoid the discomfort. After several seconds, her hand once again looked normal, except for the slight dusting of scales on the tip of her finger. *How can they shift from someone with my mass to an enormous dragon without creating matter?* Kas had told her making something from energy alone might be theoretically possible, but unlikely.

A drop of rain hit the back of her head and she looked up. Another drop hit her face, and she sensed more rain moving in quickly. "Time for me to go back to the tent," she told the dogs. A gravitational field formed to block the subsequent drops that started hitting the dogs and the ground. "Sorry, I don't have a better place for all of you," she offered quietly as she headed back to the others.

"Stephenie," Kas said as she climbed into the tent. He held open the old tome he had been reading. A small stone sitting in the gutter of the pages emitted light and illuminated him from below. The patter of rain on the waxed tarp over the tent added to the ambiance. "I think I've been translating this word incorrectly." He flipped back to another section in the book he had marked with a scrap of parchment covered in his own scribbles. "I may have been looking for the trap in the wrong city. Likely we should look further south. If this passage is correct, which I believe it to be, then what I thought to be a gulf that went horizontally from west to east, would instead be one that is just off the vertical from west to east." Kas set down the book and pulled out a map of the northern lands and held it out to her. "See, Cilwir, which I believe is a modern name, relatively speaking, is near the edge of the gulf that is further south." He picked up the book again. "Which aligns better with this other passage—"

Stephenie raised a hand. She sensed Ista needed her attention and paused a moment as the concepts of Rolf messing with the dogcart and removing something from a hidden compartment filled her mind. *Watch him and get Douglas,* she instructed. *Did Hugo force Nokki to modify a cart to hide things or was Nokki part of it? How many traitors do we have?*

"She's always in your head." Kas closed the book and tossed the light stone to the side.

"Something is happening at the border. Rolf appears to have hidden a small bundle of papers in a dogcart."

Kas shook his head. "I presume you already have Douglas involved. There is nothing you can do from here."

"Kas, this is serious. We need to know why Nokki was murdered and what those two are up to. I'm guessing they are spies, but for whom? How many others are involved?"

Kas held his breath, about to say more, then simply exhaled. "I might have found where the trap in Sandven was located. I thought my breakthrough might excite you. I guess not."

Damn it, Kas, she fumed silently. "I am, but the trap's been there for a long time. This is happening now." She grabbed the boots she had just pulled off. Douglas' surroundings overlaid her vision. She mentally spoke to Douglas. *Ista is watching him, but I want you to be ready to grab him as well.* She slipped on her boots as she watched Douglas leave the larger of the two roundhouses and head around the rear side to keep the building between him and Rolf.

"We can talk once this is done," Stephenie said, not bothering with the buckles on her boots as she slipped out of the tent and into the rain. She automatically formed a gravitation field above her head, directing the water away from her so that she remained dry. *Oh, if I could have done that as a child.*

"What?" Douglas whispered, water already dripping from his face.

Sorry, you are getting wet. I was just thinking about how I might have gotten myself burned alive well before we ever met. She walked away from the tent and checked on the unhappy horses and ponies. Their ears perked at her approach, but none of them found the cold bath from above pleasant. She slipped into the enclosure and stood in the middle of the animals, extending her shield out to keep all of them dry. The dogs unfortunately remained outside of the camp.

"He's got something in his hand, I think," Douglas said.

Her friend remained low to the ground and leaned against the wet stones of the roundhouse. Unfortunately, Rolf remained too far away for her to see through the communication stone that Douglas carried. However, Ista shared the concepts of what the guardians observed.

Yes, Ista believes it is a bundle of documents in a treated bladder to keep the contents dry. It's flat. There appears to be a secret compartment in the dog cart.

She saw Douglas perk up at the statement. "I searched the cart. The woodwork must have been pretty good."

I'm guessing that was Nokki's part of this. I wonder if Beka knows anything.

Douglas did not respond to that comment. "He's just gone over the rise and headed toward the bridge. Perhaps he thinks he'll be able to slip to the other side without being stopped or the guardians detecting him." Douglas moved from his cover and followed Rolf, moving through the grasses and uneven ground to minimize being spotted. With the sun below the horizon and the thick storm clouds covering the sky, the night had become as dark as it would ever get at this time of year.

Douglas moved over the rise that protected the roundhouses from view by anyone at the border and continued to follow a parallel path to Rolf. He had fallen further behind the young man, who now crouched low as he closed in on the small guard house and bridge.

Ista does not see anyone on the other side. The Sandvian soldiers are keeping out of the weather. We may not be able to identify their contacts.

"Lucky them."

I'm imagining a protective dome over your head to keep you dry.

"Might as well imagine me home with Ben for all the good that is doing me." Douglas sped up when he reached a part of the landscape with larger rocks and boulders that would provide some cover. "If I die from sickness, you can blame yourself."

Love you too, she replied warmly.

"I won't be able to stop him. He's too close to the bridge and looks like he might run for it. Hard to tell without more light."

Stephenie and Ista agreed with Douglas. *Take him,* she told the castle. Before she even finished the thought, four of the winged cats burst from where they had crouched among the rocks beside the bridge. Even with their size, because of their magic, the cats could levitate and fly short distances, making them nearly silent when needed.

Rolf screamed in terror, tried to retreat, and then found both arms held firmly in two separate guardians' mouths. The stone teeth pressing firmly enough to hold him, but not tight enough to tear through his flesh.

Douglas arrived quickly at a run, then slowed so that he could walk around the cats to face Rolf. "Just what do you think you are doing?"

"Please, I've done nothing wrong. I just wanted to go to Sandven and see my family."

Douglas moved closer as the cats pulled on Rolf's arms, tensioning his upper body. "Kick at me and you'll lose your arms." Terror raced across the young man's face. Douglas lifted the man's tunic and retrieved the thin package wrapped in treated skins. "I think it is time to explain yourself."

Rolf sagged and dropped his head. "I don't know anything. Only that Hugo told me to get this across the border."

He might not be lying, Stephenie said. *I'll let you handle it. Hopefully, I'll be there late tomorrow or sometime the next day. It'll depend on how much I can push the others. Let me know what you find.*

Douglas nodded his head and said nothing as the two cats walked toward the roundhouses on the other side of the rise. He looked at the two guards that had come out of their small, heated enclosure. They stopped at the very edge of the communication stone's awareness. "I've got this," he said to both Stephenie and the soldiers. The border guards accepted his statement and they simply watched Douglas and the guardians lead Rolf away.

"Damn spies," Stephenie mumbled after the connection had broken. The wind and rain picked up, but she did not feel like returning to the tent, so she remained with the horses to make their night a little better.

On a dogsled in the winter, a strong team could easily cover the hundred and ten miles from Alkmaar to the border in two days. Stephenie knew her powers could fly her there—in human form—before it was time for their next meal. However, with the horses, the same distance on the road needed at least four days. Despite the desire to deal with Hugo and Rolf, she could not risk leaving the others in case another assassin pursued them. With already having two shorter days of travel out from Alkmaar, Stephenie's only means of getting the team there in two more days involved pushing everyone beyond their limits.

She did not want to tell them she planned to put in forty miles a day. That would generate complaints even from Henton. Instead, she planned to boost the animals' endurance and hope the people did not notice the faster pace and longer days. She started with the horses while the others broke camp. The rain had stopped two turns of the glass earlier, but the clouds remained thick in the sky, and the horses and ponies had an unpleasant night even with her protection. She drew power into herself and eased their aches and directed their bodies to speed the rebuilding of the muscles that had worn down from their continued march. She knew she would repeat the process at each stop during the day.

For the humans, they would have to contend with the strain on their own. She trusted Henton with her life, and Perain near enough, but she did not like touching their minds during healing, so she hoped they could push through the pain. The drovers she knew would be the largest problem. However, Kor had spent some of his time addressing sprained ankles and other injuries, so perhaps they could manage as well.

The dogs came next. The pack growled and snipped at each other when she moved into their midst after the wet night. She examined each one closely, checking their feet for signs of injury. Five needed healing, and two others appeared to have worms. *I'll ask Perain for suggestions on how to treat that.*

By the time she addressed the pack's needs, the others had disassembled the camp and started loading the ponies. She joined Henton in putting the bags of grain on Furball's back. "Rolf tried to take maps and coded messages across the border last night."

Henton shook his head. "You suspected he wasn't innocent."

"If those two betrayed us, how many more? Nokki might have done some woodwork to create a hidden compartment in the dogcart. Perhaps willingly. Perhaps not." She sighed. "Then there is the question. Does Beka know?"

Henton put a hand on her shoulder and stopped her from picking up the sack that held their own food. "Don't become too negative. It could easily be only those two, and everyone else in Ista will feel as betrayed as we do."

She frowned. "I don't know what I'm doing. Islet is better at being queen than I am." She glanced around, but everyone else remained occupied with their own tasks. "I'm far happier out here than sitting on a throne listening to people's gripes."

Henton chuckled. "You've told me more times than I can count that you were never meant to rule." He allowed the mirth to fall from his face. "But you are no fool, and you know you need to get better at it. Listen to your sister's advice and don't ignore the rest of us when we tell you things." He tilted his head to the side. "Though to be honest, you have made terrible choices in who you've picked as advisors. For example, I know nothing about running a country. I'm just a marine that's only barely able to keep people under me alive."

"Bullshit," she responded. "You're damn good at keeping people alive. Even when they piss you off with their stupidity."

He smiled at her. "We're all trying to figure it out." He looked out across the rocky landscape. The clouds blurred together with the horizon. "I'm most at home when sailing on familiar waters, but I'm learning to navigate the politics of court life."

She grunted. "I've got the most screwed up court there ever was. This is nothing like court life." Memories of being a young girl and watching nobles dance and talk and giggle with false sincerity came to her. Her mother, who believed her the actual spawn of Elrin, had tried to keep her locked away, but Antar castle had many secret passages and hidden observation nooks.

"I wouldn't know," Henton said without regret. "I've only heard stories and observed from very far away."

She returned her focus back to the issue at hand. "I'm just worried about who is behind this. The documents Rolf tried to smuggle into Sandven were written in some code. Other marks on the map of Isa Fields were written in a dialect spoken in Lobben." She rubbed her forehead. "Is that to throw us off or was it Lobben?"

"Or Yreka." Henton shook his head. "That Senzar bitch chased you across the world to kill us because she thought you violated their secret unspoken rules about harming one of them."

Stephenie kicked a rock. "They can kill anyone deemed less than them, but don't ever fight back or they will send a death squad to kill you and everyone you love."

Henton frowned his agreement. "She could easily have arranged for someone to spy on you, even though you told her to leave us alone." The frown did not leave his face. "And she warned us there are others that don't answer to her that might come looking to cause us trouble."

"She knows what I am. I'm certain she wants to control me rather than kill me." Stephenie grabbed another sack of grain from the ground and hefted it onto Furball's back. "I've tried to avoid drawing too much attention to us these last couple of years. But we need the trade."

"Yreka will not forget about you." He took the sack with their food and put it on top of the grain. "Opening up Ista to outsiders is going to invite trouble. Just coming south to speak with Ivan has driven people to try to kill you. Twice. What happens when others come into Ista that want to harm you, or Ryia, or Kas, or Douglas?"

"We can't be completely locked away from everything else. I think Kervigar had been wrong to keep Ista a secret from the rest of the world. Yeah, he needed to keep what he was a secret, but he could have done that by changing his decor."

"Those kinds of enemies are on a whole other scale, pun intended." He picked up three straps and tossed the loose ends over the top of the supplies. "The prior ruler obviously had enemies. They killed him. If they come for us, my hope is we die quickly." He moved closer to her and lowered his voice. "Speaking of which, have you heard anything at all from the friendly dragon?"

"She wasn't that friendly," Stephenie challenged. "I hope I just pissed her off somehow and that she's not dead. It's been over two years with no word. Five lessons did not teach me enough."

Henton pulled the first strap tight and then moved on to the next one. "Did you get any sleep last night?"

She shook her head. "I need less and less." She looked up at him, her eyes moistening. "Ista and Douglas reached out while Kas was telling me about the trap, which he now thinks is in Cilwir. He got angry. I didn't feel like going back to continue that conversation." She patted Furball's neck and pushed the gelding's nose away from her pouch. "Plus, it was raining, and I wanted to offer some protection to the horses."

He frowned at her. "I don't want to get in the middle of things, but the two of you are getting as snippy as the dogs are with each other."

She put a hand on her hip. "That is not getting in the middle of it?"

He pulled the third strap tight. "I said I don't want to. But Kas keeps coming to me to complain, and I can't help but think the reason you are talking to me right now instead of him is that you want my advice."

Her shoulders slumped. "I do need some advice."

He shook his head. "I'm the wrong guy to ask for advice on love. I've not had a lasting relationship with anyone, and while I've managed to get Ryia to not hate me, she's still always on guard with me."

"Well, you told her she was too young for you." Stephenie raised a hand. "I'm not disagreeing. I think it could have been a terrible idea. She's grown a lot over the last couple of years—"

"Do you want to talk about her to avoid talking about yourself?"

Stephenie crossed her arms. "This is why I come to you. You don't let me get away with things I shouldn't."

Henton stopped, looked around, and then focused on her. "The two of you need to talk to each other and not me. That's my advice." He moved a step closer and put his hand on her shoulder again. "I get it. He's messed up. He was dead—lacked a body—for however long it was. You took the raw material from a dead deer and created a new body for him. Every bit of him is you taking his memories and filling in the gaps to make a man that you wanted. He's bound to feel insecure. Like he can't live up to your expectations. He's not interested in swords and fighting and traipsing across the world, but you are."

She sighed and looked down at her feet. "You're right. I need to make sure he knows he's enough." She looked off to the left. "Now tell me, what's wrong with me?"

Henton turned her toward Argat and started guiding her toward her horse. "You fell in love with the first person who truly saw you for who and what you are. He understood you when everyone else, including me, didn't." Henton bent down and picked up a sack of oats. Argat immediately sidestepped away until Stephenie nudged him back toward Henton with her mind. "I'm guessing you had one expectation of what life with a breathing man would be like, and reality isn't quite the same."

She lowered her voice. "You're saying I made a mistake."

"No. I'm saying the two of you need to talk to each other and work out what you each want, accept you won't get everything, compromise, and give each other the things you can give." He grabbed the tent poles and canvas and balanced it on the oats. "The two of you are good together, but you're both stuck on your own initial assumptions."

She moved closer and hugged him. "This is why I talk to you. You know how to make things better."

He squeezed her with one arm and then pulled away. "Too bad I can't give myself good advice."

She wiped a tear from the corner of her eye. "I'm aiming for forty miles today. The road from here on out is mostly flat, without too many hills. If you feel sore, let me know. I'll heal your muscles." She smiled at him. "It's the least I can do."

He shook his head. "You won't get forty miles out of anyone. Adjust your expectations."

Chapter 17

Dacian sat with Warner at a large table in a public house. Norbek's primary defenders had all fallen or surrendered before midday after the invasion. Pockets of resistance continued to emerge the following night and had resulted in another twenty of his soldiers dying from ambush attacks. While he and his younger cousins had added many empowered people to the ranks of Fotia's Faithful, the number of people who could wield magic remained a small percentage of the overall population. He ordered a redistribution of the troops to include at least one empowered holy warrior with each unit of regular soldiers. The change reduced the casualties significantly.

I just hope I can keep Fotia's followers and their damn council from exterminating too many people in their desire for religious righteousness. The centuries of purges of anyone with powers not tied to the gods never seems to end.

"We've not seen anyone with significant magic since last night," Warner said in Malinan. "Though they could be biding their time or plotting to come after us directly."

Dacian nodded his head, knowing even though Sandven did not practice the concept of burning witches, the efforts of so many others over the centuries had left them with few who could use magic. *And even fewer that understood what magic is.* "Agreed. I think once they realized the city was lost, they probably went underground."

"Literally." Warner moved a couple of small markers across a hand-drawn map of Norbek. "Some of the sewers are large enough to hold a reasonably effective group of fighters. The forces have routed at least four cells. We even found a group of women and children hiding in what is an underground market. The entrances were concealed in four different buildings."

"It gets cold in the winter. I imagine they prefer to do their shopping out of the wind." Dacian looked at a ledger. None of their nobles reported any injuries. In total, they had lost only sixteen of their holy warriors and eighty-nine regulars. More than half of those had been to a rather powerful mage. Another forty-five had injuries, but the healers had addressed any wounds that would prevent them from continuing to fight.

"It wasn't as clean as I would have liked. The soldiers are still a bit too green, but with the reinforcements arriving tomorrow, we should be able to press on to Horn Point."

They both looked up and turned their focus to the outer door of the public house. A dozen men approached. When the people reached the door, a knock sounded. "Enter," Dacian commanded.

Two Sandvians with their hands bound before them stepped into the dimly lit room, followed by two holy warriors and eight swordsmen. "Prophet," the Faithful of Fotia sang in unison before bowing deeply. The two prisoners, realizing who sat at the table, bowed as well, repeating the soldiers' statement.

"Who are you?" Dacian asked, intrigued by the admiration coming from people he expected to despise him.

"Prophet, these men claim to be members of the Faithful." The older of the two holy warriors stepped forward to the edge of the table. "They turned themselves in yesterday morning, but we had only now been able to deal with them. They carried markers of Fotia and a bundle of papers." The holy warrior who had lost most of his hair due to age set down two small disks that bore the mark of the cauldron of rebirth, as well as a bundle of papers.

Dacian reached across the table and took the papers. No seal secured the bundle, and he unfolded the pages to reveal a confusing set of script. The hand that made the marks had practice, but many of the marks had hallmarks of hesitation and someone had heavily overwritten more than a dozen lines to make the original symbols illegible. He turned his attention to the two men. "Please explain yourselves."

"Prophet, we had never expected to meet you here in Norbek. We knew the High Council Member would send someone to collect the documents, but we never hoped to be graced by someone of your standing."

Dacian searched through the emotions of the young man still in his early twenties. He wore both his blond hair and beard thick and braided. His tunic marked him as a soldier of King Ivan. A sense of pride and admiration radiated from him and his shorter, and heavier set, companion. "Have you translated the documents?"

The man vigorously shook his head. "No. We don't know the code. Only the man in Ista and the High Council Member knows it. That way, no one would know what it said."

Damn Andre, I told him Fotia commanded the Faithful to avoid Ista. Dacian nodded his head knowingly as he read the surface thoughts of the men. If he pushed too deep into their memories, they would notice his intrusion. "How long have you had these in your possession?"

The man smiled. "We have only been in Norbek for six days. Our unit rotated away from the Ista border; it took eight days to arrive here. We had them at the border for nine days—"

"Ten days," his companion said. "Ten days before we rotated out."

"Ten days." The man started counting on his fingers.

"Twenty-four days," Dacian said, satisfied that they spoke truthfully, but not patient enough to wait for the man to perform the math. "These men appear to be members of the Faithful," Dacian said to the holy warrior standing at the table.

The holy warrior pursed his lips. "Should we release them?"

Dacian shook his head. *Andre is ignoring things I have specifically told him not to do. I need to see what kind of damage he's done.* "The council will want to continue to get information. Give them back their markers, but lock them up as though none of this occurred. No one here is to speak of this to anyone. We do not want anyone in Sandven or Ista to learn of our plans, and we don't want them to know there are spies at work." He reinforced the command by projecting a sense of euphoria and obligation into the group of men.

Then he turned his attention to the two spies. "You have done great work. You can now assist us by learning what the Sandvian soldiers in Norbek are planning to do to resist Fotia's wisdom."

Looks of concern crossed both men's faces, and Dacian suspected they had not turned themselves in quietly. However, he needed to keep them from potentially telling others they had handed off the documents to him. *I need to translate the reports and then destroy them before Andre does something even worse.*

Dacian turned to Warner and spoke in Malinan. "I'm going to head back to Berl today. I have faith that you are more than capable of leading the force to Horn Point and joining up with Vikram as we had originally planned. Just avoid killing too many innocents."

Warner smiled. "There are few of those."

Dacian turned back to the others, not in the mood to argue that compassion was more effective long-term. *But this is very short term.* He met each of their eyes and continued to project a sense of peace and power that they would associate with listening to him speak. "Remember, none of you know anything about this. I will take the documents to the High Council Member today. My disciple will continue to lead the invasion of Horn Point as originally planned." He waved his hand, signaling the others to leave the public house.

Chapter 18

The drovers complained quietly as they sat in a circle eating a cold meal. Stephenie tuned them out and closed down her mental awareness. Their emotions radiated a distaste for the journey, and even for her because of the harsh pace she had set so far that morning. The feelings had not reached hate yet, but she suspected if she decided to ignore Henton's advice and push them to forty miles in a single day, that would push it to that level of contempt. *Even the soldiers think I'm crazy.*

She estimated they had managed almost fifteen miles so far, but that left another twenty-five before she wanted to stop. *It'll just have to take an extra day.* She sighed and silently informed Ista that they would be delayed. The castle updated her on the status of Hugo and Rolf, as well as the harvest. *I get people wanting to burn me. I've lived with that my whole life. But those two also betrayed the rest of Ista. And Hugo killed his own brother.* She felt a sense of reassurance from Ista and allowed the anxiety that had built to wash away.

She looked up and noticed Kas watching her from over the top of his open book. The frown on his lips disappeared when he noticed her returning his glance. He dropped his focus back to the page in front of him. *The discussion needs to happen.*

Stephenie rose to her feet and walked over to him. "We should talk," she said in Dalish to keep the conversation private.

"I am trying to puzzle out this passage. I have almost figured it out." He continued to stare at the marks on the page.

"I'm serious, Kas. We've not been talking enough."

He made a show of closing the book. "Do you not have others to talk to? You spend most of the day and night talking with the device in Ista. I warned you that it would occupy your mind and take over."

"Kas, please. We've been through that. The mental connection is not like that." She could not deny the frequent communications, but Ista did not communicate like another person. The castle acted more like an extension of herself, providing awareness of her country, not companionship. It definitely had not taken control of her mind and body, which Kas expressed as his greatest fear regarding the castle. "I know this trip has been hard for you. But it's important that we are honest with each other."

He put the book aside and stood up. "I have always been upfront on my opinion of your relationship with Ista."

"You are the most important person in my life."

"It does not feel like that." He glanced around the camp. "You are always busy with something. Running the country, communicating with the castle, talking with Henton, training Ryia. I'm just one of many things you focus on."

She bit her lip and paused before responding. She reminded herself, *you don't want to argue. You just want to clear the air.* Aloud, she said, "I have a lot of responsibilities. There are many things that steal away my time. I had hoped this trip would have allowed us to get closer again."

He shook his head. "When I lacked a body, floating around for hours every day did not really affect me. I could do little else. Now I also have things I can do." He glanced at the horses. "I have also concluded that I dislike sleeping on the ground, being cold, tired, and uncomfortable. I grew up in a city with a library, beds, and hot food." He softened his stance. "I will be glad to get back to Isa Fields, but it is still many days away, even at your pace." He forced a smile. "Which is not making anyone happy." He glanced back at his book. "We can talk more when we are home. I am just not in the mood right now and will probably say things that will not help."

Stephenie nodded her head. She wanted to ball up her fists and pound on something, but she contained her disappointment. *At least he knows when he's not ready to talk. That's at least something,* she told herself, wanting to have something positive to focus on. "Okay. We'll work this out when we get back."

She limited their pace to thirty miles or fewer per day, and two days later, as it neared time for dinner, Stephenie finally saw the half dozen buildings Sandven maintained at the border. The old buildings had originally been to support trade, but a couple of decades of neglect, followed by hasty repairs, left the stone structures in an unpleasant state.

A small summertime river marked the border with a wide stone bridge arching over the meager flow of water that emptied into a small fjord. In the winter, the river and fjord froze over, allowing anyone or anything to simply walk between the countries. However, on the Ista side, a long series of five-foot tall black stones covered in runes marked the edge of her domain. Set every thirty feet, aside from the gap where the bridge existed, these rectangular blocks protected the entire border of her country. The magic in the stones reacted to anyone coming close to them, alerting Ista of the intrusion.

Oh, to be an actual dragon with hundreds of centuries of time and near limitless power. She had no way to fathom an existence that did not march to an eventual death from age. That she might not show any signs of aging for another eight hundred years, and then still live a long time after that, had never fully registered for her. *A half-breed curse,* she reminded herself, not wanting to consider all her current friends dying, and then her making new friends, only for them to die. The idea of repeating that process again and again until she could no longer bear the pain and became a recluse always threatened her sanity and made her want to scream at the injustice.

She slowed as Ivan's border guards noticed their approach. A watcher blew a horn, and twenty men scrambled from several buildings to fall into a loose formation with spears and crossbows at the ready. Stephenie wondered which one, or ones, of that group had conspired with Rolf and Hugo.

Her pack of dogs remained a hundred feet off the road on her right. The slow integration of Dufnall and her friends with the pack had already mellowed them to the point she no longer needed to push on their minds to suppress the growls and biting. However, the sight and smell of strangers raised their hackles.

The warning horn from the soldiers alerted the two people who sat in a recently constructed guard hut on the Ista side of the border. She knew that Douglas, his friend Lukas, and the other six border guards left the roundhouse after a guardian alerted them of her approach. The rise in the landscape hid them and the buildings from her view.

She ordered the dogs to remain back and not approach the soldiers as Dufnall and the others quickly caught up with her. The Sandvian soldiers waited along the road, blocking the path into Ista. When Dufnall and Stephenie reached a distance reasonable for speaking, a man that wore a captain's uniform stepped forward. Stephenie appreciated the westerly breeze that blew away any likely odors from the unwashed men.

"Who are you and why are you here? We know southerners and their horses when we see them."

"Captain Tumi, I'm Jarl Dufnall the Younger. I have orders from King Ivan." Dufnall turned halfway toward Stephenie. "Captain, this is her Majesty, Queen Stephenie of Ista. My brother, his Majesty, King Ivan, has sent me north to Ista to finalize a trade agreement with Ista." Dufnall pulled a folded parchment from the satchel hanging at his waist. "Here are your new orders. I'll let you read them. Then I will leave you with my team of drovers and ponies before her Majesty escorts me to Isa Fields."

The young captain narrowed his eyes, but he came forward. He took the folded parchment, noticed the seal, broke it, and then started reading. His eyebrows rose several times before he dropped his arms to his sides. "Stand down, men. We are to wait here until Jarl Dufnall returns." The captain turned to his men with a grin. "Then we can go back to Horn Point."

A few small cheers went through the twenty soldiers.

Stephenie could see the boredom hanging on the soldiers that had been given the thankless task of watching a border that had no activity. *Did the traitors act from a lack of excitement, money, or orders from Ivan?* Henton had earlier argued that even if Ivan had been behind it, he had seen many countries involved in spying, including

Cothel. She did not like to think of her father as dishonest, but realized ruling a country requires some flexibility of morals.

Still, the documents bothered her. *Was the language used to distract from Ivan and to put the blame on Lobben? Or was Lobben actually responsible and Ivan had traitors in his own ranks?* She needed more information.

Stephenie brought her focus back to the forefront. "Jarl, if you'll follow me, we can cross the bridge into Ista as soon as you gather anything you need from the ponies. We have a dogcart across the border that can carry your supplies."

Dufnall bowed to her. "We'll gather what we need."

"I'll be glad to get the next hundred miles done," Ryia said, walking past Stephenie toward a wide stone bridge that spanned the river. Douglas and seven other people approached the bridge from the other side of the rise. Her pack of dogs felt eager to run with so many new people nearby, and only her mental dominance kept them in check.

Stephenie swore as Ista conveyed events happening in the round houses. *It is not your fault. Hold Hugo and don't kill him,* she told the castle. She called out loud enough so that Dufnall and the others could hear her. "I'm going ahead. Please take your time and follow when you've gathered everything." She handed off Argat's lead to Henton and hurried toward the bridge, the dogs rushing forward to cross with her. Ryia raised an eyebrow and Stephenie signaled for her to wait.

It took all of Stephenie's self-control to avoid running or flying, but anyone who watched knew she moved with purpose. At the bridge, the border guards bowed to her and welcomed her home. None of them mentioned the dogs that had rushed forward, only to line up in three neat rows behind her.

Douglas who approached the bridge as she crossed, smiled and waved to her. "It is good to have you back. New friends?" His face did not hide his apprehension of the pack of dogs.

Stephenie nodded her head. She wanted to comment on the form fitting wool coat he wore over a linen shirt, demonstrating a marked improvement of his skills, but she could not bring herself to humor. "Hugo just broke Rolf's neck." Douglas' eyes widened, and he turned his head to look to the north. "Hugo appeared to try to get the guardians to kill him, but Ista has him restrained."

"Damn it," Douglas fell in at her side as they moved quickly back the way he had come. "Rolf was getting close to breaking. Hugo's a cold bastard."

"I apologize, your Majesty," Lukas said with a bow. He had come with Douglas to help with the dogcart. "I should have remained behind to watch the prisoners."

Stephenie shook her head. The thin man with thin blond hair was almost twice her age and always willing to take blame for anything that went wrong. "It is not your fault."

When they came over the rise, Stephenie headed directly toward the smaller of the two round buildings and ordered the dogs to wait just north of the building. Her pack moved in among three of the dozen guardians that sat scattered around the area. The dogs sniffed at the stone statues, certain they represented something, but uncertain what. The stone protectors turned their heads to watch her, their movement only occurring out of sight of Sandven's soldiers.

"What are you going to do with the dogs?" Douglas asked.

"I'm uncertain. Some of them are still far too aggressive with people."

Douglas nodded in understanding.

"Do you have any idea of the motivation for the betrayal?"

Douglas shrugged. "They knew that no one here could read their minds, so they remained silent. They knew we expected you today." He kicked a rock off the tightly packed road. "I should have left guards with them."

She could not keep the irritation from her voice. "Not you as well. You left two guardians. Hugo reacted too fast, even for Ista, to realize what he intended until it happened. He just reached over to Rolf and snapped his neck." She picked up her pace and swept through the wooden door and into the thirty-foot wide single room building. The firepit in the middle of the room provided some warmth, but most of the light came from an oil lamp by the door.

Hugo lay on the floor, his arms spread out and pinned down by the two stone cats that had been in the room. The cats' tails rested over his legs, becoming an immoveable object. The black-haired man snarled at her and struggled against the stone paws pressing down on his wrists. Rolf lay crumpled into a heap, his head turned too far around and at an odd angle.

"How many have you killed?" Stephenie asked, forcing calmness into her voice. "Your young friend here. Your own brother. Anyone else?"

Hugo looked away, pain clear in the tension in his face and neck. "I've nothing to say to you."

"We let you come into Ista, and this is how to treat the citizens of the country you swore to protect?" Stephenie turned to Douglas. "Do you have the documents?"

He nodded and pulled a bundle of folded parchment from an internal pocket in his blue dyed overcoat. Stephenie took the papers and opened the complex folds so that she could see the full details. The larger outer parchment contained a map with drawings of many aspects of Isa Fields as well as marks showing the road and waystation and typical locations for guardians. The labels on the map were written in a language she did not understand.

"Everything on that is in a western dialect spoken in Lobben," Douglas said, looking over Stephenie's shoulder. "It's not widely spoken or written, but Collin, the guard with the bent nose, used to cart goods from Lobben with his father before his father died. He recognized a few of the words."

"You said the rest is in code?" Stephenie looked at the two smaller pages that had been folded up with the map.

"Yeah. None of the marks look to make real words." Douglas shrugged. "Not sure why they would use regular words on the map and not code."

Stephenie tried to see if any patterns jumped out at her, but even with her natural ability to learn languages, nothing immediately made sense to her. She handed the documents back to Douglas. "Because if they used the code to represent something that we knew, it would make it easier to break."

Douglas started refolding the documents. "That makes sense."

Stephenie moved closer to Hugo and squatted beside him. "I could rip the truth from you. That's why you killed Rolf and tried to get yourself killed." She pursed her lips. "But I find that process very distasteful."

"You don't scare me, Witch. Nothing you can do to me will make any difference."

She moved closer to his face. "I don't need to torture you." Her head tilted in contemplation. "I could," she admitted. "I healed a man dozens of times, as they tortured him daily. The Butcher, seeking information, ripped his guts from his belly or used brands to burn through his flesh to his bones, leaving the room smelling of roasted meat. You could taste the smell of him from the smoke that hung in the air." She smiled. "I don't need to do that to you. You killed Rolf to keep him silent, but you've not been able to do anything about the person those documents were supposed to be handed to."

She rose to her feet and held her hand out to Douglas. "All I need to do is go back over the bridge and tell them you confessed. I should be able to figure out who the traitor is."

Hugo squirmed, but the stone cats weighed far too much for him to free either his hands or his legs. "You will not prevail."

"Don't worry," she said over her shoulder as she walked to the door. "I'm going to keep you alive to witness what comes." She left the building, with Douglas following directly behind her, and headed back toward the bridge. Hugo's screams became muffled as one guardian lowered their bodies onto his arm and then put a stone paw over his mouth. She confirmed with Ista that Hugo could still breathe.

"Steph?" Henton asked a million questions in that one word when they crossed back into Sandven. "Douglas?" He added with a slight nod of his head.

Stephenie used her eyes to hopefully convey that she had everything under control and to ignore the initial scream that had come from over the rise. She then turned her focus to Dufnall and kept her voice low. "I apologize, but I believe you may have some traitors among the soldiers stationed here. If you do not mind, I would like to question them to find out who might have been working with a murderer."

Kor looked over his shoulder and Dufnall's four guards tensed, but none of them moved against her.

Dufnall raised an eyebrow. He started to respond, hesitated, looked over his shoulder at the men behind him, and then at Henton, Douglas, and Ryia. While Kas and Perain stood further away holding the leads of all the horses, the others left no doubt who would be the primary combatants. He nodded his head. "Of course. As Ivan's representative, I will allow you to make your inquiry. If there are traitors, they are not acting on my, or Ivan's, behalf, and we'd want to identify them."

She tried to remain calm and protect a sense of openness. Dufnall had not given her any reason to doubt him on their journey, and she did not want to make him any more fearful of her than he already was. However, people she had allowed to live in Ista had committed murder and plotted against her with others. The affront to her and her people left her drawing energy into herself. The concentration of power heated her blood, and she wanted to crush something to release the buildup.

Henton, Ryia, and Douglas fell in behind her with Dufnall, Kor, and the four guards. The soldiers watched as the line of people headed in their direction. Quizzical expressions that ranged from worry to distrust filled their faces. She extended her senses, trying to read the emotions of each of the twenty men and the five drovers. *I've not felt anything that would make me suspect the drovers, and Hugo wouldn't have known they were coming.* She tried to reassure herself of their innocence, but their dislike of her tainted her opinion of them.

"Your Majesty? Jarl Dufnall?" Captain Tumi questioned with a slightly broken voice as he sweated in the cool wind.

She did not make a mental connection to any of the men, but she narrowed her focus so that she might sense surface thoughts and emotions. The youthfulness of the men left them less disciplined than more seasoned soldiers and she immediately isolated a soldier radiating a palpable amount of dread. He continued to repeat the thought. *Don't look at me.*

Stephenie stopped in front of the man and raised the folded parchment in her right hand. "These documents were intended to be passed from Ista to someone in this group. The traitors in Ista were caught in the act and now that I've arrived, I intend to take action against—" Stephenie closed her senses as the panic of the man spiked.

The sandy-blond haired man looked over his shoulder at a second man that resembled him. She sensed the first man's desire to run and as she opened her mind again, the second man expressed anger and frustration. She glared at the first man and cleared her throat to bring his focus back to her. "Your name?"

The young man stammered. "I don't know what you're talking about." His accent marked him as someone not native to Sandven.

"You came from?"

"Lobben," said the captain. The uncomfortable expression that had earlier been on his face now narrowed to anger. "Him and his brother."

Stephenie shifted her gaze back to the second man, who stood three people away. His emotions remained more contained than the shorter first man. The three soldiers between them stepped back and out of the way. She used her senses to look for weapons and other dense objects on their persons. Each had several small knives, a handful of coins, and a metal disk embedded in the leather of their right boots. She expanded her mental search and found no one else with something embedded in their boots. *That gives me hope I've found everyone.*

The younger brother looked over at his elder brother. "Arlo?"

"Say nothing," came the quick response.

Stephenie smiled. "Dufnall, I would like to question both of these men."

"You have my permission."

Arlo tried to move, but Stephenie wrapped him in a gravity field that pressed on him from all sides. The more he struggled, the stronger she made the field. She allowed enough room in front of his chest, abdomen, and mouth that he could breathe. However, he could do nothing else. She did the same to the younger brother, then lifted them both into the air, turned them upside down, and walked toward the bridge with them floating directly behind her, five feet in the air. The younger brother cried and screamed.

The other soldiers scrambled over themselves to fall back. Their fear expressed in their quiet curses and trembling hands.

"Be at ease," Dufnall told the soldiers before following Stephenie.

When she reached the bridge, she jumped up and spun around to sit on the stone wall that prevented someone from falling to the river. "I don't like traitors," she said, staring at the younger brother. She rotated him in the air so that he could see his older brother shoot upward like a bolt from a crossbow.

Both men screamed. She turned the younger man back toward her, leaving his brother hanging over a hundred feet in the air, his head pointed toward the ground. The brother near her, his head turning red, sobbed. She flipped him right side up and dropped him on his ass to hit the ground from just over four feet. He moaned from the impact. She wrapped a gravity field around the metal disk in his boot and pulled. The leather tore and the two-inch round object flew to her hand.

She frowned. While she did not understand what the markings said, one side had the image of a large cauldron, and the other, a man with multiple hounds. "So, you're followers of Fotia." It remained a statement. The disk held no trace of power and so she knew this man likely had no abilities with magic. They always made the augmentation devices of a special alloy, which had an entangled link to one or more relays. She had found no way to block the power flowing through those entangled particles, which allowed the devices to protect themselves vigorously from anything that could mar or damage them.

She used her powers to crush the copper metal in her hand, then dropped the talisman designed for a common man on the ground. "Why don't you tell me who sent you and what your purpose is?"

The man looked down at the crushed disk and whimpered. "I am a faithful follower of Fotia. Fotia will protect me."

Stephenie glanced upward. "You love your brother, don't you? Do you think Fotia will protect him from me?"

"Please," the man said, his own gaze looking up at the man almost one hundred feet directly above him.

Stephenie let Arlo fall headfirst toward the bridge. He screamed from the sudden movement. His brother screamed.

"No! Please!"

Stephenie had not allowed Arlo to enter a free fall and continued to slow his descent in a manner that would not crush his fragile body.

He stopped a couple of feet from the ground. A whimper of fear emerged from both brothers' lips. She then flung Arlo back into the air to repeat the process if needed.

"What's your name?"

"Jonn."

"Well, Jonn. Arlo's fate is in your hands." She shrugged and bounced her heals against the stone wall of the bridge. Her own youthful appearance and casual tone created a discordant contrast to the rage in her eyes. *I am not a monster,* she reminded herself, pushing back on the hint of pleasure that wanted to escape at the power she had over the men.

Dufnall and the others stood frozen as they watched her.

"We were commanded to be ready whenever one of the Faithful brought us messages of the happenings in Ista." He looked down at his feet and the torn boot.

"And who do you hand the documents off to?" Stephenie kept her tone conversational. "It's not like you get a lot of visitors here."

He shook his head. "We rotate posts. Horn Point, then Alkmaar, then here, then Norbek." He bit his lower lip and moisture appeared at the corners of his eyes. "We were told to hold the documents until we reached Norbek. Then hand them to a priest who would come to us." He looked up at Stephenie. "A priest reporting directly to the counsel of eight. Someone reporting to the High Council Member himself."

Stephenie pursed her lips. She felt a sense of resignation coming from the man. "If you rotate, I'm guessing there are others, yes?"

Jonn shrugged. "No one said anything to me. This is our first rotation."

She looked over at Henton, Kas, Ryia, and Douglas, who had all gathered in a group. "What do you think?" she asked in Cothish.

"Kill them both," Ryia responded. "Traitors deserve to die."

Henton frowned, and Kas looked uncomfortable. "Henton has relayed what has been said. I worry about what they already took and what Lobben would want with the information."

Stephenie exhaled and looked at Ryia. "Technically, they are not traitors to Ista. Ivan might consider them traitors, but that's his call.

To us, they are people in a foreign country receiving information from traitors in Ista."

"Was that display of power wise?" Henton asked in Cothish. He purposefully avoided looking at the soldiers watching from Sandven.

Stephenie shrugged. "Perhaps not, but it's nothing compared to what the drovers saw at the roadcut, and we know they will end up talking."

Henton nodded his head.

"Hugo and Rolf going to die?" Ryia demanded, bringing back the topic of discussion. "They're traitors. Hugo even killed his own brother." She looked at the man crying silently on the bridge. "I still say these men need to be punished. We don't want them telling others what they know."

"Hugo already killed Rolf," Douglas commented.

"Even more reason Hugo should die." Ryia shook her head and tightened the grip on her staff.

"Hugo is our problem," Stephenie said. "He will be punished."

Henton cleared his throat. "You already know the correct things to do."

Stephenie nodded her head and turned to Dufnall. She switched back to speaking Sandvian. "It sounds like Jonn and his brother are acting as agents of Lobben and Fotia."

"How'd you find out about this?" the jarl asked.

"We caught their accomplices preparing to hand off the documents."

He shook his head. "No. You somehow knew before we arrived. How?"

She slipped off the wall. "Magic, my dear friend. Magic."

Arlo dropped from where she had held him. Both men screamed again. She let him fall faster this time and slowed him more abruptly and painfully, but not fast enough to do damage. She righted him and let him land on his ass like John did, bruising his tailbone as well.

The urge to fly filled her, and once she reached Isa Fields, she would find an excuse to sneak away and spend some time moving around the mountain peaks. *I really need the time to relax and feel human.* The irony that she could fly only because she was not fully human was not lost on her.

With both men on their rears, and their feet before them, she used her powers to remove and rip away any weapons, pouches, and jewelry, including the second talisman of Fotia from Arlo. The weapons and other items she flung to the side and left on the ground; the talisman flew to her hand.

"You betrayed Fotia," Arlo snarled.

"I had to save you."

Dufnall cleared his throat. "What will you do with them?"

She pursed her lips. "Technically, they are your people. I brought them onto the bridge, but I am expelling them back to Sandven and will allow you to enact your own justice as you see fit."

Dufnall said nothing for several moments. Then he turned and signaled for the captain of the border soldiers to approach. When the nervous man reached the edge of the bridge, Dufnall pointed to the two men. "I want these men held until we return to Horn Point. My brother will sentence them as appropriate."

The captain nodded his head, signaled for additional men to come forward and they took the two prisoners to one of the buildings on the Sandvian side of the border. Stephenie expected the two could escape if they had enough determination. During the summer months, they might even make it across the wilds on foot and get back to Lobben. In the winter, without dogsleds, they would run out of supplies and freeze before they even reached Alkmaar.

Stephenie turned back to the north. She expected neither of those men to know much more than Jonn had said. She frowned, though no one else could see it. "I'm sorry we had to deal with that," she said over her shoulder to Dufnall. "It wasn't how I wanted to introduce you to Ista, but I think once we start north, you'll come to appreciate what Ista has to show."

Dufnall moved forward quickly to walk by her side. "My good neighbor queen, worry not, your country has shown me far more hospitality so far than my own had shown you. Dealing with spies is much preferable to poisoners and assassins on the road."

Stephenie allowed herself to grin. "Indeed. It seems we have more than just jealous jarls to worry about."

Chapter 19

Stephenie led Dufnall and the others over the rise to the two stone roundhouses. Small trails of smoke drifted out of the openings in the roofs. The stone guardians had moved slightly, but still appeared to lounge in a nearly random pattern. Four of her own border guards helped Dufnall's four soldiers carry all the Jarl's supplies toward the dogcart.

"Those are some strange sculptures," Dufnall said as he passed within five feet of a winged cat loafing on the rocky ground. He bent down to examine the scaled surface of the stone, but he refrained from actually touching it. Kor stood nervously above him, one hand on his sword. "As you know, there are rumors of creatures with troll blood living in Ista." He turned his attention back to Stephenie and slowly rose to his feet. "Is this the source of those stories?"

Stephenie nodded her head, but she did not elaborate. *He'll see in a moment.* "I know it is somewhat late in the day, and this would mean sleeping in the open again, but I would like to put a couple of miles in before the weather turns. We've still got four days of travel before we reach Isa Fields."

The four guards and Kor glanced longingly at the roundhouses. Dufnall noted their silent protests and smiled. "When the spring grasses first poked their way from the ground, I never expected to spend so many days on my feet. Lead the way."

She nodded her head as they turned toward the smaller building, glad she did not have to convince him. "We have to take a prisoner back with us." She paused at the door. "Please prepare yourself for the first of what will be many surprises."

"Your Majesty has surprised me several times already."

Stephenie let a lopsided grin reach her lips and pushed opened the door. "You've seen nothing yet." Inside, Hugo remained pinned to the ground by the two guardians. She walked over and stood above him and held the token of Fotia so that he could see it. "We've captured the men who were to take your documents to Lobben. When we get back to Isa Fields, we can discuss what you've already shared."

The guardian shifted its paw off Hugo's mouth and the man turned his face away.

Stephenie turned her back on the traitor and looked at Dufnall and Kor. The others waited for her outside and she silently told Ista to put Hugo on one of the guardians.

Kor gasped in alarm as the two stone cats sprang to their feet, spread their wings, and then snatched the startled Hugo from the ground. Using their mouths and wings, they flung him over the back of one cat.

Hugo cried out in alarm and then grunted as the impact knocked the wind from his chest. The cat designated to transport the prisoner closed its stone wings around Hugo, locking him in place.

"Jarl, stay back!"

"Easy, Kor," Dufnall said. "If Stephenie meant us harm, we'd have been dead long before now."

Ista, have Rolf dumped in a grave away from the border. She used her own powers to move Rolf's corpse onto the other cat while she faced Dufnall and Kor. "I tried to explain to Ivan there are reasons we keep the border closed. Most people would not understand the things they would see in Ista. Rumors and stories about what we can do would spread and grow with each telling. This would draw unwanted attention, bringing people we want to avoid, and deterring those whom we want to interact with peacefully."

Kor slid his sword back into his scabbard. "I don't suppose steel will do much against stone."

"Just turn dull," Stephenie said. "Now, I'm afraid we're going to scare your guards a bit. They're already tense because of your call of alarm."

"Trolls," Kor mumbled as the cats moved into position behind her.

"No," Stephenie said. "The protectors of Ista. They are one of the many reasons no one should cross the border uninvited." She moved a step forward. "We've tried to keep their presence secret." Her voice grew crisp. "Though I imagine the man trapped on the back of that one might have informed Lobben of them in some detail."

"You'll burn in Fotia's cauldron, Witch," Hugo tried to yell, but could only just whimper it because of the compressive force of the cat's wings.

Stephenie shrugged. "I've had a lot of threats against me over the years," she told Dufnall. "You seem to have a question."

Dufnall moved forward with a hand outstretched. "Are they soft? It appears as if they have stone scales for fur." He shuttered. "The wings look like leather."

"They are stone," Stephenie said. "Feel free to touch it."

"It's warm." Dufnall brushed his fingers over the cat's head, being careful to avoid the exposed teeth.

"Hugo needs to live," she said. "Normally, they are as cold as any other stone." She exited through the door and outside she caught Henton's eye. "Five miles? It will mean arriving in Isa Fields earlier on the fourth day."

Douglas frowned. "If you weren't using my cart for all the supplies, I'd take the dogs and get back home in two days."

"I'm afraid not," Henton told his former soldier.

Stephenie turned her focus to Dufnall's guards. "In a moment, you're going to see something you won't expect. Try not to get frightened. This will be the first of many things you've never seen before."

The four men looked at Dufnall, then each other, and then gasped as the stone cats pushed open the door and exited the building. The soldiers turned to look at the other cats scattered around them and noticed all the guardians had risen to their feet and turned their heads to watch them.

"We expected to see things," Dufnall reassured them. "Let's put a few more miles under us."

*   *   *   *   *

"If trolls did not birth these creatures, how did they come to be?" Dufnall walked beside Stephenie as the pack of dogs moved around them. Kor remained a step behind and was as uncomfortable as ever.

"Magic created them. They protect the borders and the city of Isa Fields. It is hard to even scratch them."

"We heard rumors about stone monsters that move on their own. I can't imagine even an axe cutting into their skin." He continued to watch as the guardians moved gracefully ahead of them. A stone tail swaying back and forth as they walked. "They must weigh even more than your horses, and I know a horse can crush a man beneath him."

Stephenie directed a jab at a dog that looked ready to bite his neighbor. She made eye contact with the animal and it backed down, no longer eager to make a commotion. She turned her focus back to Dufnall. "They can be as light or heavy as needed. Like I explained regarding the stones at the roadcut, the guardians can create a field around themselves to adjust how much attraction they have to the ground and other larger objects. It even lets them fly for short distances."

"These are the things that killed our people who crossed your borders?" Kor asked from behind them.

"Mostly," she answered without emotion. "There are plenty of bears, wolves, foxes, and other animals that roam Ista. We often find seals near the coasts. When we've tried to convince people to turn back, we've typically herded the large predators toward the intruders to keep them from knowing about the guardians. The wise ones turned back quickly. I've also gone out to meet some, though engaged them in a way that meant they didn't see me."

She allowed the wind to blow her hair and caress her face. "We'll stop in just a couple more miles. I need to bring down some food for the dogs. Tomorrow will be a normal day."

Dacian's feet hurt. The three days of near constant travel, even with relying heavily on his powers, taxed his mind and body. The last day and a half involved significant hills and valleys as he moved through the mountain pass. The one positive remained that he had traveled alone, and that allowed him more time to consider Andre and the council. If he killed Andre, he would need to do so in a manner that did not trace back to him. Manipulating the minds of a priest or servant to either outright kill the man or poison him would be the safest route, but first, he needed to know what else Andre had planned.

If he confronted Andre, he could perhaps alter the man's mind, but doing so would leave observable changes in his personality that others would notice. With Andre's control of most of the council members, Dacian knew they would likely suspect him of treachery, and that would undermine his actual agenda. "No, I need to take it slow and methodically."

He had studied the documents each evening, but without a cypher, he expected it would take a long time for him to break the code. The last one hundred and fifty years of studying civilizations and the rise of certain powers in the north provided a foundation for that kind of work, but his interests did not include mathematics, and that limited his ability to find a numerical solution.

The road to Berl had many soldiers traveling into Sandven and messengers heading in both directions. He knew his proclamation of returning to Berl would likely already have reached Andre, but he did not want to have people stopping him along the way. To combat that, anytime he sensed people near him, he pushed against their minds, directing their focus away from him, leaving people unaware of his presence.

The stupid think I can turn invisible, but light can't pass through me. That's not how things work. He examined the soldiers standing at the gates that restricted travel between Berl and the pass. From a distance, they would see his approach, but he walked at the rear of five other soldiers that simply felt no reason to look in his direction or register the sound his boots made upon the ground. When he came within his range to affect the minds of the gate guards, he extended his mental manipulation to them, making each one want to look away from his presence. A strong mind could overcome the direction, but most never even realized something had happened. They simply felt compelled to stare at someone or something else that drew their interest. *And so I am unseen.*

Dacian strode right past the guards and through the open gate as the soldiers stopped the men he had walked behind, demanding justification for their travels. *I could have earned a fortune as a burglar of those without magic.* While one did not need magic to recognize the effect, and magic did not make one immune, those with power and knowledge at least understood the possibility and developed other protections.

The day had grown late, but with the excitement of the invasion, many people still walked along the streets of the ground city. Despite the toll on his mind, he continued to redirect attention away from him as he made his way to Berl's Stone City. A few people appeared to notice him as he passed, but eventually they turned away, remembering something more important that needed their attention.

He passed by the soldiers protecting the southernmost entrance to the Stone City and he quickly made his way deeper into the mountain where wide ramps allowed for carts to bring supplies into large storage rooms. Dacian continued moving through a section of the mountain that most of the elite would never tread. While physical crime remained low inside the Stone City, wealthy people often directed their subordinates to use the large and numerous chambers to hold ill-gotten goods. These criminal practices meant they did not like people poking around.

Dacian entered chamber sixty-three using his powers to manipulate the mechanical lock securing the door. The room could hold enough dry goods to feed one hundred people for a year. However, it now held food and goods for one of the noble families leading soldiers in Sandven. *Based on Warner's report, they should leave Gaffel in the morning and start the march to Horn Point.* He hoped the noble hoarding these supplies landed a role guarding the road, but justice seldom applied to the wealthy and powerful.

The taking of Norbek and Gaffel, and controlling the road between them, would generally meet his grandfather's desire to prevent Stephenie from easily moving south. However, Lobben needed a meatier target to justify the endeavor. "Plus, we need to keep Horn Point from sending troops to retake their communities."

Dacian stopped halfway into the storage room. Several columns of stone and mortar added in random locations supported the thirty-foot wide span of stone above his head. The ancient ceiling still had multiple cracks and several gaps where chunks of stone had calved off, but he knew of no recent failures.

The walls in this section of the mountain had also developed cracks and the one he sought conveniently remained mostly obscured behind a column built next to the left-hand wall. He removed the coded message from his backpack and levitated the papers into the opening near the top of the wall, where he stored items he did not need often and were too valuable to risk someone stealing.

With the documents stored safely away, he left the storage room, reset the lock, and headed up toward the eighth level. If Andre maintained a cypher for the code, Dacian doubted the High Council Member would keep it in his public offices. *Most likely it'd be in his private chambers, but searching both are in order. I just need to figure out where he is.*

Dacian stopped on the seventh level to steal the robes of a first order priest, knowing that the less his appearance stood out, the easier his victims found it to ignore him. After changing, he stopped a layman clerk carrying a stack of parchment. While he could get away with manipulating most people, he did not want to run into one of the council members or any of the more powerful priests that would likely be on the eighth level. The chance they might recognize the manipulation remained too high.

"Where are the council members?" He asked, while influencing the man's mind to look at the wall.

"They are meeting in the planning room," the man whispered. "They do not want to be disturbed."

Dacian picked up a recent memory the clerk witnessed of someone discussing a late dinner the council had ordered. He pushed his way further into the man's thoughts and suddenly the clerk dropped the stack of papers he had been carrying.

"Damn it. Stupid rock." He knelt down and gathered the scattered pages he believed he dropped after tripping. The man reviewed them and put them back into the proper order as Dacian continued to Andre's private rooms.

*   *   *   *   *

As High Council Member, Andre commanded a suite of rooms. His private rooms had a main greeting chamber with four passages leading from it. The passage on the far left went to a large dining hall and kitchen. The original builders of the Stone City had carved ventilation shafts to keep the air circulating and to allow certain sections of the city to have working kitchens with fires to cook food. For the less well off, they relied upon food coming from the surface city.

The next passage led to a ballroom, also with two fireplaces to warm up the perpetually cool stone. The third passage led to his private offices, where he sometimes conducted business. Dacian had been in all three sets of rooms before. The passage on the right led to Andre's private chambers. Rumors spoke of a bathing room, bedroom, library, and sitting room, also with fireplaces.

All four of the passages remained dark, and Dacian sensed no one. Instead of taking the oil lamp that illuminated the greeting chamber, he pulled a small opaque stone with a blue hue from his pouch. "Cvicat de," he said, never having learned if the sounds had any real meaning, and the stone suddenly emitted a bright light. With the thumb sized stone on the palm of his left hand, he entered the narrow passage to Andre's private office. After thirty feet, the cramped tunnel opened into a sizable room. A desk, too large to have moved assembled through the passage, sat in the middle of the room.

Dacian ran his attention around the room, looking over the bookshelves and two cabinets that leaned against the wall on the opposite side of the room. A rug covered the worn floor, while the soft stone made it easier to carve, it also meant countless feet ate away at the surface and exposed pockets of more dense material, resulting in an uneven surface.

The bookshelves drew his attention. While he counted a dozen books, many objects of interest rested on the wooden shelves. "At least twenty skulls of dogs." The tradition of Fotia's priests saving the skulls of their hounds had been an interesting side effect of their belief system. He had written three chapters in one of the journals he kept in the storage room that recorded details of the practice.

The other trinkets did not interest him, as their purpose seemed only to provide evidence of Andre's personal wealth. He quickly reviewed the titles of the books and removed each one carefully from the shelves to see if Andre placed any loose parchment between the pages. Finding nothing, he moved to the cabinets. The heavily decorated furniture had embedded locks to secure the contents. He knelt down and used his mind to sense the nature of the locking mechanism. The brass metal had a series of complex springs, levers, and catches. A long narrow pin pointing toward the front of the lock caught his attention, and he brought the light stone closer. "Oh Andre, you've covered a hole with a thin bit of paper and painted it."

Dacian stepped to the side. He did not think the needle inside the lock would launch out of the case, but that it simply struck the fingers of a hand not using a key. "A clever design, but with a fatal flaw." Dacian avoided the mechanism all together and simply generated a small field that pulled the spring-loaded locking bolt out of the opposite door. With a second field, he swung open the right door of the cabinet. The trap, which he assumed contained poison, did not release.

Dacian moved around to peer inside the cabinet. Stacks of papers, journals, and ledgers filled the interior shelves. The left-hand door had two internal latches that secured it to the top and bottom of the opening. He used his powers to disengage them and swing open the door. "Where would you hide your cypher?" He desperately hoped Andre had not memorized it.

The cabinet had three shelves and Dacian started with the top shelf that put things at eye level. He pulled out the bundles of paper and remained careful to not change the order or disturb the way Andre had stacked things. Most of the documents appeared to be meaningless correspondence. Simple orders to underlings for supplies or to make repairs on his homes in Kutenveld or Sudhold. The journals focused on personal observations about others and sometimes even Dacian, himself. Dacian even found a set of documents detailing events and data useful for blackmail. *Which is one way to influence others to give you want you want.*

The second shelf had more of the same, as well as a series of lewd drawings. A few had color ink added, but most were sketches using charcoal. "It's obvious where your pleasures fall."

The third shelf had stacks of bills that Andre marked as paid. Dacian flipped through several and almost put the stack back when he noticed the bottom shelf had a gap between it and the rear wall of the cabinet. Using his mind, he tried to feel for voids and uneven energy potentials. A smile reached his lips, and he carefully pulled all the documents from the bottom shelf, setting them on the floor directly below where they would need to be returned.

He created another field and pulled up on the back of the bottom shelf. Andre had a trap on the main lock and Dacian did not want to risk other protections he had not noticed. The old wood rotated along the front of the cabinet on a concealed hinge. Dacian put his head into the cabinet to look behind the now vertical board. The small compartment hid another bundle of papers and Dacian lifted them out.

He stepped back, turned around, and put the stack of parchment on the desk so that he could examine it. The bundle contained only a dozen sheets, but the words meant nothing to him. Ordered lines and columns on the page contained another code more complex than the one he had intercepted from the spy in Ista. The single hand that wrote these pages also differed from the one in Ista. These markings had a flourish that demonstrated confidence. The pages from Ista were hesitant and contained errors and rewritten sections.

"Damn. Who are you talking with, Andre?" Dacian flipped through the various sheets. The marks had a clear pattern, but knowing what the words meant would take time. "Perhaps even ..." Dacian looked down at his figures and noticed a slight moistness on his skin. He put the papers down and brought his light stone closer. A slight oily coating reflected in his bright light. "Bastard."

Dacian drew power into his body, lifted the papers with a gravitational field, and then quickly returned them to the hidden compartment. He closed the shelf, returned the stacks of materials from the floor, shut and latched the left door, then closed and reengaged the spring-loaded bolt on the right one.

"Did you do that Andre, or was it the person who sent the letters to you?"

Dacian continued to draw power into himself as he left the office and Andre's private rooms. He hastened through the passages until he found a dark corridor. Power coursed through him, and he directed the energy into his hands. He pushed the energy outward, accelerating the tiny elements that made up his skin. A moment later, the smell of burning flesh filled the air. He contained a scream that wanted to escape his mouth as his flesh and contact poison burned away. The palms of his hands and the pads of his fingers turned black and then cracked with his involuntary movements.

When he could bear no more pain, he stopped generating heat and instead pulled energy away, cooling the charred flesh. The stench of burnt meat filled his nose, and he stumbled toward his rooms. Lightheaded, he directed the power remaining in him to healing the damage, regrowing healthy muscles, skin, and tendons. The effort drained him, but he only had himself to blame.

Chapter 20

"Dacian, I ordered you to escort the Faithful to Horn Point. Why are you here?" Andre sat behind the desk in his private office and stared at a ledger that Dacian knew tracked the High Council Member's personal wealth. He had seen the growth in the last year's figures the prior night. Based on the records, the nobles paid for the privilege of servicing Fotia's war contracts. The quick review did not tell Dacian if the nobles believed the money went to Fotia or if they knew Andre kept it.

"Fotia instructed me to return here and pray. Potential disruptions could occur if we deviate from our defined path." Dacian avoided touching Andre's mind. The High Council Member gained his position by being more powerful and ruthless than his contemporaries. While Dacian did not think Andre posed a direct threat, the likelihood he would notice an intrusion remained too high.

"You wouldn't claim Fotia told you something for your own gain now, would you?" Andre looked up from the ledger and waited for a reply.

Dacian wondered if the man knew he projected his own behavior, but he doubted Andre had that much self-awareness. "That would be unethical." Dacian kept his hands closed and at his sides. The skin had healed, but remained red. So far, Andre had not appeared to pay them any attention. "I would lose my favor with Fotia if I did that." *Of course, you don't really believe in Fotia, do you?* He wanted to know what Andre actually believed, but he also did not want to reveal any truths by asking.

"And what can go wrong? This invasion's your plan, given to you by Fotia, as you've told the council many times." Andre leaned back in his seat, demonstrating an air of confidence. "The reports that have come in show things went well in Norbek. You burned and destroyed a significant part of the resistance. Your abilities would have been useful in Horn Point."

Dacian nodded his head once in acknowledgement. "My disciples, Vikram and Warner, are quite capable. Warner contributed much to the taking of Norbek. Fotia told me last night that you will soon receive reports that Gaffel fell with almost no casualties. It is now held with two hundred of the Faithful against any potential response from Alkmaar."

Andre pursed his lips. "That is indeed good news. My information has shown Alkmaar, and Ivan's troops at the border to Ista—a cursed land if there is one—might account for only one hundred soldiers." Andre pulled a coin from his pouch and started flipping it between his fingers. "Perhaps another twenty or so more fighters if the civilians join in. There should only be six witches and warlocks among their number."

Dacian felt genuine happiness at the report. "Even better." It pushed the boundaries of not wanting to instigate a reaction from Stephenie, but the intelligence helped to reassure him of the numbers he left in Gaffel. "With such small numbers, Alkmaar can remain isolated and alone."

Andre frowned and stopped flipping the coin. "I don't like leaving any force on our back door. Gaffel is critical to maintaining our control over Horn Point and then later driving further south into Cilwir. With the other bridge between Norbek and Horn Point destroyed, we only have a single route to move troops."

"Alkmaar is too close to Ista. It could draw attention from the north."

Andre stood up. "So what if it does? I've done some investigation on the witch queen. She's fled her home and claimed lands that should belong to us. She's got no standing army, just refugees from Alkmaar that went north."

"Fotia has said repeatedly that we do not want to wake the Ista of old." Dacian avoided clenching his hands because of the lingering pain.

"The Ista of old is dead and gone, so do not preach fear to me." Andre glanced at a map on his desk. "Between Ista and us on the west is nothing but a vast wasteland. Once we have the east, we'll have a road right to her front door." Andre looked up and waved his hand to stop Dacian from responding. "Since you are here, you can help prepare the third wave of soldiers. The new recruits need guidance and confidence. They're still very green."

Dacian bowed his head, turned, and left Andre alone in his office. He needed the war to slow down. Based on troop projections, if the nobles and generals followed Warner's and Vikram's orders, the bulk of Lobben's forces would remain occupied for the rest of the year. *Ivan has the supplies and won't surrender if they merely siege the castle. I just need Andre and the nobles to be content with a long siege.*

Stephenie pushed the group just over thirty miles to reach the waypoint situated about halfway between the border and Isa Fields. A group of five stone buildings with steeply pitched roofs sat nestled in a slight depression along the road. A guardian emerged from the largest building and four residents of Ista followed it out to see what would have sparked a guardian to move. When they saw the party approaching, they came forward, expressing their happiness at Stephenie's return and promised to take care of all the animals while everyone else rested inside.

Henton, well aware of Stephenie's possessiveness, stepped forward and took Argat's lead from her. "Douglas and I can help with the horses," he told the four station attendants. "If the four of you can manage the dog team, we'll all get this done and back inside."

The older man in the group looked toward the pack of dogs sitting away from the buildings. Then he noticed Hugo's arm and leg hanging down from under the stone wings of the guardian. Stephenie smiled. "Just leave those dogs. They're getting friendlier, but I wouldn't call them friendly. They should stay in that area for the night." She then turned toward Hugo. The man had stopped his shouting earlier in the day. The nature of his confinement caused discomfort and pain, but nothing serious enough that he would die. "He's going back to Isa Fields for judgement. He's no longer a threat."

Kas and Ryia approached, each of them carrying their personal bags.

Stephenie looked at Dufnall, Kor, and the soldiers. "Time for you to see Ista's next surprise." She started toward the building. "This is more subtle, but I expect it will impress you." At the door, she held it open to allow Dufnall and his people to go first.

"You're being too nice," Ryia said in Cothish to Stephenie as she followed Kas inside.

Stephenie tousled Ryia's hair as she walked past. "I don't have to be."

Ryia tried to avoid Stephenie's hand by ducking low, but she could not avoid the contact. "Hey."

Once Ryia got out of reach, Stephenie followed her into the building. A raised central firepit radiated heat, but instead of coal or wood, the pit contained nothing but small rocks. Six stone pillars supported the roof. Glowing crystals held in brass holders attached to the pillars brightened the room with a constant light. The clean mortar joints in the stone floor had no cracks. A series of tables around the central firepit provided places to sit. Shelves containing numerous supplies and goods lined the outer walls and fur mats lay below them to provide places to sleep.

"Goddess," Dufnall said as he moved about the room, transfixed by a light source that did not flicker and burn. He put his hand over the stones in the fire pit and quickly pulled it back. "Do you need to do anything to replenish the heat in the stones?"

"No," Stephenie said.

Ryia dropped her pack on a fur laid out near the middle of the back wall and immediately started grabbing supplies from the shelves to prepare a dinner.

Stephenie moved closer to Dufnall, Kor, and the soldiers. "The heat energy comes from deep in the ground. Ista sits on a larger reservoir of molten rock and most of the energy that runs the land comes from that."

Stephenie glanced at Kas; he had started to unpack his books at a table near where Ryia would prepare the meal. *Are you still angry?* She asked him. The fact that he did not push away her mental outreach gave her hope.

I am not angry. I will just be very glad to be home in a couple of days. You have your job to perform. I will continue to study these books until I can get to the library and to look up the reference data I did not bring with me.

She felt his dismissal and turned her attention back to Dufnall and forced a smile at the awe he experienced as he looked around the room.

"Is the molten rock how the cat's move?" Kor asked.

Stephenie shook her head. "No." She went to the door, opened it, and pulled a fist size rock to her hand before returning to one of the tables. "I'll show you something of how they work." She sat down and motioned for Dufnall and Kor to sit across from her. "I can smash this stone into smaller stones, yes?" Dufnall and Kor nodded their heads. "It can be smashed and smashed until it is sand and then the sand turns to dust." She pushed the stone toward them. "What that means is stone is made up of a lot of tiny particles that are all stuck together. They want to stay as they are, a solid chunk of cold stone."

"I can agree to that," Dufnall said.

"Metal, or any solid, is similar, just small pieces that stick very tightly together." She lifted the stone and Dufnall took it. "Metals can be heated and that causes them to melt. We can heat stone until it melts as well."

"I've never seen a fire that hot," Kor said.

"But it holds as reasonable," Dufnall challenged his friend.

Stephenie took the stone back. "When you heat something, you excite the tiny particles that are too small for you to ever see. They vibrate and move. Like ice changing to water and then to steam. It is all just different states of the same thing." She tossed the rock into the air. "The excited particles start to move too fast and the forces that hold them tightly together breakdown and allow them to slide apart, or even separate. What happens with the cats is not a result of heat, but simply a disruption of the field that holds the particles together.

That allows the particles to separate and slide against each other like a liquid."

Kor frowned, and Dufnall looked confused.

Stephenie took a deep breath, pulled energy into herself, and narrowed her focus from the macro world to the microscopic and then further. She looked for the pattern of energy fields that held all the parts of the stone in her hand together. Because multiple components made up this rock, the disruptive field she needed to craft had a great deal of complexity. Her head throbbed as she focused on things her eyes could never hope to see.

Gasps of surprise came from Dufnall as the solid rock suddenly sloshed down through her fingers. She quickly generated a gravitational field to catch the liquid stone. She bit her lip, drawing blood, as she manipulated the stone until she had formed a small bowl. A moment later, she dismissed the disruptive field, and the stone solidified into a thin vessel more than a foot in diameter.

She felt herself wobble as her focus shifted to the macro world that she lived in. For a moment, her mind could not focus on any of the energy fields around her. She felt momentarily blind, as if she had accidentally stared at the sun.

The bowl, still held in the air by her thoughts, slowly settled on the wooden table. She clenched her right hand that had held the stone, and she felt the small particles of rock her skin absorbed into her pores. They crunched as they broke down and became powder on her skin.

Dufnall hesitantly reached out and touched the surface of the thin stone bowl. "It's as cold as the stone was." He looked up. "Are you okay?"

Stephenie healed the cut in her lip, though she still tasted the blood. "It takes a lot of concentration and gives me a headache to do that. But I'm fine."

The four guards stood transfixed. Everything she did made them more and more certain they offered no protection to their charge.

"Yeah, all well and good, but that doesn't make dinner, now does it." Ryia walked past the table and grabbed some supplies from the wall behind Stephenie. "Show off."

"May I?" Dufnall asked, gesturing to the bowl.

"Please," Stephenie said as she leaned back. "It's as fragile as any stone bowl that thin, so handle it with caution. But consider it yours." She chuckled. "There are a lot of stones outside. I can always make more."

Everyone rested well that night except Hugo. In the morning, Stephenie resumed her driving pace. The others had grown used to the milage and offered fewer complaints. By the afternoon, the sky had cleared enough to present a good view of the mountain range that loomed to the west. The snow-covered peaks glistened under the rays of the sun and provided a significant obstacle for anyone wanting to traverse the land.

The next day became more of the same. Stephenie continued to distract herself from the concerns that awaited her in Isa Fields. She played with the dogs, using Perain's help to temper the hostility of the pack. She did not know what her plans would be for the animals in the long term. Her continued influence kept them in line, and without her dominance, the dogs would likely separate into two or three packs. In the wilds, they would wreak havoc on anyone or anything they came across. *At least until winter, when the food and shelter this far north became scarce. Perhaps if they are separated and kept as pets, they might learn to behave.* She doubted many of the citizens would want the risk. For now, she planned to keep them in one of the northern fields that they had not yet had a chance to cultivate.

With the mountains growing ever larger, Stephenie slowed her pace slightly so that Dufnall and his men would get the full impression of Isa Fields when they finally saw it. The rolling land undulated with hill after hill. The effort tired everyone, but as they reached the top of a rise, the grey stone walls of a castle ten miles away came into view. Ista stood proudly at the base of the mountain, offset by the trees and greenery around her. A warm breeze and the fragrant smell of lavender filled the air.

"That is my home," she breathed. The full valley that Kervigar had carved out of the mountains was still hidden by another hill ahead of them. "My sister should have a feast set for us once we arrive."

"I'm looking forward to bathing," Ryia said; Dancer's lead draped causally over her shoulder. "Eating food I didn't cook and bathing."

"The stonework is impressive," Dufnall said. "We'd never build anything that tall in Sandven. The wind would steal away any warmth in the winter. That must be five stories high."

"Four technically," Stephenie responded. "There are some very tall ceilings." She started forward again. "Wait until you see the rest of the valley."

She led them down the hill and up the next. As they crested the last rise, the bowl-shaped valley came into full view. Nearly ten miles long, the ordered city sat in the middle of colorful growth. Vibrant green trees, fields with flowers, pastures with tall grasses, and groves of deciduous trees covered everything in sight. Argat whinnied and pulled at his lead rope, eager to graze and roll in the lushness of the vegetation.

A row of black obsidian obelisks standing three feet high and spaced every twenty feet marked the boundary between the fertile land and the wild landscape they had spent almost half a month crossing.

"What are those black towers?" Dufnall asked, pointing at the forty-foot-tall obelisks scattered in a geometric pattern across the valley.

"They control the weather," Stephenie answered. A group of fifteen men and woman approached them along the road. "Isa Fields is green all year round," she continued. "The buildings are all two and three stories tall because the boundary regulates the wind."

He shook his head. "They say you have markers at the border for as far as anyone has searched. I found that scale hard to believe, but this city is unlike anything I could imagine."

"Your Majesty," Menni said, as he approached the group with a deep bow. The bearded man had become a competent stable master under Stephenie's guidance. "Your Graces," he added, again bowing to Kas, Henton, Douglas, and Ryia. The others with him bowed as well.

"Menni, perfect timing. Argat will not sit still until he's able to make himself sick on the fresh grass."

"Her Majesty informed us of your arrival, so we knew when to come greet you." The man smiled. "I'll keep an eye on all of them."

Perain stepped forward. "I can help with the dog teams, Steph. Then meet you for dinner."

Douglas walked over to Perain. "I'll help Perain. Then get cleaned up at home and come back to the castle for dinner."

"Thank you, Douglas and Perain." Stephenie patted Argat's neck as she handed over the lead to Menni. "Let me grab my personal pack, then please have the rest of our gear brought to the castle." She turned to Dufnall. "Anything you want to carry, grab it from the dogcarts, otherwise we'll have it delivered to your rooms."

Dufnall moved to the cart with his gear, pulled out a satchel, and left the rest. "Please, lead on. I'm eager to see more."

Chapter 21

Dufnall, Kor, and the soldiers stared at the stone buildings of Isa Fields, none of them having seen a city not built close to the ground to avoid the wind. The stone blocks that made the walls had sharp angles and tight seams instead of rough rock mortared together. Stephenie did not have to explain magic had formed those blocks, as the consistency of each one exceeded human stone cutting.

She led them through a garden in the middle of the city, the ancient oak trees with sprawling canopies offering shade to the short grasses under them. Stone benches and tables provided the citizens of the city a place to rest and enjoy the white marble statues of animals that marked nine points around the grove.

The dogs remained tightly packed around the guardian carrying Hugo. The four days of painful confinement had definitely weakened the man, and he spent most of his time moaning.

When they reached the base of the mountain and started up the wide steps toward her castle, she paused at the first landing with the massive fountain. She knew Dufnall and Kor recognized the images of elves among the other humanoids. Dufnall eventually turned his attention back to the spiraling towers of Ista waiting on the next landing above them.

"It looks nothing like any castle I have seen drawn in books," Dufnall said. "It has no defensive walls. No moat. The doors and windows are large and not guarded with iron."

"It's more like a palace," Stephenie admitted. She looked up at the smooth walls. While Dufnall and his men had no way of knowing,

Kervigar built Ista's walls with only a couple of feet of stone. A castle that tall in the south would have walls twenty to thirty feet thick. Memories of Antar Castle and the old tower her father allowed her to claim as her own brought a smile to her face. *Yes, Ista, you are beautiful in your own right.*

They climbed the white marble steps to another courtyard where planters overflowed with fragrant flowers, guardians lounged next to other statues, and trees provided shade and fruit. The large double doors at the top of a final set of stairs opened inward. Islet emerged onto a small landing, a stately dress of light green cloth accenting her complexion. Sir Walter stood just behind her in a gambeson similar to Henton's and Ryia's, only a lot cleaner.

"Sis," Stephenie exclaimed as she easily climbed the steps and approached Islet.

"Hold," Islet said in Cothish, putting up a hand and stepping back. "I can smell you from here. You'll ruin this dress."

Stephenie crossed her arms. "Yes, Ma'am."

Islet shook her head and looked over Stephenie's shoulder as the others followed her up the steps with a little less enthusiasm.

"Hi Islet," Ryia said when she reached the landing. "I won't hug you. I'm heading straight for the baths."

Islet nodded her head as Ryia walked around them and into the castle. Islet then turned her attention to Dufnall and spoke in Sandvian. "Jarl Dufnall, on behalf of myself and my sister, may I welcome you to Ista?" She inclined her head, but she did not bow. "We have rooms prepared for you and your men."

"I am honored," Dufnall said, bowing in the southern form. "Your Majesty?"

Islet smiled. "People do refer to me as such, though technically, I'm a disposed queen and just Stephenie's regent. I'm sure Stephenie has already told you to call her Steph, so feel free to call me Islet." She turned to her husband. "And this is Walter."

"Jarl Dufnall," Walter said. "It is a pleasure to meet you."

"Please, just Dufnall. And the pleasure is on my end."

Stephenie moved forward and then quickly embraced Islet in a powerful hug, pinning Islet's arms to her side. "I missed you. And thank you for everything."

Islet sighed and patted Stephenie's sides with her limited mobility. "You express your gratitude in a most annoying way," she mumbled in Cothish, then softened her expression. "I'm glad you are back. I did not want to deal with the Hugo situation on my own." Islet glanced at the pack of dogs and the guardian.

Stephenie released her sister. "We'll talk about it later."

"Islet, Walter," Henton said. "It is good to be home. I'll get cleaned up and help with anything that needs to be done."

"Thank you, Henton." Islet turned to look at Kas and spoke again in Cothish. "I hope your journey wasn't too arduous, and that you found some time for study."

Stephenie tensed slightly, uncertain how Kas would react to the comment. She had not informed Islet of their troubles, but Henton or Ryia could easily have communicated with Islet on their own and relayed the obvious tension.

"I believe I made some breakthroughs, but I will need to confirm the findings with additional sources from the library." He turned to Stephenie. "With your leave, I will go with Henton and clean up."

She nodded her head. "Of course."

Stephenie turned back to Dufnall. "Now that we settled all that, we'll show you around." She led the others through the double doors and into a large entrance hall. Three crystal chandeliers shaped like a swarm of flying lizards hung from the vaulted ceiling forty feet above them. The light in the hall came from crystals held in the talons of each foot. The ceiling itself was awash of colors that her unaided eyes could not decipher into a coherent pattern. Vivid red, blue, and green colors formed geometric patterns that glowed faintly, casting an odd tonal quality to the light in the room.

She allowed her mind to focus on the color of the energy patterns and when combined with the slightly off-putting ceiling, a pristine landscape suddenly came into focus, with mountains and trees and massive dragons gliding effortlessly through the air. *Kervigar was a master of art. Though he made some things only for a select few.* Stephenie understood only a full-blooded dragon, or someone one or two generations removed, would have the natural ability to perceive the image.

Dufnall and Kor turned around as they took in the view, spinning in a wide circle over the marble floor, which contained a patchwork of inlaid colors forming Kervigar's personal mark. Dufnall's four guards remained transfixed in place.

"I'm ..." Dufnall continued to move around, unable to express his thoughts in words. When his gaze fell on the massive double doors at the far end of the hall leading to the throne room, he stopped. The pair of five-foot-wide and ten-foot-tall doors glistened from the inch and a half of solid gold covering the raised surface that depicted Ista's crest with a dragon prowling around the back side of the shield, leaving only its head and tail visible.

Stephenie cleared her throat. "If you'll follow me." She headed toward one of the small utilitarian doors on the long walls of the entrance hall. "I can take you to your rooms, and once you are settled, we'll show you the bathing room."

"Jarl," Kor said, still staring at the doors to the throne room. "I ..."

Dufnall recovered his composure. "Of course. I know you would also like to refresh yourself before dinner. Please lead the way."

"Islet, I'm putting the dogs into the large storage room behind the one where we've stored the clothing and cloth. Can you arrange for someone to bring food for them? Just have it left at the door. I'll have a guardian bring it in to them."

"Of course," Islet responded.

"Thanks." Stephenie turned to Walter. "Can you lock Hugo up in the small room on the north corner and have someone tend to him? Be careful. He tried to get the guardians to kill him. I want him to remain alive, so make sure he doesn't get anything that can harm him. He's not likely to be in a fighting mood, but just in case."

"Yes, Ma'am, I'll take care of it."

She smiled. "Thank you. Alright," she looked at Dufnall and his men, "let's go to your rooms." She opened the door and revealed a long corridor with multiple doors and a grand staircase heading up. She climbed the stairs while a pair of guardians escorted the dogs down the corridor and out of sight.

"The upper floors are made of stone?" Dufnall looked at the ceiling as they climbed the open stairs. The protective railing curved over on the top and dripped down, as if to form a cascade of falling water. "And the light. I don't even see any crystals."

"Magic," she replied and took him up two more flights of stairs. The halls, doorways, windows, and ceilings all reflected a slightly overstated opulence. While the colors remained light, blues and greens accented many of the surfaces. Had human hands carved the details, decades would have passed before they completed the work. "The baths are on the third floor. I will show you all how they work, but right now Ryia is in there, so you'll need to wait." Dufnall raised an eyebrow. "The room is communal." She shrugged. "I inherited the layout and did not dictate it."

"No, that is not a problem. We Sandvians often bath or clean up in a hothouse. Doing so individually is a waste of coal and heat."

Stephenie smiled, knowing that in many places bathers made no distinction for gender, but for most of the castle residents, their Cothish upbringing left them more reserved. "So I have been told." She continued down the hall. The three people who worked in the castle approached from the opposite direction, each of them carrying various items such as water jugs, towels, and a platter of food. "While you wait to get clean, it appears Islet has made sure you have some refreshments." She stopped in front of a darkly colored wooden door. "Dufnall, this is your room. If everyone wants rooms of their own, they can have the next four. Or if they want to share a larger room, the one at the end of the hall has nine beds in it."

Dufnall looked at Kor and his guards. They looked overwhelmed.

Stephenie laughed. "Look them over and decide." She moved away from the door. "Since I smell worse than I look, I will leave you and bathe now so that you'll have access to do so before long."

"Ma'am," one of the servants said.

"Yes, Erika?"

"Once we settle the Jarl, I will bring you fresh clothing."

Stephenie smiled at the woman who remained eager to please, but refused to abase herself to gain favor. "Thank you, I appreciate it." She then turned to Dufnall and gave a small bow of her head as she walked away to head back to the third floor.

*　　*　　*　　*　　*

Stephenie closed the door to the communal bathing room and sighed. The room smelled of hot water. Ryia looked up from where she lounged in one of the dozen smaller stone tubs situated around three of the walls, each facing in toward the center of the room. A tub against the far wall could hold ten people easily.

"You feeling any better?" Stephenie asked Ryia as she slipped off her boots and socks to put her bare feet on the warm stone floor.

Ryia slipped her head below the water of the two-foot-tall tub that rested directly on the floor. Stephenie chuckled, used her powers to open the taps connected to the pipes that dropped from the ceiling into the tub next to Ryia. Her mind sensed the stopper that sat next to the drain on the bottom of the tub and she shifted that into place as she walked across the room.

Stephenie tugged at the laces that tightened the top of her shirt and slipped the dirty cloth over her head. She had shed the rest of her clothing before Ryia came back up for air.

The younger woman wiped away the water that continued to drain from her hair into her eyes. Eventually, she pulled her hair back and looked at Stephenie. "Showing off the goods?"

Stephenie slipped her legs over the flared edge of the tub and dropped to her butt. She put her back to the center of the room so that the water falling from the pipes splashed against her feet. It also allowed her to look directly at Ryia. "You've only gotten more angry as we grew closer to home. You can tell me anything."

"Because you've already seen all my secrets?"

Stephenie slid forward to get closer to Ryia, pulling her knees up to her chest. "No. It's because I like to think we're friends and you'd tell me what's bothering you."

Ryia splashed water against her face and then looked at a point on the other side of the room. "How do you put up with it? All this work to make me more effective with magic has made me more sensitive to feeling emotions. When people look at me, I know what they are thinking. What they want to do to me."

Stephenie held back her response. Ryia appeared to want to say more, and Stephenie did not want to keep her from opening up.

"Those soldiers. Even Kor and Dufnall get aroused when they look at me." She shifted her focus back to Stephenie. "I feel it when they look at you. You're like a million times more sensitive than me. Don't tell me you haven't noticed." She stared, waiting. "How do you put up with it?"

Stephenie shrugged. "I tune it out."

Ryia shook her head. "Why do you let them get away with it?"

Stephenie looked down at the hot water filling the tub. It had finally reached her belly. She wondered if she could widen the pipes to let the water fall from the cistern on the roof faster. *But then, would the heaters get it hot enough?* She turned her attention back to Ryia. "Sorry, I was just thinking it would be nice if these tubs filled faster." She forced a smile for Ryia. "But to answer your question, tell me this: do they just think these things or are they staring at you? Are they saying things or approaching you?"

Ryia frowned and shook her head. "No. But I know they are thinking it."

Stephenie leaned an arm over the top of the tub and tried to frame her point as a question instead of a fact she already knew. "When you wanted Henton, I'm guessing you were thinking about him without his clothes. Perhaps tried to steal a look when everyone would clean up in a river."

Ryia crossed her arms and glared. She tried to say something and nothing came out of her mouth.

"The point is, everyone, including you and I, will have thoughts when you see other people. It is only if they act inappropriately on them. Say things they shouldn't or try to do something they shouldn't. As much as possible, you should ignore the things in their heads they don't act on." Stephenie shifted slightly back to stretch out her legs. "And I'm not saying that approaching you to see if you're interested in some sort of relationship is inappropriate. It's if they don't accept what you tell them, then it's inappropriate."

Ryia shifted and moved to the edge of the tub. "But I can feel their emotions. This damn magic has ruined so much of my life. Made me have to leave home as a child. Made me a wanted person. It destroys any chance of me finding someone." She shook her head. "How can I ever like someone when I know the only reason they even bother is because they want to get me into bed?"

"I don't know, Ryia. I really don't. The only thing I can say is that we need to work on you being able to tune out the background noise."

"Henton's mind's quiet, though sometimes I know he feels things. Douglas was never attracted to either of us." She sighed. "Perain keeps to himself, but he'd probably jump at the chance if I allowed him." She looked down into the dirty water in her tub. "Even Walter will look at me sometimes."

Stephenie ran a hand under the scalding water coming from the ceiling. "You didn't mention Kas."

"He's good about keeping his emotions to himself."

"Way to protect me."

Ryia looked over at Stephenie and hesitated before speaking. "What's wrong between the two of you?"

Stephenie shook her head. "I don't really know for certain. He's angry that I'm not supporting his need to destroy the traps as fast as he wants. I'm frustrated he can't see that we have more pressing needs. Henton thinks he's self-conscious and worries he can't live up to my expectations. He also thinks I expected Kas to be perfect because he was someone originally unattainable, and also the first person to see me for what I am."

"Damn." Ryia leaned back against the flared part of the tub. "I guess I shouldn't be feeling so sorry for myself."

Stephenie moved to the rear of the tub so that the water cascaded down on the back of her head. "You're a beautiful woman, Ryia. People will find you attractive and have desires for you. If you allow them to get to know you, those desires might move from purely physical to something more."

She sighed. "You need to find a way to get lavender into the water. I forgot to bring the box from my room." Ryia looked over at Stephenie and said nothing for a long time. Finally, she spoke. "I don't know that I want anyone right now. I thought I wanted Henton, but not anymore. He was right. I'll likely look like this for dozens of years. What if I live to be a hundred and only look like I'm thirty?" She bit her lip. "Does not wanting to deal with that—with other people's feelings—mean there's something wrong with me?"

"No," Stephenie said sharply. *She's worried about living to a hundred. Depending on who's guessing, I might live to a thousand.* She did not want to think about repeating a cycle of everyone she knew dying of old age again and again. *How many times will that happen before I no longer care and crawl into a hole? How many times before the dragon in me no longer sees people as beings and I become cruel like them?* The falling water hid her tears.

The door opened and Erika came into the room. She curtsied to each of them and approached with a bundle of clothing.

"Thank you, Erika," Stephenie said. "Please set them someplace they won't get wet." Stephenie reached up and turned off the taps. The tub had become nearly full and the falling water had splashed out to create a wide puddle around her tub.

"Yes, Your Majesty. Do you need anything else?"

"No, thank you, Erika."

Chapter 22

"I would like to thank you for such consideration to Kor and my guards," Dufnall said as he reached for the plate of venison in front of him. He turned to look at Stephenie at the head of the table on his right. "I wouldn't have expected the gracious treatment, not after you had to pay for your own accommodations in Horn Point."

Stephenie handed a bowl of currants to Kas, who sat to her right. "As you already know, most of the city is empty. We don't have anyone to act as an innkeeper. That role just isn't needed."

Dufnall chuckled. "I hardly noticed. I'm afraid my attention continues to be drawn to other things." He looked around the dining hall with more dragon themed chandeliers over their heads. He rested a hand on the long stone table as thin as a finger with sculpted edges and curved legs that should never support the weight. Unlike her bowl, the table had embedded magic that reinforced its structural integrity. "Even the smallest things amaze me."

Henton, who sat further down the table, with Islet and Walter between him and Kas, cleared his throat. "You can see this is why we continue to ask you and your people to not tell others about what you've seen here. Likely, most won't believe you, but for those who do, it will just drive more to try to cross the borders and we don't want to have to constantly turn people away."

Dufnall nodded his head and looked at Kor and the four soldiers who sat on his left. "We will honor the original agreement, more so now that we understand the reasons for your requested discretion."

Stephenie picked up a crystal glass that Erika had filled with wine purchased from Sandven the prior year. She took a small drink and set the glass down on the table. "If you would like, after you get a tour of the city tomorrow, I can ask Ryia to continue providing you with more training."

Stephenie saw Ryia lean forward so that she could look around Henton. Ryia's eyes did not roll, and her sharp tongue remained silent, so Stephenie took that as a sign of agreement.

"We definitely would like to continue more of what has been explained on the road. Perhaps when we are not walking for the whole day, we can make more progress." Dufnall smiled to remove the sting from his words.

Islet swallowed the food in her mouth. "I understand you had concerns about assassins following you."

Dufnall turned his attention to Stephenie's sister. "Indeed. I sent word back to Horn Point about what happened when we went through Gaffel. Most likely, Ivan's soldiers that patrol the roads would have already found the bodies. I hope Rokr can be dealt with appropriately without starting a war with his faction."

"The merchants we saw on the road would have found the bodies as well," Kor added. "We warned them. I'd guess some of them would have cleaned the bodies of anything of value."

"Are you worried about internal rebellion?" Islet asked.

"Rokr's brazen attack on us was a surprise," Dufnall continued. "I do fear he might try a more direct rebellion. However, my brother is not without his own loyal soldiers."

Islet continued. "Do you think he was the one that tried to poison Stephenie?" She asked as she put another chunk of meat into her mouth.

Stephenie noticed Douglas and his husband talking quietly at the end of the table. Perain leaned in to respond to them. *Douglas is probably glad he remained behind,* she mused. *I can't blame him.*

"I know little of the event," Dufnall replied to Islet before turning to look at Stephenie.

Stephenie nodded her head. "Someone poisoned the water jug in the boarding house. Fortunately, I drank the water before anyone else.

Anyone could have added the poison. It wasn't the assassin on the road."

Stephenie drained the rest of her wine and stared at the empty glass. She felt Kas' annoyance at having to sit in the room and be excluded from the conversation. "This can be broken just by singing," she asked Kas in Dalish, remembering a random discussion they had weeks ago.

He looked up from his plate. "If you can find the correct sound frequency that causes the crystal to vibrate. I do not recall the correct technical term for the effect." His tone was dismissive.

She hummed while looking at the delicate glass.

"I imagine it needs to be at a higher pitch." Kas continued to eat, but he watched her.

Stephenie knew she could make the crystal vessel explode with a radiating burst of gravitational energy, but the idea of doing it with her voice intrigued her. She increased her pitch and watched with her mind's eye. The heat of her breath caused the air in front of her to tumble and swirl as the extra energy imparted from the temperature differential caused it to rise slowly higher. The glass itself slowly became more excited. Energy from internal vibrations increased. She adjusted her voice until she observed the internal energy in the glass spike quickly.

"Damn," Ryia said just after the top of the glass shattered, sending pieces of crystal scattering around her.

Stephenie looked at the stem of the glass that remained in her hand. The residual red wine dripping down her fingers. She looked up and Kas frowned at her, his plate of food now contaminated with sharp fragments of her glass.

"Sorry," Stephenie said, setting the base of the glass down on the table.

"Allow me," Erika said as she hurried from where she had stood at the wall. She quickly grabbed both Kas' plate and hers with one hand and then tried to shift the crystal fragments from the table onto the stack of plates in her other hand.

"Thank you," Stephenie said to Erika. "Sorry, Kas," she said softly in Dalish. "It was interesting to see the energy build in the glass. It grew quickly right before it broke."

"I imagine it did. The sounds you made caused it to vibrate until the internal structure could not remain in one piece." He watched Erika take away their plates. "I hope she brings a new one. I was not finished eating."

"You'll need to teach me to do that," Ryia demanded from down the table.

Stephenie wiped the wine from her hand on the small towel Erika had left behind. "Sorry about that," she said to Dufnall. "I hadn't intended to make such a mess."

"That was quite impressive." He set down his fork. "May I speak with you privately?"

Stephenie looked down the table. Everyone had stopped eating after she broke the glass and had not resumed yet. "Sure." She pushed her chair back and then waved everyone down. "Please, remain seated and continue eating. We'll be back." She stood up. "Follow me."

Dufnall rose and Stephenie led him out of the dining hall, down a long passage, and into a small sitting room with a table that contained a board game Stephenie enjoyed playing with Henton and Islet. "Please have a seat," she said as she settled into a wingback chair with thick padding.

Dufnall sat across from her. "You're not human, are you?"

Stephenie chuckled. "My sire was not a normal man. I never met him, but I understand he can take many forms."

Dufnall nodded his head. "Your display on the bridge after the assassin's bolt." He looked around the room, though nothing in the sitting room contained any overt displays of dragons. "I had wondered about the imagery on Ryia's staff when I first saw it, but no doubt remained in my mind once I saw the power of this place." He held his gaze, though she felt his heart racing. "When I saw the entrance hall, I knew what I saw as a young man was not drink."

Stephenie leaned forward. "Dragons have hid away from most of the world for at least sixteen hundred years because elder dragons ordered it. Apparently upon pain of death if they do not comply. I know little to nothing about those events. But in my blood is the ability to control raw power, unlike most others. My very existence has made me enemies. Powerful enemies. People that would like to make me their pawn, or dead, regardless of the cost to others."

Dufnall swallowed. "I can't say I understand, but I promise I will keep your secret."

She sighed. His fear filled the room, though he remained outwardly calm. "I knew when I agreed to allow you to come to Ista that you would see enough evidence to likely come to this conclusion." She leaned back, sinking into the corner of the chair. "I have no intention of threatening you or harming you."

"If I may ask, what happened to the prior inhabitants?"

"My sire slaughtered the dragon that built this country and all the people that lived here. Then, a few years ago, he started manipulating people to try to kill me. I did not know what I was and simply followed a lead that drew me to Ista. I wanted to beg him to leave me alone, or at least kill me and leave my friends alone. It wasn't until I arrived, that I learned my true nature."

"I guess being renamed after a preferred brother is not that bad in comparison."

Stephenie laughed. "Probably not, but I'm not trying to see who has a worse lot in life."

"I would definitely like to learn more from you ... and Ryia, before you send me back home."

Stephenie rose to her feet. "It would be my pleasure. However, it can wait until tomorrow. I'm still hungry, and I'm sure I've managed to make everyone else quite uncomfortable sitting there without us."

Stephenie crossed her bedroom and set down the mug of water on the table near her side of the bed. She watched Kas as he stood near the door, his attention in the book he held open in his hands. "Are you ready to talk?"

He looked up, sighed, and closed the book. "I am still angry, but yes, we need to talk."

She moved her hands, looking for something to do with them. "Please, tell me what has you so angry with me? I keep looking for what I can do differently, but ..."

He dropped his hand and held the book to his side. "I do not know." Resignation filled his voice. "We want different things. You want to be outside. I prefer the library." He shook his head. "However, the real issue is you do not consider me your first priority."

She moved closer, but she did not reach out to touch him. "You are."

"I am not. I warned you that allowing the castle into your mind would be an issue. It is always there. Always watching me. Always judging me. I can feel it there when we have a mental connection. You converse with it when you are talking to me."

She wanted to deny his statements. However, they had a certain truth to them that she knew he would argue.

"My big ask has always been to help me destroy the traps. But on our trip, you barely acknowledged the effort." He paced to the right. "I am not a fool, and I understand we could not head further south, but you did not even attempt to help me look where I originally thought the trap was located. You could have at least tried."

"Kas, I understand your need, and the moral reasons behind them, but the trip to Horn Point had always been about doing what we needed to do for the people of Ista."

He snorted. "Another group of people that come before me."

"You've always known my history and background."

"Stephenie, when we met, you were a princess running away from your mother. You have said countless times to Henton and others that you are not fit to rule. Before we came to Ista, you had no intention of being a queen."

She swallowed, biting back the angry retort in favor of one that she hoped would de-escalate the argument. "I made those statements when I thought everyone who ever met me would want to burn me as a witch, regardless of the truth. We came north to try to stop the damn dragon that started this whole mess from continuing to try to kill me and those I care for. We remained here because of Yreka and the Senzar threat. Because of what I am, Ista accepted us and the people who now rely upon us. I cannot simply do whatever I want, when I want to." She looked away and fought to avoid clenching her fists. "I keep looking for options that reduce my responsibility, but I can't just let these people suffer. For them to be left at everyone else's mercy, simply because it is more convenient for me."

Kas raised his own hands in uncertainty. "And that is the problem. I do not know what I expected from you, but I honestly thought I would remain your priority."

Her voice dropped, afraid of the answer. "Do you still love me?"

Kas hesitated for a moment and then nodded his head. "I do, but right now, I am not able to share you like this."

She felt the tears running down her face, but did not bother to wipe them away. "So, what do you want to do?"

He bit his own lip. "I need time. I'll move my things to the bedroom down the hall." He stepped forward, a hand halfway outstretched, but then he stopped and lowered his hand. "I have tried for a long time to ignore the castle. I did not want you to bond with it because I knew it would become this permanent connection to you. It would always be in your thoughts. I need to figure out how to deal with that." He turned away, moisture in his own eyes, and quietly left their bedroom.

The tears fell unchecked down her face. She stood there for a long time before crawling onto the top of the bed and crying herself into a fitful sleep.

Chapter 23

Stephenie led Dufnall up a set of narrow steps and over a three-foot high stone wall. The branches of the nearby maple trees hung down, and she had to push them aside to descend into the walled off grove. These stones, unlike those used to create the buildings, remained natural and rough, with green lichens covering much of the exposed surface.

"I'm uncertain of why some parts of the land were sectioned off," she told the eager jarl. "And with the wind, it doesn't stop the seeds from spreading, but for the horses, sheep, and sled dogs, the areas with gates make great animal runs."

"I've never seen most of these plants," Dufnall said as he pushed through the branches. "Most of what we have in Sandven is root vegetables."

"We have some of those as well."

"It never gets too cold here?"

Stephenie shrugged. "Not what your people would call cold, but some of those from Cothel have complained. In the dead of winter, Isa Fields will get cool to help reset the plants, but it doesn't freeze. Plus, the obelisks will also radiate illumination when the sun fails to come over the horizon."

"My brother would kill me, but I think I might like to return for a longer stay and learn more once all the trade negotiations are complete."

"I promised to kick you out, and I definitely will do that. However, you would be welcome to return as long as your brother would not accuse me of manipulating you."

Dufnall reached up and tugged on a leaf, felt its surface, and examined the five lobes before he released it to spring back overhead. "I've spent much of my life reading and studying things. I'm not completely useless. I do practice with my spear and sword, but if I had a choice, I would avoid the tedious parts of life."

She turned away from Dufnall and looked out over the gently sloping ground. The trees grew in a haphazard pattern in what had become something of a wild forest. Various plants grew up among a layer of smaller fallen branches that made walking through the grove interesting, but not difficult. *Avoiding the tedious parts of life, now that is a goal.* She resumed walking, saying nothing aloud. An eighth of a mile later, they came to another wall and a set of stairs formed by larger stones jutting from the wall. Stephenie climbed over the barrier and into a field that still had most of the wheat standing. The tops of many of the stems had already broken and fallen to the ground.

Dufnall finished climbing down the steps and looked at the partially harvested field. "What am I looking at?"

"One of our wheat fields. We've been harvesting it, but we don't have enough people, and those we do have, have had to experiment with how and when to harvest. The yields are low and I expect most of the crop left has gone too long." She slid her hand along a nearby stem, stripping all the kernels into her hand. "The seeds are now breaking off on their own. The early harvest got covered in mold and made people sick." She tossed the grains into the field. "The good part is it appears to reseed itself. The problem is getting it brought in to store and consume."

"I know some kinds of wheat grow not too far to the south of Sandven, but this variety is not a northern crop."

Stephenie nodded in agreement. "We've got mills in the city to grind this into flour. There are granaries to store the grain. We just don't have the people with the knowledge." She turned to Dufnall. "It is why I want to allow some people from the south to immigrate. A few people who know how to work the fields can teach others and that can make us self-sufficient."

Dufnall squatted down to examine the crop. "I believe I can convince my brother to allow it, but he won't like the loss of the tax money if you don't need him." Dufnall looked up. "He'll also realize he won't have power in the relationship. It's not like he'd be able to starve you out long term. A war with you would be pointless with your stone cats."

Stephenie recognized her mistake in admitting her goal, but suspected Dufnall already knew the implications. *He's shrewder than I give him credit.* Aloud, she continued, not bothering to conceal the truth. "We have fewer guardians than you might expect and a large area of uninhabited land to protect."

He stood up. "There are jarls in Sandven who fear you might try to take over the southern countries. That you want power and land because they believe that what little they have, you'll still want it." He used his arms to include everything around them. "There is nothing in Sandven that can compare to this. I believe I've been around you long enough to know that you do not hunger for conquest. I will try to convince everyone of that fact."

Stephenie smiled. "Thank you. I …" *What's happening, Ista?* She allowed the castle to relay a conversation occurring at the border with Sandven's Captain Tumi and another man.

"What is it?" Dufnall asked.

Stephenie shook her head and continued to listen through the guardian that lounged under the bridge. The stone and distance between the guardian and the speakers muffled the sounds. Her stomach dropped when she understood the warning the man brought.

She pushed the conversation to the back of her mind. "Lobben has invaded Sandven. They took Norbek with an army of holy warriors and are likely moving east."

"What?"

"Do you trust me?"

Dufnall nodded his head. "You've had plenty of chances to kill me if that had been your intention."

Stephenie drew in power and formed a gravitational field around Dufnall's legs and hips. "I won't let you fall." She adjusted the field so that he lifted into the air. She monitored the pressure on his body to avoid causing pain. He muffled a cry of surprise as he moved slowly upward until he hovered above the tops of the nearby maple trees. She wrapped a similar field around herself and rocked upward.

She flew both of them back toward the castle. A second field blocked the wind from Dufnall's body, keeping his sensation of speed down. Stephenie did not bother for herself, instead she let the wind rip through her loose hair and across her face, relishing in the rapid pace. Less than a count of fifty later and they had traveled the mile and half back to the castle, where they landed just outside the door.

Ista already had the guardians gathering the others and Stephenie led Dufnall back into the castle. She took him down a passage off the left side of the entrance hall and into the map room. She started pulling large sheets of paper from deep shelves and spread the maps over a massive wooden table that consumed the center of the room.

"Steph?" Islet said, coming into the room with a guardian behind her to hasten her pace.

"I don't think I should wait for the others, so I'll let you pass on what we know." She separated two more maps, spreading them across the table. "There is a runner that came to the border wanting to warn Dufnall that Lobben has taken Norbek with a large number of holy warriors and other soldiers. He believes they planned to march east from there."

"Are you certain?" Islet asked.

"I'm certain there is someone at the border making the claim. I'm leaving for the border shortly. I want to hear what is being said directly."

"I should come with you," Dufnall said.

Stephenie shook her head. "You did well flying that short distance, but I'm going to go much faster and if it is just me, I can go a lot farther without needing a break."

"My brother needs to be warned."

Stephenie nodded her agreement. "I believe the runner said that was already done, but I will confirm."

"Where are the others?" Islet asked.

"Henton, Douglas, and Walter are in the city searching Hugo's house. Kas is still in the library. Kor and Ryia are with the others in the training field."

"I won't ask how you know all that," Dufnall said.

"Magic," Stephenie and Islet said simultaneously, and then grinned at each other.

"I'm leaving now. I don't want to startle anyone at the border with a guardian, and I don't want the runner to leave."

"Be safe," Islet said and offered a quick hug.

"Dufnall, I'll let everyone know what is happening soon." Stephenie hugged her sister once more and then exited the room. She stopped in her bedroom to grab her sword as she made her way out of the castle. With the limited workers, she encountered no one else.

Outside, she flew into the air and streaked across the sky. Unlike with the trip from the field to the castle, where she kept them mostly upright, Stephenie angled herself more horizontally to reduce the wind drag, but not so far as the force her neck into an uncomfortable position. She climbed to a little over three hundred feet up and pushed herself forward as fast as she could.

She used Ista and the guardians as mental beacons for physical direction and flew a straight line from Isa Fields toward the border encampment. What would otherwise be over a hundred miles following the road, required traveling only half the distance in the air. The rough and rolling ground that sped beneath her provided none of the normal obstacles.

Power coursed through her body, but over the last two years, she had grown much better at using lower energy fields to affect and control higher powered fields. The indirect nature took more concentration and understanding, but it did not require her to draw all the power through her own body. *Skill over raw potential,* she reminded herself of the mantra Kas often repeated to her. The thought brought a tear to her cheek that the wind dried immediately.

Even with her more careful usage of power, the constant flow of energy still took its toll, and by the time she neared the border, her insides felt raw and burned.

To keep from revealing more of her abilities and scaring the soldiers, Stephenie reduced her altitude and skimmed the ground well before anyone could see her in the sky. Flying just above the ground required more concentration to avoid large rocks and the dips and rises in the landscape, but soon she saw the round houses and she touched down just north of them. Her body and mind sagged when she stopped drawing power into herself, and she stumbled with exhaustion.

At least I'm not bleeding. Hemorrhaging from the nose and eyes because of overextending oneself remained a consistent indicator of witchcraft for those that believed in the southern gods. Priests and holy warriors tended to have so little power, and relied upon their augmentation devices, combined, those factors meant they did less damage to their own bodies and seldom cooked their own brains.

She took a few moments to steady herself before she walked out from behind cover and headed toward the bridge. She knew from Ista that all of her border guards continued to confer with the Sandvian soldiers. When they saw her approaching along the road, they rose to attention. Her sudden appearance without supplies or transportation sparked fear in Captain Tumi and the Sandvian soldiers. Her own guards remained startled, but they had seen her appear without warning before.

She did not speak until she had crossed the bridge to join them. "I understand something has happened. Please tell me what you know."

"How? How did you know already?" The Sandvian Captain asked. "How are you here?"

"Ma'am," Loke said, bowing his head. The border guard pointed to a young man with a braided beard sitting against the bridge's abutment. "That man, Edis, came north on a dogcart to warn us about Lobben attacking Norbek."

Stephenie started walking toward the young man, and Edis quickly rose to his feet. He looked at her closely because he witnessed the others deferring to her, but he did not appear to recognize her. "Hello Edis, I'm Queen Stephenie. I understand Lobben has invaded Sandven."

Edis' eyes bulged, and he stammered a quick apology. "Yes, Your Majesty."

Stephenie nodded her head, not wanting to draw this out too much. "You're not in trouble, Edis. However, I really need to hear what happened and have you tell me everything you know."

The twenty-something nodded his head. She could tell he remained skeptical because of her apparent age. "Fotia's soldiers marched from Lobben. It was horrific."

Stephenie tried to keep her voice level. "Tell me the specific details. How many? How did they attack? What weapons? How many died? What they did next. What you did."

Edis swallowed. "It happened in the dead of night. I was asleep, but I was told by those who witnessed it that some of their priests threw fire, smashed houses, and unleashed lightning. Somehow, they simply walked through the gates without the alarm being raised. Then they surged through the city barracks and slaughtered the guards and the jarl's men."

"Lightning? Are you sure?"

Edis nodded his head. "I heard the thunder several times. When I realized no rain fell, I went outside and saw the flashes of light. It was as if the sky fell upon the city."

Damn, that doesn't sound like normal priests. Stephenie let Ista know her concerns that this attack had Senzar support. *But what do they expect to gain?* She wondered to the castle. Unfortunately, Ista had no comment for her.

"I did not stay to see the end of the battle. They sent many of us away to warn Gaffel and Horn Point. At Gaffel, they told us we needed to warn Alkmaar. Two of us were selected. At Alkmaar, we were told Jarl Dufnall had come to Ista." He looked back at the camp in Sandven. "I came north to provide the warning to the Jarl."

"When did this happen?"

"This is the eighth day since the invasion."

Did my going south trigger it? Ista did not answer her. "How many invaders? Did you see their numbers?"

Edis shook his head. "I did not see them, but some elders said there were well over a thousand, perhaps two, maybe three."

Stephenie breathed a sigh of relief, even if it might appear inappropriate. *No one could mobilize that many troops that quickly. This was planned before my trip.* She then felt a pang of irritation about feeling good that her actions might not have caused the invasion. *People still died and suffered.* She returned her focus to Edis. "And you left before the battle was over, so you don't know the outcome."

"The outcome was not in doubt. Fotia's Faithful killed most of the defenders before anyone knew there was a battle. They knew where to find our soldiers and the Lobben cowards killed them in their sleep." Edis' hands clenched. "Those who could take power from the Goddess did, but they were overwhelmed and died quickly. They captured and killed many of those trying to flee the city. We escaped through a sewer they didn't appear to know about." He looked to the ground. "There were only ten of us. Some went faster than others. Most made for Horn Point. I finally managed to get a dog team in Alkmaar so I could come here. Others going to Horn Point got dog teams in Gaffel."

"And you believe they were going to continue east?"

Edis nodded his head.

Ista, send four guardians south, one each to Alkmaar, Norbek, Gaffel, and Horn Point. Stephenie frowned at the hesitant response. *I realize they won't have support and their access to power will diminish. Keep them out of sight. I just want the guardians to watch so we know what is happening.*

After Ista agreed, Stephenie felt four guardians to the west take motion. She turned back to the exhausted runner. "Thank you, Edis. Please remain here for now." She looked at Captain Tumi. "Thank you. If the invaders turn north, please know that you and your soldiers will be welcomed into Ista. I won't make you fight them alone."

The Captain nodded his head. She turned and headed back into Ista. To her border guards, she said as she passed, "I need a little while. I'll provide guidance in a bit."

Islet, she told Ista, asking for her sister's communication stone to activate.

Islet activated her stone almost immediately. "Steph, are you okay?"

Fine, she responded as she increased her pace. *I also want to speak with Kas, Henton, Ryia, and Dufnall. Can you get them all stones?*

"Yes, I can do that."

Thank you. Have everyone make the connection from different rooms. Not every stone transmits at the same speed and even I can't take the echoing when everyone is standing together.

Islet gave a knowing grin. "I can stand it even less than you."

Reach out when everyone is ready. She broke the connection and continued toward the closer of the roundhouses. Inside, she gathered supplies while she ate some of the readily available food. She considered her current exhaustion with the distance and time that she would need to reach Alkmaar. *I should be able to do that, but can I make Norbek?* She did not know if she could manage the full journey without a significant rest.

She knew from the maps she had reviewed just before she left that in a straight-line Alkmaar was roughly the same distance she had just flown, about sixty miles. Norbek would be closer to another eighty, and having never been there, it would hamper her ability to fly a true path. The guardians could cover the ground quickly, even off the road, as they could fly over most obstacles. Without flesh, they would not tire like her and could travel without stopping. Their only consideration really being the need to stay out of sight. "They should all be in place before this time tomorrow."

Stephenie paused in her gathering of supplies. *Islet, Dufnall.*

Dufnall stood with Walter in a small room. "What is this? I can see you as if you are in the room, but when I turn the stone, you move. Now I see Her Majesty as well, but her room overlaps with the one I'm in."

Stephenie forced herself to separate out the visual image from each person, only focusing on one at a time. *It will get worse in a moment. Try not to pay too much attention to the visuals. Imagine closing your eyes. It might help, but everything exists only in your mind.*

"Steph," Ryia said, her hair tangled slightly from being outside. The room she stood in was dimly lit.

"How is this possible?" Dufnall asked as he sat down, a hand coming over his eyes. "I can still see everyone and the rooms they're in."

"We don't normally have multiple connections," Henton said. He appeared and also sat down in a chair. "It will be hard to focus, but try." Even Henton looked pale. "Steph, Islet informed us of the invasion. Have you learned anything else?"

Stephenie noted Kas had joined their conference. "Okay, now that everyone is here, I'll tell you what I know." She slipped a meat pie that one of the border guards had left near the fire into the sack she had picked up from the shelves. "Lobben invaded Norbek about eight days ago. They had a lot of priests and holy warriors helping. Apparently, many of them used fire, gravity, and lightning to decimate the defenders."

"That seems like some powerful holy warriors," Henton said.

"I'm worried there might be some Senzar involved," Stephenie admitted. She repeated her statements in Dalish for Kas, then returned to Sandvian. "I'm going to fly to Alkmaar to see what's happening there. The runner's information is just what he knew at the time. He left before the battle for Norbek was complete, and a lot could have changed in eight days."

"Steph?" Henton's question contained a warning.

"The flight to the border didn't take too much out of me." She hoped her mental projection to them concealed the exhaustion she actually felt. "If they are not under siege yet, I'm going to tell them to come north and let them into Ista."

"Steph, that is risky," Henton protested.

"If they try to flee with an army at their back, they won't have the time to gather food and supplies. We don't have the resources to feed them, so they will need to carry everything they can. If they leave before an army is chasing them, they can do it in a more orderly fashion."

Dufnall looked unwell. "Do you think they are coming north?"

Stephenie shrugged and quickly repeated the details for Kas. She grabbed a waterskin and went outside to a rain barrel to fill it. "It would be a risk to leave Horn Point behind them. Ivan would likely send his soldiers north. They may have left a large force at Gaffel or simply split their soldiers and sent some to both Alkmaar and Horn Point. The runner said warnings went to both."

Islet drew Stephenie's attention by moving. "I agree. If there is an army coming north, we should consolidate as many soldiers as we can."

"Are we sure they are coming?" Ryia asked.

"I've sent some guardians south to act as spies. We'll have better information when they arrive." Stephenie capped the waterskin.

"They might have left Alkmaar alone, at least for now. The force there is not significant."

Dufnall nodded his head slowly. "There are only eighteen soldiers at the border now, leaving out the two traitors. Alkmaar had around fifty or a hundred. Not certain. We could assume some people would take up arms, but the city is not set to defend itself against an invasion. The walls are more for animals and bandits."

"I will try to make Norbek after I tell Alkmaar they are welcome to go north. I want to see what happened firsthand and try to get a measure of what Lobben's plans are." Stephenie again quickly repeated the conversation for Kas.

"What do you want me to do?" Kas asked.

"If they recruited numerous priests and are using augmentation devices to bolster their forces, we need to put a stop to it. Can you change your focus to that trap?"

Kas nodded his head. "The research I did last year indicates it is buried somewhere in the mountains. However, I found little of explicit details. No mention of a city. No landmarks. We had a hard time finding Mertor's trap. I would expect the builders of this trap to similarly concealed it."

"If you can't find anything more, we do it the old fashion way," she told him before switching back to Sandvian for the others. "We'll see if we can deal with the priests of Fotia the same way we dealt with those of Mertor. Find a holy symbol, use that to locate a relay, and use the relay to locate the trap."

"Not on your own," Ryia said. "You can't do that alone."

She switched to Cothish. "Ryia, I won't. I'm hoping this is not my sire causing trouble again. Perhaps it is just a regular bastard who wants to conquer their neighbor."

"Will you be able to help Ivan?" Dufnall asked. "With the might of Ista at your back? My brother would be indebted to you."

Stephenie shrugged. "I can't take on an army by myself and I don't have the guardians to spare to send them to war. However, we might be able to remove Fotia's priest from the battle." With her bag of supplies, she headed back toward the bridge. "We will attempt to rout Lobben's forces by removing their magic."

Dufnall did not look placated. "I only hope jarls like Rokr didn't support this."

Stephenie nodded her head. "I'll reach out again once I have more details." She broke the connections and took a moment to allow her head to clear. The overlapping rooms and people, even when separated, made her head throb. *Please, not my sire and not the Senzar.*

Chapter 24

Islet gathered the others, including Douglas, Perain, and Kor, and brought them back to the map room. *I suppose this might need to be renamed the war room.* She did not like the thought. The last time she faced such a painful event, her older sister, Kara, had died at the hands of the Senzar during their invasion of Esland.

Islet let everyone sit in the chairs before she spoke. "We need to start taking action to prepare for the worst. If Lobben's eventual goal is Ista, then I expect to see forces coming north through Alkmaar. They might have already taken the city."

Dufnall cringed at the statement but said nothing.

Henton looked at the maps scattered across the large table. "It's been a little while since I really looked at these, but we might still want to watch our western side." He slid a map of Ista out from under one of Sandven and Lobben. "We know the mountains go all the way north to the sea, but that doesn't mean Lobben knows that. And there are passes through the mountains around the border, which they might know about. The path might not be good for moving an army, but smaller squads could make it. Last year, Steph told me more than once that people approached the boundary stones before turning back."

Islet nodded her head. "I imagine Ista and Steph have a sizable number of guardians covering the western shores and borders." She sighed. Dufnall still appeared at a loss for things to say, and Ryia simply stared at the table. She expected Kas mentally communicated with Henton for a translation, as Stephenie's husband appeared agitated. She looked up as Walter put a comforting hand on her shoulder. "Thank you," she mouthed to him. To Henton, she continued. "What makes that side of the country hard for invaders, makes it hard to send anyone to guard it, especially with our limited numbers. If they waste time sending people to cross the border, we'll know and have plenty of time to react."

Walter sat down next to Islet. "As Islet said, it's pointless to do anything now."

Islet watched Henton consider his words before speaking. "My point was more that what we thought to be hunters could have been spies checking out their options last year."

Dufnall cleared his throat. "I know her Majesty said that runners were bringing the warning to Horn Point, but I can't help but feel I should do something more than sitting here." He glanced around, his movements hesitant and stuttered. "There are at least fifty soldiers in Alkmaar and eighteen at the border. Instead of having them come north to Ista, I could lead them south, and perhaps help hold, or retake, Gaffel. It's definitely possible for soldiers to move off the roads, but wagons and supplies really need the cleared paths. Gaffel sits at the crossroads that leads here as well as Horn Point. It's strategic."

Islet shook her head. "There are things we can do now before we have more information, and there are things that need to wait." She sympathized with Dufnall; she had wanted to rush to Kara's aid when she learned of the invasion of Esland. However, her then husband had wisely stated they needed to bolster their forces before charging in. At that time, they had few troops along what had been considered a friendly border. *Not that bolstering troops had helped against the Senzar magic.* She pushed away the memories. "I would recommend not throwing small groups of soldiers at a target that Lobben is bound to consider extremely important. They will come in force, because, as you said, it is the only path they have."

"And if they are coming north," Ryia said, "we need to be ready here." She looked up and met Islet's gaze. "I can start working on drills with my students. The three of them have some combat skills, but—"

Islet raised a hand. "I appreciate the initiative, Ryia, but I think it would be better to focus on training them for healing. They are not skilled enough in combat, and if we pushed them to the front, against a large force of priests and holy warriors, then they would be the first targets." She noticed Kas' frown at her use of the terms and assumed Henton had translated exactly what she said. *Or Kas has learned those words in Sandvian.* "We need to keep those in Ista with magic to the back and focus on healing anyone that is injured."

Ryia frowned. "I'll have to be at the front. You need someone with magic to defend us. If not, our people won't survive." She glanced at Kas and switched to Cothish. "You'd be best to stay back and help with the healing. No offense, but you've not been training with Henton and me."

Kas frowned. "I need to research where the trap in Lobben might be located. The only thing I ever found was that they had hidden it within the mountains, but I do not even have a city name." He looked at Islet. "I should be doing that now. I have little I can offer for advice with battle plans." He pushed his seat back and stood up.

Islet nodded her head. She could see the hurt in his face, and wished Ryia had not provoked him, but both their statements held truth. "Please let us know as soon as you find anything." She watched as he left the room and then turned back to the others.

Henton spoke as soon as the door closed. "Of the people in Isa Fields, we can probably recruit up to half to fight, but that includes a fair number of older men and women."

"We need people to bring in crops," Walter said. "I think that southern wheat is beyond saving, but there are root vegetables that are ready to harvest. You need to leave some people for that."

Dufnall looked between Islet, Walter, and Henton. "Do you plan to take a stand and fight them? How many can your guardians deal with?"

Islet pursed her lips. "Stephenie has said they are powerful. But depending on who we face, our enemies may have significant magic. I would guess that if it is just common priests and soldiers, the guardians could defeat the entire army."

Dufnall raised his eyebrows. "That is a serious defense. Can't you spare some to fight on Sandven's behalf? I implore you to come to our aid. We will be forever in your debt."

Islet sighed. "I wish it were that simple. Stephenie is the one that you would need to convince. But part of the concern is concealing Ista's presence and avoiding drawing the wrong people here. We know that those with enough power can destroy them. There are hundreds of guardians that no longer exist, and no way at this time to create new ones."

"Because of the dragon?" Dufnall asked.

Islet tried to remain impassive. "We don't know who destroyed all of them, but that is what we believe." She leaned forward. "I know Steph, she will do everything she can to help Sandven. Her plan is to find the trap and disable it. If the invasion force suddenly loses all of its magic, that will generate a lot of chaos and allow for an easier defense."

"If Sandven hasn't already fallen. What if they are not coming for you, but are just coming for Horn Point?" Dufnall continued to look between them. "You are only assuming this is due to you. Sandven and Lobben have been peaceful, but only just. They've hated our Goddess beyond memory. Perhaps this new prophet simply motivated them to take action."

Henton slid some maps around. "That is also a possibility. We've been wrapped in our own issues for so long it is easy to forget other people have their own problems and conflicts." He studied the maps for a while longer. "I don't know as much about soldiers moving over land, but my guess is, that assuming they had the forces to move on after they secured Norbek, they are likely either already at Alkmaar and moving north, or are closing in on Horn Point."

Walter leaned forward to look at what Henton observed. "They could do both if they have enough soldiers."

"Isa Fields has no external defenses," Douglas said from the far end of the table.

"Save for the distance to get here," Perain offered.

Douglas continued. "If someone makes it across the border and defeats the guardians, we don't have a way to protect the city."

Islet took a deep breath. "We don't have the details from Steph yet. She'll let us know soon if Alkmaar has fallen or not. If not, then they may have decided it was not worth the time and trouble to remove the small garrison, and their aim is really Horn Point." She sat upright. "The border from here is four days away, perhaps three if people march hard." She looked toward Douglas. "While Isa Fields does not have any wall to protect it, it would be best to keep everyone here and let Ista use the guardians to wear down any army that crosses the border." She pushed her chair back without fully addressing Douglas' concerns. *I don't have that answer.* "Henton, Walter, Douglas, Perain, please look at the city and see what defensive options we have. We also need to look for places to secure anyone that is too old or young to fight." She looked at Ryia. "I know you hate it, but please work on improving your students' skill with healing."

"What about me?" Dufnall asked. "I can help."

Islet smiled at him. "You and Kor can use magic. You should join Ryia's students. If things go badly, we'll need all the healers possible."

Ryia stood up. "Come on, Dufnall, Kor. I'll break you of your pointless rituals and show you the truth."

Chapter 25

The sun had dropped low on the horizon by the time Stephenie reached Norbek. To the west, she could see the full mountain range about twenty miles away. The tops of the snow-covered peaks remained obscured by the clouds that had come and gone through the day. With her stop in Alkmaar, and pauses to rest during the flight, most of the day had been spent before she arrived.

The fear of Senzar mages possibly remaining in Norbek drove her to approach the city from the top of the small, lone peak that overlooked the city. She approached covertly by descending with the mountain behind her, using the dark background to hide her flight. Just over two miles from the city walls, but still high enough up the mountain to observe Norbek and the surrounding area, she landed among a copse of small pine trees.

The outer fields, perimeter walls, and buildings occupied a flat section of ground. Obvious signs of fighting easily stood out to her. In one field, soldiers supervised men digging a mass grave for the bodies that they had unceremoniously stacked in a pile. Inside the walls, she noticed several sections where buildings had collapsed. Other sections of the city showed evidence of burning, some still smoldered. From her vantage on the mountainside, she thought she saw more bodies hanging from hastily constructed gallows.

Stephenie ground her teeth, saddened by the wanton need for destruction that so many people seemed so eager to unleash on their neighbors. "Why? Why the need to destroy so much for the benefit of so few?"

She crouched down among the trees to take advantage of the bed of fallen needles. Her head throbbed from all the power she had drawn through her body. Even with the stops, the flight to Norbek had taxed her greatly. While she had not yet started to bleed from her nose, she did not want to push herself further without more rest.

She opened the bag of food that Lami had replenished in Alkmaar and ate a hearty dinner. After finishing her meal, she leaned against the rocks behind her and closed her eyes. It took almost no time before she fell asleep. Her dreams oscillated between Kas coming to her to beg for forgiveness and her bones exploding from drawing too much energy into herself.

She woke feeling drawn and uncertain. *Kas,* she pleaded to the universe and knew the futility of the effort. Until he felt willing to talk more, nothing would change between them.

She looked to the southwest. The sun had dropped below the mountains and illuminated the clouds with a deep crimson. Ista informed her that Islet and the others had attempted to contact her earlier to check on her, but the castle chose not to disturb her sleep. *Thanks,* she said, grateful for being allowed to rest. *I'll reach out in the morning once I know more.*

Stephenie shifted her position, took care of nature's call, and then finished the food and water she had brought with her. Those activities allowed the sun to fully set before she resumed her descent of the mountain.

She flew along the surface, dodging trees and boulders, dropping down vertical cliff faces, and staying concealed until she finally reached the foothills of the mountain. The inhabitants of Norbek had cultivated the surrounding land with fields and pastures, each lined with fieldstone walls. She did not sense anyone within her range outside the city's fortifications, and the sheep appeared unsupervised in a nearby field.

Stephenie flew closer to the city walls, remaining low and staying beside the fieldstone walls to mask her approach. She could see soldiers illuminated from behind as they patrolled the tops of the walls and she brought herself to a stop to look for a pattern in their movement. The men on the wall spent most of their time watching the interior of the city and seldom turned to look out into the dimly lit fields. Quiet conversations reached her ears. Without the noise of an active city, nothing obscured their voices, which highlighted a lack of discipline.

She continued to approach, flew over the defensive ditch, and stopped less than ten feet from the wall. Her mind remained focused on the people not only on the wall, but also those out of her sight patrolling the street next to the wall. A boisterous laugh came from someone just out of her range, drawing the attention of a pair of men to her left.

Power flowed into her, and she rocketed into the air, sailing over the wall to land well inside the city next to a stone building set three-quarters of the way into the ground. Her feet moved the moment she touched the ground, taking her toward the center of the city and away from any of the patrols that had possibly seen her.

Stephenie found it challenging to avoid additional soldiers walking the streets. The narrow gaps between the buildings made it hard for her to separate out the minds of those inside their homes and those keeping the people there. However, she felt the press of time. With the night lasting only four turns of the glass before the sun rose again, she forced herself to take risks she might avoid if any of her friends had been with her. *They can't bitch about what they don't know about,* she mused to Ista, who echoed her sentiment about doing as she pleased. The knowledge that Ista did not always support the wisest decisions was not lost on her, but very few times in her life had she actually been unsupervised. Even once her life fell apart and she fled Cothel to search for her father and brother, Henton, Douglas, and the others had joined her mission, providing companionship and advice. *And someone to watch over me.*

The smell of burnt flesh and charred wood lingering in the air brought her out of her memories. She navigated the twisting streets to one part of the city she observed as having some of the heaviest destruction. Dark stains speckled the ground and buildings. Without a recent rain, she knew the larger spots marked places where some people took their last breath.

She moved closer to a building with a front wall that appeared to have collapsed inward. *A few priests together could do that,* she decided. *Even a single particularly strong and practiced one could.* While she had never spent a lot of time with the holy warriors of Felis in Cothel, she had watched them practice from a distance and had a general idea of the range of power the augmentation devices provided.

She stopped in front of another building. *Now, this one?* Large stones covered the street, scattered about as though the building had exploded outwards. Not just priests, but most people who used magic seemed to exert more power pushing something away instead of pulling it toward themselves. Stephenie did not understand the reason, but assumed the behavior came from a psychological limitation that imposed body mechanics on their mental models. *Too afraid of smashing their own faces by pulling?*

A sigh escaped her lips. The city did not feel like thousands of invaders had taken residence. *The numbers on the walls. The numbers in the streets. This is a holding force.* She moved away from the abandoned part of the city and headed toward the north, hoping to get a sense of how many people currently resided in the buildings that remained standing.

As she walked, her mood soured. "This might have been a waste. What can I confirm by just looking at what's left?" *Do I go on to Horn Point or let the guardian be my eyes?* As a single person, she did not want to face a large force, let alone one lead by possible Senzar mages.

She kicked a stone out of the street and pondered her options. The flight here had drained her, but she had nothing conclusive. *Disturb someone in their home and ask questions?* She shook her head. *They probably didn't see the actual event. Stop a patrol and interrogate them?* Ista responded favorably to the idea of abusing the invaders. Stephenie suspected her castle still felt considerable anger at Stephenie's sire for the destruction he brought to Ista's charges. *Fine, you talked me into it.*

Stephenie moved back toward the center of the city and expanded her search, looking for minds that continued to move longer distances, compared to those that might simply pace about their confined homes. It did not take long before she sensed a squad of eight men approaching from the east.

She stopped walking and put her back against a shop that had a shingle above the door with a painted loaf of bread. The building blocked the light of the mother moon that penetrated the thin cloud layer, concealing her in shadows. Inside the structure, she felt four people. The next building appeared to hold over thirty, though those people remained tightly packed together.

Priest or no priest? She mused as she waited for the men to reach her. *Priest,* she answered herself as one of the eight men stopped and looked in her direction.

"You? What are you doing out of your house?"

Stephenie sensed a trickle of power going into the man that spoke. The other seven ceased their quiet conversation and looked around, finally picking up their priest's focus.

"Step away from the building." The man's accent marked him as not coming from Sandven.

Stephenie opened her mind to sense their emotions, and she felt the confidence of youth and inexperience. *Good,* she told herself, happy to not face a group of seasoned warriors. The short sleep she had on the mountain had allowed her some recovery, but she did not feel at her full capabilities. *And I'm not going to transform here to give me more endurance.*

She stepped forward into the street, allowing the moon to illuminate her, though she kept her body turned to conceal the sword she carried. The group of men continued purposefully in her direction. "It's a girl," one soldier said, and a sudden flare of lust assaulted Stephenie's senses. "My turn to go first."

Stephenie narrowed her eyes as she probed the surface thoughts these men broadcast into the world. She knew exactly what the man intended before he reached for his pant ties. A second man, just as eager, drew his sword and advanced only a step behind the first.

Memories of shame that Ryia fought with surfaced in her mind, and Stephenie's inner rage took over. *I only need one or two alive,* she growled to Ista. Power flowed into her, and the second man's drawn sword flew from his hand. He tried to catch it, but it left his grasp far too quickly. The blade flipped in the air, and Stephenie caught the weapon's handle as she surged forward. The first man looked up, no longer worried about his pants ties. He did not have time to react as she drove the broad, three-foot long blade through his leather armor covered chest up to the crossguard.

The first man's arousal faltered with the severing of his heart. He stumbled back from the force of her blow and looked down at the handle. Stephenie drew her own rapier before he stammered something unintelligible and fell to his knees.

The second man had stopped, stunned into inaction. She felt he might be as young as seventeen. Seeing her move, he raised his hands before him, and her swing cut through both wrists. A gravitation barrier defected the spray of blood back toward him. Her magically enhanced follow-up sliced through the boiled leather armor he wore to protect his abdomen.

The priest shouted something in his own language and Stephenie heard the name Fotia. A wave of energy hit her, sliding her back a foot before she disrupted the field that had formed. He continued shouting as the five remaining soldiers drew their weapons and sprinted forward.

Stephenie formed a gravitational bubble the size of a candlestick and blew a hole through the priest's right shoulder. *You'll live until I have time to question you.*

The second wave of energy hitting her disappeared, and she turned her focus back to the soldiers. The closest, a middle-aged man with a poorly fitting helmet, made a wild swing that she easily deflected with her sword. A gravitational field stopped a thrust from a younger man with three missing fingers on his left hand.

Her rapier, lighter than the swords the soldiers carried, moved faster, and she jammed the tip of her narrow blade past the noseguard of the middle-aged man's helmet. She felt the thrust break through the bone behind his eye and continue into his brain. A mental push sent the man tumbling backwards and freed her blade to target the next rapist.

The man with the missing fingers had physical conditioning, but he fell for a feint that left him open. She sliced through his unprotected shins and then drove her blade deep into his armpit as he fell to one knee.

The priest tried to hit her with another burst of energy, but the focus and power behind the blow had diminished and she simply ignored the effort.

The three remaining soldiers turned and ran. Stephenie used her powers to lift the two swords that the dead and dying soldiers had dropped. She mentally flung them like spears at the two farthest men, striking each in the back, severing one's spine. The other tumbled, bending the sword that extruded from his chest.

The third man, she hit with another candlestick sized blast of gravity that tore through his head, sending blood and brains across the street.

She turned back to the priest, who had his left hand pressed on the bleeding wound that rendered his right arm limp.

"Witch, Fotia will destroy you!"

Stephenie used her mind to fling the blood from her sword and then casually sheathed it. She moved toward the priest, who wore chain armor over his brown robes; his bald head reflecting in the growing light. She knew that soon the sun would rise back over the horizon.

The man continued to move backwards and mumbled things in his own language. She sensed power flowing through the augmentation device into his wounded shoulder.

Stephenie increased her pace and the man stumbled. He turned to look behind himself, and by the time he turned back, Stephenie had closed the distance. Her hand hit him hard in the chest and he started to fall. She grabbed the medallion resting on his sternum and yanked it down and forward. With his backward momentum, the metal chain holding the medallion broke, tearing the flesh at the back of his neck.

He hit the ground with a thud and a gasp of pain. "Please," he begged in Sandvian after he caught his breath.

"You allow these criminals to rape women and girls." The growl in Stephenie's voice vibrated the ground.

"Fotia's hounds follow their instincts," the middle-aged man stammered. Tears glistened on his cheek and the smell of urine rose from a darkened spot on his robes.

Her instincts screamed at her to rip and tear, but Stephenie forced herself back a step. *I'm not here to slaughter people.* However, the memories of these men abusing a woman and then killing her as she pleaded for mercy still lingered in Stephenie's mind and the merciful part of her fell silent. "Rapists die." She began to crush his balls with a gravity field and then stopped.

I need information. The memory of that purpose surfaced within her, and she took a slow breath. "This invasion," she said, forcing calmness into her tone. "What is the purpose? When did the planning start? Who's driving it?"

The holy warrior struggled for a moment, his body in obvious pain, and then he used his left hand to force himself into a sitting position. "I don't know what you want to know."

She narrowed her eyes. Her mind searched outward to look for any other soldiers that might have heard the commotion and would interrupt her. After filtering out the people in their homes, she did not sense anyone approaching.

She turned back to the priest, his fear and terror giving her the confidence to connect her mind to his. He did not even struggle against her intrusion. "How many of you were in the force that took Norbek?" She hoped the questions would spark memories.

The man shook his head and winced. He put his left hand behind his neck to stop the flow of blood down his back, then returned it to the shoulder wound that still bled. "I'm part of the second wave. We followed behind the first wave to relieve those that took Norbek."

"How many?" Stephenie demanded again as she sifted through his incoherent thoughts. She did not speak his language, so she needed to rely on impressions and visual memories instead of his words. *So weak. In Cothel, he would never have gone to battle as a priest or holy warrior of Felis.*

"There were almost eight hundred of us."

"Not eight hundred holy warriors. How many of you?" She narrowed her eyes as he translated the words in his mind for her. "Seventy-five. And how many in the first wave?"

"I ..."

"About three-thousand troops, with over four hundred priests." She raised her eyebrows. Cothel had more overall priests and holy warriors, but that meant a significant percentage of the invasion force had magic. "How long have you been a priest?"

The man opened his eyes wide and his panic grew.

She pushed back on his fear of betraying Fotia. "So, this olive-skinned man calling himself the Prophet of Fotia recruited you, and hundreds like you." Her own eyebrows rose. "Most in the last two years."

"Stop," the man said as more details leaked from his mind.

"Dacian went back to Berl, but his disciple Warner went forward to Horn Point with the initial invasion force."

"Stay out of my thoughts," the man pleaded.

Stephenie snorted, absorbing numerous details of the invasion that he continued to think about. "I'm just tasting the surface thoughts," she snarled. "I don't want to know your depravity." She bit her lip and considered what she had picked up from the man. *Is this Dacian one of Yreka's people or another faction that she said would find out about me? Damn, I'm blind without information.*

"Please, I promise, I'll make sure no other girls are harmed."

Stephenie winced. His statement came with the memory of the murdered woman pleading to live. She broke the connection just as she blew a hole through his forehead. A vacant stare filled his eyes; the former contents of his skull covered the ground behind him. Several moments later, he collapsed onto his side.

Her skin crawled, and she shivered as she tried to push the memory of watching the girl suffer from her mind. Unfortunately, she knew the visuals, sounds, and smells of the event would never truly leave her. *I should know better. I should have learned by now. Damn it.*

Ista offered her comfort and reminded her of her friends waiting for her to return. Stephenie bit her lip and brought her attention back to the chaos she left. Eight dead men littered the street. A sudden fear of the retribution the soldiers would exert on the locals made her consider killing the rest of the invaders, but she felt the trickle of blood in her nose and knew that unless she wanted to transform, her body had reached its reasonable limits.

I can't just slaughter everyone. The pleasure she had experienced with the eight she just killed worried her, but the memories of the remains her sire left for her to clean up grounded her. Before other soldiers could happen upon her, she made her way down the street and toward the rear wall of the city. She would rest on the mountain slope before returning to Ista.

Stephenie stole several blankets, as well as food and water, before she flew out of the city and returned to the mountain. The sun climbed back over the horizon as she reached the copse of trees she had used earlier. This time, her dreams included images of a Senzar horde crawling up the mountain slope like spiders surging from a nest.

Once she gave up on resting, she grabbed the augmentation device she had taken. The raised image of a bald man stared at her. *At one time, I believed the gods would punish me for even handling one of these.* She shook her head at the foolish ignorance she had grown up with and simply made a mental connection with the medallion. She felt the same general sense of intelligence from it as she had from any of the other augmentation devices she had handled, and the device now allowed her to make simple requests. The original makers of the augmentation devices required some magic to use them to avoid common people gaining the power to resist their rulers.

Where are your sources of power? she asked it in the old Denarian tongue. Few people outside of the nobility, or those aligned to one of the southern gods, spoke the Denarian language. She assumed that the same empire that once ruled all the lands around the Sea of Tet had created the traps at the same time. The need to communicate with the technology kept the language relevant and limited the drift in the pronunciation and meaning of the words.

Instead of the augmentation device providing her an answer, a pattern created from an energy field formed above the metal surface. Unlike combat functions, requests for protected information required a challenge and response. She made note of the intricate image just before it faded away. The symbol likely represented a name and not a normal word, but she could not ignore the Denarian influences in the mark. She fixed the image in her mind and added a small accent mark to the edge of the symbol and projected the visual in her mind to the device.

The augmentation device responded immediately, not with words, but with an understanding that the closest relay transmitted its power from the southwest. Using a mental model of the maps she had reviewed, she felt the relay sat about seventy miles to the southwest. This device also had entangled connections to two another relays, the second one around one hundred-and-fifty-miles due west. The third one lay almost two-hundred-and-sixty-miles to the southwest. "Berl for certain, and Kutenveld for the second," she mumbled, trying to recall the cities in Lobben. She mused on the third one and could not decide if the relay was in Wetzen or Vinkeg. "Doesn't matter," she admitted. If she needed to go that far south, she could isolate that relay when she got closer.

She reached out to Ista and confirmed the guardians at Alkmaar, Gaffel, and Norbek had arrived. The one headed to Horn Point proceeded slower because of the increase of soldiers along the road. *What's the status of each?* Stephenie waited as Ista relayed the concepts and visuals from the guardians' point of view. *Alkmaar has people already heading north, but still no invaders. Gaffel is heavily occupied.* The guardian at Norbek had found a perch further up the mountain slope. All four of them could only observe from afar.

Thank you, Ista. Please connect me to Islet. Stephenie gathered her stolen blankets and supplies while she waited. *When I get back, I'm going to always have a pack of supplies ready. I've grown too complacent.* With Islet still not having made contact, Stephenie lifted into the air and flew north in a manner that would conceal her presence from anyone in Norbek.

On the other side of the peak, she rose higher into the air, increased her speed, and headed directly toward Isa Fields. If she flew over the top of the mountains instead of going back through Alkmaar and the border camp, she could reduce the total distance to get home.

"Steph," Islet said after Stephenie had traveled nearly forty miles. "Sorry, we were in the war room—map room—discussing options."

Stephenie nodded her head as she flew into a thick cloud. The moisture condensed on her face and hair as she rose higher. She used her mental awareness of the energy potentials around her to avoid hitting any mountain peaks. *I'm heading home,* she told Islet. *I'm pretty sure there are at least three Senzar responsible for the invasion.*

"Damn," Islet swore. Stephenie could see the others in the room as they watched Islet holding the stone in front of her. "I knew it was only time before they came for us."

Stephenie bit her lip. *They recruited many older people as priests. I believe Fotia's council normally focuses on younger kids like the priests did in Cothel. These new priests appeared to have only been trained to go against regular people and very weakly skilled witches and warlocks. Not against us. Their mission was always to siege Horn Point.* She angled down, sensing the ground had dropped away as she came over a ridge. However, the light grey haze of the cloud remained the only thing she saw. *There is a third and fourth wave of soldiers coming out of Berl. The second-wave priest I killed thought he was supposed to go to Alkmaar and take that to avoid anyone coming from behind them. However, all the other activity is concentrated to the south.*

"Do you think this is just about someone's personal power play to take over Sandven?" Islet lifted a glass of wine to her mouth and drank more than a sip. "Perhaps it has nothing to do with us. Uncle had a Senzar mage ruling Kynto from the shadows for years. That had nothing to do with us. Could that be the same here?"

Dufnall looked expectantly at Islet. "Does she know anything about Ivan? Has Horn Point fallen?"

She had already considered that perhaps these Senzar might just be later generation people looking to grow their personal power, but instinct told her a deeper motivation drove this invasion. *Not sure on Horn Point. The guardian is still heading there. Gaffel has probably two or three hundred soldiers occupying the town. The guardian can't get close enough to even know if the original inhabitants still live. The Lobben soldiers are targeting anyone with a hint of magic. They definitely believe it's a holy war.* She emerged from a cloud and saw pockets of green spread through the mountain valley below her. *But that doesn't mean they won't eventually come for us, and perhaps they just took Sandven because they wanted to secure the supply lines and we are the actual target.*

Islet nodded her head in understanding. "I would love to have spies in all those locations with communication stones."

If only we had enough spares to risk them. We sent two to Cothel. She reached out instinctively and sensed both of the stones moving further away from her. *Please make it to Josh,* she told herself.

"Stephenie doesn't know about Horn Point," Islet told Dufnall, who appeared to have grown impatient.

Even if this has nothing to do with us, if we can remove the power of these priests by turning off the trap, then that could give Ivan a fighting chance. It sounded like four hundred holy warriors and another twenty-five hundred soldiers had moved on from Norbek. Assuming some of them have remained behind in Gaffel, and along the road, there are still likely two thousand people, along with a couple of Senzar, going against Horn Point. Stephenie shifted to the right and lifted herself higher to avoid the next peak along the mountain range. *I have an augmentation device and know where three relays are. I'm hoping we can locate the trap quickly. Is it too soon to ask if Kas has found a location yet?*

"I'm afraid so. He's in the library looking, but he said there is not much beyond the trap being in the mountain range."

Understood. I'll be home before dinner. Without waiting for a reply, she closed the connection. *Damn it, Caridelis, you were supposed to prepare me for the Senzar.* She knew enough to not even imagine insulting or threatening a dragon for fear they would later read her mind and learn of the slight. *I hope you're still alive. I could use your help.*

Chapter 26

The journey back to Isa Fields left Stephenie bleeding from her nose. She stopped several times, but her body had not been able to fully recover since the initial flight. Islet had dinner ready for her, and after she had cleaned herself up, everyone gathered in the dining room. Everyone saw the weariness in her and allowed her to sit and begin to eat before asking her questions.

"To start with," Stephenie offered, her mouth full of roasted meat. "The guardian I sent to Alkmaar has patrolled around the southern side of the city, checking the approach from the road. I think all of Ivan's soldiers are already on their way north. I'm not sure how many residents will decide to stick it out, but most of them left with the soldiers." She swallowed and then added more food to her mouth. "Regarding Gaffel, Lobben overran the town. Right now, the troops appear fixed and not planning to move. Based on guardian's limited scouting, I think they have at least two hundred soldiers on station in the town built to support less than a hundred."

"What of Horn Point?" Dufnall asked. "Forgive my insistence, but I worry over my brother."

Stephenie nodded her head. "The guardian arrived. The only real defensive walls are around the castle. We can't get a close look, but the city appears to have surrendered to the Lobben forces. We've not detected any significant conflicts occurring, so right now, most of the people appear unmolested."

Dufnall shook his head. "Could Ivan's soldiers have retreated to another position?"

Stephenie shrugged. "The guardian's only been able to scout a little of the area. Are there other defenses nearby they would have retreated to?"

Dufnall looked at the plate of food in front of him. "No. Our internal fighting over the years generally left the populations alone. The castle is the only real defensive position."

"It is not your fault," Kor said.

"Does Horn Point's castle still hold?" Henton asked. "Were you able to get the guardian close enough to see that?"

Stephenie swallowed. *It is a good thing my magic seems to always burn off what I eat and more.* She grabbed the glass of wine and drank it all to wash down the food. "I had it go into the gulf and approach from underwater. Fortunately, the castle is close to the shore." She set the glass down. "It's surrounded by soldiers." She confirmed the current situation had not changed with Ista. "So far, no significant fighting has occurred at the castle. The castle is definitely under siege. That may be a good sign. Perhaps they might be looking for specific terms of surrender. They might not want to actually kill him."

"I thought these bastards were religious fanatics," Ryia said. "Since Ivan's also a mage, that won't sit well with them."

Dufnall swallowed, though he had yet to eat anything. "Is there anything we can do to help my brother?"

Stephenie pursed her lips and glanced at Kas, who had joined them and sat on her right as normal. "Any breakthroughs?" She asked in Dalish.

"No. The library's references on the traps are old and incomplete."

She turned back to Dufnall. "The best thing we can do is try to disable the trap, which will remove the magic from all of Fotia's priests. Hopefully, we can cause a loss of morale and many of the soldiers might abandon their commanders. I believe many of them are green."

"How long will that take?" Kor asked. "I can't see Ivan holding out against hundreds of their holy warriors for many days, let alone weeks or months. Those that can take from the Goddess are not an organized group. Ivan likely only has a few dozen with the ability in the castle. Once summer passes, no one will have the stomach to sit in siege."

"I implore you to send your guardians," Dufnall begged from his seat. "If they are as powerful as you claim, as we've seen, you could route this invasion."

Stephenie sat back. "I understand your need. I really do, and we will help you and your people, but there are mages involved with this effort that are incredibly powerful. I suspect at least three, but there could be more."

Dufnall bristled. "You believe these are the people you defeated in your homeland. With the power of this Ista, how can they be a threat? Are they that dangerous?"

Stephenie held Dufnall's angry gaze. "These are people who have not forgotten how magic works. They are people used to ruling others and see nothing wrong with slavery and throwing away lives. It's possible they could destroy the guardians. The amount of energy the Senzar can leverage varies, but their advantage is their education." She softened her tone. "These people might have no ties to the armies we already defeated. The Senzar seem somewhat fragmented as a group. We know of at least some who acted as shadow rulers for decades. It's likely others currently rule countries around Tet right now."

"I still don't understand why you won't send the guardians." Dufnall tossed his napkin on his full plate.

"Because this invasion could be a lot of different things. It could be what it appears, Lobben wanting to take over Sandven. They could also intend it to draw me out to see what I'm capable of. Or it could be to pull away my defenses so that Senzar invaders can reach Isa Fields and kill everyone here." She sighed and leaned forward. "Before I arrived, a large portion of the guardians were destroyed. While there seems to be a lot of them, there are not that many for the size of the country, and they are not as powerful the further they get from Ista. I will go south personally and attempt to rout the Lobben army. We can hope that Ivan resists the siege, and whoever is behind this wants the castle more than a fast victory."

Henton cleared his throat. "Could Ivan get aid from the jarls south of Horn Point? There are a lot more people living in the south. I recall Cilwir being twice the size of Horn Point. Plus, the maps show at least four other major cities."

Dufnall shook his head. "I don't know who was in Horn Point at the time of the invasion. Typically, the jarls will make a trip to see Ivan during the summer, but if there was enough warning, many of them probably fled. Some would support Ivan, others would be happy to see him fall. However, those that support him might not want to risk exposing themselves to attack from those that don't."

He put his hands to his head and leaned his elbows against the table. "I apologize for the demands. If my people are not likely to fight for Ivan, I should not expect it of you, who are still waiting for basic trade to be allowed again."

Stephenie felt his anguish. "I will not abandon your people, but we will need to hope that your people can hold out long enough for what I can do to make a difference."

"How long?" Kor asked.

"I don't know. Finding the trap will require that I visit at least one or two of the temples of Fotia to access the relays—the big metal statues. From those, I can get a direction and distance to the trap."

"Assuming they work the same as the other relays," Henton said. "And if they are like Felis' relays, they are huge, and you won't be able to move them to triangulate the trap's position."

Douglas set his glass down. He had finished three glasses of wine already. "I agree with Henton. It won't be like going against Mertor's priests. You found that trap only because those assassin-based priests had a mobile relay that we could carry with us."

The tension had not diminished in the room. Henton's normally restrained emotions radiated from him. Douglas broadcast a general sense of disapproval. Walter feared for his wife. Only Kas, Islet, and Ryia had their emotions under control, and each for different reasons.

"If anyone has a better option, I welcome the suggestion. However, I believe there is at least one Senzar mage in Horn Point leading the armies, probably two. This Prophet has two disciples of foreign origin that are supposed to be there. The priest I questioned in Norbek had heard that Dacian, Fotia's Prophet, returned to Berl. If any of these people are as skilled or as powerful as Yreka—"

"Then they could kill you," Islet said, finally speaking up.

Stephenie nodded her head. She looked at a loaf of bread sitting within arm's reach; the aroma made her mouth water, and she decided she could eat a little more. She grabbed the loaf and tore off the end. "I need a couple days, perhaps more, to recover. Then I will fly to Berl. There is a relay there. Perhaps the trap is close and I can get a solid fix on it. If not, I'll at least know the direction and can fly to the next closest relay."

Henton leaned forward. "That is over two hundred miles, even going directly there. The journey to Norbek wore you out." He used a hand to indicate her current appearance. "You're ready to collapse. Berl is further."

"I know."

"You'll need backup," he said.

"You'll need the staff," Ryia added, the steel capped weapon always by her side. "You might encounter the Senzar. Assuming they are not as powerful as Yreka, it might beat them. Henton killed two of Yreka's underlings with it when I lost my hand." She held Stephenie's gaze and did not look down at the appendage that had been painfully regrown over six months.

"I won't take your staff," Stephenie said.

"Then take me with you," Ryia countered. "You can't do everything alone."

"I'll make your third," Henton said. "Perhaps that crossbow can deal with one or two of them. You weren't able to deflect the bolt, and you looked like crap after getting hit."

Stephenie shifted her gaze back and forth between the two of them. Their determination evident to everyone. "Doesn't mean they don't know something that I don't."

"You need support," Henton countered.

Islet set down her fork and pushed her still full plate away from her. "The Lobben forces are not currently coming north. If the Senzar threat is in Horn Point, even if some troops start north, we should be able to deal with them. Take Henton and Ryia with you. They can help protect you better than anyone else. We'll continue to make preparation here just in case."

Stephenie chewed on the crusty bread and then set what she still held in her hand down on her plate. "Very well." She smiled at them. "In truth, I would like the company."

"How will you get there with the two of them?" Dufnall asked. "There isn't enough snow for sleds and carts won't make it over the rough ground. Do any of you even speak the language?"

"We'll fly," Stephenie responded. "With the extra weight, I imagine it will take us a couple more days to make Berl, but it will be faster than hiking through the back country. I can't predict anything beyond that because I won't know what the situation will be there." She pushed her chair back without answering the second question. "I'm going to get some rest and see how I feel in a day or two." She rose to her feet. The uncertainty of this plan weighing heavily on her, and even Ista's sense of confidence did not compensate for it.

Stephenie sat in the chair in her bedroom. Kas stood near the door. "Do you think it is wise to attempt to destroy the trap with just the three of you? The effort to deal with Mertor nearly resulted in everyone's death and there were not any Senzar present."

"Now you don't want me destroying the trap?" Stephenie had not wanted the anger to fill her voice, but she could not contain it. "I'm doing what you've been asking me to do for the last three years."

Kas crossed his arms. "Is that why you are doing this? To appease me?"

"I'm doing it for many reasons." She grabbed the bowl of dried lavender from the side table and hurled it into the fireplace, breaking the bowl. Islet had suggested the fragrant aroma might relax her, but it only succeeded in making her angry. "I can't help but think the invasion has something to do with me. I've got no proof, but if it does, then all those dead people are my fault." She stood up. "We need Sandven to be a friendly country, not occupied by someone ruled by men who take pleasure in burning people with magic." She took a step toward him. "I'm doing it because I want you to love me, and this seems to be the only thing you care about."

Kas straightened. "If you think this is the only thing I care about, then you do not really know me." He shook his head. "Sacrificing yourself will not fix things between us."

"Thanks for the confidence in my ability. Thanks for believing in me."

"Your dragon friend has not kept her promise to train you. I lacked any ability to bridge the gap to fight people with that skill and power. The library has very little meaningful details. I am terrified of what will come." He threw his hands into the air. "This is pointless. You never listen to my advice."

"Bullshit. I listen all the time. I consider everything you say. Sometimes I'm just not able to do what you want."

Kas shook his head. "I need to step away before I say something regrettable. If you need me, I am sure Ista will tell you where to find me." He turned, opened the door, walked out, and slammed it behind him.

She let the tears fall down her face and did not bother moving. *This is another reason I need to go. At least we won't be fighting.*

Five days later, Stephenie, Ryia, and Henton gathered early in the morning to depart for Berl. Islet, Walter, and Dufnall rose early to see them off.

"I expect at least a hundred people will arrive in Isa Fields in the next day or two, then another four to five hundred over the following days," Stephenie said. She had dispatched another guardian to monitor the progress of the people who left Alkmaar. "They appear to have brought a fair amount of supplies, but I fear it won't be enough to get them through the winter. The guardian watching Alkmaar has seen less than fifty people remaining."

"That is one way to grow our population," Walter said. He seemed to realize the statement fell flat as soon as it left his mouth. "What I mean is those coming can hopefully help with some things we've not been able to get to. If they want to leave once this is over, we won't hold them."

Stephenie allowed the silence to hang in the air for several seconds before she spoke. "Use the speaking room to communicate with Ista. I've asked her to be more active in telling you things."

Islet nodded her head. "Of course." She moved forward and hugged Stephenie. "Come back to us. All of you."

"Don't get your royal self into a knot," Ryia said. "We'll be back."

"Make sure Perain continues to work with the dogs," Stephenie said. "And keep Hugo alive. I want him to know that we've killed his god."

Stephenie looked at the main doors of the castle, but Kas had not yet come to see her off. She forbade Ista from telling her anything about Kas' location, and the castle so far had honored the request. She bit her lip and turned to Henton and Ryia. "Ready?"

They both nodded their heads.

Stephenie looked back as the castle's door opened and Kas emerged. He came down the steps and approached. "I could not determine any specific location for the trap. But the few references I did find indicated it might be near a series of old mountain rooms and passages. The city of Berl is a likely candidate."

Stephenie put her arms around him and hugged him. "Thank you."

He squeezed her back. "Please be safe."

Stephenie nodded her head. "We will be." She stepped back, feeling about to cry. She wrapped their lower bodies and the packs in a gravity field, and then turned back to Walter, Islet, Dufnall, and Kas. "I'll make sure you stay aware of our progress, but don't expect anything for at least three or four days."

"Love you, Sis."

Stephenie lifted the three of them into the air. She glanced at Kas, but he seemed hesitant and uncertain. To avoid drawing out their leaving, she turned slowly away from the castle and those that had gathered to see her off, and then continued to rise before gaining speed.

Chapter 27

Dacian's conversations with Andre had continued to get more disconcerting over the prior eight days. Ever since Fotia's army arrived at Horn Point, he suspected Andre had found a different source of information. Andre had tried to hide his knowledge of events taking place hundreds of miles to the east, but Dacian felt certain that Andre had the knowledge.

"Warner, how are things going?"

His cousin, reporting from within a building near the outskirts of Horn Point, frowned. "The nobles are eager to take the castle. They are certain Ivan does not have any meaningful defense and they are not listening to me or Vikram."

"Do they not understand that Fotia has commanded that Ivan is converted to Fotia's fold? He is not to be killed."

Warner snorted. "They are too busy trying to enrich themselves. Two of them rampaged through a section of the city they were supposed to contain and instead executed over a hundred people, calling them followers of Elrin. Then they had their soldiers take anything of value in those homes and businesses."

Dacian sunk into his chair. "Not even fear of Fotia will keep these people in line."

"Your doctrine is a little too forgiving. Far more so than what Andre and the council had preached for years. They claim their interpretation of Fotia's scriptures is more historically correct." Warner shook his head. "And many of the priests seem to agree, since they are also benefitting. Some of the ones we recruited are still under our influence, but they are tempted by personal wealth. They grew up with nothing and are now part of the magical class."

"Damn. This whole endeavor is falling apart."

"I hate to say it, but I wish you were here."

"I have not found a cypher yet and haven't figured out his plans for Ista." He sighed. "I'm still certain Andre has someone with a communication stone providing him information. Have you or Vikram found anyone that might have a way to send him the information? Andre's been more coy these last couple of days, but I'm certain he is getting reports from someone other than me."

Warner waved someone forward and Vikram came into view. "You find anyone suspicious?" He asked the darker man.

Vikram shook his head. "Nothing for certain. A couple of the more difficult nobles have disagreed more than normal. Acting like they have a different set of orders than what we've been providing. I've sensed them wanting to dismiss us and do their own thing, which has been to take the castle and forget the siege."

"If they do, it means they won't feel the need to protect the supply lines, and that will reduce the troops on the roads even further."

Warner nodded his head. "The city fell too easily. We should have tried to reduce the number of soldiers more."

Dacian snorted at that comment. "You know I tried."

Warner continued. "They left less than a third of the people we told them they should station on the roads. If your northern queen wanted to come south, she'd find it easy enough to do so."

"I need to report to Andre shortly." Dacian looked down at his left hand. White lines from numerous cuts covered his palm. "I am eager to be done with this."

"I am as …" Warner suddenly looked confused, as if he did not remember where he sat and that he had been talking. A loud impact occurred out of Dacian's view. Warner momentarily regained his composure. "Vikram!" Warner spun around and the connection dropped.

Dacian tried to hang on to the mental image, but everything had happened so quickly, and the room had almost no illumination. *Was that blood splattered on Warner's face? Who could have attacked them?*

Several thoughts ran through his mind, including Stephenie coming south to protect Horn Point.

Dacian commanded the stone to reestablish communication, but no one activated the corresponding stone. He tried again multiple times and then switched to trying to connect to the stone Vikram carried. Neither answered. He used his stone to determine the distance and direction of the other stones. They both resided in the same location and did not appear to be moving.

"Damn it." He ordered the stone to connect with his grandfather, though it was not at one of his specified times. Despite multiple attempts, he received no response.

Dacian threw a pewter water mug across the room and it crumpled against the wall. "If someone killed my cousins ..." He could not push aside the fear that they had been executed. *The look on Warner's face. Like someone had addled his thoughts.* Given his own tendency to manipulate people's minds, it did not fall outside of reason that someone with the skill could have done something similar to his cousins. Although they were only eighth generation, and near the last generations to be considered part of a household, they had far more power and skill than most. *Who has both the skill and motivation to kill them?*

To kill a protected member of any household carried significant repercussions. Stephenie has done so with at least two, if not four, people before. Does she know of us? He needed to inform his grandfather, but the next designated time for contact was not for two more days. *It is time Grandfather told me who she really is.* He only hoped his grandfather actually knew.

Too many possibilities existed. "Damn it." He stood up, hid his communication stone back in the crack in the wall. Already late for his meeting with Andre, he cut his palm and then wrapped it up as he headed to meet with the High Council Member. His mind shifted to the next problem. He would no longer be able to provide Andre accurate predictions and information on the battle unless one, or both, of his cousins actually survived.

Dacian walked into the main temple and then into the back rooms to the council chambers. He found it hard to concentrate as he moved through the hall and stepped into the large chamber with a series of tables pushed together. Five other men beyond Andre sat around the table. Kev, Andre's spy, stood near the far wall with a woman servant. He ignored both of them as insignificant.

He tried to shake the weight off his mind as he tried to expand his awareness around the room, but his focus continued to return to Andre. *How is he in my head?* Dacian closed down his thoughts, trying to protect them from whatever device the High Council Member might be using.

"Prophet," Andre said from where he sat at the head of the table. "Please sit and dine with us. The other council members here would like to hear what you have to say."

A servant he had not noticed approached from his left and held out a tray with a crystal glass filled with wine. Dacian tried to shake his head to decline the invitation, but the servant held the tray so that it blocked Dacian's path. He took the glass. "Thank you," he mumbled, but had no intention of drinking the contents. *I need to get clear of this room.*

"Please sit," Andre repeated.

Dacian focused on Andre and doubled his efforts to clear his muddled thoughts. *If you somehow ordered the deaths of my cousins.*

"Please, eat. We have decided to have a feast."

Dacian forced a smile and sat. He could not remember why he wanted to leave the room. *Something is wrong,* he tried to remind himself before he forgot again. *I need to get out of here.* "I am fasting to remain pure for Fotia's messages," he managed to say, and then tried to turn away, but found he could not look away from the man at the head of the table.

Andre raised an eyebrow, as if to ask if that could be true based on Dacian's extra weight. "What news does Fotia send to us?"

"The same. It is imperative that Ivan join our cause. We need to convince him of the merits of Fotia's teachings."

Andre nodded his head. "Please look over the reports we have received from the various nobles on the front. There is a request to send a force from Gaffel to Alkmaar."

Dacian still tried to shake the sense of detachment that filled his mind. He took the stack of papers from the servant who held them out on a platter, and then Dacian placed them on the table before him. The words on the page seemed dense and written in a strange language, though the symbols looked familiar. He flipped through several pages. He could not focus on the words, almost as though he had forgotten how to read. *I need to get out of here,* he repeated to himself. Then a memory surfaced as he noticed the slight moisture on the parchment. *Bastard.*

He fought against the pressure on his mind, but he found it impossible to draw power into himself. A moment later, another person seemed to appear from out of nowhere right next to him. *They are blocking my attention.* He tried to slow his breathing and pull energy into himself. The new man grabbed him around the neck and forced open his mouth. Another person appeared from a space he had ignored and poured the glass of wine into his mouth. Dacian struggled, but he could not stop the men.

Eventually they released him, and he coughed and spit out as much of the wine as he could. However, he felt a numbness spreading from his gut. A shiver spread through his body. The pressure eased from his mind and suddenly he noticed yet another man standing in the room. The man had green eyes and a narrow jaw that marked him as an outsider. His left hand resting on the handle of a sword with a ruby in the pummel.

"Dacian, I would suggest not fighting against the poison." The man's voice was calm, and he spoke in Denarian with an accent that marked him from the distant south. "It's not intended to kill you, just make you manageable. Our friends have goals that exceed your own, and I intend for them to achieve them."

"Well said, Kamari." Andre leaned back in his chair. "If Fotia's Faithful are not yet taking the castle in Horn Point, please tell them to begin right away."

Dacian felt his heart sink. The man could only be a kiwa, an outcast assassin hired by one of the families. He knew from Andre's command to start the assault that there had to be at least one more in Horn Point. *They killed my cousins.*

Chapter 28

The sky remained mostly clear as Stephenie flew Henton and Ryia over the mountains. She navigated around the tallest peaks instead of going over them, as she found that it became harder to breathe if they got too high and she did not want to subject her friends to that struggle. The highest peaks in Ista towered above everything else, and Stephenie herself had not attempted to fly to them, even on her solo journeys. Fortunately, those formidable mountains lay west of her intended path.

After about twenty miles of travel, she found a sheltered valley and set them down near a melting snowfield. Enough small woody growth filled the valley, and they quickly gathered a pile of material to create a fire.

"You know this is not your fault," Henton said after knocking the ice from his boots to sit down on a rock five feet away. "Even if the Senzar have invaded because of us, it is still not your fault."

Stephenie let out the breath she had been holding. "I've been wondering how many of these bastards have been in the north for decades, or even more. That sixth-generation piece of shit secretly ruled my uncle's country. He wasn't directly tied to the Senzar invasion, just enjoyed all the benefits of being an ultra-powerful, long lived, sadistic pig among all the normal people."

"Yvima was a bastard," Henton agreed.

Ryia warmed her hands over the fire. "I never had to deal with that one, but obviously you survived him."

"Kynto and my uncle did not survive his death," Stephenie countered, leaning over with her elbows on her knees. "How many people did my uncle's mercenaries kill when they saw his weakness and then took over his country? My actions triggered all of that. My decisions."

Henton shook his head. "And if you hadn't stolen Cothel's money back? Duke Burdger, or his son, would have ruled Cothel. If not them, it definitely would not have been your brother."

Stephenie reached out and sensed the location of the communication stones on their way to Cothel and breathed some relief. She continued to look at her hands. *But could I have made other decisions to have protected Josh without so many dying?*

"Some people just need to die," Ryia said. "Once they do certain things, they deserve what they get."

Stephenie looked up. The anger and hate Ryia still felt drove her to continue to improve her ability to fight. Unfortunately for Ryia, the people that deserved her vengeance had already been killed by Ryia's friends. "There are many that do, but what happens when justice for those that were wronged results in suffering for others that are innocent? What happens when the result of justice is worse than leaving it alone? Does righteousness keep the executioner from having any guilt? Does burning down a city to warm people on a cold night make sense?"

Henton shrugged. "You do what you can with what you know. If you had blankets you could give a city full of freezing people, and chose to burn everything down instead, then that's wrong. But if the only choice—that you knew at the time—was to burn it or everyone would freeze to death anyway, then burn it and try to figure out the next step the next day." He pulled a pouch of berries out of his backpack that sat next to him and tossed it to her. "But you know this already."

She caught the food and slowly nodded her head.

"This plan is crazy, isn't it?" Ryia asked abruptly. "I mean, the only reason you found Mertor's trap was the stupid priests didn't think about leaving an obvious trail because they were so isolated. What are the chances these Fotia morons are that stupid?"

Stephenie appreciated Ryia's change of topic, but it did not remove her sense of despair. She looked down at the food, dumped a handful of the tart berries into her hand, and then tossed them into her mouth. "I should have thought to put spies in the cities of our southern neighbors. My father would have done it. I've not thought enough about what it takes to run a country."

"Don't start," Henton snapped. "Islet had been an actual queen for years, and she didn't think to do that either. More importantly, we didn't have the people to send. Let's just deal with what's before us." He pulled some more food from his pack and removed the cloth from around a baked pastie. "In fact, let's change the topic completely. When this is over, I want you to consider buying some long ships and running them during the summer for fishing along the eastern shore. You named me Duke of the Waves. I want to own the title."

She let a small laugh escape her lips and then nodded her head. "I don't like eating fish, but since the rest of you all do, we can start building some roundhouses close to where the border road bends to the west. It's only ten miles from the bend to the shore and clearing a road there won't be too much work."

"I like the plan," Henton said, a wide grin on his face.

"Speaking of plans," Ryia said. "How are we going to deal with a bunch of hostile people in Berl? None of us speak their language, though Perain said most of them will speak Sandvian." Ryia looked at Henton's head. "And the crazy priests there shave their heads. I'd look like shit if you take my hair."

Stephenie raised a hand to Henton. "I didn't change my hair before. I'm not doing it now." She frowned slightly. "Though I could trim it. It's definitely a lot more work now that it's in the middle of my back."

"I didn't say anything," Henton responded. "Ryia brought it up."

"Do they have rules that only bald heads can enter their temples?" Ryia moved away from the fire and sat down next to Stephenie. "I could wait outside to make sure no one comes in while you ask the relay where the trap is."

Stephenie reached over to her own backpack and dug around until she pulled out a fur hat. "Even our fully haired northern friends wear hats in the summer on cool days. I imagine it's colder if you don't have hair. We should be able to cover up our heads to move around the city."

"And the temples?" Ryia's blue eyes revealed her skepticism.

"I doubt they would allow me to walk up to their sacred altar and put my hands on the relay, bald or not. We'll have to sneak in during the night, get a sighting, and then hope we can find where the trap's hiding."

"I'm going to put a dozen gold crowns on us getting caught and chased out of the temple." Ryia pulled out a small journal. "Any takers?" She looked up. "Come on, it's worth the bet."

"Ryia," Henton said, his disapproval heavy in his voice. "We aren't going to bet on how this mission is going to go."

She frowned at him. "I just want a record of who's right and who's wrong. What's it to you if I make a little coin while I'm at it?"

"Really?" Stephenie asked. "You could go into the treasury room and take any money you need at any time. Not that any of us have any need for the money when we're in Ista."

Ryia shook her head. "How did you think I planned to pay for any losses?" She used her stick of charcoal to make some marks in her journal. "Is that twenty crowns for each of you?"

Stephenie laughed. "No, because I'm pretty certain you're more likely to be correct than wrong. I don't like one-to-one odds. Give me four to one and I'll take your bet."

"Fine, four to one, but you know I'm still going to win." Ryia smiled at the two of them. "Now, what odds do you want on someone spitting in whatever food we order when we are in Berl?"

After the fire burned down, Stephenie flew them another twenty miles, setting down in one of the mountain passes that could potentially allow east and west travel through the World's Backbone. The protected valleys had a deeper snowpack near the peaks and thicker tree and vegetation cover on the lower slopes. The campsite sat on the Ista side of the border, but Stephenie would easily take them into Lobben the next day.

They set up the tent two hundred feet from a crystal-clear river that flowed west and would eventually end up in the lowlands. A family of white foxes watched them as they built a fire and prepared their dinner. The curiosity of the two pups brought them within only a few feet of Henton.

The foxes eventually lost interest and departed after Stephenie, Henton, and Ryia consumed the meal that Ryia prepared. Stephenie sensed a bear at the very edge of her range, but so far, it showed no interest in their campsite. No other people, just the peacefulness of nature.

Tired from the effort of keeping the others aloft, warm, and protected from the wind, Stephenie climbed into the tent early and fell into an uneasy sleep. Dreams of Kas and a desperate sense of longing filled her mind.

She awoke before the sun had set for the night and climbed out from under the blankets. Neither of the others had slept yet. As she emerged from the tent, Ista sensed her wakefulness and immediately informed her that the Lobben soldiers had taken Horn Point castle. The priests and holy warriors of Fotia easily overwhelmed the defenders. Ista did not know the fate of anyone inside the castle, but many soldiers appeared to die when the invaders breached the walls.

Damn it. Keep an eye on Gaffel and monitor for any change. There is nothing we can do for Horn Point at the moment. Hopefully, Ivan lives. We should wait to tell Dufnall and Islet until we have confirmation. Ista agreed.

The futility of this mission weighed her down and she considered simply returning to Isa Fields. She heard Ryia and Henton talking. However, Ryia noticed the change in Stephenie's mental activity and their conversation stopped. Wanting to give them their privacy, Stephenie had no intension of inquiring about the topic.

Ryia and Henton, sitting across from each other by the fire, looked at her with a questioning gaze. A trail of smoke blew toward the northeast passing between the two of them. She nodded to them both, not having the energy to tell them that this effort might be too late to matter.

She took care of nature's call, and then, unable to sleep more, headed the two hundred feet from the camp to look at the river. The water in this mostly flat section of the valley had dug a shallow channel no more than three feet deep. However, the fast-moving water had washed all but the largest of boulders downstream, leaving a relatively smooth riverbed.

She drew power into herself for warmth. After staring at the river for a long time, she shed her clothing, tossing them in the general direction of a lichen covered rock. *Transform without fire,* she instructed herself, wanting to put the probable death of Ivan and those in the castle from her. Power continued to flow into her, and she again concentrated the energy into her hands. The pain built, and she relished the punishment for not being able to stop Lobben. After a moment, she focused on controlling the amount of energy flowing into her body. *There's a tipping point,* she told herself. *Just enough to trigger the change, but no more.*

She sensed Ryia and Henton approaching her from behind. She ignored them and concentrated on slowing the draw of energy as she approached the transition point. The pain ate away at her composure, but pain filled her so often that she forced herself to simply let it exist in her mind.

The tips of her fingers elongated as the flesh of her hands shrunk. No trace of wasted energy escaped the scaly skin. She allowed more energy into herself as the change cascaded up her arms, leaving her feeling smaller and emaciated. Her face changed at the same time her chest and upper body narrowed. Muscles moved locations, their attachments no longer in the same place. *Wings,* she pleaded, but a hollow feeling let her know nothing more than a pair of small bony protrusion formed on her back as the transformation raced down her rear and legs, ending with taloned toes.

"Is everything alright," Henton asked. Stephenie could hear the concern for her in his voice.

She nodded her head, which had small red horns above and behind her ears that protruded an inch beyond the surface of her hair. She had felt the heat of the energy that escaped from her back and legs. "I've been trying to not burn away all my clothing."

"That change was so smooth and controlled," Ryia said. "I barely saw any flames, and you didn't even growl or curse."

Stephenie turned to face them. Her chest was flat with no hint of breasts. She thought she looked less human than some of her prior transformations; however, her current form was obviously designed to walk upright on two legs and not on four feet. "Do I look worse than normal?"

Henton started to talk, but Ryia beat him to it. "No. Are you still trying to decide what this form is supposed to look like? It's always stunning regardless of how you create it."

Stephenie snorted. Her reptilian nose was now embedded in her upper jaw that extended outward with her pointed lower jaw. "Is it wrong to want to become one of them?" The sound of her voice had changed as her tongue and throat had elongated. *At least then, I would die before the rest of my dragon kind and not have to watch them wither away.*

Ryia closed the distance to her. "You need more flesh. You're now my height." Ryia carefully ran her fingers down Stephenie's scaled arm. "But your scales are so smooth."

Stephenie looked over at Henton. She could tell his appreciation for her current appearance did not reach the same level of approval as Ryia.

"You do look very thin."

She nodded her head. "I feel empty. I could eat a whole deer at this point."

"Then go hunting," Ryia said. "You've burned a lot of energy flying us around today. And you'll need to do it again tomorrow and the next day and the next."

She patted Ryia's hand, careful to not scratch her friend with her sharp claws. "Thanks for reminding me. I had forgotten how far we needed to go." She smiled to take the bite out of her sarcasm, but then feared the rows of pointed teeth might have frightened Ryia. "I think I will hunt."

"Bring something tasty back for us," Henton said. "I'll take your clothes back to camp."

She closed her green reptilian eyes. "I've told Ista to conceal this until we know more, but Lobben took Horn Point castle this evening. I fear Ivan might be dead."

Henton's disappointment showed in his shoulders. "Damn it."

"If either of you wants to turn back, I won't force you to go on."

Ryia shook her head. "Let's kill the bastards. They took Ivan's castle; we kill their god." She reached out and hugged Stephenie. "Go get something to eat."

Stephenie hugged Ryia back, then turned and dove into the river. The cold water felt refreshing against her scales. She would deal with human concerns later.

The next day took them over the border between Ista and her two southern neighbors. They traveled along the western side of the mountains, which appeared lusher with taller pine trees filling the valleys and lowlands. More wildlife prowled the denser vegetation. From their vantage point a few hundred feet above the ground, they could see more rivers and streams spreading out from the mountains.

Stephenie broke the day up into four shorter segments, allowing them to cover almost fifty miles before she rested for the night. She knew she could go further in her lizard form, but the act of transforming also exhausted her, and forced her to consume large amounts of food. When she returned to her normal form, it left her feeling bloated, as if too much of her existed. How the dragons shifted forms from huge thirty-foot long lizards of death to delicate human, she did not know.

She spoke to Islet the day after that. The first wave of people from Alkmaar arrived in Isa Fields and she had visual conformation from the guardian in Horn Point that the invaders had executed Ivan. The soldiers around Horn Point also changed their formations, some preparing defenses against anyone approaching from the south, while others appeared to prepare to march north again.

Chapter 29

Islet looked up from the papers on her desk. Her hand had cramped, and she welcomed the chance to stop recording the names and details of the people who arrived from Alkmaar into the ledger. "Kas, I'm glad you came." He stopped next to the pair of chairs before her desk. "Please, sit."

Kas looked at the chairs and decided on the one on the left. He sat down and put his hands on his lap. "I was told you had something important you need to discuss with me."

Islet nodded her head and now weighed Kas' attitude against writing the occupations of another seventy people. *I don't have a choice; I need him to comply, especially with Dufnall in despair.* "Kas, with Ryia gone, I need someone to help train everyone who has magic. I need someone to help keep Dufnall occupied."

"I do not speak their language and they do not speak any of mine."

Islet picked up a piece of paper. "We have new people. There is Lami, plus four other residents of Alkmaar, and one of the soldiers from some country called Semr. Apparently, it is a ship ride and two hundred miles from Horn Point. I have not had a chance to look it up on the maps. That is eleven people who need to learn more about magic." *And two that need to take their minds off their pain.*

He leaned forward. "Again, I do not speak their language. I cannot help. Was there anything else?"

Islet let the caring expression fall from her face. "I get you are angry at Stephenie for some reason. No, I have not asked her what is going on between the two of you. It is not my business. My business is protecting the people of Ista. You have skills we need."

"I have other tasks that are more important."

Islet shook her head. "Spending your entire life reading through books is not what we currently need."

He stood up. "If this is all you want to talk about, I am done."

"Sit down." The hardness and command in her voice returned him to his chair. "I get the fact that your people died trying to destroy the traps. I understand your need to pursue that effort. However, I don't understand why you even care about that anymore."

Kas sat back, a puzzled expression on his face. "You do not understand? There are creatures in another world being drained of their life so that we can use that life energy to supplement the power of people who have no business even using magic."

"I get that. But you care about nothing else, so what is the point if you save these creatures in another world? You care about none of the lives around you. You don't care about the people of Ista or Sandven enough to even learn more than a few words of their language in nearly three years. You don't care enough to help Ryia teach the people, forcing her and Steph to learn things on their own."

"Stephenie is unable to learn anything from me. Her skills and abilities far exceed mine. The way I learned to use magic does not apply to her. It is a waste of my time."

Islet nodded her head. "You claim to care about these creatures so much that you throw away a chance at a second life and a new body, so that you can do nothing but research. Sure, you've found several traps, at least theoretically, but they are scattered all around the Sea of Tet. You don't train yourself to deal with the people that use them. You expect Stephenie, Ryia, Henton, and others to deal with the traps you find. And when they don't just get up and run off on your personal mission, you throw a fit."

"I could crush you with my mind," Kas said. "I am not without the ability to fight."

"But you can't actually interact with a trap. You don't have the ability to see the energy fields. You don't have the ability to respond to the challenge. You need Stephenie to help you with that."

"You called me here to insult me?"

Islet shook her head. "No. I called you here to get you to help. You want to stop people using the traps and break them of their reliance on the augmentation devices, then educate people to have an alternative. Give the people you look down upon the skills necessary to eliminate their need to use the devices."

Kas opened his mouth but said nothing.

"Yes, I'm aware you consider most of us simpletons and brain damaged imbeciles. But whose faults is that? The people who don't have access to the information, or the person who sits here and complains and refuses to share what he knows."

Kas looked away. "I am not good enough."

Islet pushed a piece of paper aside. "You're not good enough? Do you mean morally good enough or not skilled enough?"

Kas looked up. "Skilled. I tried to help Stephenie, but it only confused her most of the time. Ryia rejected my help, saying I always talked nonsense. I am not a good teacher. I never was. I lived a simple life. My family had wealth, and I had access to libraries and studies."

Islet did not look away. "That makes you a useless noble, or at a minimum, a wealthy merchant brat." She shrugged. "What do you want me to say? I am not sorry for you. I don't have sympathy for what slights you think have been sent your way. If you want my respect, you will act like a man and do what is best for everyone, not just focus on your single-minded goal." She picked up the quill. "You've seemed to overlook the fact that before you can throw countries and societies into complete chaos by toppling their leadership and access to magic, you need to put an alternate system in place. That alternate system is teaching people the truth. Giving them the means to be successful. Otherwise, you really don't care about life, you just want to be right."

"You know nothing about me. I have seen war. My first wife Sairy died at the hands of terrorists. I watched my friends slowly die from lack of food when the Denarians sealed us into our city. I then starved to death myself. A thousand years might have passed, but for me, it feels like only five years. I remember the smell of death throughout the city. People desperate enough to eat the dead. The ghosts of people watching as their friends ate their bodies. This war is fresh in my memory, not a history lesson that everyone forgot. You have had centuries to do the right thing, but all you did was forget all the knowledge and skill my people once had. Everything I knew and loved is gone. I am alone in a world that makes no sense. A world full of people that do not know the basics of magic or the life I lived."

Islet moistened her lips. "I had not considered how fresh your pain was."

"And how futile it is. My people died and the rest of you learned nothing. You only made it worse. You think I do not realize I can do almost nothing to change how things are?" He shook his head. "Perhaps when these invaders come, I'll die for real this time, and the world can just rot."

She leaned forward. "If you want to talk about it, I'm here whenever you want." She swallowed. "I know something of despair and wanting to turn away from the world."

Kas straightened. "I am okay. I am sorry for my outburst."

She hesitated a moment. Islet did not believe him, but she could not force him to talk. "Kas, I know you may not agree, but we still need your help. Instead of letting the army invade Ista and kill everyone here, we can resist and fight. Win this battle and then continue your war against the traps."

"Is there a point?"

"There may be. If you can use your knowledge to quickly train people how to heal, it could save the lives of people who do not use augmentation devices. You need people like those in Sandven to resist the people who perpetuate the lies." She noticed his softened expression. "I've asked Douglas to help translate for you. I don't expect you to spend every waking minute teaching magic, but I need you to teach them for at least half of each day." She noticed the shift in his posture and felt confident she had convinced him. "Douglas is about as happy about this as you."

"Very well," Kas said, and he rose to his feet.

"Kas, I am serious about being here if you want to talk. You are correct, we don't understand what you are going through, but if you share your pain, we will be there for you."

He nodded his head, turned, and then left the office.

Chapter 30

Stephenie's pattern of travel continued for two more days. While she did not bother to speak with anyone in Ista, she knew that Henton and Ryia, who each carried a communication stone in the event either of them became separated, continued to speak with Islet regularly. She allowed them to inform Islet that a large contingent of soldiers left Horn Point and headed toward Gaffel. It would take several days before they knew if the force headed for Alkmaar or Norbek, but it appeared those in charge at Horn Point did not consider southern Sandven a current threat. If that meant the jarls had thrown in with Lobben, she did not know, but the odds favored that possibility.

On the fifth night out from Isa Fields, they camped where they could see the smoke from Berl's surface city. The next day, they flew out of the mountains and to the northwest side of the Berl, where the roads to Kutenveld and Sudhold merged before continuing as a single road into Berl. They avoided notice by remaining low in the sky and staying away from any of the smaller outlying communities. They had to walk nearly five miles back to Berl. However, they had already consumed most of their food, which lightened their packs, and the approach to Berl remained mostly level on a well-maintained road.

They each wore their hats, with Stephenie and Ryia concealing most of their hair under their outer coats. Their Sandvian supplied wool and fur garments marked them as outsiders, but these stood out much less than the lighter linen and silk cloth that they had either brought north from Cothel or had acquired from those that had died over twenty years ago in Ista. The people they met along the road did not question them, though several watched them closely.

"So many people in brown robes," Henton said as the surface city came into view. "We likely need to find some local clothing to blend in."

Stephenie only nodded her head. Her attention fell on the fields and pastures for animals surrounding the city's stone walls. She wondered if the additional rains and snow that fell on the western side of the mountains changed the native vegetables and grains these people grew. She stored the information away in case it could augment Ista's food production.

Once inside the walls, the city looked much like Horn Point, with the buildings extending down into the ground more than above the surface. A mixture of sod and tile roofs kept out the weather. The streets, made mostly from packed clay and rock, remained free of debris and garbage. The strong winds blowing through the mountain pass carried away the worst of the city odors, leaving only the hint of sulfur from burning coal.

Above them, and to the east, the Stone City had been visible well before they actually reached the outer fields of Berl. A distinctive manmade line stood out, created by the exposed walkway that wrapped around the western and southern side of the mountain leading into the pass. Smoke and steam escaped from several holes in the mountain's side, giving it the appearance of generating its own cloud.

The people inside the surface city's walls looked at them with distrust, but no one actively harassed them. They found a couple of merchants willing to accept their Sandvian coin, and Ryia purchased three sets of brown robes with yellow circles on their chests. The hats they currently wore resembled the fashion in Berl close enough that they did not replace those.

"And I see a lot of people with hair," Stephenie told Henton in Cothish as they used a narrow alley between a couple of buildings to pull the robes over their other garments.

"I'm less worried about someone on the street than someone inside a temple," Henton responded. "Speaking of which, I'm pretty certain we passed a temple just a street back."

Stephenie nodded her head. "The augmentation device I have is tied to a relay high up inside the mountain. I've checked a couple of times on our way into the city. I don't need to use the one tied to the device if there are other relays in the city." She frowned. "However, even in Cothel, many of the temples of Felis don't have actual relays. Too much cost and effort for the original builders to create that many, I expect."

"Maybe they have a smaller one that we could steal?" Ryia offered. "That would be ideal."

Stephenie knew that would make triangulating on the trap much easier. *But the chances are slim, and even if we had one to carry around, the entrance to the trap could be sealed up, or miles away. I hope this isn't going to be a fool's errand.* The ability to locate the traps had been another contentious point of disagreement with Kas over the years. He wanted it to be easy, but she knew the original builders wanted to keep them hidden.

She looked up over the top of the low roof at the Stone City. *They could have also hid it in that labyrinth.*

She pulled the wool robe down and wrinkled her nose at the smell. "Let's check the temple you saw, and we'll hope to get lucky. Perhaps we can win the wager against Ryia," she added, hoping to prove to the others that the fate of Sandven had not demoralized her completely.

Henton frowned. "Well, you've just ruined the chance it'll work out in our favor."

"Don't blame me," Ryia said. "I'm just in it for the coin."

The temple building was twice as long as it was wide. A pair of dogs lounged at the entrance, tied to the structure with ropes long enough to allow them to move inside or outside the open door. She projected a sense of peace to the curious animals and patted their heads as she entered.

No windows illuminated the interior, though five fires at the far end heated cast iron cauldrons with a steaming liquid boiling inside of them. They had added something sweet to provide fragrance. However, condensation covered the stones and wooden poles supporting the roof, and the additive did not remove the smell of mold and mildew.

Stephenie examined the energy fields in the building and felt no sources of power coming from the carved and painted wooden statue behind the cauldrons. *It's never that easy.*

An older man with a pronounced limp approached from where he had sat. He said something in the local language and Stephenie shook her head. "I'm sorry," she said in Sandvian. "We've only been in the country since the start of the summer. We've not yet learned your language, though we have found enlightenment through Fotia."

The older man looked at each of them in turn and then nodded his head. "Fotia is not one to coddle the weak. Through pain comes enlightenment." He looked at Henton and then back to Stephenie. "You are his daughter?"

Stephenie forgot how young she looked and then nodded her head. "My sister and I lost our mother years ago. Our father has been lost in his grief for some time, but since we came here to learn of Fotia, we've found some peace. Our suffering brings us closer." The man frowned and Stephenie realized her statement had not triggered any sympathy.

"What do you want?"

"We were looking to find a teacher at one of the temples. Are there many temples in Berl?"

The man slowly nodded his head. "Many."

Great, someone who does not like talking about his god. "Are there any with the metal altars? I am told you can feel the strength of the connection with Fotia through the metal statues." She focused on the surface thoughts he broadcast, hoping her statements might trigger a memory she could utilize.

"Only senior members of Fotia's Faithful are permitted into the main temple in the Stone City."

Stephenie picked up a sense of resentment from the man. *Excluded from that privilege, I assume.* "Thank you for the information." She turned to Henton and Ryia, gave them a knowing look, and they all exited without saying anything else. Outside and on the street, she walked between the two of them. "I think that confirms we need to get into the mountain."

"Great," Henton said. "Even with the robes, we stand out. Our camping supplies. Our weapons. Can we hope they let just anyone into the mountain?"

She shrugged. "The man felt excluded, so I'm guessing you need to have a certain social status." She looked up at the walkway. "Or have a half-breed mongrel that can fly."

"Can we get some food first?" Ryia asked. "I hate to die with nothing but trail food in me."

They spent the rest of the day quietly asking laborers and street merchants about the Stone City. The people who had been willing to share any details had only ever seen the three lower levels that contained storage and living spaces for servants. Wealthy merchants and lower nobles occupied the next two floors, while the elite of the Fotia and wealthy nobles lived on the seventh and eighth levels.

Several people confirmed the Prophet lived inside the mountain on the eighth level. While he would conduct sermons in the main temple for the most worthy, the man and his two disciples had conducted sermons in the other two temples in the Stone City, as well as many of the larger temples in Berl's surface city.

Stephenie cut the information gathering short when she grew more concerned at the reactions their questions generated. Neither she nor Ryia had sensed anyone following them, but she could not keep her mind focused on the task. Thoughts of remorse at not stopping Ivan's death continued to surface and her frequent distractions left her wanting to find a place to rest. *I could have sent guardians. Did I let my fear of what might happen topple Sandven's government?*

"What's the plan?" Ryia asked as they sat in the corner of an eatery that only had cauldrons of stewed root vegetables.

Stephenie forced herself to swallow another spoonful of the mushy food. "Same as before, we fly up to the walkway, enter the top level, use the medallion to find the relay, get a location, hope the trap is easy to find, and get out."

"Steal some robes that mark us as at least acolytes," Henton added. "And put one of Balkr's crossbow bolts through any Senzar we see."

"I think our weapons and packs would make markings on robes meaningless," Stephenie challenged. "Plus ..." She could not help but stare at a knot in the wooden table. After a moment, she shook her head. "I've not seen any in an easy place to steal. It's not like when we had Kas with us and he could just float through walls as a ghost."

"Guards?" Ryia asked slowly, her own attention directed at the wall behind Stephenie.

Stephenie shrugged. "Choke them until they pass out, then tie them up and hide them somewhere out of sight." She pushed the disgusting food away. "I'm hoping we won't encounter many in the middle of the night on the top level. I'm ..." She shifted her attention to the door but saw nothing that would have merited her change of focus. She shook her head, trying to clear her thoughts again. "What was I saying? Oh, yeah, I'm counting on the guards being mostly on the lower levels to keep people out, not on the top floor."

Ryia shook her own head and then turned her attention back to Stephenie. "We've got a long time before it turns dark. Where are we going to wait?"

"We could find a room and rest," Henton offered. "Sleep when you can. We might not get a chance later."

Dacian kept his eyes closed. He found it difficult to breath, as though a pile of stones rested on his chest, but he knew the feeling came from the poison's effects on his muscles. The entrance of Andre and Kev into the small room had woken him. He knew the futility of feigning sleep with people who could sense thoughts, but he had no desire to open his eyes.

The boot against his side forced Dacian of cough. He struggled to shift his body, but the recent dose of poison left him too weak. His body now constantly burned energy to heal the damage of the chemicals destroying his organs.

"How do you like my friends?" Andre asked.

Dacian looked up from the floor. Andre wore a new robe and Dacian thought the threads of the yellow sun on his chest contained gold. He refrained from responding. He knew it might provoke Andre into hitting him again, but he needed everyone to believe him close to death. *If I can keep them from giving me more poison …* He did not want to get his hopes up. Escaping Andre would not require much effort. However, with Kamari's sword in the mix, he doubted he could escape even if he made a full recovery. *I need to get away without that bastard knowing.*

"Nothing to say?" Andre asked. Pleasure evident in his eyes. "The good news is Kamari wants to keep you alive." He shrugged. "At least for now."

Dacian coughed again. He forced himself to breath slowly. "Who is he?"

Andre tisked and shook his head. "Dacian, do not play the fool with me. I know you and Kamari have secrets you don't want to share." Andre crouched down. "What is special about this Queen Stephenie? Why have you been avoiding working hard to make sure we avoid Ista?" Andre picked at a piece of dirt on Dacian's robes, looked at it between his fingers, and then flicked it away. "Why does Kamari want to draw her here? Why does he want to make it look like you killed her?"

"I've never met that man before," Dacian said honestly. "But whatever Kamari is after, will not benefit you."

Andre pursed his lips. "Fotia Faithful are poised to rule all of the north. Everything from here to the top of the world. I don't know what your goal was, but I know it wasn't to benefit me."

Dacian licked his chapped and split lips. He wanted something to drink, but doubted he could trust anything given to him. "You do not believe in Fotia, Andre. Just your own power. You've made an ally of an assassin. Your new friend will leave you dead when he has what he wants. Had you followed my lead, you would have ruled all of Lobben and Sandven."

Andre stood. "You love to manipulate people. Once Kamari has what he wants, he will kill you, and then leave. He has not once wanted to be the center of attention, unlike you."

Dacian watched Andre swallow and knew he had planted at least a seed of doubt. Andre's greed would prevent the man from changing course, he knew that much. *But Kamari will likely kill Andre before he leaves. Kiwa don't leave witnesses. At least I have that.*

"Kev will remain here to make sure you stay alive. You've screwed up his mind, so my little pet is worthless to me now." Andre turned and left the room, shutting and locking the door behind him.

Dacian looked over at Kev and the young man moved closer with a wet rag. He sighed and allowed the man to wipe the dirt from his face, not that he had the strength to resist. *Why send a kiwa to kill Stephenie? Who is she and who wants her dead?* Placing the blame on him, that he understood, it would draw Yreka into conflict with his grandfather and not whoever ordered their deaths.

Chapter 31

Islet leaned over and inhaled the fragrant lavender in the large planter at the edge of the courtyard around the castle. Just on the other side of a cut marble wall the loose stone of the mountain climbed away from her. She doubted that Ista would allow anything to fall from the steep slope and crash down to disrupt the castle grounds, but that required faith in a magical construct to value her life. A castle with a definite personality and memory.

She tried to consider Erika's regular advice to be more trusting of everyone and everything. The woman had willingly taken up the role of castle servant and proved easy to speak with. Over the last year, she had become one of Islet's trusted friends. Walter faced his own demons and grew frustrated when he could not fix her problems. Stephenie's friends had always been hers, and Islet never found a casual and open relationship with them. Erika provided the perspective of a woman who had lived her entire life in a harsh environment and that eased some of Islet's anxiety. "Never overlook the beauty of the moment," she whispered, repeating Erika's often repeated reminder. The second half of Erika's advice felt more bleak. "You might not live to see the next." However, the Sandvian woman never spoke the words with remorse or despair. Only a simple acknowledgement that everyone's time remained too limited to worry and fret.

"Embrace the moment," Islet reminded herself. "I wish it was that easy."

She heard footsteps behind her and turned quickly, though the guardian five feet away remained unmoving and uninterested. "Kas," she said at his measured and somewhat hasty approach.

"Ma'am," he said with a bow.

Islet raised an eyebrow. "That is more formal than normal."

He nodded his head. "I am trying to be respectful and show contrition."

"Kas, one thing about family is we might not always get along, but we do try to forgive and forget." She forced a smile. "I do appreciate the gesture. What is it I can do for you?"

He nodded his head and looked back toward the city. "I am worried about Arno, the mercenary that had been in Ivan's army, and who claims to have converted to worship the Goddess."

Islet nodded her head and started walking toward the castle. "Is he disruptive to your teaching?"

Kas shook his head. "No. The trouble is, I believe him to be far more skilled than he lets on."

"How so?"

Kas shortened his normal stride to keep pace with Islet and then looked down. "In several ways. First, he seems to struggle to not be effective in the magic I have everyone practicing. It simply comes too easy for him, and he does not know how to make it look hard. Second …" He pursed his lips and then continued. "I need to admit I did not enjoy being told to help train the others. I have been difficult with Douglas and the students. I have instructed them, but I have been rude."

Islet said nothing. She felt change required admitting one's faults to oneself, but she also did not believe that doing so deserved a reward.

"I made a comment about Sarel being … It was not nice. It was under my breath and in the language from the dragons that the senior Senzar had used. I saw the smirk on Arno's face. He covered it quickly, and I pretended not to notice, but if he understood the language, I fear he could be a Senzar spy."

Islet found herself unable to breathe. The memories of her captors sifting through her mind, looking for anything of use, left her feeling vulnerable and exposed. *You are free,* the rational part of her brain repeated again and again until the rest of her decided she needed to breathe again.

"Islet?"

She gasped, air returning to her lungs. She took several deep breaths and then swallowed. After a moment more, she continued. "We knew it was a risk. Henton argued endlessly it was a risk." Her hands shook, and she stepped close to a planter so that she could lean against it for support.

Three guardians moved close and surrounded them. She felt some relief at Ista's awareness of their conversation and her distress.

Kas did not offer her a hand, but he softened his tone. "I am not capable of fighting a Senzar mage. No one here has the skill and power. We could have Ista send the guardians to eliminate him."

Islet's mind cleared at the discussion of murder. "Are you absolutely certain he is a Senzar mage?"

Kas frowned. "No. It is just a belief. However, the risks are too great to ignore, should he be one."

Islet nodded her head. "I'm glad you brought your concern forward. But I'm not ready to execute someone just because there is a suspicion of guilt." She frowned. "I can't believe I'm even saying this, but perhaps he is Senzar, but not actually a threat."

Kas frowned. "After all that has occurred, you believe them to not represent a threat?"

"I'm saying not all of them may agree and perhaps he is looking for a place of refuge."

"He has hinted to me multiple times—as well as directly asked—for permission for the new students to have a tour of the castle and the library. He has also inquired with others about when Stephenie is expected to return and what she is doing away from Ista. He has asked about her abilities, such as being able to fly." He shook his head. "She had failed to conceal too many things from the people living here."

Islet resumed walking and set a brisk pace toward a side door in the castle's southern wall. While she might agree with some restrictions on people learning about Stephenie's powers, restricting her ability to explore her powers helped no one. "What are our options besides having Ista kill him?"

"If he is what I fear, no one in Isa Fields can secure him."

"And asking him directly is too risky," she admitted aloud. "Our advantage right now is that he hopefully doesn't know that we know."

"That is correct."

Islet walked up the narrow steps to the stone door and opened it. The foot thick door swung easily on the pivots sunk into the top and bottom of the door jamb. "What of the weapons and magical artifacts Stephenie keeps hidden in her secret rooms?"

Kas shook his head. "I am not sure Ista would allow me into those rooms. I know Stephenie, Ryia, and Henton reviewed the collection again before they left. I do not know if they took any, but she had stated several times before that Ista informed her that Kervigar had secured them in the vaults because they presented a danger to the user, as well as others."

The door closed effortlessly behind Kas, sealing itself closed. Islet paused in the long hall and looked at the now solid outer wall. Even the gap needed to allow the door to rotate had filled in with stone. She turned to Kas. "Let's go to the speaking room. I have questions for Ista."

Kas nodded his head and followed her to the storage room with all the markings on the floor and walls. A guardian already waited inside. Islet smiled at it. "Thank you, Ista."

Kas stood with his arms crossed. "Any questions you have for the castle could more easily be asked of Stephenie directly."

"First," Islet said, raising her thumb into the air. "Stephenie is dealing with a lot trying to infiltrate Berl's Stone City, locate the trap, and stop the invasion. I'm," she turned to look the guardian in the face, "not going to add worry and concern to her already difficult task. Ista, please refrain from telling Stephenie what is going on unless everything falls apart."

The winged cat simply stared back at her.

"I mean it. She can't just fly back here and deal with this, so there is no point in causing her to panic." She turned back to Kas and raised her index finger. "Second, even if I felt good about sending Ista to kill this man, unless he spends part of each day far enough away from everyone else, we risk him hurting others while we try to deal with him."

"Then what do you propose?"

"Ista's walls, floors, and ceilings appear to have survived a dragon attack. I'm hoping they could hold in a Senzar mage." The guardian before her nodded its head. "What about the interior doors?"

The guardian tilted its head, approximating a response of uncertainty. Then it moved to the walls and Islet read out its reply. "Dragon has destroyed doors, Senzar, perhaps not."

She frowned. "Any better ideas? Ista? Kas?"

"How would you even get him sealed into a room?" Kas asked.

"Well, you said he's been asking to come to the castle. Through you, I could apologize for not meeting with each of the new students personally and offer to have them meet with me. You could lead them to a room where we could then have the doors sealed."

"If the man is what I fear he is, he would likely suspect something. You risk him sensing that no one was in the room and grow suspicious." Kas raised a hand. "And before you suggest being in the room and asking him to wait, he would likely read your mind. It is even likely he would read my mind, or the mind of whoever escorted him to the castle well before you got him to your room."

Islet shivered. "Then we need to do it in a way that does not cause suspicion and prevents him from learning anything from anyone who knows about this." She bit her lower lip. "This will make it hard for you to continue to teach him."

Kas shrugged. "I continue to use Cothish to speak with Douglas and Douglas translates into Sandvian. The language barrier could help. But as time goes on, I suspect my suspicion will indeed leak out."

She took a deep breath. "We have to act. If we remove you suddenly, especially if he already suspects you might have realized something, then it might force him to act. If we wait, he's likely to act, either on whatever original goal he had, or once you give him more reason to suspect that you know."

"I am in agreement with that logic."

Islet's mind raced. "In that case, I will not tell you the plan. The less you know, the less he might learn. For now, return to your normal schedule." She moved to the door of the speaking room and opened it. "Your next session with the students is tomorrow, yes?"

"Correct."

"Thank you for bringing this to me." She extended her arm to allow Kas to leave the room ahead of her. He bowed his head and walked out. She allowed the door to close behind him and turned back to the guardian. "Ista, I am really going to need your help here."

Walter, Erika, and Menni helped Islet shift a heavy free-standing bookshelf with doors against the wall. They had already moved in a rug, a desk, and three chairs. A painting of the valley with trees exhibiting fall colors had come from an antechamber leading to Stephenie's personal offices.

"How much more do you want to move?" Walter asked, and then wiped his brow.

Erika stepped back and leaned against the desk. She and Menni had not asked questions, realizing Islet would not answer them.

"Erika, can you please move the desk supplies from one of the unused offices and place them in the drawers and on the top of the desk? We want it to look like an actual office."

"Of course, Ma'am."

"Do you want me to help?" Menni asked and Islet nodded affirmatively.

After the two of them left the room through the main door and into the front hall, Islet walked through the door on the opposite wall and examined what they had done in the adjoining room. The work to make it appear to be an inner office left quite a bit to be desired. They had carried in a desk and a single chair, but no other effort had been made. This rear room had a second door as well, leading to a smaller hallway that ran along the rear of the castle. She suspected they had intended this hall for servants to have easy access to the storage rooms, but no documents of the castle construction existed that she knew of.

"It is quite late already," Islet admitted. "Erika will get her cousin first thing in the morning, hopefully, before Kas starts teaching everyone."

"I don't like this," Walter said as a pair of guardians moved down the rear passage toward the room. "If this man's as powerful as Yreka, he'll rip this place apart."

Islet nodded her head as she examined the wooden door separating the room from the hall. Her plan rested on two-inch-thick stained oak boards to keep the man contained. Islet knew from Stephenie that magic permeated the inner core of the door because it blocked everyone's ability to sense through them. *However, can it resist destructive magic? Can the guardians resist destructive magic?* She stepped aside as the pair of guardians moved to the doorway between two rooms. One sat down directly behind the door, the other moved to the corner, remaining hidden from sight of anyone looking through the opening.

"We'll have two more in the front room, ready to shut the door as soon as Arno enters. There will be two waiting in the room across the far hall. These two, and four more waiting in the rear hall."

Walter nodded his head. "Ten guardians would hopefully be enough." He moved closer to her and put his hands on her shoulders. "But why you in this back room? Can't someone else be the bait?"

Stephenie would stop me if she knew, but I can't risk anyone else. "We're already going to put Erika's cousin at risk, asking him to escort the new students to the office. I'll stand next to this back door and as soon as Arno is in the first room, I'll exit and shut the door. The guardians should be able to keep him from breaking out and Ista will seal the doors."

He kissed her forehead. "I'll be—"

"In the next room with the door shut," she said firmly, not wanting to continue the debate. "We don't want him sensing anyone else waiting for him." *Not when you'll be as frantic as me.*

"In the next room with the door shut," Walter reluctantly agreed. "I truly hoped being at the end of the world would keep us safe. We just draw more and more attention to ourselves, it seems."

Islet heard Erika and Menni putting things on the desk in the front room. She squeezed her husband and then peaked into the room to see the progress. "This looks good. Thank you. Menni, please say nothing of this to anyone and go get some rest."

"Yes, Ma'am," he said, then gave her a small bow before leaving the room.

"Erika, please bring several pitchers of water and a few days of food that will not spoil and hide them in the bookcase. Then get some rest."

She nodded her head. "Yes, Ma'am. I'll fetch Rugga first thing in the morning, as you asked. I'll send him to you as soon as he arrives."

Islet thanked her and then led Walter up to their bedroom. She knew neither of them would sleep much. Her own nerves would make her toss and turn through the night, and Walter would refuse to drink his sleeping aid because it would prevent him from waking in the morning.

Chapter 32

After purchasing food for another five days, they found an inn that catered to people from Sandven and rented space in the back room to rest. With the war, several other merchants occupied the space, and had done so since before the invasion started. Their timing had been poor, and they had missed the opportunity to get through the pass before the soldiers had arrived. A few of their number argued that fortune favored them, as they avoided the fate of arriving in Norbek or Horn Point only for the armies to arrive and occupy them.

Stephenie, Ryia, and Henton said little, offering only the story about a dead mother and a grieving father. The dozen other merchants did not press for more, and only professed a hope that the conflict would soon end so they could get back to business.

The three of them left the inn shortly after the sun fell below the horizon. While it still did not yet get truly dark, the days continued to quickly get shorter and the nights longer and dimmer. Since her first trip to Norbek, the night had grown to around five turns of the glass, even if it did not start until well after most reasonable people wanted to turn in for sleep.

The route toward the mountain took them to the northern edge of the surface city in order to avoid the industrial section near the ground entrance to the Stone City. Now that the distractions of the day had faded, the sounds of forge hammers and bellows filled the night, suggesting a strong demand for instruments of war.

With Stephenie and Ryia using their senses, they avoided the soldiers patrolling the streets and approached the near vertical cliffs making up the exterior of the Stone City. The four ground entrances to the mountain remained heavily guarded, the closest one just under a quarter mile south of their position.

Stephenie looked up and reached out with her senses to look for people on the crenelated walkway two-hundred feet above them. "There are five people at this end of the walkway," she told the others. Ryia nodded her understanding, but she did not sense them herself. Henton quickly pulled back the string of Balkr's bow. It required only a limited force to set the mechanism, as the deadly projectile generated its own forward momentum. He waited on loading one of the two precious bolts, but still pointed the weapon into the air.

When the people on patrol moved south along the walkway, she lifted herself, Henton, and Ryia into the air, guessing at the mental range any of the five guards might have to sense their flight. To provide a margin of safety, she flew north of the end of the walkway, and then came back south along the side of the mountain to land at the very end of the platform. The patrol she had felt continued moving away from them.

"Now where?" Ryia asked as she crouched down, her staff held sideways near the ground to avoid drawing attention.

Henton pulled one bolt from the satchel at his side and loaded the crossbow. "Only for Senzar," he said.

Stephenie nodded. They had already agreed he would take no actions unless she or Ryia pointed out a target. She closed her eyes and pushed her mind to look for other people nearby. The thick stone of the mountain blocked her ability to sense anyone inside the city, and the five soldiers patrolling the walkway continued to head south. Before long, they would follow the curve of the mountain and would move out of visible sight.

"We don't know anything about what's inside," she mused aloud. The lack of planning and scouting made her nauseous, but they had already consumed too much time. Sandven had fallen and now the Lobben troops marched north.

Henton crouched down beside her. "The change of guards could be imminent, or it could be a long time away. We might take this group and question them, or we could make our way inside and look for someone else."

Stephenie weighed the consequence of the outside patrol going missing compared to someone inside the mountain not arriving at their destination. "It's late. I'm hoping there won't be that many people up." She rose and moved forward in a partial crouch, having decided. "We leave the people outside alone. If we take them out, someone might realize intruders entered from the walkway. Inside, they won't know how we got in."

Ryia and Henton followed closely behind her. When the patrol disappeared around the curve of the mountain, she rose to her full height and walked to the large opening they had seen from the surface city earlier in the day.

The parapeted wall on the outer edge of the walkway had mount points for ballistas, but no weapons currently pointed toward the city. *Are they there in case their own people revolt or just in case the city fell to an invader? Either way, those that carved the walkway into the mountain felt the need to defend the Stone City.* Lists of precautions she had failed to make in Ista ran through her mind. *Should I plan for the day when Isa Fields is full of trained mages? What defenses should I put in place now?* Ista reminded her of the guardians. *But does assuming the worst of people actually make them distrust you and then plan to betray you? Look at Hugo and Rolf.* She knew those two likely acted from religious motivations, but she could not dismiss the idea of creating future enemies from current behavior.

She ignored a series of normal sized doors set into the mountain. Her senses told her the doors led to small rooms filled with various items of wood and steel. *Likely locked armories.* The entrance they sought lay just ahead.

"I don't sense anyone," Ryia whispered to Henton, and Stephenie agreed with her assessment.

The large open entrance had a lip of stone overhanging the top, which could block some, but definitely not all, of the weather expected in the north. A pair of fluted half columns, carved out of the mountain, flanked either side of the passage and supported the lip of stone twenty feet above them. Other swirling ornamentation carved into the mountain side spread out from the columns. Time and the elements softened the sharp edges, causing the loss of detail in many of the reliefs. However, they still showed a great deal of skill and artistic beauty.

Inside the mountain, the large passage ran at a sixty-degree angle toward the south. A pair of wooden doors, currently open, could close to block out the worst of the weather. A handful of lamps burned low, providing bubbles of illumination in the darkened interior.

Stephenie did not wait for any discussion and moved into the well-trodden passage. Henton and Ryia followed close behind her, each keeping their own watch for threats.

She continued to extend her senses, trying to look around corners and through the stone. Muddled hints of people living further in the mountain remained on her periphery, but no distinct signatures of thought formed in her mind.

After a hundred feet, they neared an equally large passage that branched to the left and went deeper into the mountain at an angle. A mind obscured by stone began to solidify to her senses. She signaled the threat to the others with a quick motion of her hand and then approached the corner of the intersection. No one appeared to her senses in the larger passage, but she peaked her head around the corner just in case. More oil lamps, including one just above her head, illuminated the passage.

She focused her attention on the lamp above her and pulled the energy from the flame, causing the light to sputter and then cut out. She repeated the process with the nearest lamps down each of the three branches of the intersection. The tunnel fell into darkness, but her night vision had always been excellent, and her mind needed no light.

The person she sensed grew closer and she knew this man came from a smaller passage down the left branch. An eternity later, a man dressed in a wrinkled robe, fur hat, and fur slippers opened a small door twenty feet away. He emerged carrying a small candle enclosed in a housing to provide light.

Stephenie extinguished the candle as soon as the door closed behind the man. A muffled curse in the local language escaped his lips. However, he had no chance to say anything more as she wrapped him tightly in a gravitation field that compressed his chest and blocked his mouth and nose. Panic and fear immediately radiated from the middle-aged man.

She motioned Ryia and Henton to follow as she closed the distance. She felt the man's attempts to struggle against her field and she rotated him to face her. Her eyes could see the details of his overweight face. She felt his limited attempts to draw in power, but they seemed instinctual and not practiced.

"We are looking for the main temple with the metal statue of Fotia. Tell me where it is and I'll let you go."

The man's panic continued to build, as he could not get any air. Stephenie allowed him to gasp in a breath, but then blocked him from a second one. "Which way?" She released his left arm, and he quickly pointed behind himself, down the large side passage they had just entered.

"Thank you," she said. However, she continued to restrain the man. She tried her best to tune out his fear of death as she continued to starve his brain of air. His muscles flexed and contracted, pressing against her field until he fell unconscious. She immediately relaxed the energy blocking his chest from expanding and his mouth and nose from opening. She monitored him as she lowered his body gradually to the floor.

Ryia had already rushed forward and began binding his hands and feet. Finally, Ryia put a balled-up piece of stolen fabric in his mouth to gag him only after his breathing had returned to normal.

Stephenie continued to watch for anyone else that might approach them, but the passaged remained clear.

"Is there any good place to hide him?" Henton whispered.

She looked with her mind. Multiple side passages appeared to lead off the larger one they stood in, but she did not know where they went. She shook her head, moved to the door the man had emerged from, and with her powers, lifted the man inside. *Theoretically, the side passage should have less traffic than the main one.* She shut the door. "We just have to be fast and hope no one else finds him."

They continued down the large passage, and after only four hundred feet, Stephenie's senses detected what felt like large wooden doors six hundred feet ahead of them. She could not tell if they blocked the whole passage or not. However, she sensed no one else in the area, and she moved forward. As they grew closer, her mind confirmed an expansive room behind the doors.

I just might win that bet with Ryia, she thought to herself and then looked down at the stone beneath their feet. Like the passage leading to the outside, countless people had worn away the softer parts of the stone, leaving ridges, lumps, and bumps. *I wonder who cut this passage and if it had grown larger overtime because of people trying to smooth out the floor.*

Henton bumped into her back. "You okay?"

She shook her head and continued moving forward again. "Yeah. Just distracted."

"Sarge, watch where you step," Ryia said softly. "The floor's got some rough spots."

Stephenie glanced down and stepped around a sizable depression, then increased her pace toward the doors, now less than a hundred feet ahead of them.

"Anyone inside?" Henton asked.

Stephenie extended her senses again, probing through the carved wooden doors, but she could not sense anything on the other side. She continued to probe, and as they approached the doors, she noticed the pair of lamps hanging from hooks on either side of the ornate doors. They burned a fragrant oil that permeated the air and burned her nose. However, the lamps had decorative metal work that looked like a pack of dogs running around the base and she found it hard to turn away from them.

"Steph?"

She shook her head. "Sorry, no, I don't sense anyone inside." She put a hand on one door and pushed. The heavy door resisted her effort and she enhanced her strength with her powers. A moment later, the door pivoted on the metal rods that extended into the floor and ceiling. The steel and stone complained about the movement, and she pushed it open only far enough for them to slip through one at a time. She then pushed the door closed, despite the noise it created.

A couple of lamps burned at the far end of the large temple chamber, illuminating the metal statue of a bald man that the true believers thought represented what their god Fotia looked like. The fifteen-foot-tall statue sat on a stone block so that it appeared to take up most of the thirty-foot tall far wall.

She walked toward the statue, heading down the center of the room between the rows of stone columns supporting the ceiling. Halfway into the chamber, she stopped. *Why am I constantly looking at the floor?* She tried to turn around, but found her mind still wanted to look at something on the ground.

A tingling and pressure in the back of her head finally became irritating enough that she realized it had existed on and off during much of the day. "Ryia, what do you sense?"

"I ..." Ryia's voice broke with hesitation. "What kind of stone is this mountain made of?"

Stephenie barely raised a gravitation field to deflect a sword aimed for her skull. She felt sluggish and unable to focus. "Shield yourselves!" she shouted as she turned, trying desperately to see who had attacked her. *A ghost? Where is the bastard?* She ripped her sword from its scabbard and tried to concentrate, but the weight on her mind pressed so hard that she could not think. Her attention continued to come back to the floor again and again.

"Out of my head!" She swung an arc around her, knowing instinctively that something or someone tried to close on her. *What is it? Ista? Ista?* Her ability to form a coherent thought kept slipping away, and she lost her connection to the castle.

A grunt of pain drew her attention, and she saw Ryia stagger and drop to her knees. *Out of my head, damn you!* She drew in energy, realizing she had not even started building up an internal reserve.

"Fighting makes it painful," a voice said in accented Cothish. "Please, fight," he said sweetly. "I like it when people fight me."

"Who are you?" She demanded. Panic hastened her rapid spinning, but she remained unable to lift her focus from the floor. *He speaks Cothish. Had he followed us in the city and listened to our plans? Who is he? What's he done to Josh?*

She could not follow up on the thoughts; another man chuckled and then spoke in Sandvian. "Witch, as the High Council Member of Fotia, I order your death. Talon, end her."

Something sharp pierced her lower back and pain radiated out as a blade twisted, cutting and tearing muscle and organs. Her mind still did not register the presence of anyone near her, but she knew her mind lied to her. She flung energy outwards, pushing anyone near her away with the force of a charging horse.

"No one dominates me," she swore, trying desperately to control her thoughts. Memories of the Senzar who had invaded her mind north of Antar and took over her body drew a growl from her lips. "Asshole, Prophet," the words drawn out as more power entered her body.

She heard laughter from several people, but she could still not see or sense anything around her.

"Yreka's pawn," the sweet voice said, shifting to use Denarian. "You might be a Prime, but you're an infant." A moment later, she felt herself flipped over, and then the air left her body as she smashed into one of the stone pillars supporting the ceiling. Blood leaked from a new hole torn through her left shoulder.

Damn these Senzar, she swore. More power flooded into her and the lamp above her head extinguished because it lacked the energy to continue to burn. She pushed raw energy from her, and lightning shot from just in front of her toward where the laughter had come from. Unable to focus or see the energy fields, she had no idea where to direct her attack and the electricity discharged into a random spot on the floor.

Henton cried out in pain, followed by a grunt and the sound of someone hitting the floor.

"Bastard!" She pushed herself to her feet, feeling blind, but her eyes continued to focus on the floor. Her sword lay somewhere in the room, but out of her field of view. "Ryia? Henton?" She called and heard no answer.

Another blade, or perhaps the same one as earlier, plunged into her right side. She felt an arm around her neck and a hot breath in her ear. "Demon. Elrin's spawn," a different and deeper male voice whispered in Sandvian. Her brain did not see who hung on her side, but logic insisted someone did and her left hand certainly clutched someone's arm. The blade twisted in her side. She heard more grunts of pain from Henton and Ryia.

No! She screamed mentally and pushed against the fog in her mind. Ahead of her, she made out two men standing next to each other. Both wore brown robes, but one had green eyes and a narrow face. He looked at her with a conviction born out of a sense of power and control.

"I told you, struggling makes it fun. But I'm here to kill you so the Senzar don't get to control you. We don't fail our tasks." He chuckled. "I'm just glad I remained in Berl instead of trying to pursue you into Ista like my companions. I would have been so disappointed to only have your pet friends to kill." He walked forward with an easy swagger. "But once I'm done with you, I am going to enjoy examining that staff."

He turned his head for a pointed look at Ryia, who she finally saw. Her friend lay on the ground in a fetal position, clutching the staff desperately.

"Not my friends," she growled. Her awareness of the people in the room disappeared again as the pressure in her mind returned.

A growl escaped her lips and the temperature of the room plummeted as she gorged herself on power, pulling in energy from the floor, the air, and the man who clung to her and stabbed her a third time. *No flames,* a clinical voice in the back of her mind said. Her fingers changed first, growing into the arm of whoever held her. A scream in her ear deafened her, but the power continued to flow into her, driving the rapid change on her flesh.

With the increased energy, she felt her thoughts clearing again and suddenly she remembered that she could see energy currents. Thousands of energy channels filled the large open space. The chaotic visual noise made her nauseous. Many of the pulsating fields emanated from what she knew must be the sword the man carried. More than half of them leading directly to her head.

She tuned out the screams of agony the man with his arm around her neck yelled into her right ear. She focused on the mental assault coming from the weapon. Her initial reaction of pushing the mental connections away from her did not work as they reformed faster than she could respond.

Raw energy leaped from an area near the sword. *Shithead.* The power crackled through the air, following a pathway he had created between himself and her forehead.

She dove to the left, using her mind to move her body faster than muscles alone could ever propel her. Her hands still gripped the arm of the man who tried to choke her, and she pulled him with her, shifting the channel of energy from her body to his in the process.

A boom of thunder filled the air, and she felt every muscle in her body contract as electricity flowed through the man, into her, and then into the ground. The sudden collision with the floor and powerful shock gave her a new moment of clarity. She knew the man that had grabbed her, and now lay on top of her, would die shortly from the energy that had passed through both of them.

With her ability to think returning, multiple people came into her awareness. She turned her focus toward a man and a woman that stood over Henton and Ryia. Ryia had not moved, but the staff still protected her. Henton appeared injured and bleeding on the floor just outside of Ryia's protection.

Three quarters of the way down the chamber, and off to the side, a young man stood over another who sat on a bench. Fear radiated from the young man.

A bald man with an augmentation device stood frozen in place next to the man with the sword. His face filled with disbelief. "She can't beat us. How is she doing this, Kamari?"

"Shut up, Andre." The green-eyed foreigner cleared his throat. "You can't win, little girl."

Just as suddenly as her awareness came, it began to disappear again. *They are mine,* she swore. The floor shook slightly, and she pulled on the connections the sword tried to reestablish to her mind. Just as with any intelligence, the faster and more dominant mind often gained control during the initial phase of establishing the mental link. The intelligence of the sword did not know how to behave when Stephenie reacted faster. Whoever created it, made it to befuddle and distract others, but they never expected its victims to embrace the connection.

The failure of design allowed her to gain control of the weapon. *How do you function?* She demanded it in a dozen languages and eventually found it responded to emotions and not words. The need for it to obey her and stop confusing her friends flowed from her. She forced her belief that the sword belonged to her into the weapon, using her possessive rage against the device.

The green-eyed man staggered and dropped the sword. Her mind cleared completely, and she used her powers to pull the sword toward her, catching it with her left hand as she flung the corpse off her and leaped to her feet.

No longer impaired by the mental noise that had blocked her from realizing the threats that had awaited them in the room, she reexamined the current situation.

The man standing over Henton held up his augmentation device and chanted something in his local language. She closed the fifteen feet to the priest and swiped her razor-sharp talons through the man's face, breaking bone as they tore through his eyes and nose. His jaw ripped out of its socket to hang by skin and muscle. Blood sprayed into the air as the man twisted around and crumpled to the ground.

Ryia looked up from the floor, the normally transparent spherical shield generated by the staff shimmering with blue as the woman tried to use magic against her friend. Stephenie swung her stolen sword at the woman and cut through the plate armor protecting her right arm.

"Behind you," Ryia shouted.

Stephenie continued running past the woman, but she felt a channeled gravity field rip through her left arm, missed its initial target of her heart.

Focus, she told herself, trying to avoid letting the rage and possessiveness take over her actions. She slowed and turned as Ryia rolled over to Henton to envelop him in the staff's protective field.

"You can't beat us," the man said in Cothish. "We've been sent to kill you and we won't fail."

Stephenie reached out to the stolen sword and concentrated on projecting the idea that everyone other than her friends could see no one else. Thousands of threads burst from the sword toward the people in the room. Other threads swirled from the green-eyed man like snakes fighting to break free of a predator that caught them.

"Shit," the man finally cursed. Hundreds of quick gravitational beams leapt from his position. Ryia's staff blocked any that would have hit her or Henton.

Lightning leaped from Ryia's staff and struck the woman who had previously attacked her, as Stephenie launched herself into the air. Stephenie did not fly directly in the man's direction, avoiding another burst of gravitational beams. Instead, she flew around the far side of the columns and approached from his side. She hacked at his head with the stolen sword, hit him with magic, and punched him with her closed fists. The man crumpled to the ground, but she did not relent until she ripped his head from his body and scattered his limbs.

"Queen Stephenie," one of the men called from the far end of the hall. The man's voice lacked strength. "I did not know."

She stood upright, her backpack having shifted uncomfortably and threatened to fall over her head. The man seated three-quarters of the way into the room had spoken. Now that the sword did not affect her thoughts, she smelt the musty odor of incense and sweat under the iron taste of blood. The man standing over the one sitting trembled.

The bald man who had stood next to the green-eyed man broke free of his terror. He swatted at the air in front of him with a sword. "Bitch! Demon!" He continued to turn, trying to find a target, but his face looked toward the floor at his feet. "Fight me. I'm the High Council Member. I'm your better."

The sitting man slipped from the chair and got to his knees and prostrated himself on the stone floor. "Forgive me," he said in the language of the dragons. "I believe they have misled my family. I am not with the kiwa and never intended you any harm."

Stephenie felt the High Council Member calling upon the magic of the augmentation device. He tried to form a wave of force toward where the Prophet begged from the ground. She drove her own beam of energy through his head. A moment later, the man crumpled into a heap.

She commanded the sword to stop disrupting thoughts. When she looked down at her blood covered hands, she noticed that instead of the normally emaciated fingers and arms she had grown used to seeing, her flesh had filled out normally. She also did not have the hollow and empty feeling. Her eyes narrowed, and she realized she had absorbed the dagger that had been in her side when she transformed.

Stephenie looked at the man who had grabbed her. The memory of how light he had been when she threw him came back to her. With horror, she noticed most of the flesh on his arms and the side of his face had been eaten away. Her right sleeve, as well as the armor and clothing around what had been the man's chest no longer existed. *I used his body as raw material.*

"Steph," Ryia moaned, helping Henton to his feet. "You okay?"

Stephenie turned to her friends. "Are you?"

"Alive," Henton said with a stilted voice.

The man who stood over Dacian trembled as he stared at her. The sword no longer redirected his attention to something else, and he could again see her in her lizard form.

"Who are you?" she asked. Her own sense of the man registered a form of mental damage, and she wondered if he had a head wound. Tears of fear leaked from the young man's eyes, but the man did not move.

"The man's name is Kev," Dacian said, still not lifting his head from the floor. "I am weak from poison, but if you permit me to explain, I will tell you what I know."

More energy flowed into her and she began to form a channel to release energy into the Prophet. *Slow down,* she hissed at herself. She held out her right hand and her own sword flew from where she had dropped it. "What generation Senzar are you?"

The man pushed himself up so that he knelt on the floor. Stephenie watched carefully for any hint he might use magic. She also sensed Henton had regained his feet and carried the crossbow again. Ryia supported his weight, and pain no longer radiated from him. *Good girl, heal our wounded first chance.*

"I am not of house Senzar," he said, his voice that of a professor. "My grandfather, Galeno, is head of house Hezin." The dark circles under Dacian's eyes and his sunken cheeks suggested a period of abuse. "House Senzar is powerful. Yreka, head of her house, made a request of my grandfather. She asked that we take control of Lobben and Sandven and prevent anyone from traveling north and to discourage you from traveling south. In exchange, Yreka returned control of Jelonis, a port city my family once owned long ago." He swallowed. "We did not know who you were and were under strict orders to not directly interfere with you."

Stephenie's mind raced. She had assumed the name Senzar represented a race of people recently descended from dragons. *It makes sense now.*

"You are as young as they say. Just twenty-one years?" he asked.

Implications continued to flood her thoughts and she allowed herself to connect to Ista for reassurance. "I am," she admitted after several moments of silence. The changes to her mouth and throat made her voice deeper even than any of her other transformations.

"We were told you were just kiwa, an outcast, with no family. Perhaps born as a sixth generation like me, but that Yreka had plans for you."

Stephenie looked back at the scattered remains of the man who had carried the sword now in her hands. "That man said something about me being a pawn of Yreka and the Senzar. He knew I was a prime. Yet you say you did not know."

Dacian shook his head. "I do not know what my grandfather knows, but I honestly believe he is unaware."

"Steph, we need to get moving," Ryia said. "We've made a lot of noise."

Stephenie signaled Ryia and Henton to hold. "Who is that?" Stephenie indicated the man who had carried the sword. "Was he with you?"

Dacian shook his head vigorously. "That man was named Kamari. He is seventh generation and a kiwa. Yreka expelled him from her house long ago and he's spent at least a hundred years working as an assassin."

Stephenie's brow ridge rose. "I've found its frowned upon to kill protected members of different houses. Isn't that a death sentence when it happens?"

Dacian forced a small laugh. "Depends on who, and how it happens. Most kiwa are actually protected by other houses and used to unofficially eliminate competitors and enemies. A kiwa found in someone else's territories will likely die, but centuries of fighting for their own place in society have made them adept at hiding."

She lifted the sword in her left hand. "Like this device that screwed with my ability to focus."

He nodded his head.

"Steph?" Ryia pushed again.

"Please understand that my goal had simply been to occupy Sandven with minimal death. Andre, the High Council Member, and Kamari poisoned me, killed my cousins, and took control over the invasion force."

She looked at the man. His once bald head had several days of growth. His robes had multiple stains and tears. Her even more sensitive nose detected days of sweat and a general lack of hygiene. *A prisoner, quite likely, but that does not make him an ally.* "Why shouldn't I kill you for what you've done?"

"I see now that Yreka wanted to keep you isolated to avoid you learning. Your power would challenge her position. I could help educate you on things no one has told you yet."

Stephenie growled and moved closer. "More people wanting to control and manipulate me."

"If your goal is revenge, please spare Kev. He was a spy for Andre and I had to manipulate his thoughts. This has locked him in a state where he is obsessed with me and has grown to despise Andre. He's become less verbal as a result."

Stephenie stopped. "From what I heard, you brought hundreds of augmentation devices to the followers of Fotia. Where did you get them?"

"I used all the viable ones I found. There are no more."

"That wasn't my question. Did you find them in the trap room?"

Dacian's eyes lit up. "You are aware of how these devices work?" He nodded his head at her glare. "Yes, I found them in the trap room."

Stephenie sensed multiple people waiting outside of the temple doors. *I'm running out of time.* "You can take me there?"

Dacian nodded his head. "It is outside of the Stone City, but it is not far."

She sheathed her sword. "Henton, kill him if he moves. Ryia, search the man I tore apart and get the scabbard for this sword." She rushed forward to the relay and realized her now longer taloned toes had cut holes into the front of her boots. *Damn it,* she swore, knowing that her footwear had been ruined without a replacement. She pushed the problem aside, jumped onto the stone base, and put a hand on the warm metal. She quickly responded to the challenge the relay demanded of her, then asked for confirmation of the trap's location. While she believed Dacian, she did not trust him. *North about three miles.* She broke contact with the relay and headed back toward the others.

"If you will permit me, I want to get a device from my rooms, assuming it is still there," Dacian said, a frown forming on his face. "It will allow me to contact my grandfather. It could even allow you to speak with him, despite our being thousands of miles away from him."

"You have a communication stone," she said. "We first have to escape the mountain alive."

Dacian stood up with Kev's help. "Andre sent those most loyal to him with the army. This is because most of the people my cousins and I recruited are only barely trained. As a result, my cousins and I trained many of those that remain here. We took the effort to instill in them a sense of awe for us."

"Mind manipulation," Ryia snarled, her staff pointing at him.

"Very subtle and not damaging, but effective," Dacian replied. "The point is, I should be able to get us out of the city without the need for fighting."

Or perhaps to mass people against us, Stephenie considered.

"I do not want to be your enemy. Your very presence changes so much. You would be the head of your house. Do you even know which house that is?"

"We need to destroy the trap," Stephenie said, ignoring the question. "You can take us there."

Dacian nodded his head.

"How many people will this sword work against at one time?" she asked.

Dacian shook his head. "I am sorry, I do not know. I fell victim to it before they poisoned me and locked me in a cell. It's definitely powerful, but I don't know the extent of its powers."

Henton approached, a pronounced limp in his left leg and a cowl in his hands. "Pull it on and if you pull it down, it might cover your face." He glanced at the sharp nails extending through the front of her boots. "Hopefully, people won't be looking at your feet."

Dacian nodded his approval. "When we have time, I could show you how to mentally deflect people's attentions to hide your presence. However, your man is correct, seeing you in this form would frighten people and they would believe you a demon. Unless you change back, hiding will be required."

Stephenie tried to ponder the man before her. She needed him. *Or what he claims he could do for me. But they are manipulative bastards. When will he betray me as well?* She looked at Kev and noticed that while the younger man helped Dacian, Dacian tried to limit that burden.

For now, she decided and slipped the cowl over her head and then pulled down the hood to obscure her face. "We need to go to the trap and destroy it before I change back." Henton handed her his gloves, knowing that the talons made her fingers too long for her own.

Henton then returned to holding the crossbow toward Dacian. "How do you plan to explain the dead?"

Dacian continued to lean on Kev. "There are four dead members of the high council and the kiwa. I will tell everyone that the kiwa poisoned me and killed the council members. Then the three of you responded to my request for Fotia to free me from the murder's grasp." He took a long breath. "I'm still weak from the poison, but I exaggerated the effects to keep them from giving me too much. I should be able to muster enough strength to influence those outside the doors to make them believe, and they can relay the story to everyone else."

Stephenie curled her lip at the blatant manipulation of people's thoughts. "Do not damage people's minds."

He immediately shook his head. "It is but the most subtle of suggestions. Nothing that impacts their personalities."

"I will be watching. Attempt to betray us, and you and a lot of others will die." She motioned for Henton and Ryia to fall in ahead of her so that she could disappear in the back of the group. She slid the dead man's sword into the scabbard and strapped the second weapon belt around her waist. *I know, Ista. I don't like this either.* She connected her mind to the sword and prepared herself to visualize disappearing from the awareness of the people outside the doors.

Chapter 33

The morning had come as quickly as Islet feared. Her breakfast had no taste, and she had barely been able to hand Sachi to Erika after Erika had returned with her cousin Rugga. The good-natured man accepted her request to fetch the students one at a time in the order of her choosing. He had, with no hesitation or questions, accepted her explanation of wanting to get to know the students.

Islet tried not to yawn as she listed to Torun, the first, and oldest, of those with the ability to use magic, tell her about the home he had left in Alkmaar. While he remained grateful for a place to come to escape the threat of Lobben, he hoped to one day return with his wife to the city of his birth. He also asked if they had any word from Horn Point and if his son still lived. The young man had joined King Ivan's army to build his fortune.

By the time Islet explained that they did not have any details from Horn Point, Rugga knocked on the door, implying the hourglass Erika had provided him had drained halfway. She called for him to enter and the door opened. Rugga stood waiting at the threshold.

"Torun, it was a pleasure to have spoken with you. If we hear anything about your son, I will make sure to get word to you right away."

"Thank you, Your Majesty. I never expected to have the honor to speak directly with you." The man stood up and bowed.

She nodded to him and then looked around him to Rugga. "Please return Torun to the school and bring the next student." She made a point of looking down at the paper on the desk. Her mouth grew suddenly dry and she felt her heart race. She looked up at Rugga. "Arno is the next on the list." Torun exited the room past Rugga, and Rugga was about to close the door when she spoke again. "Oh, I am going to step away for a moment while you go back to the city and return with Arno. If I'm not here, just ask him to have a seat and wait for me."

"Yes, Ma'am," Rugga said, bowed his head, and then closed the door.

Her breath rushed out of her, and she clenched her fists to hide the shaking of her hands. *I need to use the chamber pot.* She leapt to her feet, the urgent need driving her out of the hastily constructed office. She passed Walter, who had waited in the rear hall while she spoke to the first student. "I'll be right back."

After she addressed her physical needs, she rushed back to the pair of rooms. Walter grabbed her and wrapped her in a lasting embrace. "You'll be fine. Calm yourself. Your sister always says powerful emotions are easy to read."

Islet leaned her head into his shoulder. "I honestly would rather die than be a captive again. I keep telling myself I'm free, but it's hard to believe myself sometimes." She remained in his arms for a long time, simply listening to the fast beat of his heart and inhaling his smell, tinted with traces of the lavender soap he said felt good on his skin.

Eventually, the six guardians in the hall shifted, leaning their heads toward the north side of the castle.

She pulled away from him, her hands shaking again. "I wish I could still ask Felis for aid. But the god I grew up with never actually existed." *That is the problem with knowledge. You can never go back to the blissful ignorance of your past.* She took a deep breath, kissed her husband, and walked into the rear office.

Walter moved to the next room, and she heard him shut the door. She led the two guardians to the front office where they took their positions. She pulled the door partially open, then retreated into the rear office, stood near the back door, and forced herself to breathe slowly. *Stephenie, I don't know how you manage to face danger and be so calm. I wish I had your abilities.*

"Her Majesty will meet with you in this office," she heard Rugga say as he approached the outer office, having come in through the side entrance on the north of the castle.

"This building's walls are strange," came a second voice. The pitch was high enough to make the speaker androgenous, the accent thick enough to mark the speaker as not native. "Do you know anything about that?"

"I'm sorry. I don't know what you mean. I'm not normally in the castle. I'm only helping because my cousin said she needed help today. It seems Her Majesty's daughter is unwell, so my cousin has too much work."

"Interesting."

Islet felt her heart racing, and no matter how hard she tried, she could not get it to slow down.

"Your Majesty?" Rugga asked. Islet assumed he stuck his head into the room by the sound of his voice. The door between the rooms stood ajar, but it blocked her view of the front office.

"She appears to be in the next room," the other voice said.

"Please wait inside," Rugga responded. His voice was clearer and louder, making Islet assume he pushed the door all the way open.

"After you," the other voice said.

No. Damn it. She took a deep breath and spoke. "Arno, I will be right with you. Rugga, please check with Erika. She needed help bringing some supplies to the kitchen."

The closest guardian in the rear hall shook its head. *Damn it.*

"Rugga?" Islet did not hear a response and she felt her mind wander. *Is that a stain on the floor? What does it remind me of?*

Good girl, she heard in her head.

She stumbled as the guardians in the rear office slammed closed the door between the rooms. The sudden mental break left her disoriented.

A cry of pain came from the front room and then a man's long wail of pain. She tumbled backwards onto her rear, and before she knew it, a guardian had dragged her into the hall. The door in front of her slammed shut.

"Islet!" Walter shouted as he emerged from the room he had been in. "Did he hurt you?"

She shook her head. "Ista, is Rugga safe?"

The nearest guardian shook his head yes, then no.

Through the doors, she could hear someone screaming and the sounds of something breaking.

She looked at the guardian. "Is Rugga out of the room?" The guardian nodded its head. "Take me to him."

Walter helped her to her feet, and they rushed through the rear hall and then through a side passage that led to the front hall. Three guardians stood around the sandy blond who lay on the floor. She reached the prone man's side and knelt down. Burns covered the left side of his face and chest and blood smeared his temple. She also thought he had broken his left arm. She applied pressure on the bleeding wound, ruining her dress.

"Kas! Ista, get Kas and Lami."

The nearest guardian tilted its head, expressing the insult it felt at being asked to do something it had already done. Menni had been instructed to watch from afar and fetch the others as soon as Arno and Rugga were halfway to the castle. While Islet could have sworn days had passed, Lami, Kas, and Ryia's three original students rushed down the hall before much more of Rugga's blood pooled on the floor.

"Arno attacked him." She got out of the way as the healers closed in. "I believe at least one guardian had to yank him from the room by the arm."

As she spoke, something slammed into the door, followed by a cry of pain. Islet knew that the doors and walls blocked a mage's ability to sense through them. But she felt less certain about other magic escaping. Five guardians now filled the hall, waiting to get closer to the door.

"We should get Rugga to a bedroom," Lami commanded, his authority earned by years of healing those in Alkmaar, though fear of what existed on the other side of the door shown in his eyes and the eyes of everyone else.

"Follow me," Walter said, his hand on his sword.

Chapter 34

Getting out of the temple had posed the first challenge. The soldiers that had responded to the noise doubted Dacian's version of events until suddenly they accepted his word and believed everything the Prophet told them. Stephenie saw the connections between their minds and Dacian, but the connections coming from the sword to these people overwhelmed anything Dacian did. She monitored the sword's behavior and found that it instantly made connections to anyone around her, except for those she actively concentrated on excluding from the effect.

She continued to move around the soldiers so that she did not stand behind Dacian, which might impact his ability to redirect the men's suspicions. While allowing this man to change people's thoughts bothered her, the alternative left her killing anyone that blocked their escape. *And I don't want to do that.*

The senior most guard wanted to sequester Dacian in a safe location until they could search the city and deem it safe. Dacian used his powers to convince them that the events of the night required discretion and that he would address their concerns as soon as he returned from doing Fotia's bidding.

While Stephenie eventually narrowed in on the fields he created, she did not understand the subtle manipulations because without a connection to the minds of the men, she could not observe the nature of how Dacian altered their thoughts. Her own prior attempts resembled a brute squad breaking through doors. *Not that I want to start altering people's thoughts, but I would like to understand how to do it without damaging their minds.*

The five of them eventually managed to leave the soldiers to the task of covertly cleaning up the dead. Dacian then led them down to the first level and out of one of the secondary exits of the city. From there, they left the surface city and traveled north into the foothills of the mountains. Stephenie found her feet hurt inside the boots, but she had no intention of transforming back until they finished with the trap. Instead, she focused on watching the sunrise as they picked their way through the undergrowth. *Anything to take my mind off the discomfort.*

Dacian's reliance upon Kev grew as the difficulty of the ground increased. Eventually, they reached a place where Stephenie had to fly all five of them up a tall cliff to a small ledge. Square holes in the side of the mountain face hinted at a long removed wooden structure that might have provided access to what appeared to be a shallow cave over fifteen feet high. Someone countless years earlier had filled in the opening with rubble, stone, and soil to create a natural-looking wall. Time had allowed grasses and even small trees to take root. Stephenie could sense the tunnel on the other side of the obstacle, but without someone to guide her, finding this access point would have taken days or weeks.

"Vikram and Warner helped me make that opening," Dacian said, pointing to a gap in the rubble near the top of the cave. "We reinforced the interior with some logs. It's only been two years, so they should not have rotted yet."

Stephenie climbed up the steep pile of rocks, her taloned toes digging into the ground through the front of her boots. Her fingers easily found handholds. The small opening, about ten feet up the slope, still appeared to have the logs bracing the sides. The solid stone of the mountain made up the ceiling of the original opening. She signaled the others to follow her, and she crouch-walked the half-dozen feet to the other side of the barrier, where she then climbed down to the floor of the passage.

Dacian, helped by Kev, followed next, with Henton and Ryia on their heels. Dacian activated a light stone and handed it to Kev to hold before them. The extra illumination allowed Stephenie's excellent night vision to see a long way into the mountain, but aside from a few scattered rocks that had rolled away from the barrier, the ten-foot-wide passage remained empty. The fifteen-foot-high ceiling had vaulting to help support the natural stone, which she did not sense as having any magical reinforcement.

"It's at least a couple miles or more before we reach the trap room," Dacian said.

Stephenie wished she could get a reading of the trap's location from the augmentation devices, but she suspected that limitation had been a security precaution from the original builders, as the relays created complex challenges that changed for each request, whereas the augmentation device challenges remained consistent. "Then we should get going."

They walked in silence, with Stephenie in the lead. She used her mind to search for threats and obstacles. In her current form, the continual energy draw did not physically tax her as much as normal, but the hyper alertness made her uncomfortable and she fidgeted with the weapons hanging from the two sword belts.

"We are almost to the chamber," Dacian finally said, confirming what Stephenie had already sensed. "The room is circular, with a high ceiling. The round cylinder of the trap sits in the middle on a pedestal."

"And there is nothing dangerous to us in there?" Henton asked.

"The room is full of magical artifacts, though most appear related to the construction of the trap and the augmentation devices. I finalized the assembly of over four hundred unfinished devices in there, depleting everything that remained. Nothing disturbed me, or my cousins, while we did that." He glanced over at Stephenie. "There are storage cabinets, chairs, workbenches, and ledgers. Besides that, there are some handsomely carved statues situated at seventy-two-degree increments around the walls. The largest is directly across from the entrance."

"What?" Ryia asked.

Dacian turned to Ryia. "There are five carvings that are equally spaced around the room."

He and Kas would get along well, Stephenie decided. *Always trying to be too damn precise.* "We'll get a good look shortly," she told Ryia as they moved around a gentle bend in the passage.

Stephenie stopped at the threshold of the room, just as the crystals in the ceiling illuminated, generating a harsh light a little too blue for daylight. The ten-foot-tall metal cylinder glistened and reflected a blue tone. Raised runes and markings covered the surface of the cylinder, and aside from the dust that had settled on any of the flatter surfaces, the three-foot diameter device showed no signs of tarnish or damage from where she stood.

"Prophet?" Kev asked, wonder filling his voice.

"Yes, Kev, this is an amazingly wonderful room. Long before any of us were born, people developed technology that no one has recreated in countless generations."

"You sound like you don't want to see it destroyed," Henton remarked. He stayed several feet back, Balkr's crossbow still pointed to the ceiling, but ready for use.

Dacian turned slowly to face him. "I'm a student of history. I relish the study of what we lost. Learning what existed when my ancestors abandoned these lands three to four hundred years after the elven wars." He breathed slowly, working through some obvious physical pain. "In truth, I have never heard of these devices being destroyed. I know that people of sufficient sensitivity can respond correctly to the challenge and gain command of the device, but to destroy it?" He shrugged. "At least while the source of its power still exists?"

Stephenie opened her mind and felt her senses overwhelmed with energy floating about in the room. The floor, ceiling, walls, tables, and everything permeated different fields. "Definitely a preservation field throughout."

Dacian turned back to her. "Yes. You will become quite thirsty the longer you remain in the room." He glanced back at Henton. "Over the period of half a day. The field that keeps the contents in a consistent state is not harmful in short durations."

Stephenie turned her focus to Dacian. "We've disabled a trap before, so I have some idea of what I face. However, your actions destroyed the government in Sandven and today we killed what I assume is the leadership of Lobben. I expect fighting and chaos to see who takes over will soon follow."

Dacian nodded his head. "The High Council Member controlled most of the other seven on the council, and so he effectively ruled the country. The king is a figurehead with no actual power." Dacian leaned against the wall behind him for support. "Unfortunately, I am certain Kamari, the assassin, has at least one companion in Horn Point, or he did several days ago when they took me. I had two cousins that I am fairly certain I saw die. They appeared to lose awareness of their surroundings while I spoke with one of them."

"And the piece of shit implied at least one, if not more, has gone to Ista." Stephenie glanced at Henton, but he did not provide a look that implied he felt the need to say he told her so.

"Dufnall can't take Sandven back on his own," Ryia said from where she stood next to Henton.

Stephenie turned back to Dacian. "I've let you live so far. You've helped me find the trap, and I don't think you've sent me into an ambush. But you can't just walk away now. You've left a mess of both countries. You've effectively achieved what Yreka wanted, have me confined in Ista, or occupied sorting through this mess before it's safe enough for me to trust my southern border."

Dacian looked uncomfortable. "I am uncertain what I can do."

"You're their prophet, or some bullshit like that, right?" He nodded. "And you said you influenced a lot of minds to trust you."

"When I am not suffering the lingering effects of poison, I am quite adept at convincing people to give me what I want, yes."

Stephenie glanced at Ryia and Henton. Both of them gave her a worried expression, uncertain of where her statements led. She did not trust the man. She did not like his methods, but she needed an immediate solution. "I need you to take over Lobben and rule it. Do whatever is needed. Dissolve the council. Overthrow the king. Whatever is needed to get the army under control."

"I am not sure exactly how I would do that. The nobles who led the force are working on Andre's prior orders, which likely said to disregard what I told them. There is a kiwa among them, and whoever that is, they will probably still come for you, and for me as well."

Stephenie pondered the issue for a moment. "The assassins are a separate problem. Let's first focus on how we get the armies to stop killing the Sandvian people and pivot them into acting as a temporary holding force until I can reestablish a working government there."

Dacian lifted his hands, palms up, showing he had no suggestions.

Ryia shifted her feet. "The priests and anyone carrying an augmentation device are about to lose their connection to power. That's going to cause chaos." She looked at Henton. "If only we could time it with Dufnall raising an army to strike."

Stephenie shook her head. "Ivan's forces were either killed or fled. I'm not sure they would even support Dufnall immediately. Didn't he say Ivan has a couple of kids?"

Henton nodded his head. "In the south. That assumes one of the jarls thinking they could take over has not killed them."

"And if we coordinated things, people would likely suspect the invasion was caused by me and Dufnall as a means to overthrow the country." Stephenie frowned at the thought and shook her head. "Besides, we don't have time to plan anything. We need to stop them from advancing on Alkmaar and Ista." She bit her lip. "I hate reinforcing lies, but I have an idea of how to get you in control of the country, Dacian. It will probably have long-term consequences when Fotia never returns, but it will buy us time."

Dacian crossed his arms. "I had really hoped to leave this country."

"Some bastard has to pay for what's happened," Ryia snapped.

Stephenie held his gaze with her reptilian eyes. "What are a couple of years to someone like you? They will pass before you know it." She turned around and entered the trap room. "You will answer to me in how the countries are run."

Dacian took Kev's arm and followed Stephenie. "I will support your decisions, Prime. I cannot speak for my grandfather, but I believe he will do so as well, once he learns the truth."

Stephenie ignored the man and continued to drift into the room as Dacian disengaged his arm from Kev and sat down on a wooden chair.

"It really feels dry in here," Ryia said, following Stephenie. "And the air smells funny." Ryia stopped in front of a set of wooden tables against the right-hand wall. She walked past the books and supplies that sat in neatly organized piles to a seven-foot-tall stone carving of a naked man halfway exposed from the surface of the wall.

"It is the preservation magic." Dacian motioned for Kev to sit in the next chair. "The walls, floor, ceiling ... everything seems to radiate it into the room."

Stephenie still found it hard to sort out all the fields in the hundred-foot-diameter room. She frowned at not finding any defensive measures. *The entrance had just physical concealment. Did the builders consider that to be enough?* She did not have an answer, and she knew the longer they waited, the more Sandven would suffer.

Her path through the room drew her to the trap. She moved around it, looking at the markings to identify a smooth spot where she expected it to present her with the challenge. She stopped on the side opposite from the entrance. A circular spot two-thirds of the way up the tall metal cylinder had no markings. "I think I found it."

Ryia continued her path around the edge of the room. "Whoever carved these naked men thought highly of themselves, or men are far less gifted now."

Stephenie ignored her younger friend's statement and put a hand on the trap's surface, feeling warmth where an expectation of cold existed. The device reached out with a mental connection at the same time a complex pattern appeared on the smooth surface. Stephenie responded by projecting a mental image of the challenge symbol with the accent that indicated she was a recent descendant of a dragon.

Her awareness and sense of self lurched. She no longer had a body, her consciousness simply existed in a vast void. The void had no color. No smell. No sound. It did not even have light or darkness. She simply floated in nothingness. Even her connection to Ista felt broken, leaving her isolated and alone in her head. Unlike when the sword made it impossible for her to concentrate on Ista, she now had no sense of the castle at all. Instead, she felt another presence. Something malevolent and angry.

She immediately worked to contain her memories and the idea of herself. "Fotia," she called out in this place that existed within metal and crystalline structures.

"Why have you come? What is it you want? Stephenie, daughter of Duvargintik."

She fought against the trap as it ripped memories and knowledge from her. Unlike Ista, who she had welcomed into her mind, the trap needed to stay out of her thoughts. "Fotia, I need to send a message to all of those carrying an augmentation device." The words hurt to form in her mind. The trap's personality felt nothing like Mertor's. This one liked the suffering of others. *It likes pain.*

"I do like pain," the empty void replied. Then suddenly she found herself in Vinerxan, in the dungeon under the castle, where she healed Orlan to keep him alive as The Butcher cut and burned his flesh.

Stephenie took a deep breath, once again having a human body and form. A chill ran through her. The torture she helped to perpetuate represented a low point in her life, even though she had no choice in the act. However, instead of Lord Rilan standing over the table with a dull knife, a bald man with sharp eyes and a heavily muscled torso took his place. She realized instantly that the trap had made a mistake. While the disturbing stench of blood, urine, and decay filled her nose, the fact that she once again had a mental image of her body, allowed her to focus on containing everything that made her real. She clamped down on her memories and thoughts. "Mine," she growled at the projected image of the man.

"What is it you want to say to my Faithful?" The man's tone had grown cold, as if he had lost a toy that he intended to play with longer.

She considered being polite, but in her limited experiences with traps, they had formed the personalities of the devices from living people, and some of that personality leaked out in the doctrine of the religious followers. So far, Fotia had been hostile and seemed to respond to authority, not kindness.

"You could send a message yourself," the trap said, as though it spoke to a child.

Stephenie knew she could send emotions and impressions to those holding augmentation devices if she knew the correct command. However, that kind of message only contained feelings and remained limited in complexity. This ability normally resided with the high priest, or others who controlled their churches. She did not want to send a simple message, but one with an active voice and words. That required using the trap.

Her tone grew hard. "Tell them you are displeased with their behaviors. Your Prophet, whom you had explicitly chosen, had conveyed your commandments, but the corrupt council had betrayed the Faithful and killed King Ivan. In the land of the gods, you have made a pact with the Goddess of the north and will tolerate no attacks on her followers. From this day forward, you will withhold your powers from all but your Prophet as punishment for disobedience. Once the Faithful learn to live by your Prophet's messages and repent their sins, you will consider returning. Until then, they must suffer for the betrayal they committed."

The image of Fotia before her narrowed his eyes. "You shut down and killed Mertor. Now you plan to do the same to me. I do not wish to be terminated."

Stephenie felt herself fragment. Pain radiated through every part of her being. She blinked several times and instead of her mind being within the trap, she lay crumpled on the floor with her chin pressed into her chest and the back of her head against the wall. She heard screaming and saw a bright flash of light and felt the floor rumble, but she could not feel the right side of her body.

More light flashed through the room and a body flew through the air. A detached part of her mind recognized Kev as the young man collided with the ceiling before dropping to the floor with a sickening thud.

Henton and Ryia walked backwards toward the passage with Dacian supported between the two of them. A large naked stone statue pursued them.

Stephenie struggled to breathe as she sorted through the pain of a broken arm and crushed ribs. *Shit.* She closed her eyes and pulled energy from the room. She opened herself like a damn breaking. Power flooded into her body, and she directed it to healing the worst of her injuries.

The stone statue changed directions; the trap aware that the larger threat had regained consciousness. Stephenie rolled away as a stone foot slammed down into the floor where her legs had been. "Fotia, you've picked a fight you won't win this time," she yelled in the old tongue.

The statue swung a fist at her, and she lurched backwards, narrowly avoiding the stone. Her breath came with the taste of blood and a throbbing in her side. The construction moved as fast as one of Ista's guardians and her healing remained incomplete.

She unleashed the raw energy in her, aiming for the ten-foot-tall statue's chest. The lightning flashed around its surface and discharged into the walls, ceiling, and floor, leaving the statue unmarked.

Damn it. She considered the weakness of Ista's guardians and launched a gravity wave at the statue's neck. Her field fell apart before it struck the automaton and she leapt backwards again to avoid the stone fists.

Ryia ran at its back and swung her staff, but the stone being kicked backwards, balancing on one leg. The staff tried to raise a protective barrier, but it crumbled, and Ryia flew across the room, striking the wall near the entrance.

Henton released the bolt from his crossbow. The projectile slammed into the statue's back and exploded with a flash of light. However, the statue did not appear to even notice. The flattened bolt fell to the floor and the stone monster continued to charge after Stephenie.

Stephenie ran, her feet unbalanced by her toes sticking out the front of her boots. *Ista? Ideas?* She felt the castle assessing the current situation from her memories, but it had not yet provided guidance.

"Steph," Ryia said, her volume hindered by a lack of breath. "Nothing the staff has can hurt it."

Stephenie felt relief flow through her to know that Ryia had somehow protected herself from the worst of the blow.

"The crossbow did nothing," Henton shouted as he helped pull Ryia to the confines of the passage.

Stephenie continued to retreat, her feet slipping because she had trouble gaining traction on the smooth floor. She shifted to the tips of her feet, letting her talons dig into the uniform stone as she continued to keep the trap between her and the ten-foot-tall statue. Her head still hurt from the initial blow, and she had trouble keeping out of this guardian's reach. "Just this one statue?" She called out to her companions.

"So far," Ryia said, her voice stronger. Lightning again leaped from the staff, this time aimed for the trap.

"No!" Stephenie shouted.

The trap redirected the lightning back into the passage, but with ten times the energy. Stephenie heard Ryia cry out in pain and then nothing.

Damn it. Stephenie dodged left as residual electricity shot out in all directions from the cylinder. She absorbed the white-hot bolt that connected with her leg. Her pants leg, already singed slightly from her transformation, blackened and fell away. She limped backward as the statue continued its relentless approach. Using her mind, she flung books, chairs, and supplies at the stone monster. The creature knocked aside the larger objects and ignored the smaller ones.

Ista? The castle informed her no way existed to block the power traveling through the entangled particles. *Yeah, that much I know.* Stephenie felt herself growing tired. *I can't keep this up.*

Her left boot slipped again on the smooth floor, and she caught herself with her powers. She pushed away with her right foot, ripping a gouge in the smooth floor as she tried to get out of reach of the statue.

The stone fist struck her hip, breaking her pelvis and sending her across the room. Her powers kept her from hitting the wall and energy flowed into her broken bones, knitting them back together just in time for her to scramble away from the statue again.

"Steph!" Henton called from the passage.

"Bastard," she whimpered. "Ryia?"

"The staff saved me. Mostly."

Stephenie again felt relief flood through her as she maneuvered closer to the passage. Tears leaked down her face as the pain in her hip and chest built. "I need you to act as a diversion."

Ryia hesitantly came to the edge of the passage as Stephenie circled around the trap, her attention on the opposite side of the room. "I need you to run past it and give me time."

"Uh ... maybe."

"Can you do it?" She growled, her focused already narrowed on the floor about a third of the way around the trap on the left of the passage.

"Yes."

"Now!" Stephenie shouted and then dropped to her hands and knees, trusting her friend to act. In her mind, she examined the microscopic fields holding the stone particles together. In her lizard form, shifting focus away from the macro world happened faster, but with no less pain. Power burned her body as she concentrated on weakening the bounds of the stone that made up the floor. She lost much of her awareness of the world around her, having only a vague sense of Ryia running at the statue with lightning flying.

While the people that constructed the room had simplified her task by purifying the floor and walls into a monolithic structure, she needed to disrupt a huge section of the floor. Not just wide, but also deep. Blood ran from her lizard nose, and she felt her heart racing.

Ryia grunted in pain and Stephenie barely registered Ryia's hasty approach with the statue chasing her around the trap. Stephenie winced as she pushed the fields further toward the statue. "Jump!" She yelled at Ryia and had to trust her friend to succeed.

She felt the statue step into the liquefied stone because new material entered her disruptive field, shifting the contents she had focused on. Her senses expanded as the statue fell forward. She only managed to generate a depth of about three feet, but the statue's right leg fell all the way through the liquid stone, and it tumbled forward. A wave of cold stone few into the air.

Stephenie ripped her attention away from the field and generated a repulsive wall of gravity to direct the splashing stone back down toward the statue. Much of the stone solidified the moment her field dropped, reestablishing the bonds between the molecules. But enough of the floor remained liquid long enough to encase the majority of the statue. The automaton's left leg and the back of its head and upper shoulders remained above the uneven and wavy floor. Stone dust and droplets of rock skittered across the uneven ground, as they returned to the natural state before hitting the floor.

Stephenie scooted back, her head burned, and for a moment, she remained blind to the energy fields around her. The statue's left leg continued to move, but the rest of it appeared unable to break free of the floor. She held her position and watched, hoping the statue could not escape. She wiped blood from her lizard nose, but more appeared.

"Steph," Ryia said, rushing back to her and wrapping her arms around her. Blood and burn marks covered the right side of Ryia's scalp, where some of her hair had melted away. Evidence of further damage existed on her shirt and pants.

Stephenie held Ryia as she breathed slowly. Her perception of the energy fields slowly returned, though she still felt like someone coming into a dark room after staring at the sun. Her ability to differentiate anything but the strongest of patterns had not yet returned.

Henton and Dacian appeared at the edge of the passage. They looked at the chaos in the room and waited. "Any movement from the other statues?" Henton asked.

Stephenie looked around, both with her eyes and her mind. The preservation fields, combined with her changing focus, continued to make the room feel like looking into a dense fog. "I've not seen them move yet."

"That one was bigger than the rest," Ryia said, slowly releasing Stephenie and moving back to her feet. Ryia's hair was a tangled mess, with missing sections and melted ends. The smell of burned flesh lingering on her. "The other statues looked like they are just part of the wall, not just in a man-sized alcove like that one."

"Poor Kev," Dacian said as he looked at the broken body. "He had been a loyal spy for Andre. I had not intended to break his mind so badly." He looked at Stephenie. "To see your power. I'm at a loss for words." He turned to the floor. "The fluid motion of the stone defender is not even something I had considered. Then for you to bury it in the floor."

Ryia helped Stephenie to her feet. "We're not done here yet," Stephenie said, irritated by Dacian's more clinical tone. "The piece of shit personality refused my order and then tried to kill me." She turned to the others. "Wait in the passage, just in case there are other defenses."

"You okay, Steph?" Henton asked. "You took a beating. I thought it might have killed you."

She lied and nodded her head. She felt the throbbing in her chest and hip the worst of all, but the burned-away scales on her leg came in next. However, her ability to sense the fields had nearly recovered. "We need to deal with this thing, and now I'm mad."

She waited for the others to retreat to the passage and then she went back to the opposite side of the trap. Her taloned hand touched the warm surface. This time she held her sense of self in reserve, locking it away protectively from outsiders. She responded to a new challenge, allowing the trap much less access to her mind. A moment later, she again existed in the void of nothingness. However, instead of waiting for the trap to construct a reality for her, she forced an image of the trap chamber into her thoughts. Fotia resisted, but then the room appeared around her as she first saw it, with the bald man standing next to the metal cylinder.

"This time we are doing it my way," she demanded. She caught a reflection of her face in the smooth part of the trap and her neck had elongated as well as the front of her head. Long red horns protrude half a foot from the top of her scaled skull. Her green eyes glowing with an inner light.

"I am designed to survive at all costs. I will not let you destroy me," the man said.

She shot forward and drove her taloned claws into the man's side, easily lifting him off the stone floor with her right hand that seemed three times as large as normal. "Can you see my inner nature now? I can be as cruel as you. Send my message."

Fotia squirmed, and Stephenie sunk the talons from her left hand into his other side. The man seemed as small as a child. "You are a construct. A device. A memory of a spiteful person. I have proven my authority with the challenge. I have given you an order. Obey!"

Fotia's eyes closed and the room shifted. She no longer held him in her grasp, but he remained diminished in size as she looked down upon him as if she had truly taken on the full form of a dragon. She felt the message go out to all of the augmentation devices. The location of every device came back through the relays, with more than half of them located in Sandven. Each one registered in her mind like a tiny beacon. Confusion and disbelief came back through the network of devices from those holding them.

"I have granted your request," the man said. "Will you not give me mercy and allow me to continue to exist? I am what is left of the man who went by the name Fotia. In building me, the man was consumed. You would murder me in deactivating me."

"I order you to release the being from the trap and cease activity. The life you claim to have exists only because you are killing something else."

"Do you not live because you kill animals to eat them?"

Stephenie nodded her head. "But those who use you are killing that being in the other world in order to dominate and harm others. Your argument is a false premise. They do not need to use that power to survive, and you are not a living person, just a device." She focused her mind. "Shut down," she demanded, pushing her will upon the device.

The man before her disappeared and the void returned. She struggled to breathe. Fotia intended to trap her within him to kill her in a last act of revenge. Grabbing the lingering power within the device, she pushed her mind from the cylinder and gasped when she once again felt her own body.

She sagged to her knees. *I've killed again.* Despite what she had told the trap, she knew from her dealing with Mertor that the intelligence with the traps had something of a life, similar to Ista. "But my position is still more correct," she mumbled, knowing she did more good than harm.

"Steph?" Ryia's voice held a lot of pain now that the adrenaline in her system had faded.

"Are you okay?" Henton asked. "Dacian says the trap is disabled."

Stephenie took a deep breath and stood up. The statue's left leg had stopped moving, and when she reached out to the augmentation device still in her pouch, she sensed the limited power it absorbed from the environment, but none of the entangled energy that actually provided its functions.

She pulled more energy into herself, strengthening her right hand and arm. With a growl, she slashed downward across the smooth surface of the trap. No longer powered from another world, the normally indestructible metal ripped and tore under her talons. *Now I am done. The bastard can never be reactivated.* She knew that without the surface that displayed the challenge, even with environmental energy, no one should be able to provide commands to reawaken the device.

Exhausted, she stepped down from the platform and limped around the right side of the cylinder, avoiding the statue, just in case it still had a different source of power and could break free of the floor. "It's done."

Chapter 35

Stephenie considered transforming back to her human self when they reached the rubble wall obscuring the exit, but she did not trust Dacian enough to risk being that weak and exhausted in front of him. *If I'm this tired and damaged in this form, I'm likely to pass out as a human.* Instead, she sat down with her back against the wall. Dacian sat against the opposite wall and further down the passage. He looked ashen and weak, though he had not been directly involved in the combat. *Poison. The most effective way to kill one of us.*

She reached out to Ista. *Is Islet available?* The castle confirmed Islet carried the communication stone and that her sister rested in her office. Ista also relayed the events that had occurred with Arno. *Why didn't you tell me?* Stephenie ground her teeth, but then calmed down as Ista conveyed both Islet's and the castle's own concern about providing distracting news. *I get it, but I'm not happy about it, even if it was the correct decision. Let me talk to my sister.*

"Stephenie," Islet said from her chair. Her posture and pale skin conveying Islet's physical and mental exhaustion. "Are you well? Henton and Ryia?"

Stephenie nodded her head, projecting a human image of herself to Islet. *Yes, we are all safe. The trap is disabled, and a message sent to all the people carrying the augmentation devices.* She scratched an itch on the side of her head where her small horns extended from her skull. *Ista informed me of what's happened. Are Rugga's injuries as bad as she believes?*

Islet bit her lower lip. "I shouldn't have involved him. I had hoped to use someone who had no knowledge of things to keep everyone safe. However, I think the bastard read my mind even though I was in the other room."

You did very well. I'll see what kind of help we can provide Rugga once we return.

"Kas and Lami did good work on him. Erika is staying with him to make sure he doesn't need anything."

I'll try to get home as quickly as possible. She shifted her position, her damaged boots now annoying enough that she considered going barefoot. *The man you captured is an assassin. Ista said he's damaged one guardian, but the others in the storage room overcame him enough to subdue him. It was an excellent idea to use a pair of rooms like you did. Ista can keep one door closed and let the guardians in and out of the other one. You might write him a letter informing him of the food and water you left and that he won't be starved to death. It might keep him from trying to do more damage that would force the guardians to kill him.*

"Thank you. I'll write a letter. We were at a loss for how to deal with him." Islet leaned forward and put her arms on her desk. "Did you kill the Senzar that were there?"

Stephenie shifted her head from side to side. *It's complicated.* She quickly relayed all the details of their day in Berl, the sword that obscured thoughts, the dead kiwa, and Dacian's help. Once she had updated Islet on their current state, she leaned back against the stone behind her. *I need to figure out what to do about Lobben and Sandven. Dufnall likely doesn't have enough loyal followers to take control directly. We need to get him support and have the Lobben forces withdraw in an orderly fashion, but I worry destroying their god might cause total chaos, even with my demand they follow Dacian's orders.*

Islet nodded. "I'll ask Dufnall to think of ways we can help him take the throne. He might simply turn things over to his nephews. Assuming they live, they would be next in line."

Please work on determining his desires. We need functioning trade, and this shitty war will put those efforts back by at least a year.

"Assuming one of the other jarls doesn't take over. We still don't have an army to prop him up with."

Stephenie pursed her lips. *No, but we have money. I know there are mercenaries we could hire.* She looked over at Dacian, who motioned to her to get her attention.

"Prime," Dacian said from where he sat a dozen feet from the edge of the rubble that blocked the passage entrance. "My grandfather is trying to contact me. Do you want to speak with him? I can introduce you."

Stephenie did not feel up to meeting the old man, but she needed to assess what the head of Dacian's house knew and make sure he supported her goals for Lobben. "Yes, that is fine." *Islet, I need to go. I'll contact you later.* Islet nodded her understanding and Stephenie broke the connection.

Henton glanced in her direction, his crossbow still armed and loaded with their only remaining bolt. Ryia sat next to Henton, her staff sitting across her lap. She looked pained and more exhausted than Stephenie felt.

"Grandfather," Dacian said in Denarian from where he sat, the small oval stone held before him. "Yes, I am alive. However, someone sent at least two, and likely three kiwa to disrupt our activities." He nodded his head. "I am nearly certain they killed Warner and Vikram when they were in Horn Point. The one in Berl, named Kamari, was working with Andre. They poisoned me and took me prisoner. I believe they wanted you to believe Stephenie had killed us." He shook his head. "Grandfather, I believe Yreka has misled us. Stephenie is not an outcast." Dacian frowned. "I know I was not supposed to interact with her, but, Grandfather, she is a prime." He pushed himself to his feet and moved closer to Stephenie. "As you can see," he said, holding out an arm toward her. He swallowed and nodded his head. "Of course." He held out the stone. "He would like to speak with you." Dacian nodded his head and then handed Stephenie the stone. "I assume you know how to activate it."

She forced herself to her feet, took the stone, and instructed the stone to open the connection that currently requested her to respond without answering Dacian directly. A brightly lit office with wooden walls, bookshelves overflowing with books, and a man with long bushy hair appeared before her. The man, appearing to be in his mid-forties, smiled at her from a stuffed armchair, though his eye betrayed the youthful appearance granted from a strong affinity with magic. She suspected he had lived for well over two centuries.

"I am Galeno," he said with a firm voice. He rose to his feet and bowed to her in a manner similar to the custom of Cothel. "I must beg forgiveness from you, not only for my actions, but the actions I ordered my grandson to perform. Please tell me that none of your protected house have come to harm as a result."

Stephenie narrowed her eyes. "I am not yet certain how many people in Sandven have died. Lobben murdered King Ivan, along with many of his loyal soldiers and advisors."

"Forgive my involvement in those tragedies. Dacian's purpose had been solely to occupy both countries so that you do not journey south from Ista. I was informed you were just an outcast that Yreka had pursued for punishment. She only wanted you contained until she decided what action she would take."

Stephenie kept her expression calm. "I told her to leave me alone. To leave Cothel and my brother alone. Did she send those assassins after me? Has she done something to Cothel? One of these assassins spoke Cothish."

Galeno remained expressionless. "Yreka is powerful. She has enemies, but almost none that have the resources to oppose her openly, at least not until you disrupted their plans three years ago." He slowly turned. "Many of her enemies would not hesitate to resort to using kiwa to eliminate those that anger them. I have known her to do the same. However, I do not have any confidants within her household." He gestured to the accommodations around him and then sat back down in the chair. "Others, I know, do have spies, but House Hezin has been in decline for many centuries. Hezin, the source of my line, had several offspring at the same time, and many of them competed for control over his legacy. Instead of rising to prominence, the household ripped itself apart from the inside." He looked wistful. "Senzar had fewer children with humans and elves, and he spread their births over the centuries. That line remained fairly stable." His curiosity finally got the better of him, and he leaned forward. "Do you know your family line?"

The realization of household names coming from the dragon that spawned the offspring clicked with her. *If I tell him, what does he gain?*

How many others heard me say his name? She tried to weigh the consequences carefully and felt energy flowing into her from the frustration of having too little knowledge to make an informed choice.

Dacian shifted uncomfortably. He could not hear Galeno's side of the conversation, but she suspected he could sense her energy draw. "What do you gain by that knowledge? How does it benefit you and harm me?"

Galeno smiled. "That is a wise question." He sat back, taking on the role of a studied instructor. "If a household already exists, as a first-generation descendant, you suddenly become the head of that house. You might inherit a powerful group of people. Those at the top might resent you and challenge you, or they may see you as a means to raise their fortunes." He picked up a small statue of translucent green stone fashioned to look like a dragon with its wings extended and teeth bared to strike. "There are only a handful of fourth generation people left in the world, and one ancient third generation man. Most houses now are led by sixth generation descendants. And many more houses have simply disbanded because those of subsequent generations don't have the power to compete against the other houses. You are a prize anyone would want to claim and control." He set the dragon figure down on a small table in front of him, so that it remained in view of the communication stone. "I imagine trying to control you would be a fatal mistake."

She snorted. "Just as insincere attempts to appeal to the vanity that I know I have are."

Galeno nodded his head. "A valid assessment. My flattery of you is due entirely to my surprise and appreciation of what you represent. I never expected to ever hear that another child would be born from a dragon. I truly believed they had disappeared from the world and the families would eventually die off." He leaned toward the communication stone again. "However, I suspect I understand what Yreka is now doing."

Stephenie failed to contain herself and asked. "What is she doing?"

"She wanted me to keep you in the north without directly doing anything to you. I imagine that was to honor her agreement with you, as well to limit the chance I would learn what you are." He pointed to Dacian, who stood within the range of the stone. "My grandson fancies himself a scholar and has spent decades in the north studying the fall of the civilization north of the Boundary Mountains, what those of you around that inland sea call the Rim Mountains. He knew of the Lobben god and the culture and language. Which allowed him to play a role and forced Yreka to involve me." He sighed. "As I mentioned earlier, House Hezin has been in decline for centuries. Dacian's proximity had value for her, so she granted me concessions. I would have expected her to return south. Go back to her base of power and bolster her forces after her interactions with you."

"She hasn't?"

Galeno shook his head. "No. I am uncertain where she's currently located, but I know it is in a country on the west of those mountains your people call the World's Backbone. Given what I just learned about you, I imagine she's hoping to find you have a sibling somewhere."

Stephenie could not prevent her eyes from widening. *That piece of shit.* She knew her sire had raped the queen of Calis before going to Cothel and creating her. No child came of that because the queen had killed herself. *Could he have dozens of children floating around? Yreka wants to find someone she can dominate and mold into her pet, since I refused her.* She told herself without transmitting the thoughts through the stone.

"I see you understand the threat."

Stephenie's mind raced, but she took a moment before responding. "The man, or kiwa, who tried to kill me knew what I was. He had a sword to befuddle my mind and perhaps other magical devices. My sister has used resources we have in Ista to capture another likely assassin. Could Yreka have found what she is searching for and then sent them to kill me?"

Galeno frowned. "It is possible, but I would imagine she wants to acquire and train anyone she finds. She normally takes a long-term view and would not likely act so rashly, especially as Dacian was on the path to contain you. Why disrupt him as well? My guess is that one of her enemies has spies in her household and learned of you from someone Yreka has informed within her circle of mostly trusted family."

"What do you propose as an informed response?"

Galeno smiled again. "You are far more stable than what the stories of primes would imply." He picked up the dragon statue again. "I never met one. I was born long after all the primes had died, and even longer after the dragons had disappeared. But I have always understood that a child of a dragon often exhibited animalistic tendencies. Let it be known that I will have no one in House Hezin hinder you. I will order my grandson to not speak a word of what you are to anyone and to leave the north this very day."

Stephenie shook her head. "No," she snapped. "Dacian will remain in Lobben and take control of the country and the armies. I just destroyed the trap of Fotia and told all of his followers they are being punished for not following the word of their prophet. He can leave only once Sandven is restored and Lobben is no longer a threat."

Galeno nodded his head in acceptance and said nothing else.

"He will also answer any questions I might have about these stupid households and this society of people who feel they should rule the world."

Galeno agreed again, but then raised a hand. "You may be angry at the world, and the events that have led to this moment, but I suggest you understand people like you, me, Yreka, and Dacian, do in fact rule the world. Fair or not, beneficial to society or not, it is a fact. A fact that others in positions of power will defend with the bodies of anyone they can throw at someone who would challenge their positions of power."

Stephenie's hands tightened around the stone, but she accepted the lecture. *He's right,* she admitted to herself. Her own certainty that she had the right to call herself queen, even when she did not want the role, rose in her mind. Her sudden ordering of Galeno's and Dacian's actions had felt natural. It did not take magic to covet power and control. *I'm just like everyone else,* she admitted sadly and then softened her grip on the stone. "Understood."

Galeno accepted her statement. "I will offer you any advice you want, whenever you want it. However, I am not in a position to challenge any of the other families. Dacian's taking over the throne in

Lobben would not be out of the realm of reason, so that should not cause a conflict within the houses. However, his change of stance on allowing you free passage may irk Yreka. I will have to deal with that somehow. It may even trigger more kiwa coming north."

She looked over at Henton and Ryia and knew they had been far more vulnerable than she had. "I don't like assassins."

"Neither do I."

"I will give the stone back to Dacian. We will need to find a way to communicate after this."

Galeno bowed to her again. "Agreed."

Stephenie broke the connection and turned her focus to the man she still had not decided if he deserved to die for the pain and destruction he caused, or if the choice had not really even been his. *I've killed thousands, perhaps even more than he has. Though most of those were not intentional.* Intellectually, she knew he claimed to have set out to minimize the number of people who died as well. "I do not like to order people's obedience, but your grandfather agreed that you will take over Lobben and help fix the mess here and in Sandven."

Dacian bowed his head to her. "It is a burden I will bear as payment for the decisions we made. I am not sure exactly how I will achieve it, but once I recover my strength, I can enforce my control over the nobles."

Stephenie turned to Henton. "Can I have your communication stone?" Henton nodded his head, fished his out of his backpack, and carried it over to her. She took it and handed it to Dacian. "So that you can communicate with me. Do you have a spare one that allows you to communicate with your grandfather?"

He took the stone from her. "Only if I am able to recover the stones from my cousin's. I can use this stone to sense their location, but I can't risk leaving the country at this time. I expect some amount of panic and fear from the Faithful of Fotia. It will take time for the armies to regain their command and control over the soldiers and for any directions I provide to be received and accepted."

Stephenie nodded her head. "Stabilize things as quickly as possible, then we can work out a transition plan." She signaled for Ryia and Henton to get ready to leave. "Then I want you to look at how to train those with magic to perform healing without augmentation devices. That will be the first priority to establishing a long-term functioning society."

"Should I tell them that their power comes from the Goddess?"

She pursed her lips. "It might be necessary at first, but we need to prepare them for the truth about magic." She bent down and picked up her own backpack. "I need to get back to Ista as soon as possible."

Chapter 36

They escorted Dacian a quarter of the way back to Berl and then turned around to make their way north. Stephenie trusted the man to know his own strength and have enough of a sense of self-preservation to either return to Berl immediately, or to hide out until he recovered from the poison.

Stephenie, Henton, and Ryia said very little until they found a secluded valley where they could set up their own camp and rest. The rough land, injuries, and total exhaustion they each felt meant they stopped within five miles of Berl. After they erected the tent and built a small fire to make dinner, Stephenie told them about her experience with the trap and then her conversation with Galeno.

"You really think that's what Yreka's up to?" Henton asked. "Could you actually have siblings?"

Stephenie looked at her scaled hands and considered the question. "Everyone is trying to manipulate me. They all want something." She looked up. "But yeah, we already know my sire tried the same thing in Calis. Only Queen Eayn killed herself instead of bringing a half-breed into the world."

"Well, she wouldn't have known she'd have a half-breed," Henton challenged. "But she likely thought she was carrying a demon based on what Duvargintik told your mother."

"That means the piece of shit likes to go after queens?" Ryia looked at each of them. "He raped two that we know of. Are we needing to look at queens for all the other countries between here and Cothel? South of Cothel?"

Stephenie reached up and felt the horns on her head. They extended a good four inches above her hair. *The bone and flesh I absorbed from that man.* She shivered again.

"What?" Henton asked.

Stephenie frowned, though she doubted her face made the correct expression. "Something I haven't mentioned yet, because I don't like the implications." She held up her hands.

"I noticed you're not as thin as normal," Ryia said, and Henton agreed.

"When I transformed with that man trying to choke me, I somehow consumed part of him." She looked down at her larger than normal feet, with her talons extended through the front of her boots. "It's unnerved me."

"Something like how you regrew my hand? Only I had to constantly eat."

"Or used dead deer as raw material to create Kas' body," Henton offered.

She nodded her head. "I think so. I consumed raw materials from him." She rubbed the tips of her fingers together. "It made me realize that I can heal almost instantly, but it requires that I have spare minerals and resources within me. I can't just create matter out of nothing. If I've not eaten recently, or have healed too much, I'm not able to heal as much."

Ryia nodded her head. "I think that might be part of why I also feel drained when healing someone else. Some of me transfers over to the other person."

"Agreed," Stephenie said. "I'm terrible at healing others, but thinking back, I think I've pushed part of myself into others as well." She sighed. "But right now, I'm more demon than ever before. Sucking flesh and bone off someone to make this body. If Josh could see me now."

"Your brother has a lot of issues." Henton waved a finger at her. "Don't start feeling guilty about any of this."

"Yeah," Ryia said. "I think you're beautiful, just as you are. Don't change back if you don't want."

Stephenie chuckled. "I don't mind this form, but I also like my human body as well. I am not going to remain in one or the other all the time. I'll assume either form as it pleases me." She ran her fingers the wrong way against the scales on her arm. "Plus, fewer issues with clothing catching on me as a human."

"Let's focus on more important things," Henton said after he shifted into a position that took the pressure away from the location of the stab wound had he received. Ryia's healing had done enough to close the wound and knit his organs back together, but the recently mended flesh still hurt.

Stephenie pulled her boots off. "That's not a small list. We've got the assassin Islet captured. Ista has him under control, but there's likely another one around. There's the lack of food for Ista. I think Dacian can get Lobben under control pretty easily, but not sure about Sandven." She leaned back herself. Her feet had formed blisters under her scales from the boots, even with repeated healing. She pushed energy into them to fix the damage once again.

"Sandven will be the problem," Ryia said. "Dufnall isn't really cut out to be a king. He's a bit too … soft on people."

Stephenie shrugged. "Not all rulers need to wield a club. He might use reason and logic to win people to his position."

Ryia's eyes rolled far enough to convey her thought on that topic.

Stephenie did not completely disagree. "I hate to leverage them, but we could look to hire mercenaries to stabilize the country. Ista has enough wealth to easily do that."

Henton tossed a stick to the side. "Not to be skeptical, but could we keep mercenaries in check? Also, shouldn't we see what he wants to do before you take over the country on his behalf?"

Stephenie pondered the statement. *I'm effectively dictating to Dacian the priorities for Lobben. If we had someone to do the day-to-day administration of Sandven …*

"You're plotting something," Ryia said.

Stephenie nodded her head. "Empire building." She looked at the tent. *It could also help with Kas. I would not have to spend so much time running each country, especially if Islet will rule Ista's people.* "I'm about to collapse. But think about this while I sleep. Yreka arranged to overthrow the countries directly south of us. Now we have to rebuild them. If she finds another kid my sire could have scattered about, I fully expect war to come at us."

"You saying you want a buffer country?" Henton asked.

Stephenie shook her head. "Not like that. Not as something to discard and abuse. What we need is both countries stable and secure as fast as possible so that we are not wasting time dealing with local distractions. However, that means rebuilding the countries with people who will do what we want." She pushed herself to her feet. "Should I just be honest and admit that would make me an empress over the region?"

"What of Ista?" Henton asked.

"Islet has made a good regent. I'll need someone to handle the day-to-day task for all three countries if we want to focus on trying to find any siblings I have before Yreka does."

"Assuming she hasn't already." Ryia tossed a rock toward the fire. "She's had a couple of years' head start."

"I know. Think about it and be honest with me. Is it a good idea?" Stephenie turned away and moved to the edge of the camp. She pulled off her blood covered and damaged clothing, not trusting herself to transform back into her human form without emitting excess energy as flames. She focused on draining off the residual energy in a controlled manner to bring her body safely to the transition point. Her exhaustion made the process difficult, but after a false start, she dumped power into a nearby stone, making it red hot.

As she shifted back, she found herself a bit bloated and uncomfortable, as though too much flesh existed. It did not feel like overeating, but that too much mass existed throughout her body. *How do I get rid of the excess?* Ista had no answer for her. Kervigar, the castle explained, always compressed his mass when in smaller forms. What that meant, Stephenie did not know for certain.

She put her spare clothing on, climbed into the tent, and fell immediately asleep. Ryia and Henton remained up for a while longer, eventually eating the food that still simmered in the pot.

In the morning, Stephenie transformed back into her lizard form. The extra mass that made her uncomfortable as a human helped to reduce the pain and make the transformation much easier. Once they packed up their gear, she flew everyone north. She remained transformed and simply used the improved energy handling to fly longer and farther each day. On the third morning, after disabling the trap, the three of them arrived in Isa Fields.

Islet, Stephenie said through the communication stone, consciously projecting an image of her current form.

Her sister's eyes widened. "You've grown horns."

Stephenie smiled. *I have.* She kept her expression light. *Do they become me?* She turned her head from side to side.

"The red is deep and striking. They appear to shift color slightly as the light shifts."

Thank you. Her expression became more somber. *How is Rugga? Ista keeps telling me he's doing well, but what is your opinion?*

Islet leaned back. "At first I was worried. But now he claims he wants to keep the burn scars. Kas and Lami healed most of his injuries. We've given him a room in the castle until he wants to go back to his home."

Only the strong survive. Scars are the mark of facing Dalkin and not cowering.

Islet lifted an eyebrow. "You sound like a northern more every day."

Stephenie shifted her flight to the left, banking around the mountain ahead of her. *We'll be home soon, but before I arrive, I want to ask you a question.*

Islet leaned forward in her chair. "Of course, Steph. What do you need?"

Stephenie let out a deep breath. *I don't want to make you feel any obligation, so please tell me no if you don't want the responsibility. However, Yreka is likely searching for another prime so that she can train them and make them her pet. If she succeeds, I fear war will come to Ista. I expect with the mess in Lobben and Sandven, and with her plotting, I will need to be away from Ista for an extended period of time.*

Islet swallowed and then forced a smile. "Steph, if you need me to continue my duties here, I will."

A laugh of relief escaped Stephenie's lips. *Thank you. I love you, Islet. You're a great older sister. I didn't want to impose on you.*

Islet leaned sat back in her chair. "Steph, to be honest, I need to keep myself busy. I don't want to drown in the nightmares that come from too much time to think."

Understood. Stephenie closed her eyes and allowed the icy wind to fling her hair about her head. She knew of Islet's fears, but had no way to fix them. *Do you think Dufnall is capable of ruling Sandven? I'm giving Dacian orders for how I want him to rule Lobben, and with what I fear is coming, I need Sandven to do what I want without delays. If I had to put someone else on the throne, I will.*

Islet frowned. "I've spent some time talking with him. He lacks confidence, and he doesn't have a base of power. The average person might support him, but what of his nephews and the other jarls?"

Half the country is under Lobben rule right now. We'll have to contend with detractors, but can he do it? She frowned. *Does he even want to do it?*

"I think he can, if he has enough support." Islet shrugged. "I don't know if he wants the job."

Stephenie nodded her head. *Can you gather the others in the in the map room? Henton, Ryia, and I will land soon, take care of the assassin, and then join you.*

Islet rose to her feet. "Of course." She walked toward the door as she continued. "I've been talking with Kas as well. He's been through a lot more than I realized. I think our talking is helping the both of us. I hope you don't mind."

Stephenie shook her head. *I don't mind. I have a lot of things to tell the both of you in private as well.*

Stephenie approached the castle from the west and kept the mountain range behind them to obscure their approach from anyone in the valley that might be watching. While Islet had captured one assassin, Stephenie had not raised her concern that additional killers might have come with Arno and might still lurk in the city. She did not want to panic her sister with her own fears.

Stephenie touched down on the fourth-floor balcony and pulled her wind-blown hair back behind her horns. She took a deep breath and tried to allow the sense of safety and protection she once felt when in the castle to fill her. However, the fact that an invader had made it into her lands ate away the calm she desired.

"You want us with you, right?" Henton asked, dropping his backpack to the stone tiles and unstrapped the crossbow from the outside. "Unless you think he could take over our minds and make things worse."

Stephenie pursed her reptilian lips and asked Ista to show her the situation in the room. She turned to her friends. "Arno threw a fit for the first couple of days, but since the guardians have continued to bring him food and water, he mostly sleeps on the floor."

"We want to help," Ryia demanded, her own heavy pack unceremoniously dropped from her shoulders.

"It should be safe enough," Stephenie decided. "But the two of you stay behind me." She removed her own pack and lowered it to the floor. Ista informed her that a guardian would come to bring all three packs to their rooms. Stephenie thanked the castle, opened the glass-paneled door, and entered the long hall that connected the main rooms on the upper floor.

Ryia and Henton fell in directly behind her and the three of them descended to the first floor. On the first floor, they walked silently to the rear hall, and then to the rear storage room. Henton paused a moment to arm the crossbow and place the last bolt into the weapon. He nodded his head and then Stephenie opened the outer door.

They entered the room already packed with six guardians. Stephenie led the way around the stone cats and pulled open the door between the two storage rooms.

Arno instantly woke from his sleep at the intrusion and drew in energy. Stephenie growled, and the man froze in place, his brown eyes wide. He remained in an awkward position, halfway from laying on the floor to a crouch.

Her voice deepened. "I ripped Kamari apart, leaving pieces of his body scattered across the temple of Fotia. If you don't want your brains to decorate these walls, you will remain very still and draw no power."

The brown-haired man did not move.

Stephenie snarled, her sharp teeth showing. "So, kiwa, you call yourself Arno?"

The man nodded.

"I grant you permission to speak, Arno." Stephenie clicked her razor-sharp talons on the handles of both swords. "Do you deny you came here to kill me?"

"No, Prime." Arno looked at the sword that had belonged to his companion.

"And you harmed someone in my household."

Arno's brows pinched together. "The servant?"

"Rugga," she corrected, her taloned toes scraping the stone floor.

"What do you plan to do with me?" His face fell, resignation removing any remaining traces of confidence.

Stephenie continued to watch the room for any changes in the energy fields. She sensed only a small trickle of power flowing into the man and assumed he did not even realize he made the small draw. "Who else is with you? We assume another of your number was in Horn Point. The person who killed Vikram and Warner. Any others?"

"Am I sentenced to death?"

Stephenie crossed her arms. Instinct demanded that she rip his beating heart from his chest and eat it, but the rational part of her mind objected to murder. *And I don't want to eat people.* "That depends on you," she said, realizing she had not actually decided. "If you were to leave the north and never return. Never do anything to harm those under my protection. Take any partners with you when you go. Then I might consider allowing you to leave my country."

Arno slowly finished standing, moving out of the uncomfortable crouch he had been maintaining. "Nia was in Horn Point on the first of the month. She was to follow the soldiers north and regroup with me if possible."

"We found your communication stone," she said, knowing from Ista what Kas had found when they searched the home they provided him. "I assume it is to contact her, yes?"

Arno nodded his head.

"So, who sent you to kill me and mine?"

Arno considered his words for several moments. Almost no emotion leaked from his mind. "Colette of Irwan House had taken us in. She learned what you are. If the Senzar bitch gained control over you, she would crush Irwan House." Arno continued, offering an explanation. "Yreka killed Collett's father, and Collett wants revenge."

Stephenie's lip rolled at the mention of Yreka. "And with your failure, I am assuming this Colette will send others. Do you have a way to contact Colette?"

He nodded his head. "Colette did not know you had matured into your powers. She believed you to be too young. Please, understand, this decision did not originate as malice toward you."

"Killing me out of kindness?"

He shook his head. "Out of self-preservation. But, given your obvious power, if you let me live, I will inform Colette of the error of that decision. She wouldn't send anyone else to harm you if she knows the truth." He bowed his head. "Please forgive our errors."

Stephenie let out a deep breath and dropped her arms to her sides. She would ask Dacian to validate the likelihood of those statements as soon as she could. "I need to confer with someone, but assuming what you've said is true, then I will have you escorted to my border, where you and Nia will need to return to the south without interfering any further in Sandven and Lobben. Nor will you harm Dacian or his family. Nor anyone in Cothel."

The tension left Arno's body, and he nodded his head.

"I also want Colette to contact me." Stephenie pushed down the rage burning in her. "Had she done so in the first place, she would have learned I'm not an ally of Yreka. Your interference has played into Yreka's hands and has killed far too many."

Arno bowed his head. "Forgive us."

"We'll see." Stephenie motioned for Henton and Ryia to leave the room. She followed them out and closed the door so that Ista could seal it. She signaled them to remain quiet as they left the second room and entered the hall.

"Are you sure about that?" Henton asked. He removed the bolt from the bow and carefully released the tension from the string.

Stephenie clenched her hands, her sharp talons pressing into her scaled flesh. She slowly released the tension in her body and met his eyes. "If I start killing, I am afraid I won't stop." She pushed back on the memory of ripping apart Kamari's body. "I could easily become the monster I don't want to be." She looked down the hall. "I will confirm the story with Dacian before I do anything."

"Another one of these bastards who thinks they can kill anyone in their way." Ryia spit on the floor. "Sorry." She used her boot to rub it away, but it only smeared on the stone.

Henton swallowed. "Ryia, don't let the hate consume you."

Stephenie nodded her head and put an arm around Ryia's shoulder. "Henton is right. It will eat you up. I fight against it constantly." She smiled. "Despite how I look, I want to keep my humanity."

A tear fell from Ryia's eye, and she leaned her head against Stephenie's chest. "Steph, I will try. I want to be like you. I don't want to see more faces when I close my eyes."

Stephenie kissed Ryia's forehead. "We are always here for you."

Ryia squeezed Stephenie and then pulled away. "I promise to talk more with both of you."

Stephenie let out a long breath. "Good." She started walking toward the map room. "I'll check with Dacian on what the man said. Hopefully he spoke the truth and we just learned the name of another house that doesn't appear to like Yreka."

"That would be good information," Henton agreed.

Stephenie entered the map room first. She knew Islet, Walter, Kas, Douglas, Perain, Dufnall, and Kor sat around the table. Fear burst from everyone except Islet and Kas as soon as they saw her. She stopped at the head of the table, with Ryia and Henton behind her.

"You have horns," Douglas said, recovering from his shock before the others. "And no boots?"

Stephenie smiled. "I outgrew the ones I was wearing."

"It is good to see you," Islet said, rose from her seat, and quickly moved to hug her.

Stephenie returned her embrace, but she looked at Kas. *This is what I am. Can you accept it?*

He nodded his head. *I told you I will not abandon you because of who you are.* He compressed his lips and hesitated a moment. *I owe you an apology. Islet has pointed out some flaws in my logic. As well as some behaviors that I am not proud of. I have not figured how to feel good about Ista, but I am trying.*

Stephenie ignored the comment about her castle. She could not change that aspect of herself. *I have an idea for how I can spend less time worrying about ruling.* Kas raised a mental eyebrow. *It involves me becoming an empress and leaving the day-to-day things to others.*

That is an interesting idea, Kas responded.

Stephenie released Islet and glanced at Kor, whose hands shook. *Though there is more I need to tell you,* she continued to Kas.

There always is. He gave her a timid smile. *I want to thank you for destroying the trap. I know I have been unfair in my expectations.*

Ryia moved toward Kor, her staff at the ready.

"Your Majesty," Dufnall said, putting a hand on top of Kor's. He rose to his feet and bowed deeply.

To Kas, Stephenie said, *I have not given you the priority you need. I will do better.* Stephenie reached out and put a hand on Ryia's shoulder. "Dufnall, regardless of how I look, you can still call me Steph." She avoided licking her lips for fear of how that would appear.

Islet stepped back and resumed her seat next to Walter, drawing his stare away from Stephenie and toward his wife.

"It is true what she is," Kor said to Dufnall.

"Yes," Douglas agreed. "She's a menace to her clothing and tailor."

Stephenie chuckled, though the vocalization did not sound like her to her own ears. She grinned at the former soldier as she unbuckled the two sword belts she wore. "And now to my cobbler."

"Allow me," Henton said as he came forward to take her weapons.

Stephenie handed both weapons to Henton, and he placed the crossbow and swords on a table that sat against the wall. She turned her attention back to Dufnall. "I am sorry about Ivan and everyone that suffered or died."

Dufnall nodded his own head, he but held his tongue.

Stephenie held his gaze. "I need someone strong to restore the governance of Sandven. I need someone who can quickly cement control over the jarls and bring everyone together." She moved behind the chair at the head of the table, but she did not sit down. "I fear far worse things are coming and that we'll have little time to prepare."

Dufnall shook his head. "As I've told Islet, I'm not next in line for the throne. I have two nephews that might still live. I could never disgrace Ivan in that way."

Stephenie rested her left hand on the back of the chair. "I am truly sorry for what has happened in Sandven. I don't know if Ivan's sons still live. Or if they do live, if they are under the control of Rokr, or some other jarl. However, I cannot wait to see." She motioned for Ryia and Henton to sit. "Fotia's Prophet has taken control of the armies that were left in Berl. He's sent dispatches to the forces in Sandven, informing them he is now Fotia's sole voice. He is using his powers to build a base that will see him control the entire country."

"The man that started all this," Dufnall sneered. "The man that had my brother killed."

"Dacian has many things to answer for, but he was a pawn in a larger scheme. Others triggered the death of Ivan. Dacian's goal was simply to capture him." Stephenie softened her voice. "His control over Lobben is fragile at the moment, but I intend for him to rule the country, probably for several years."

"He started this, and you support him," Kor demanded.

Stephenie shook her head. "He did not start it." She took a deep breath. "It is true. This current conflict centers around me." She lifted a hand to quiet Ryia, who she felt about to speak. "I have my own choices to answer for, but I didn't start it either. I'm not the instigator. So many others have agendas. I'm certain I only know a fraction of those involved." She pulled out the chair and sat down. "Up to this point, I've not been a driving force because I had no way of knowing the scale of things." She took a deep breath. "But I'll be damned if I continue to simply ignore things and let the world crash down around us. I'm determined to forge my own agenda and put an end to those that think they can control me."

Stephenie let her statement hang for several moments. "So, Dufnall, I need your answer. Will you rule Sandven on my behalf, or will I need to tell Dacian that I will need his forces to control both countries indefinitely?"

"You expect me to rule in your name?" Dufnall questioned.

Stephenie tried to ease the anger burning within her. "In part. I will leave the day-to-day function of ruling to you, but I'll expect your strategic coordination with me. Ista has enough money to stabilize your economy, and I believe we can hire a strong enough force to ensure the other jarls are brought in-line."

"Rokr needs to pay," Ryia said without her normal fire. "He tried to kill you multiple times."

Stephenie nodded her head. "Dacian will eventually take full control of Lobben, even from King Boraue. His troops will need to stay in Sandven long enough to avoid chaos and anarchy. I want him to withdrawal them, as I fear the soldiers still have too much hate for those with magic. But that transition needs coordination."

Dufnall nodded his head. "I don't want that bastard ruling Sandven."

"Good," Stephenie said. "You will need to cooperate with him, but you do not need to like him. The first thing I will need from you is thoughts on mercenaries."

Dufnall swallowed and Stephenie felt his resignation. "If we can get some ships, we can sail east to Fosen. I've heard their pirates will do almost anything for enough money." He lifted his attention from the table. "Though I'm not sure I would trust them."

"Never trust mercenaries," Stephenie agreed. "We use them only long enough for you to win the loyalty of your own people. I'm hoping the ancient threat of Ista will help keep people in line."

Henton cleared his throat. "What about trusting assassins?"

Stephenie lifted her gaze to Islet, Walter, and Kas. "Good work capturing Arno," Stephenie said in Cothish. "I am proud of the ingenuity."

"Thank you," Islet said. "Ista was also a big help in making it work."

Stephenie felt Ista's pride in Islet's statement. "I have some good news regarding the assassins. The three that were sent to kill me should no longer be a threat. We killed one in Berl, and we confronted Arno as soon as we arrived. I believe they had not expected me as I am now. So far, all of those who've seen me became immediately contrite. And I confirmed what Arno told me with Dacian. Likely, I think we've found a couple of new allies."

Douglas raised an eyebrow. "Do you think you can trust him? Yreka become contrite when she saw you, but it sounds like she's still plotting against us."

Stephenie did not feel comfortable sharing the potential she might have siblings yet. "Yreka's been very specific about avoiding us. I don't believe that will last, but these possible allies hate her as much, if not more, than we do."

Henton leaned forward. "And now that we know more of the people involved, we can make better decisions. Our weakness has always been our lack of knowledge, but now that is changing."

"Exactly." Stephenie pulled a map toward her. She felt Kas' confidence in her and she smiled. "Now, let's start planning."

www.ingramcontent.com/pod-product-compliance
Lightning Source LLC
Chambersburg PA
CBHW030639260626
47157CB00007B/2399